Also by C. K. McDonnell

THE STRANGER TIMES

This Charming Man

The second *Stranger Times* novel

C. K. McDonnell

PENGUIN BOOKS

TRANSWORLD PUBLISHERS
Penguin Random House, One Embassy Gardens,
8 Viaduct Gardens, London SW11 7BW
www.penguin.co.uk

Transworld is part of the Penguin Random House group of companies
whose addresses can be found at global.penguinrandomhouse.com

First published in Great Britain in 2022 by Bantam Press
an imprint of Transworld Publishers
Penguin paperback edition published 2023

Copyright © McFori Ink Ltd 2022

A CIP catalogue record for this book
is available from the British Library.

ISBN
9780552177351

Typeset in Van Dijck MT Pro by Jouve (UK), Milton Keynes.
Printed and bound in Great Britain by Clays Ltd, Elcograf S.p.A.

The authorized representative in the EEA is Penguin Random House Ireland,
Morrison Chambers, 32 Nassau Street, Dublin D02 YH68.

Penguin Random House is committed to a sustainable
future for our business, our readers and our planet. This book is made
from Forest Stewardship Council® certified paper.

In memory of Ian Cognito
R.I.P. (Rage in Perpetuity)

PROLOGUE

The hunger.

The damned hunger.

Phillip had never felt anything like it. Having been born into first-world comfort, he'd never before known true hunger. Sure, he'd missed the odd meal, or been famished while looking for the only open chip shop at 3 a.m., but this was something else entirely.

This was not that sort of hunger.

He tried to keep to the shadows as he walked. He didn't want anyone to see him and the bright lights of the city hurt his eyes.

It was unseasonably warm. Only in Manchester could hot weather in summer be classed as unseasonable, but there it was. Six days into a heatwave and there was already talk of a national hosepipe ban. That was quite some achievement on a rain-soaked island.

It had started yesterday – the hunger. At first, he'd mostly ignored it. He'd told his mum he reckoned he was coming down with something. It was Saturday so there was no need to phone in sick at work. He'd texted the lads to say that he wasn't up for going out, and he'd been branded a lightweight. As soon as he'd woken up this morning, though, he'd realized that something was wrong. Very wrong. His mouth had felt different. He'd cried out in shock when he'd looked in the mirror, and had bitten his own tongue in the process.

A quick google had yielded nothing of use bar a couple of joke websites. He couldn't find anything that explained how you could grow teeth like that overnight. They were so damn sharp, too.

He'd called his dentist to make an emergency appointment. It was going to cost a fortune but he was freaking out. Then he'd ordered an Uber to take him there. As he'd stood waiting in the foyer of his building, the light streaming in from outside had hurt his eyes. He'd remained there, phone in hand, watching the little car icon on the screen make its way to his location painfully slowly. Then he'd tried to step out into the sunlight . . .

His screams had attracted the attention of a couple of passing girls, no doubt on their way to soak up the sun somewhere, and pulled them out of their happy chatter. They'd run over and found him lying in the doorway, writhing on the floor. One of them had pulled his hands away from his face and her friend had screamed. Phillip had legged it up the stairs and back into his apartment, where he'd shut the blinds and tried to calm himself down.

This had to be a joke. Someone was playing a sick joke on him. Only how could they do that? Had someone spiked him with something? Keith. That prick. He said he'd stopped doing that kind of thing but Phillip didn't believe him. He'd sent the guy an angry, accusatory text but had received what seemed like honest bafflement in response. Phillip had ignored his attempts to call.

If it wasn't Keith, then he didn't want him knowing about this. The idiot would tell everybody.

Desperate, he'd phoned NHS III. The woman on the other end of the line had laughed and told him to stop wasting their time with silly pranks.

Phillip had gone back to the mirror. His appearance had changed beyond just the teeth. His skin was paler, except on the right side of his face, where the sun had hit it – it looked as if it'd been burned. It was red and blistering, painful to touch. And, despite being in the middle of a heatwave, he felt cold.

It was only as he'd raised his hand to his scarred face that he'd noticed how long his fingernails had become. That was when he'd really freaked out. Huddled on his bed, he'd rocked back and forth as the tears streamed down his face. Once that had passed, a bit of clarity descended.

Whatever this was, it was a medical issue. He needed to go to hospital. He didn't want to phone for an ambulance as there'd be more questions. He couldn't take anybody else laughing at him. No, he'd wait for the sun to set and he'd walk to the hospital. It was only about fifteen minutes away.

That decided, he'd calmed down a bit. At least he had a plan.

He'd spent the rest of the day feeling hungry but had been unable to eat. Never mind negotiating his new dental work, everything he'd put into his mouth had made him want to retch.

His phone had told him that sunset was at 9.26 p.m. He'd waited until 9.30 p.m. and then he'd pulled on his thick black hoodie. Mr Black – that had been his nickname in the group.

As he'd prepared to leave the flat, he'd gone to check his appearance in the hall mirror and he hadn't been there.

All day he'd studiously avoided using the V-word, even in his own mind. It was too ridiculous. Too stupid. Too . . .

But now . . . He didn't have a reflection. How could he not have a reflection? This all felt like a nightmare he was unable to wake up from.

He'd sat down and tried to think. He'd seen a couple of stupid horror movies in his time. Who hadn't? But they'd never been his thing. Still, everyone knew the basics. You had to be bitten, didn't you? That's how you became a . . . He hadn't been bitten. He'd hooked up with that Spanish chick a few days ago. She'd been a bit kinky, but there hadn't been any biting. There had been the redhead last weekend. Maybe this was an STD? Was that it? If it was, then the solution was still the same.

In the absence of any better ideas, he'd left the flat and headed towards Manchester Royal Infirmary. And also, it was what the hunger wanted him to do.

It wasn't long before he reached the hospital, but then he kept on going. He told himself he was building up to it. A bit of a walk would calm him down. He knew it would be difficult to explain all this, so he just needed to take some time to clear his head and then he'd go in. They were medical people, after all – it was their job to be understanding about stuff. Even stuff like this.

Then he found himself on Oxford Road, standing in the shadows of a doorway, opposite one of the student bars. He watched people come and go, and then he noticed a girl stagger into the street. Her mascara was running and she looked worse for wear – like she was possibly going to be sick. It was only when he found himself preparing to cross the road and follow her that he stopped himself.

What the hell was he doing?

He knew the answer.

Hunting.

Not in the normal, looking-for-action way either.

His mouth was salivating.

He ran.

He didn't know to where, he just ran.

And ran.

And ran.

People. Lights. Screeching traffic and raised voices. Everything blurred as he ran for all he was worth.

He stopped only when he collapsed from exhaustion.

He was lying on the ground. Heavy machinery loomed around him. A building site, then. Could be anywhere. It wasn't as if there were a shortage of them. There'd been a big write-up in the *Evening News* last week – Manchester's building boom.

'Hey, sir. You cannot be here, sir.'

The voice came from behind him somewhere. It sounded Eastern European. Phillip was too exhausted to move.

'I said . . .' The figure of a security guard in a hi-vis jacket appeared upside down in Phillip's vision. He was holding a torch and peering down at him. The man's eyes widened and his voice softened. 'Are you all right?'

As the guard shone his torch in Phillip's face, some instinct caused Phillip to hiss.

Before he knew what was happening, he was up on his feet.

The security guard stumbled backwards and the distant streetlight caught the terror in his face. 'What the hell are you?'

Phillip didn't answer. He knew now. He knew.

He watched as the guard panicked and fumbled for his walkie-talkie, causing it to tumble to the ground. Phillip wasn't in control any more. The hunger had him.

And so now Phillip walked, stopping every now and again, trying to retch. As much as he wanted to, he couldn't make himself throw up. The hunger had receded, leaving an all-consuming revulsion in its wake. Memories of what had happened kept coming back to him. What had he become? How could this happen to him? Was he being punished?

It was late now – the small hours of the morning. Phillip had only a vague idea where he was. It wasn't an area he normally would have ever considered walking through. There had been that one time, when he and Jeffers had driven over here looking to score some weed, and that had been an unpleasant experience. In ordinary circumstances he wouldn't have been caught dead here. The irony.

A couple of teenagers skulked out from an alleyway in front of him and looked him up and down. Phillip averted his eyes and walked on.

'Hey, mate – you all right?'

They were following him now.

He ignored them and kept walking.

Another voice. 'We're just trying to be friendly.'

'Yeah, don't be like that.'

He quickened his pace but it sounded like they matched it.

'You're being rude now, boy!'

'Maybe we should teach you some manners?'

Up ahead, Phillip saw what he was looking for. What he hadn't admitted, even to himself, that he was heading for, but there it was.

A figure was walking unsteadily along the pavement. A young woman. Even from a distance you could tell. She was barefoot, a pair of high heels dangling from her right hand. She stopped at a set of traffic lights along the dual carriageway.

He ran.

He could hear the boys behind him, shouting as they took off after him in pursuit. It didn't matter, though. He was faster now. Faster than he'd ever been. His feet barely touched the ground.

In front of him, the girl pressed the button for the pedestrian crossing then hugged the pole to keep herself upright. The road was one of the main arteries in and out of the city, and even at this time of night it was busy with traffic in both directions.

Along the carriageway, a large HGV clanked as it hit a particularly big pothole. Phillip realized he could hear more now.

Smell more too.

Every sense was heightened.

He could tell the girl in front of him was wearing Coco by Chanel, and she smelled of rum and Coke. The warm night air also carried the scent of cigarettes and her sweat.

The HGV trundled on.

The girl was still leaning against the pole. Oblivious. Focused on the little red man. Waiting for it to switch to the green one so she could continue her weary trudge homeward. These lights always took for ever.

She was desperate for the toilet.

As Phillip accelerated towards her, he knew that. How could he possibly know that?

It was all a matter of timing.

He had judged it to perfection – he could do that now.

The key was not to think. To do.

To be undone.

The first thing the girl knew was the gust of air as something rushed past her and jumped.

The first thing the HGV driver knew was the *thunk* as something hit the front of his cab. Hard.

He slammed on the brakes, causing his load to jack-knife across the road. The car behind, which had just accelerated to make it through the changing lights, was forced to swerve on to the central reservation to avoid going into the back of him.

The driver gripped the wheel tightly, his heart pounding as adrenalin surged through his body. The lorry finally came to a stop.

What had he hit? What had he hit?

He sat back and only then did he notice the blood splattered across the windscreen.

Something was on fire.

Somewhere behind him, a girl screamed.

CHAPTER 1

Hannah stopped to stretch her hamstring.

It didn't need stretching – at least no more than the rest of her did – but she'd quickly realized that it was either do that or just be the sweaty, unfit person leaning on a fence at the edge of the park, trying hard not to throw up or break down. Today was day one of the new her. She had to admit that the running-to-work idea had seemed a whole lot better two nights ago when she'd first agreed it with herself. She'd been on her second bottle of wine at the time. What kind of an idiot takes advice from a drunk person, even if that person is themself? And who on earth takes up jogging in the middle of a heatwave?

The 'new her' initiative had been spurred on by the events of the last couple of weeks – namely that she'd had to take time off work to sort out getting 'the old her' divorced from the pathetic waste of oxygen and Armani suits to whom she'd been married. It had involved a trip to London as that was where Karl's lawyer was based. Given that he was 'the wronging party', as opposed to 'the wronged party', you'd think Karl would have made more of an effort to be accommodating, but Hannah knew better. In Karl's world view, he was always the wronged party. He had no doubt constructed in his head a detailed narrative as to why he was the victim. Hannah had made sure that he hadn't been allowed the chance to share it with her.

It hadn't been as bad as she'd expected. Well, it sort of had, and it sort of hadn't. She wanted almost nothing from Karl, but the utter bastard had still found ways to be awkward. According to him, she'd co-signed a lot of loans and mortgages during their time together, none of which she recalled. It turned out that her drive for emancipation was very inconvenient and he'd be obliged if she just pack it in.

It all looked as if it'd drag on for ever, until Hannah had picked up some of the paperwork relating to these complex financial arrangements and noticed something interesting. Namely, that her signature on the documents was not her signature. Karl had been forging it for what appeared to be years. He denied it furiously, of course, saying, variously, that she must have forgotten, been drunk, or been suffering from the effects of a phantom prescription-drug problem she absolutely did not have. Still, things became a whole lot more convenient after the signature issue had been raised.

The entire thing had been sad in a way. If nothing else, despite how annoyingly good Karl had looked, it had reminded her that she was doing the right thing. She'd married a selfish child and, while it was embarrassing to admit, at least she was finally fixing her mistake. And so it goes.

Still, though, the going was the important bit. And Hannah could say many things about her three months working at *The Stranger Times*, but it sure did put everything else into perspective.

In her first week, she'd discovered that monsters were real, as was magic, and that a group of immortals known as the Founders secretly ran much of the world, having achieved this immortality through the literal draining of the lifeblood of people known as the Folk, who were, well, magical types. When you realize that you have somehow remained entirely ignorant of how the world really is, of the wonder it contains, and of the eternal battle that wages beneath the surface, well, it does rather make your philandering husband's roving eye – and other body parts – seem like not that big a deal.

Hannah moved on to pretending she was stretching her upper body. One of the many reasons the running-to-work idea had been so stupid was that she now realized it meant she would be running against the steady tide of the suited and booted walking towards the big shiny offices of the city centre. From her flat near Piccadilly Station, it was, theoretically, a reasonable but doable route, but she hadn't factored in the number of people she'd have to run around. Worse still, the number of people who would witness her discover just how monumentally unfit you could become while eating your emotions and washing them down with stuff that typically just generated more emotions.

Hannah decided to throw in a lunge and immediately regretted it. Her groan caught the attention of a young guy in his twenties, who looked up as he passed. Was that a smirk? Cheeky sod. She proceeded to execute a second lunge, on the other side, because otherwise it would be admitting that the first was an ill-conceived error of judgement.

Hannah didn't know any of these people walking by, so why

was she so obsessed with what they thought? It was ridiculous. C'mon, girl – snap out of it. Finish your run to the office where a nice shower awaits, in the lovely new bathroom the builders will have finished by now.

Since taking up her position at the paper as assistant editor, Hannah had faced many challenges. The first week aside, with its numerous near-death experiences and shocking revelations, there had since been bigger battles, principally relating to how a professional organization should be run. Vincent Banecroft, editor-at-large and arsehole-in-charge, was 'challenging', in the way a cat sanctuary might use the word to describe a moggy that attempted to rip your face off while you slept.

There was the ongoing battle to stop Banecroft from treating the staff like they were a massive inconvenience whose presence was preventing him from running the paper how he wanted. Hannah had assumed that Banecroft had simply been in a foul mood during her first week in the job, given how he'd shot himself in the foot (literally) on her first day. It turned out that had been him on his best behaviour.

Then, Hannah had been forced to stretch the paper's budget to cover renovations to the building. This was because Stella, the girl technically referred to as their intern, was now staying on the premises, along with Banecroft and Manny, who was their printer (amongst other, rather harder to explain roles). Come to that, there were technically four people living on the premises, if you included the spirit that co-habited Manny's body.

Grace, the office manager and general mother hen, had been very unhappy with these living arrangements, but Banecroft had insisted. Amidst the sea of revelations during Hannah's first week was the discovery that their intern had powers – powers she could not control and which resulted in Grace's house almost being demolished. People would be interested in Stella now, and that made everyone nervous. The offices of *The Stranger Times* sat in an old church – the Church of Old Souls – and were protected by what was euphemistically referred to as 'Manny's friend'. It wasn't a perfect solution, but then nothing was.

The new arrangements meant that the paper's bathroom – consisting of a cracked toilet, a cracked sink and a shower that looked like it would leave you dirtier than when you got in – was not fit for purpose. While Hannah was away, the builders were in to finally sort it out. She'd been worried about the timing, but their availability had been limited and, seeing as they were the only ones willing to do it for the money, there hadn't been any other choice.

Still, Hannah assumed it had all gone OK. At least, she hadn't received any texts or messages saying otherwise. She had spent yesterday reading through the last two editions of *The Stranger Times*. Before she'd left, she'd worked day and night to get the features sections for the following two weeks mostly done and edited. The other articles, despite assurances that everyone would chip in with the editing, and that Ox would turn the spell-check on his computer back on, were 'variable' in quality.

There had been some regrettable errors on the captioning side of things, with pictures turning up in the wrong places. Hannah strongly suspected that the article 'Mysterious Beast Sighted in London Sewers', which had ended up with a picture of the 'right-wing personality' Katie Hopkins on it, may have been less error and more Stella enjoying herself. Still, overall, they had been reasonable editions and Hannah had read them with mixed emotions. She had, of course, wanted them to be good, but not too good. Everybody wants to be missed.

She looked at her watch. Time to get a move on. Banecroft was a stickler for punctuality – other people's, in particular. Hannah started to jog again, tugging subtly at her outfit in a few key places to stop it from sticking to her with the sweat.

The church came into view at the far end of the park. She had to admit that the sight of it did rather make her heart leap. It could've been the first warning of the heart attack for which she was possibly heading, but she didn't think so. Despite everything, she enjoyed working there. She liked the people she worked with. Not Banecroft. Nobody liked Banecroft – quite probably including Banecroft – but she liked the rest of them. She also found it interesting work. Fascinating, in fact, now that she knew there was far more going on in the world than she could possibly have imagined.

As she exited the park and crossed the road, her excitement at being back was largely dispelled as she was forced to dive to the ground to avoid being hit by their new toilet, which had just come crashing through one of the upper windows.

CHAPTER 2

Hannah staggered to the top of the stairs, nearly putting her foot through the dodgy step fourth from the top as she did so, and all but fell into reception. A small crowd of her co-workers was there to greet her, although there was a notable absence of 'welcome back' banners. Reginald, Ox and Stella all stood there, looking as if they thought the building might be on fire but they wanted to be one hundred per cent certain before evacuating.

Reginald, demonstrating catlike reflexes, caught Hannah as she stumbled in. 'Nice of you to drop in,' he said with a waggle of his eyebrows, before noticing how sweaty she was. He quickly placed her back on her feet, took a bottle of scented sanitizer from the inside pocket of his waistcoat and cleaned his hands.

'What is going on?' panted Hannah.

'Oh, you're back – finally!' said Ox.

'I was on holiday, Ox.'

The group turned as another crash emanated from the main office space aka the bullpen.

'You are an appalling excuse for a human being, Vincent Banecroft. Do you hear me? An appalling excuse.'

It was a popularly held opinion but the voice expressing it on this occasion belonged to Grace.

'With the Lord as my witness, you are a terrible man!'

'If your Lord had witnessed the one-ing disgraceful job those four-ers were doing, not even he would have been able to forgive that two.'

The second voice belonged to Vincent Banecroft, although his sentence made no sense to Hannah.

'Don't you dare talk about the Lord to me, you ungodly mess of a man.'

There came another crashing noise.

Hannah looked round. 'Isn't anyone going to break them up?'

'We did the first few times,' offered Stella, her face covered by a curtain of freshly coloured purple hair as she looked down at her phone. 'This has been happening a lot.' She was interrupted by the sound of something wooden breaking. 'Although this is a bit of an escalation.'

'Why didn't anyone call me?' asked Hannah.

'Because,' said Ox, 'Grace told us the first person to bother you while you were off on your divorce holiday would answer to her.'

'And what?' countered Hannah. 'You're all suddenly terrified of Grace?'

The group took a step back as something heavy thumped against the office wall, causing it to shake alarmingly.

'Not suddenly,' said Reggie.

Hannah shook her head. 'It's this fearlessness that really makes our journalistic team stand out.'

'Resorting to violence,' thundered Banecroft, 'is the last resort of the feeble mind.'

There was a collective wince. Grace took particularly unkindly to any suggestion she wasn't smart.

'Oh, is that right, Mr Banecroft?'

'Put that down,' said Vincent, sounding suddenly more placatory. 'That's . . . That is technically classed as a deadly weapon.'

'I hope so.'

'Right,' said Hannah, stepping towards the door. 'Stella, quick as you can. Summary, please?'

'Grace was already pissed as Banecroft found a way around his agreement not to swear and blaspheme in the office, and then, yesterday, he fired the builders.'

Hannah turned on her heel, outraged. 'He fired the builders?'

'That's exactly what Grace said, right before she stormed in there.'

'Excellent,' said Hannah, with a sigh. She took a deep breath, marched across the room and threw open the doors to the bullpen. The other three dived for cover as she did so.

In her head, she'd planned to say something charming and suave-sounding like, 'It is lovely to be back' or 'Did you miss me?' The carnage, however, rather threw her off her stride.

'Grace – put that sledgehammer down this instant!'

CHAPTER 3

Hannah took a deep breath. 'OK, we're going to discuss this like adults.'

Behind her, Stella scoffed derisively.

'Stella! That's not helping.' Hannah felt bad about her aggressive tone. 'On a side note, loving the new hair.'

The compliment was greeted with what was possibly a mumbled thanks.

Hannah was now in the middle of the bullpen. She looked to her left and to her right, where Grace and Banecroft were standing on opposite sides of the room, glaring daggers at each other. In two minutes, Hannah had managed to relieve Grace of the sledgehammer and, in a pre-emptive move, confiscate Banecroft's blunderbuss.

'OK,' said Hannah, 'let's start with the basics.'

'This is a waste of my valuable time,' complained Banecroft. 'I'm a busy man and I should not have to deal with this horse-two.'

Hannah clapped her hands once. 'Excellent, let's deal with this to start. Why have you seemingly abandoned the use of the English language for some numerical hybrid?'

Banecroft smiled. 'Stella?'

At this, Stella stomped into Banecroft's office and, moments later, re-emerged holding a large wooden display board with windows on it numbered one to twelve. It looked like something off a TV quiz show. Numbers one to ten had already been pulled back to reveal ten of the most commonly used swear words in the English language. Numbers eleven and twelve remained unopened.

Hannah studied it for a moment before the realization hit. She rolled her eyes. 'Let me guess—' But she never got the chance.

Grace pointed in Banecroft's direction. 'This appalling man is breaking the terms of our agreement.'

'Ah,' said Banecroft, 'but I think you'll find I am not. If you like, I can go through the precise wording of the agreement?'

Judging by the loud, collective groan with which this was met, Hannah guessed it wasn't the first time Banecroft had offered to do so.

'All right,' said Hannah, keen to move things along. 'I get it. You've got around the agreement by having a chart with swear words on it, then you can just say the corresponding number.'

'Yeah,' said Ox, from his spot of relative safety at the far side of the room. 'He's been ceremonially revealing one every morning for the last two weeks.'

'Indeed,' said Reggie. 'And then conjugating it, using it as a noun, as an adjective, et cetera.'

Hannah looked at Banecroft. 'It's interesting you only did this when I left.'

He shrugged. 'I wanted to do something to improve morale while we were short-handed.'

'Did you?' said Hannah as she looked round the bullpen at the after-effects of Grace having picked up some of the bricks from the building supplies in one corner and used them to try to really improve morale by killing Banecroft. 'It seems you've done a bang-up job on that front.'

'Also,' added Reggie, 'now might not be the time to bring this up, but really, aren't eight, nine and ten essentially the same word? They all mean a gentleman's gentleman, after all.'

'Ah,' said Banecroft, 'but they have different uses. For example, I can call you a nine-head but not an eight- or a ten-head. Similarly, you could be the rather more esoteric eight-womble, but that doesn't work for—'

'Can we stop discussing it, please!' interjected Grace.

'Sorry, Grace,' said Reggie quickly.

'OK,' said Hannah, 'setting this matter aside for a moment, why has the building work not been completed?'

At this, everyone decided to talk at once, each growing louder and louder in an attempt to drown out the others. Hannah let things run for about thirty seconds before piercing the air with a loud wolf-whistle.

'Right, let's try that again, one at a time.' Hannah looked at Grace. 'If you wouldn't mind?'

'The builders turned up last Monday and were working away until somebody told them to shut up.'

Hannah turned to Banecroft.

'We were trying to hold the weekly editorial meeting, which you were not at.'

'I was on holiday.'

'Excuses, excuses,' he continued. 'I asked them to keep it down while the meeting was going on.'

'I see,' said Hannah. 'And how exactly did you phrase your request?'

Banecroft shrugged. 'I have a certain style to my communication. Those uninitiated in the nuances of it may find it abrasive at first.'

'He used numbers one through to five extensively,' clarified Ox.

'And did the builders understand that?' asked Hannah.

'They didn't,' said Stella, 'until he had me bring out this stupid board so he could point at it while he talked to them. Things got a bit heated then. Well, one of 'em – I don't think he could read that well, but judging by his attempt to punch Mr Banecroft's lights out, I think he got the gist of it.'

'It is this newspaper's job not only to inform, but also to educate,' said Banecroft.

'Anyway,' said Hannah. 'So the builders left?'

'Yes,' confirmed Grace, 'but after an awful lot of begging I managed to get them to agree to come in and finish the job over the weekend. Out of office hours when there was nothing going on to disturb.'

She looked pointedly at Banecroft, who nodded. 'And then, as the boss, I decided to fire them. Now, we're all caught up. Can we move on?'

Once again everybody began to talk simultaneously. Hannah threw her hands up in the air, at which point she noticed the reek emanating from her armpits. She pinned her arms by her sides, suddenly feeling very self-conscious. Luckily, everyone she worked with remained oblivious to her odour issue as they were either busy being Vincent Banecroft or distracted by shouting at Vincent Banecroft. In addition to the mountain of hassle Hannah now had to sort out, it dawned on her that she wasn't going to be able to take the shower she so desperately needed.

Amidst the hubbub, something attracted her attention. A high-pitched sound. She'd heard it only once before but it was the kind of noise that stuck in one's memory – thanks to its distinctive and highly irritating nature, and because of the rather dramatic circumstances in which she'd first heard it.

As Hannah had expected, Dr Carter was standing in the reception area, looking in at them. The noise had been her giggle. Hannah had met the woman on two occasions. The first had been very brief, when the woman had been introduced to her as *The Stranger Times'* lawyer who had just secured Hannah's release from a holding cell in a Manchester police station. The second had been when Dr Carter, surrounded by storm troopers, had had her role as the representative of the Founders – the secretive cabal of immortals that was a conspiracy-nut's dream come true – revealed. One of the many reasons the giggle had stuck in Hannah's brain was that she'd heard it while hog-tied on the ground, having found herself face to face with a demented psychopath moments beforehand.

Even in heels, Dr Carter barely touched five foot. She sported a wide grin and possessed the kind of blonde hairdo that you could set about with a crowbar and a blowtorch and not put a dent in it. She also wore a suit that looked on the crazy expensive end of the tailored range. She held a leather briefcase.

The rest of *The Stranger Times* staff gradually fell silent as they also became aware of Dr Carter's presence. It dawned on Hannah that only she, Banecroft and Stella knew who the woman was.

Dr Carter's grin widened to the point where it took up more of her face than really should have been humanly possible. 'Is now a bad time?'

'Not at all,' said Banecroft. 'Perfect timing. Stella – please reveal word number eleven.'

CHAPTER 4

Seeing as Banecroft's private office contained two chairs and three people, Hannah went looking for something to lean on in order to give their 'guest' the spare seat. This was trickier than she'd imagined, as everything in the room looked permanently on the verge of collapse, including the man himself.

Hannah hadn't been in there for two weeks. She was trying to decide whether, in the months leading up to her holiday, she had built up an immunity to the multi-sense assault that entering her boss's lair entailed, or if it really did look and smell even worse than it had done previously. Dazzling sunlight hit the spectacular oval stained-glass window above his desk, but by the time the rays reached the other side of the room, they somehow managed to look tired, dirty and dispirited with their lot in life. As Grace had pointed out on numerous occasions, the space didn't attract rats, which went to show that even vermin had standards.

After a couple of tentative attempts at finding a suitable resting spot, Hannah took up station beside the side-window. Her position meant that she was standing side-on to the desk Banecroft and Carter were sitting either side of. Like an umpire in a game of verbal tennis.

Dr Carter had come right in and, without looking, sat down in the guest chair. Infuriatingly, there had been no squelching noise as she'd plonked herself down on discarded food, or worse. People like her always seemed utterly in control of their environment and it was incredibly bloody annoying.

Banecroft threw himself into his own chair and looked into a mug briefly before drinking its contents with a grimace. It was even odds that it had been cold tea or warm whiskey.

'Dr Carter,' began Banecroft, 'to what do we owe the pleasure of this visit? Actually, scratch that – isn't there some kind of rule where we have to invite you in?'

She leaned back in her chair and surveyed the room as she spoke. 'Vinny, sweetie, I'm your lawyer, not a door-to-door salesperson.'

'Speaking of which, I wish to officially fire you as our lawyer.'

'Ahhhh,' said Dr Carter, pulling a clownish sad face. 'Was it something I said?'

'Not at all. I just feel that your position working for an evil empire does not mesh with this newspaper's mission statement.'

'You have a mission statement? Last I heard, you don't even have a working toilet.'

Banecroft leaned forward. 'And how do you know that?'

'If you want to keep something secret, sweetie, can I suggest you don't have screaming rows about it with your staff?'

Banecroft sat back and nodded. 'Fair point.'

He kicked off his slippers and placed his feet on the desk, knocking a pile of books to the floor in the process. His socks sported enough holes and unhappy stains that they resembled a couple of puppets that had fallen on hard times, possibly by way of serious drug problems and a run-in with a threshing machine.

'I was rather hoping we might talk in private?' said Dr Carter.

'I'm afraid that isn't possible. In these more cautious times, our organization has a policy that if one of us has to meet with beings of pure evil then another member of staff has to be present. It's political correctness gone mad.'

As Dr Carter executed her giggle Banecroft made no effort to hide his wince. Hannah couldn't help but wonder if the woman had deliberately weaponized it to throw people off.

'Oh, deary me. Is Vincent Banecroft frightened of little old *moi*?'

Banecroft had a quick rummage in his earhole with his little finger. 'Speaking of which – out of curiosity, seeing as you're one of the Founders, how old exactly is little old you?'

Dr Carter clucked her tongue. 'Now, Vinny. You know better than to ask a lady her age.'

'Let's not stretch the English language to breaking point by calling you one of those.'

Dr Carter turned to look at Hannah. 'Why is it, do you think, Ms Willis, that, despite his appalling manners and frankly horrific personal hygiene, women still find Vincent here so utterly beguiling?'

Hannah looked at Banecroft, who was picking at the nail of his big toe, which was poking out of the top of his left sock, and then back at Dr Carter. 'That is one of life's great mysteries.'

'That it is,' said Dr Carter. 'Still,' she said, turning back to

Banecroft, 'if I promise to behave myself, could you perhaps excuse your secretary so we could talk in private?'

'First,' said Banecroft, 'she is my assistant editor.'

Hannah would say this for Banecroft – he did not put up with anyone insulting his staff. Unless, of course, the person doing the insulting was him.

'And second, of the people in this room, she is not the one to whom I most strongly object to being here.'

'Of course not,' said Dr Carter smoothly. 'I merely meant that Ms Willis might want to excuse herself so she can change.'

'Why?' asked Banecroft, looking baffled.

'I jogged into work,' explained Hannah.

'Well done you,' said Dr Carter, making no effort not to sound patronizing.

'Well,' said Banecroft, 'we can't all stay young by drinking the blood of virgins or whatever the hell it is you monsters do.' He pulled a bottle of whiskey from his bottom drawer and poured a large measure into his mug, before taking a swig directly from the bottle. 'I'd offer you a drink but . . . Actually, no, I wouldn't. So, what can we do for you?'

Dr Carter tutted. 'Honestly, Vincent, you don't need to go out of your way to be insulting.'

'You're right, I don't. You've put yourself directly in my way. Now, I'm having a trying morning so, can we cut to the bit where you tell me what you want so I can say no, and we can both get on with our days?'

Carter nodded. 'Very well. I've got a story for you.'

'We do Loon Day once a month – come back next Tuesday.'

'I think you'll want this one. Last night, a man jumped in front of a truck on the Princess Parkway. He died instantly. No other casualties, although I believe the poor driver is suffering from shock.'

'And?'

'And,' continued Dr Carter, 'this man was . . . unusual. Initial reports indicate that he had over-developed incisors, very pale skin, elongated fingernails, was dressed in black . . .'

Banecroft squinted. 'Hang on, you're telling me he was a—'

'No, I'm not.'

'It sounds a lot like you are.'

'They don't exist. I'm asking you to look into it.'

'I don't work for you.'

'Consider it a favour.'

Banecroft looked at Dr Carter and then at Hannah. 'It would appear that the good doctor has grossly misunderstood the nature of our relationship vis-à-vis her being one of the baddies.'

'I think you know all too well, life is never that black and white. And believe me, Vincent,' said Dr Carter, looking down at her skyscraper heel as if suddenly surprised and fascinated by its existence, 'in the waters you find yourself swimming in, it would be advisable to have a favour in your pocket.'

'Like a life preserver?' quipped Banecroft.

'Precisely.'

'As these waters contain sharks.'

'Indeed they do.'

'And, apparently, vampires.'

Dr Carter said nothing in response to this, but her smile disappeared and she locked eyes with Banecroft for a long moment.

'I don't swim,' said Banecroft. 'So, I'll take my favour now.'

'All right,' said Dr Carter. 'I do know an excellent bathroom guy.'

'I'm sure you do, but no, we don't need a bathroom guy.'

'Ms Willis's sweaty aroma would suggest otherwise.'

Hannah flinched. Direct hit. The woman really did have an eye for weakness.

'My stipulation for looking into this,' said Banecroft, 'involves another of our employees: Stella. You might remember her?'

Dr Carter raised both eyebrows. 'The teenager who exhibited inexplicable and undocumented powers when last we met? Yes, I have not forgotten her.'

'Good,' said Banecroft. 'Because you will – forget her, I mean. Not just you. Your whole organization will forget she ever existed, and you will show no interest in her or her abilities ever again.'

'Under the terms of the Accord—'

'Yes or no?' pressed Banecroft.

Dr Carter drew a deep breath then let it out. 'Fine. We will take no interest in the girl, assuming she doesn't make a nuisance of herself.'

'And I suppose I'm going to have to take your word for that?' asked Banecroft.

'I suppose you are.'

'OK. Be warned, though – I don't take people reneging on agreements very well.'

'Oh, Vincent,' said Dr Carter, 'are you threatening to spank me?'

'No. I'm threatening to drive a stake through your cold dead heart.'

It spoke to the length and ferocity of the ensuing stare-off that, despite standing in a stuffy room in the middle of a heat-wave while wearing sweat-soaked running gear, a shiver ran down Hannah's spine. It was finally broken by Banecroft belching.

'One question.'

'Only one?' asked Dr Carter.

'For now.'

She nodded.

'Given you're an organization that, one assumes, has considerable resources at its disposal, why do you need us to look into this?'

'Because of its nature, it's possible that it's something related to the Folk. Let us just say that after recent events, relations between us and them are strained. Therefore, in this particular instance, we would rather it was not us who went poking around.' She opened her briefcase, took out a thin Manila folder and placed it on the desk. 'Here is a copy of the initial police report.'

Banecroft nodded.

'Now, Vincent, sweetie, if we're done, you'll have to excuse me. I've a busy day ahead and I have to burn this outfit now that it's been in this office. Can I send over a crack team of sanitation experts?'

'No, thank you.'

'Perhaps just the gift of a flame-thrower, then? See if you can't brighten up the place?'

'It's a sweet offer, but no.'

Dr Carter stood. 'Very well. Can't blame a gal for trying. Vincent, always a pleasure. Ms Willis, don't forget to stretch. People who aren't used to physical exercise often cramp up after attempting it.'

'Thanks,' said Hannah, 'I will.'

Hannah was aware after she'd said it that there was nothing in those words that served as any kind of retort to what had gone before. Despite that, she'd used a tone of voice that definitely implied there had been.

Dr Carter stopped for a moment, smiled at Hannah and then exited the room.

'Well, well, well,' said Banecroft.

'That was surprising,' conceded Hannah. 'Are you sure that was a good idea?'

'Quite probably not, but I wanted to see her reaction when I mentioned Stella.' He stood up. 'Come on, you and I need to go down to our cellar.'

'We have a cellar?'

Banecroft shoved some papers round on his desk. 'If that shocks you, this next bit is going to blow your tiny mind.' He walked towards the door and paused. 'Before we do, have you any deodorant? Not for nothing, but the woman does have a point. You really could use a shower.'

Not for the first time, Hannah marvelled that the man seemed simultaneously to have the worst and best sense for people. The worst, because nobody in their right mind – in general, and in Banecroft's foul-smelling fog in particular – would ever dare to make such a comment about another person. The best, because without looking he ducked to avoid the hardback book Hannah felt compelled to throw at his head.

CHAPTER 5

Hannah successfully managed to intercept Grace by overtaking Banecroft in the hallway that bypassed the bullpen and led directly from his lair to reception. Hannah had heard the warning jangle of their office manager's bracelets in the distance, like an accessorized herd of angry buffalo coming over the mountain.

As far as Hannah was concerned, Grace had every right to be livid with Banecroft. The woman was a saint for putting up with him as long as she had, and that was before he'd broken the golden rule; by circumventing their swearing agreement and then firing the builders he had betrayed Grace's trust not once but twice. The peace between a self-proclaimed woman of God and a widely considered Satan-in-an-editor's-chair held only because Banecroft knew how not to push it. Or at least he had.

Grace had a letter grasped firmly in her right hand and a face like thunder.

'Grace,' began Hannah, putting out her arms to halt the head of steam built up by the office manager. 'Just the woman I need to talk to.'

Banecroft pointed at the stairs. 'We're supposed to be—'

'And we will,' snapped Hannah. 'In a minute.'

Hannah guided Grace back towards the reception desk at the far end of the room, while Banecroft grumbled something about clucking hens.

'I'm afraid,' said Grace, 'that *that man* has left me with no other option.'

'I know,' said Hannah. 'You're right. You're absolutely right.'

Two minutes later, Hannah met Banecroft on the ground floor at the bottom of the stairs.

'It's about time.'

'Sorry,' said Hannah, holding up the envelope Grace had handed her. 'I was just dealing with our office manager resigning because you're an insufferable arse.'

'Fine,' said Banecroft. 'We'll organize interviews for her replacement tomorrow.'

'Absolutely,' said Hannah. 'And how will we do that?'

'Just ask . . .' Banecroft stopped himself.

'Grace?' supplied Hannah. 'Was that the end of your sentence? Because if you and I were to get trapped in this cellar we apparently have, this week's edition might be a tad late or badly spelled, but if we lose Grace, odds on this place would have no electricity or running water by noon.'

'Actually,' said Banecroft, 'seeing as I booted out the builders with immediate effect, I think you'll find we have no running water now.'

Hannah shook her head. 'How on earth do you think that proves your point? Speaking of which, we need a fully functioning bathroom and you will be apologizing to those builders.'

'Oh, will I?'

Without another word, Banecroft headed down the hallway towards what had been their old bathroom and was, by now, supposed to be their new and improved bathroom. It was being expanded by knocking through to a locked storage room which turned out to contain two hundred and thirty-two cans of Spam with no best-before date or explanation as to how they got to be there. Hannah knew there were two hundred and thirty-two because when they'd finally given up on finding the key and broken the door down a few weeks ago, Ox had counted them before he'd put them on eBay. Thankfully they didn't sell. Come to think of it, she had no idea what Ox had done with them, which was a bit of a worry.

Banecroft pointed at the door and Hannah opened it. She'd been expecting a botched job, or at least a half-finished building site, but that was not what confronted her. Instead, the bathroom of her dreams lay before her. Yes, she really was that sad – she had dreamed about this bathroom. In the dream, however, there wasn't a hole in the ground where the toilet was supposed to be.

The tiles were a shimmering pattern of blue and white, and the sink looked nicer than the one she'd picked out from the catalogue. The shower unit was a very good size and it had two heads. If anything, it looked as if the builders had used a better standard of materials than she'd paid for. She turned her head a little as she didn't want Banecroft to see, but the sight of such a beautiful bathroom made her feel a little emotional. She wanted to move her desk down here. In fact, she would quite happily come and live here permanently.

'It's . . . It's beautiful,' she managed.

'Yes,' agreed Banecroft. 'Look at that finish, too. Given they were the cheapest quote, they've done a spectacular job. Almost too good to be true.'

She'd known Banecroft long enough to realize when he was building up to something. 'And?'

'What?' said Banecroft, the picture of innocence. 'They've done an awesome job. Can I ask – was their quote surprisingly low compared to the others?'

'It might have been.'

'And, in your experience, how many tradespeople have quoted cheaply and then gone dramatically over and above when it comes to the standard of work they provide?'

Hannah placed her hands on her hips. 'Can we skip to the bit where you prove yourself right for firing them? I mean, at least in your own mind.'

Banecroft shrugged. 'You are no fun.' He pulled a tile off the wall and held it aloft in triumph. 'Ta-da!'

Hannah stepped across to peer at the spot where the tile had been. Her eyes fell on a small gap in the brickwork. She studied it then looked back at Banecroft. 'OK, obviously the tiling wasn't done perfectly.'

'What? No, it's not that.' Banecroft slapped the various pockets of his suit. 'Wait. Hang on. Here it is.' His hand dived into his inside jacket pocket. 'It's not the tiling. It's what was behind the teeny-tiny hole between the tiles.' With a flourish he produced an object about the size of an AAA battery.

Hannah's stomach started to sink. 'Is that a . . .'

'Camera?' finished Banecroft. 'Yes. Yes. It. Is.'

Hannah slouched against the wall and surveyed her surroundings, this porcelain-clad Eden having been forever sullied. Come to think of it, Banecroft would've sullied it eventually – one way or another – but not this dramatically.

'Oh God,' said Hannah. 'I hired peeping Tom creeps to fit our new bathroom.'

'No,' said Banecroft cheerfully. 'No, you did not.'

Against all experience, Hannah dared to hope. 'Really?'

'Really. It's far worse than that. Follow me!'

As Banecroft led her out and around the side of the building, Hannah had to shield her eyes from the dazzling morning sun. Banecroft was so giddy he was dangerously close to breaking into dance.

'Come, come. Quick as you can. So much to see.'

Hannah had to admit that she hadn't paid a great deal of attention to the exterior of the Church of Old Souls. She knew about the garage/shed where Banecroft kept his surprisingly nice Jag. She also knew there were numerous bits of the building that needed repairing, because Grace had asked Manny nicely to help out, and he'd gone up on the roof to fix some tiles and one of the more persistent leaks. Yet Hannah was still surprised when Banecroft moved aside the bins and a large piece of yellow tarpaulin to reveal a set of angled metal doors. They looked like a coal chute. Banecroft threw them open with a flourish to reveal a set of stone steps.

'I've just realized who you remind me of,' said Hannah. 'Willy Wonka.'

'Because of my wonderful childlike innocence and way with people?'

'No. It's the unhinged quality and evidence you don't get out much.'

'For a woman who employs peeping Toms, you can be very cutting.'

'I thought you said they weren't peeping Toms?'

'They weren't, but I'm trying to get you used to that concept, so that the leap to the next one isn't so harrowing.' He waved her down the steps. 'After you.'

Reluctantly, Hannah went. Banecroft flicked a switch beside the door, and a bare bulb's worth of wan light was cast round the room.

It was a large space with stone walls. An aroma of dank decay forced Hannah to place her hand to her nose. At one end of the room were discarded bits of furniture, tins of what was probably paint, and what looked like, inexplicably, yet more cans of Spam. At the other end, in stark contrast, sat what looked quite a lot like a tomb.

'Is that a . . .'

'Grave?' finished Banecroft. 'Yes.'

'Creepy.'

'Oh, if you think that's creepy, hang on to your sweat socks.'

An area in front of them was cordoned off behind a dust sheet. Hannah's sense of foreboding would've been heightened if there were anywhere else for it to go.

She jumped as Banecroft pulled the metal doors shut behind them with a clang.

'Don't you think this place could do with airing?'

'Not just now.' He indicated the dust sheet. 'You'll have no doubt surmised that area over there is under our brand-spanking-new bathroom.'

Hannah didn't say anything, but approached the dust sheet slowly. Gingerly, she tugged at one corner, then, annoyed with herself, pulled it aside firmly. There was evidence of recent work having been carried out. On top of the dusty floor was a layer of fresher dust. The kind you got from cutting through stone.

Hannah looked around. 'OK, I don't get it.'

'Really?' asked Banecroft.

He moved across and pulled on a piece of cord that was hanging from the ceiling. A trapdoor in the ceiling flew open and light flooded in.

Hannah peered upwards. She was looking into the shower unit. 'Oh God. I think I'm going to be sick.'

'Yes,' said Banecroft. 'Don't you miss those heady days when you thought you'd just hired peeping Toms?'

Hannah doubled over and her mouth flooded with saliva. Maybe it was the exertion of running in this morning, or the humidity of the cramped cellar, but she doubted it. It was the horrible reality of what Banecroft was laying out.

'Before we proceed any further,' Banecroft went on, 'is it just me or is "peeping Tom" really far too nice a phrase? It sounds a bit "cheeky scamp" or "rapscallion", doesn't it? As opposed to "disgusting sex pest". When we're done here, I'm going to write a strongly worded email to the Oxford English Dictionary. Mind you, what word do we think is strong enough to do justice to this set-up?'

Hannah looked up again, reconfirming her worst fears. 'That is . . .'

'The shower, yes. The builders you hired installed a camera, so that whoever is down here can see whoever is in the shower, then snatch them, naked as a babe, and' – Banecroft moved across the room and heaved aside a large wardrobe to reveal a gate of thick metal bars – 'whisk them away through here, which leads into Manchester's glamorous sewer system. Look at that. All those whimsical remarks I made about digging a tunnel to escape this place and I never realized we already had one.'

Hannah looked from the trapdoor to the metal gate and back again. 'I hired a building firm of serial killers?'

'Be fair – serial killers who do exceptional tiling work. And, actually, no.' Banecroft tossed what looked like a bin lid off a rickety old wooden chair and sat down. It groaned alarmingly, but surprisingly held his weight. 'Think it through. It'll come to you.'

Hannah tried to take a deep breath and gather her thoughts but she could hardly breathe. 'All right,' she said. 'Nobody is going to all this trouble to grab just anyone.'

'Correct,' said Banecroft. 'And while many may wish me dead, they're unlikely to want to talk to me first. Certainly not while I'm naked. While it's possible, let's temporarily park the idea that this is an ill-judged attempt at winning you back by your philandering husband. How did all that go, by the way?'

'You want to talk about that now?'

Banecroft raised a hand. 'Excuse me. Just trying to lighten the mood. Let's also assume nobody is trying to kidnap the Rastafarian who does our printing. So . . .'

Hannah really was going to be sick. 'Stella.'

Banecroft nodded. 'Stella.'

Since the 'incident', as they referred to it, when a monster broke into their offices, only to be emphatically rebuffed by the spirit that co-habited Manny's body, it had been agreed that Stella would stay in the offices twenty-four-seven unless accompanied by another member of staff. It had to be said that Stella had neither agreed to this idea nor liked it at all. It was supposed to be a temporary arrangement, although it had been in place for three months now.

'Wait a second,' said Hannah. 'Manny's friend. Wouldn't she be able to protect Stella if anyone tried to . . .' She pointed up at the trapdoor. 'Well, do all this.'

Banecroft nodded. 'See, you almost got most of the way there all by yourself.'

'Oh, don't be such a patronizing arse.'

'Temper, temper.' Banecroft stood up again. 'To be honest, I've been giving that some thought too. I've got a theory.' He moved over to the metal doors and threw them open again, flooding the room with sunlight. 'MANNY!' he roared at the top of his lungs.

Hannah heard something crash in the distance.

In one fluid motion Banecroft pulled a packet of cigarettes from his pocket, fished one out and lit it. He took a deep drag and exhaled, before looking out at the world.

'It is so nice to get out of the office. The weather is rather good, isn't it? I didn't realize. I assumed it was warm because the heating was stuck on again.'

Hannah moved to stand beside him – to get away from the trapdoor more than anything. Being nearer to fresh air helped too.

She caught sight of Manny stumbling around the corner. Surprisingly, he was pulling on a pair of trousers. He regularly had to be reminded of their importance, so clearly Grace must have recently had one of her words about it. His long white dreadlocks – normally wrapped around his neck like an elaborate headdress – were trailing behind him, almost touching the ground.

'We here. We here. What g'wan?'

'Ah, Manny,' said Banecroft. 'Good of you to join us. Would you mind assisting me with moving something down here in the cellar?'

Manny gave Banecroft a look before taking a step towards the stairs. He jerked backwards suddenly, like a marionette pulled by invisible strings.

'Problem?' asked Banecroft.

Manny looked sheepish and rubbed the back of his neck. 'Sorry. She no go.'

'I see,' said Banecroft. 'She won't or she can't?'

'The second one.' Manny wore a pained expression on his face.

'I wonder where else she can't—'

'Thanks, Manny,' said Hannah, trying to sound cheerful as she cut Banecroft off. 'Don't worry about it. We'll be fine.'

'Y'sure?'

'Absolutely.'

After giving them one last confused look, Manny turned and slowly walked away.

Banecroft glared at Hannah. 'I wanted to find out exactly what areas that thing can cover.'

'By "thing", do you mean the powerful ancient spirit that lives inside Manny? The one we know nothing about – other than one, it protects the building, and two, it really doesn't like being messed with?'

Banecroft gave an almost imperceptible nod, conceding the point. 'Well, now we know she can't go in the cellar, so that's three things we know about her.'

'Actually, four things,' said Hannah, who was starting to feel a little bit more human now she'd got over the initial shock.

Banecroft looked at her expectantly.

'We know that somebody out there knows enough about whatever she is to know that she can't get into the cellar.'

Banecroft nodded. 'There is also that.'

'So,' said Hannah, 'are we going to call the police?'

'Oh no. Where's the fun in that? No, we're going to find out who went to all this trouble, and then we're going to crush them into teeny-tiny pieces. The police won't get us that. Whoever's behind this, they're involved in all this woo-woo nonsense, and we know the police are a black hole when it comes to that.'

'But—'

'But nothing. We get PC Plod on this, odds on the whole thing winds up being dismissed as a big misunderstanding, or else the work of one rogue workman who will have conveniently disappeared.'

Banecroft did have a point. Last time around, the police had wanted nothing to do with their troubles. Well, all bar one of them, and things had gone very badly for him.

'We need to find out who's really behind this thing and nip it in the bud. You were in the meeting with Dr Carter, same as I was. She was my number-one suspect – and she still might be. But does all of this' – he waved a hand into the cellar – 'feel like the actions of a woman who would give us a guarantee of Stella's safety in exchange for looking into a story for her?'

Annoyingly, this was another good point.

'Maybe it *is* her lot and she doesn't know?'

'Maybe,' conceded Banecroft. 'We're not going to figure it out by standing here, though. Luckily, as a result of my entirely unwarranted reputation for being a tad . . .'

'Monstrous?'

'. . . mercurial, I was able to fire the builders without the reason for their dismissal being clear. I imagine they – and whoever is really paying them – will be particularly keen for them to come back and finish the job. In the meantime, we need to find out who that is.'

'Right,' said Hannah. 'I'm on it.'

'No,' said Banecroft, 'you're not. I need you to look into that unexplained death for the good doctor as, now more than ever, we want that guarantee of Stella's safety.'

'Agreed,' said Hannah. 'But Ox or Reggie could—'

'They haven't—'

'Don't say it.'

Banecroft grinned. 'They haven't a pre-existing relationship with a member of the local constabulary.' He helpfully threw in a mime of the large eyeball on a stalk that had appeared from the top of DI Tom Sturgess's head the last time they'd met.

Hannah closed her eyes and sighed. 'God, I hate you so much.'

'Come on now, we all have to do our bit for the team.'

'Yes,' said Hannah, walking off. 'By the way, I told Grace she could dismantle your stupid bloody swear board while we were down here, you absolutely one-ing six.'

'Til Death Do Us Part

In a case that is set to make legal history, Mr Alan Aldridge from Coventry has applied to the courts to divorce his wife, Margaret, in spite of the fact she passed away six years ago. He alleges that she has been haunting him ever since and, although he has moved house twice during that time, her spirit has persisted in following him everywhere.

'It's a nightmare,' claims Mr Aldridge. 'Every time I bring a lady home, Margaret starts chucking pots and pans about, moving ornaments, changing the speed on my Barry White records.' He goes on to say that while he loved his wife, he is 'a man with needs. The missus is cock-blocking me from beyond the grave. One more lady runs out the house screaming and I'm going to get chucked off Tinder! Our marriage vows said 'til death do us part, and that's a promise I expect her to keep.'

CHAPTER 6

Dr Charlie Mason and DI Tom Sturgess walked together in awkward silence. The last time they had come into contact, things had ended badly. On the drive over to the morgue at Royal Oldham Hospital, it had occurred to Sturgess that, along with Mason, there were now quite a few people on the list of individuals he had pissed off. He was well aware that he had a growing reputation in that particular area.

Still, that didn't mean he'd been wrong. He and Mason had fallen out because the man had clearly been sharing privileged information about a case with 'interested parties'. The case in question had been the unexplained deaths of John Maguire, a member of the homeless community, and Simon Brush, a young man who had been attempting to become a reporter with *The Stranger Times*. The interested parties had been very definitely outside of the force. When Sturgess had come up against them, he'd found himself suspended from duties, his career in tatters, and with a splitting headache. Then he'd . . . Well, that was it – he didn't remember.

He did recall being rung by Hannah Willis from *The Stranger Times* and her asking him to get her in to the station to see her colleague who was under arrest. Come to that, it was Sturgess who had arrested him. After helping Hannah, they, along with her boss, the odious Banecroft, had headed off to try to find . . . someone. The next thing Sturgess remembered was waking up on his own sofa. Try as he might, he wasn't able to remember much more about the case. The more he tried, the less it seemed to help, and the worse his migraines got. Occasionally, in dreams, he'd see flashes of images – a terrifying beast; a man with a demented grin, laughing at him; and a knife, dancing in the air before his eyes.

He'd been subsequently suspended from the force pending him being shoved out the first available door for good and so, on a whim, Sturgess had gone to Italy to see his sister, Cathy. For the last five years she'd been asking him to come out to Venice, and, when he finally said he'd visit, she'd been equal parts delighted and bewildered. She and her husband, Sergio, had two kids, and she didn't come back to Manchester much – not since her and Tom's mother's death.

For his part, DI Tom Sturgess didn't take holidays, at least not ones that HR hadn't forced him to. Those he spent at home, texting colleagues while attempting DIY projects he was doomed never to finish, just waiting to go back to work. He mowed his back garden only when his neighbour stuck a passive-aggressive note through the door asking him to. The last time he'd attacked the lawn, he'd broken two mowers before eventually hiring a landscape gardening service to sort it out on his behalf. The woman had taken one look and gone off in search of a scythe.

The job was his everything. He was a workaholic, and a

dangerously obsessive one. He knew that. Still, he was good at what he did. He knew that too.

Cathy was a mean detective in her own right, albeit on a strictly amateur basis. She'd known her baby brother was in some kind of trouble, but she hadn't pressed. Once he was in Venice, Tom had met his niece and nephew for the first time and discovered he liked being an uncle. The kids were bilingual and as bright as buttons.

Much to his relief, the headaches that had been plaguing him stopped. It had happened around the same time as the text messages had started. The sender had referred to themselves as a 'concerned citizen' and told Sturgess that his work looking into the more 'unusual' cases that came the Greater Manchester Police's way was vital, and that they wanted to see it continue. He'd replied, asking who it was, and had been ignored. He'd blocked the number repeatedly, only for it to somehow become unblocked each time. Failing all other options, he'd tried to ignore the messages.

However, when he'd received the email informing him of his forthcoming disciplinary proceedings, a text had arrived five minutes later from the concerned citizen, asking him if he'd like it all to go away. He'd be able to return to Manchester, retain his rank, and be allowed to investigate the cases he wanted. He'd also be able to do so with what was described as 'improved resources'. He wasn't stupid. He knew he was being offered the chance to make a deal with the devil. The thing was, they had him, and the concerned citizen – or CC, as they signed the texts – knew it too.

He had to know. He had to find out what the hell was going on. The inability to abide an unanswered question went to the very core of his being. So he'd laid down conditions. He would do the job – he wouldn't be looking the other way for anyone. He'd share information and chase up any leads he was given, provided it benefited his investigation. CC had agreed. And so it went. He was now compromised. He could dress it up how he liked, but that was the reality of the deal.

He could tell himself that he was different to Dr Mason – that he wasn't covering anything up – but who was he kidding? Nobody starts off utterly compromised. It's a death of a thousand cuts. Tiny increments until one day, you've become the thing you feared most. What choice did he have, though? Take the deal or find himself a disgraced former copper with no friends on the force. It wasn't just the job; it was what the job meant. Without it, he'd never get the answers he needed. Still, Sturgess couldn't pretend he was on the higher ground any more, not when he'd received a text from CC in the early hours informing him that he had a case, forty-five minutes before he got the official call.

As Mason pushed opened the doors to the mortuary, Sturgess decided to break the silence. 'So, did you get to go to the wedding in the end?'

'What?' asked Mason, sounding surprised.

'The last time we spoke was after Colin from the lab upstairs' stag do, and you were annoyed as you hadn't been invited to the wedding because your ex-wife was going.'

'Bloody hell,' said Mason. 'That's one helluva memory.'

Sturgess tried to smile. The irony. This he could remember perfectly.

'No,' said Mason, with a grin, 'but that turned out to be a blessing in disguise. Yvonne, my ex, went to the wedding and, get this' – he slapped Sturgess on the back with barely contained glee – 'she got pissed and got off with the bride's father. The bride's *married* father.'

'Wow!' said Sturgess, not entirely confident of the reaction expected from him in this situation.

'Yeah,' said Mason happily, 'so now Yvonne is *persona non grata* and I've been invited over to Colin's on Saturday for a barbecue!'

'That's good.'

'Isn't it?' said Mason, dancing what looked like, to Sturgess's untrained eye, a bit of a salsa. 'His missus has a lot of single female friends. It will be a target-rich environment, if you get my meaning.'

Sturgess did. He imagined most of the corpses in the mortuary did too. Mason wasn't exactly subtle. Generally speaking, Sturgess's small-talk abilities were poor; however, they were immense in comparison with his capacity for laddish banter. He nodded, hoping that would cover all eventualities.

It appeared to, or at least Mason was too enraptured by his unrealistic visions of a British summer barbecue being like a trip to Hugh Hefner's Bunny Ranch to notice, much less care.

'I bloody love a barbecue.' Mason stopped beside a gurney upon which lay a body covered by a sheet. His face dropped. 'Oh. Ehm. Probably not the best of segues, that. So this is the body you're here for.' He placed his hand on one corner of the sheet but didn't lift it. 'Can I ask – I thought you were on your uppers?'

'I'm sorry?'

'I mean, no offence, mate, but I thought you were looking at suspension and . . .' Mason left the sentence hanging.

Sturgess could see from the expression on the pathologist's face that he realized his barbecue-based delight might have made him overly chatty. It was clear he was now regretting venturing into this territory.

'That all got sorted out.'

'Oh, right.'

'So, about this body?'

'Yes,' said Mason, handing Sturgess a surgical face mask before pulling up his own. 'It's a weird one, all right – even by your standards.' He drew back the sheet.

Sturgess resisted the urge to pull away as the sickly-sweet stench of charred flesh assailed him. The body before them was badly burned from head to toe, its lower jaw hanging open as if locked in a never-ending scream.

'From my understanding, the deceased was hit by an HGV moving at high speed.'

'Well, thirty miles an hour,' said Sturgess.

'Oh, yeah,' said Mason. 'Princess Parkway, wasn't it? Still can't believe they changed the speed limit there from forty to thirty. No need for it. I got a ticket on it last year. Big dual carriageway.'

Sturgess didn't say anything. It was hard to take his eyes off the body. The mouth in particular.

'Anyway,' said Mason, refocusing. 'The reduced speed limit was of no benefit to Mr Crispy here.'

'Have you come up with any explanation for the flames?' Sturgess had interviewed the HGV driver personally and the man had sworn blind that the first he'd seen of the victim was when he'd stopped the lorry and got out. The body had been lying in front of the vehicle, tallying with the female witness's account of how the man had leaped into its path, thereby avoiding going under the wheels. None of which gave any insight into why the body had burst into flames.

'Honestly,' said Mason, 'we're stumped. No accelerants on the body and, from what I'm told, he went up fast. If there was something on his clothes, it burned away quickly and without leaving a trace. Plus, his clothing survived reasonably intact. Like *he* was the thing that burst into flame.'

'Spontaneous combustion?' asked Sturgess.

'I mean, yeah – that's technically what it is, but we've none of the why. While spontaneous combustion is a recognized if unexplained phenomenon, there's no recorded incident of it occurring due to a massive trauma such as a vehicular collision. I've sent some queries out, but I've not heard of anything like that.' Mason waved a hand up and down the body. 'And seeing as the driver had an extinguisher in his cab and doused him quickly, if he'd not done so, this dude would've ended up a lump of gristle.'

'Right,' said Sturgess.

'And then there's the teeth,' said Mason. He took out a pen and pointed at them. 'Overly developed canines, to be exact.'

'How unusual is that?'

'Well,' said Dr Mason. 'Some people's canines are just naturally pointed, but not to this extreme. You can get it done as a cosmetic procedure, though. There's a temporary version involving resin or, if you're full-on mental, you can get them filed down and have caps put on. But . . .'

'But?'

'This is neither of those things. This is, for want of a better word, natural. How firm is your ID on this guy?'

'Reasonably,' said Sturgess. 'The flames were put out fast enough that we recovered a wallet containing ID identifying him as Phillip Butler. We also have a phone that's been verified as belonging to Butler. The general build, height, et cetera fit what we know.'

'Right,' said Dr Mason. 'Only I rang his dentist, ahead of his records being sent over, and there's no suggestion that Mr Butler was sporting this kind of a messed-up grill when they saw him last.'

'OK,' said Sturgess, 'so it's possible this might not be him.'

Both men looked at each other, neither giving voice to the point that if it was Butler, he'd somehow grown the teeth recently.

Mason broke the silence. 'We're doing a DNA test to confirm. Oh, and by the way, the dentist did mention that Mr Butler had an emergency appointment booked in for the day before he died, but he never showed up.'

'Interesting,' said Sturgess. 'Anything else?'

'Oh, we've not even got to the weird bit yet.'

Sturgess raised an eyebrow.

'We did the content analysis of Laughing Boy's stomach. No drugs, no accelerants—'

'Were you expecting to find something?'

Dr Mason shrugged. 'No, but, like I said, we're still mystified by the flames. Y'know what old Sherlock said about once you've eliminated the impossible? We did find something else, though . . .'

Sturgess resisted the urge to roll his eyes as Mason played it out. 'And what was that, Doctor?'

'Blood. But not his.'

'You're kidding?'

Mason shook his head.

'And it's—'

'Human? Yes. We're running it for DNA. And before you say it, I have asked the lab to rush both sets of tests.'

'I appreciate it.'

'All part of the service.'

Sturgess was all set to turn away but stopped himself. He lowered his voice. 'Charlie, can I ask . . . Everything you've just told me, you say it like it's nothing. I mean, I know you deal with a lot here, but still.'

'Are you asking how I keep my chipper demeanour?'

'If you like.'

'Drugs,' said Mason, with a chubby-cheeked grin. 'I'm on these really good ones. My GP is a happy-pill dispensing machine. Do you want his details?'

'No, I'm good.' After an awkward pause, he added, 'Thanks.'

'No problem. You're a single man, aren't you, Tom?'

'Yeah.'

Mason slapped his hands together. 'How would you fancy coming to a barbecue? I could use a wingman.'

Sturgess pulled his phone out of his pocket. 'Sorry, I've got to take this.' He answered the phantom call. 'Sturgess. One second.' He put his hand over the mouthpiece and turned to Mason. 'You'll ring me when you have any update?'

Mason nodded.

And then, because life is not only weird, but also occasionally unforgiving, Sturgess's phone rang for real. He looked at the device and floundered. 'I must have hung up or . . .'

Mason turned and walked away. Sturgess didn't quite hear what the other man said as he did so, but he could guess.

CHAPTER 7

It's funny how the human mind works. Hannah hadn't really processed just how insane the set-up Banecroft had shown her in the cellar was until she had pulled Grace aside and explained it to her.

It was Grace's look of disbelief, her genuine gasp of horror that really brought things home. The office manager then used her left hand to steady herself against the reception desk and her right to bless herself again and again.

'We must call the police,' she said a little too loudly.

'We can't,' said Hannah.

'What are you talking about?'

'Banecroft—'

'That man doesn't even use a shower!'

'That may be,' said Hannah, 'but I'm afraid he's right about this. We have to assume that somebody is after Stella, and the most important thing is to protect her. Oh, damn it!'

Hannah caught Grace's disapproving look.

'Sorry, I just remembered that before I left, I promised Stella she could come and stay in my spare room for a couple of weeks. I totally forgot that with all the . . .'

'She definitely cannot do that,' said Grace.

'I know,' said Hannah, 'but we also can't tell her why. The poor kid doesn't know which way is up and she's terrified of everything right now, including herself. She almost ran away last time there was trouble. We can't risk it.'

'Where would she think to go?'

'I don't know,' said Hannah, 'but she might be more concerned about protecting other people than looking after herself.'

'Oh no,' said Grace softly.

Hannah placed her hand on Grace's arm. 'Don't worry, it'll be OK.'

'And you are quite sure about the police?'

Hannah tried to keep her voice calm. 'They can't deal with this kind of stuff. They didn't last time. Banecroft is right. The best thing we can do is find out who's behind it and then make sure they can't try anything like it again. That's the most sensible thing.'

Grace nodded. 'There are a couple of men in my church. Big men. God-fearing but also a little on the wayward side.' She licked her lips nervously. 'If I asked them, they could go round to these builders and knock some heads together.'

Her last words sounded as if she were repeating something she'd heard on a TV programme. Hannah knew that Grace, despite her religious ways, loved a good crime drama.

'That won't be necessary,' said Hannah, although she wasn't exactly sure she was correct in that. Banecroft had been a little vague about their endgame. 'First off, let's find out who got them to do this and we'll take it from there. It makes more sense to investigate than to tip our hands.'

'Where the hell is everybody?' roared Banecroft from the other room.

For Grace's benefit Hannah rolled her eyes. 'Banecroft might be a monster but destroying someone who's crossed him like this is what he lives for.'

'If everyone isn't in this room in thirty seconds, I'm going to lose my one-ing two.'

It took over ten minutes for all the staff to gather in the bullpen. Even with Banecroft's impressive vocal range, he hadn't been able to reach Reggie, Ox and Stella, who had gone to make use of the facilities in the nearby Admiral's Arms pub.

Banecroft and Grace had stood there, pointedly not looking at the pile of firewood to which his swear board had been reduced while he and Hannah had been downstairs. Hannah had interspersed her awkward small talk with firing off furious texts to the other three, telling them to hurry back. She was relieved when she heard them coming up the stairs.

'About time,' thundered Banecroft. 'It's barely mid-morning and half my staff has already trooped off to the pub.'

'We had no choice,' said Reggie. 'This office is now entirely lacking facilities.'

'Yeah,' agreed Ox, 'and it turns out Dennis is pretty hardcore when it comes to the toilets-are-for-customers'-use-only rule, so I had to have a . . .' He caught Reggie's alarmed look just in time. 'Diet Coke.'

Banecroft shook his head. 'Unbelievable.'

'To be fair,' said Hannah, 'people do need to use the bathroom somewhere.'

'No, they don't. Neither Bernstein nor Woodward used a bathroom for the whole of nineteen seventy-three.'

Nobody said anything to this. Some lies are too big even to begin to grapple with.

'So . . .' said Hannah. 'Moving on.'

'Yes,' said Banecroft. 'We have a story about a vampire to look into. Hannah will be taking point.' He jabbed a finger at Ox. 'And you, as our resident vampire expert, will be backing her up.'

Ox pointed at Reggie. 'Actually, he's the one who knows all about vampires.'

'Really?' asked Banecroft.

Reggie nodded.

'Well, that's no good,' continued Banecroft. 'I need you to drive me somewhere.'

Reggie pointed back at Ox. 'Actually, he's the one who can drive.'

'Excellent,' said Banecroft. 'That worked out well.'

Ox looked like a man in a game of pass the parcel who'd been left holding the package when the music stopped, and who had just noticed it was ticking.

'Whoa,' he said. 'Hang on. I've got that big story about the crop circles outside Warrington to finish.'

'Indeed, you do,' said Banecroft. 'On top of that, you're now working for this paper's special operations department. Think of it as a promotion.'

'Does it come with a pay rise?'

Banecroft barked a laugh. 'Good one. I knew one of you was funny, but I never could remember which one it was.'

'But,' continued Ox, 'can't you drive yourself?'

'No,' said Banecroft. 'It turns out you need a valid licence to do that. Typical nanny-state nonsense.'

Ox nodded in Stella's direction. 'You had her drive you last time.'

'I did,' said Banecroft, glowering at Ox, 'but she has important work to be doing here.'

'I do?' said Stella, looking up from her phone expectantly.

'Yes.' Banecroft turned towards Hannah.

'Ehm . . . yes,' said Hannah. 'We . . . need you to do some filing.' She cringed.

'Oh, brilliant,' said Stella, folding her arms and letting her hair fall back over her face. 'That sounds way better than the vampire thing or whatever "special operations" means.'

'Excellent,' said Banecroft, choosing to ignore the sarcasm entirely. 'Glad that's all settled. You two,' he said, pointing at Hannah and Reggie, 'are Team Vampire. Along with following up with the police, you've got that source to chase up.'

'We do?' said Hannah.

'Yes,' snapped Banecroft. 'The thing.'

Hannah and Reggie exchanged a look.

'I'm afraid I've no idea what you're talking about,' said Hannah.

'The thing,' Banecroft repeated irritably. 'I gave it to you last week.'

'I wasn't here last week.'

Banecroft slapped his pockets. It was like watching a particularly awful close-up magician. His search yielded three crumpled packets of cigarettes, which he tossed on the desk in front of him, a half-eaten pork pie and, then, a tea-stained envelope.

'This,' he said, handing the envelope to Hannah.

'This is addressed to me! And you opened it?'

'I was covering for you while you weren't here, so I was doing everything instead of almost everything. No need to thank me.'

'On that, at least, we are agreed.' Hannah opened the envelope and pulled out the note inside. 'This is from Mrs Harnforth.' Hannah had met the paper's owner only once, but she left an impression.

'I know. I read it – obviously!' Banecroft clapped his hands together before Hannah could respond. 'Right, along with all of the above, this afternoon's editorial meeting is happening right now.'

The announcement was met with a chorus of groans.

'But,' protested Reggie, 'I haven't had time to prepare.'

'Ha,' said Banecroft, 'I take it back. *You're* the funny one. Last week you suggested a special feature on what noises ghosts make. Prepared. That's some funny stuff.' He snatched his collection of half-empty cigarette packets from the table. 'You've all got until I come back from having a pee to get what we will laughingly refer to as your thoughts in order.'

'But we haven't got running water,' said Grace.

'Yes,' said Banecroft. 'The good Lord has blessed me with many gifts, including male genitalia. Ergo, I can pee anywhere. Out of windows, in woods, in that plant pot beside your desk . . .'

'Don't you dare,' warned Grace.

Banecroft waved a hand theatrically in the air as he left the room. 'Too late!'

Grace looked round the room. 'He wouldn't, would he?'

Her colleagues avoided her gaze.

'If you'll excuse me,' she sighed, 'I need to go and burn an asparagus fern.'

CHAPTER 8

Stanley Roker leaned back on his stool, pushed away his glass and belched loudly. Susan, the girl who had served him every day for over a week now, was long past the point at which she felt obliged to hide her disgust.

'Jesus, Stanley.'

Stanley said nothing in response. Instead, he reached into his pocket and popped a couple of the antacids he now took before, after and, often, during meals.

Everyone knows there are five stages of grief. What is less well known is that there are five stages of sympathy. Stage one is the sympathetic ear. Susan had lent hers for the first two days. Concerned nods, a tilt of the head, listening to Stanley as he told her his woes. She had tried to give him numbers to ring and suggested people to talk to.

Stage two is the pick-me-up. She'd spent less than a day on this. Stanley wasn't one for the ra-ra speeches and Susan was too Mancunian, by both birth and nature, to be able to pull off the requisite level of positivity.

Stage three is tough love. This was certainly more in Susan's wheelhouse. She'd given Stanley the mother of all rollocking bollockings, so much so that another customer – a middle-aged woman with a maternal air and a yappy dog – had felt moved to intervene, berating Susan for her lack of compassion. That same woman proceeded to sit there and listen to Stanley for about an hour, during which time she rocketed through stages one to three at record speed. She'd absconded after her dog had decided to bite Stanley on the ankle, and left a large tip in her wake by way of an apology to Susan.

Stage four is sullen silence. Susan had essentially given up on Stanley – as, to be fair, had Stanley. He kept coming back, though. He'd been outside the door again this morning, waiting for her to open up. And so now they existed in a state of mutual indifference, like a married couple who'd realized long ago that they'd made a mistake but didn't have the energy to bother to fix it.

Stage five is inversion. At this point, the sympathizer finds themselves having completely reversed their initial position. Susan was now dangerously close to this point – switching from sympathizing with the man who had been kicked out by his wife, to being entirely on her side. Over the last week, she had discovered that sympathy is a finite resource, and she was beginning to fear that Stanley Roker had used up her lifetime supply of it.

She didn't understand what he was doing here. Really, a pub was the perfect place for the level of deep personal depression in which Stanley was engaging. She'd stopped short of suggesting he find one, assuming that if someone like Stanley was steering clear of purveyors of alcohol it was probably for a very good reason. Or perhaps that was where he went when she closed up for the evening. Whatever the reason was, she doubted it was because he was worried about his health.

It was barely lunchtime and the man had just finished his second milkshake, after dourly gobbling up three chocolate-chip cookies, a slice of caramel cheesecake and three triple-scoop bowls of ice-cream. Despite the amount of money he was spending there, Susan was growing more and more concerned that he was bad for business.

The Spoonful of Sugar was a dedicated dessert bar. It sold joyful self-indulgence – treats to lift the soul and temporarily derail the diet. Stanley, an overweight pile of sweat-soaked misery sitting at the counter and hogging the eatery's air-conditioning, was a terrible advert, both for the experience and for the products being sold to the general public.

It was like a chicken shop whose new mascot was a rooster mid-coronary. A gin-maker with a tearful, mascara-streaked woman as its poster model. A hairpiece company that showed you what a man really looked like while wearing a hairpiece. People were coming in, seeing Stanley grimly gorging his way to an early grave via the medium of highly calorific confectionary, and were leaving again without indulging in anything bar the use of the bathroom. He was a one-man government health warning.

He slammed a fist against his chest, unleashed another belch and looked down at the forty-eight flavours of ice-cream. 'Right. I will have—'

'No,' said Susan, who hadn't even realized she was going to say the word before she blurted it out.

'What?'

'No, Stanley. I'm cutting you off.'

Stanley shook his head, as if trying to clear away the cobwebs, and looked at her again. 'What?' he repeated, before adding, 'Can you even do that?'

'Watch me,' said Susan. 'Thank you and goodbye.'

'You're throwing me out?'

'Yes. I am.'

Stanley reared back and straightened himself up to his full unimpressive height. 'You and whose army?'

Susan drew a baseball bat from under the counter and gripped it tightly.

Stanley looked at it. 'You're a dessert shop. Why do you have a baseball bat under the counter?'

'There are some very angry diabetics out there.'

'Well, I'm not leaving.'

Susan didn't consider herself a mean person but everyone has their limit. 'Yes, you bloody well are. To paraphrase your wife, get the hell out and never come back.'

Stanley looked aghast. 'I told you about that in the strictest confidence.'

'Bugger off, Stanley. You've told anyone that would listen. You told the bloke who came in to fix the coffee machine yesterday, and he didn't even speak that much English.'

Stanley shook his head. 'Right. This is it. This is the moment. I thought I'd hit rock bottom when I was attacked by some demented demon, or when my wife left me, or when I was informed that a week later she'd shacked up with that bastard

Maurice Glenn. But no, this – this moment, getting booted out of a bloody dessert shop. This is rock bottom. There is no possible way for me to sink any lower than this.'

It shouldn't really be possible to identify someone you have seen only twice in ten years just by the sound of them clearing their throat, but Stanley was able to do precisely that. He hung his head. Why did he insist on dangling his unmentionables in the wind for fate to boot him in, time after time after time?

Behind him, Vincent Banecroft spoke in an unnecessarily cheery voice. 'Hello, Stanley.'

CHAPTER 9

Ox thanked the barman and arranged the trio of drinks into the requisite triangle for optimum carrying efficiency. It was coming up to lunchtime but Banecroft had ordered himself a double whiskey, this Stanley fella had gone with a lemonade, and Ox had plumped for a water, mainly because he had barely enough cash on him to cover the cost of the other two drinks. He could try to mention the money to Banecroft, but the man didn't take subtle hints.

The short drive from the office to the Northern Quarter had been a barrel of laughs – Banecroft had complained about almost everything they'd passed. Still, Ox had got to drive the Jag, which was pretty cool. After many years of good service followed by several years of erratic service, Ox's own car, the Zombie, was now suffering from a waterlogged engine. The damage was the work of the Fenton brothers, to whom he owed money – when they couldn't track him down, they'd pushed the car into the lake at Heaton Park in frustration. The council had fished out the vehicle and returned it to him, so it was now parked outside the flat he shared with Reggie, hopefully drying out in the heat.

Beyond the name of the street, Banecroft hadn't told Ox anything about where they were going. He hadn't told him anything about why either, only that Ox was going to be working on 'special operations'. Ox had to admit, it was a cool-sounding phrase, but he remained infinitely suspicious about what it would entail. Out of all the *The Stranger Times* staff members, he considered himself to be the one who was dealing with the revelations about the existence of the Founders and all that the best. His reasoning for this was simple: he'd always been convinced that dark forces were secretly running the world. All right, he'd been way off on the nature of those forces, but still.

In contrast, Grace, who had always been religious, was leaning hard on that now. Praying at her desk, crucifixes and bottles of holy water all over the place. Reggie was reading and rereading old copies of the paper, looking at every story they'd ever reported in a different light, obsessing over what was real and what wasn't. Stella – well, it was hard to tell what was going on there. He hadn't witnessed anything himself, but Hannah had mentioned that Stella actually had some powers. While Ox had wanted to know more, nobody seemed inclined to discuss it, least of all Stella herself. The poor kid was feigning boredom, but deep down, you could see she was terrified of everything – even herself. Manny, on the other hand, was, well, Manny. He appeared to be as he'd always been, although it was hard to look at him in the same way – a demonic angel appearing out of a man will have that effect on your perceptions.

And then, of course, there was Banecroft. Who knew how this was affecting him? It was impossible to tell if he was drinking more, because that was like trying to determine whether the ocean had more water in it than usual. You could have a go, but you'd need a team of dedicated scientists and a lot of fancy equipment to figure it out.

Ox navigated his way around the fruit machine and saw the two men sitting in the back booth where he had left them, engaging in what looked like a very stilted conversation. The pub's other patrons were all sitting outside, enjoying the sunshine, like normal people. In contrast, Ox's two companions were staring at one another as if competing to see who would die first.

Ox had never met Stanley Roker before today, but that didn't mean he hadn't seen him around. The fella had been waiting in reception last week, when Ox had come back from reporting about that UFO sighting over in Tameside – or, rather, the 'yet another dipshit with a drone' sighting. Initially, Ox had been antsy – the occasional debt collector had come looking for him at work in the past – but Stanley wasn't there to see him. A few minutes later, Grace had shown Stanley in to Banecroft's office, but the two men had a blazing row almost immediately and Stanley had stormed back out. While the row had been big on volume, it had been light on info. The bits Ox, Reggie and Grace had overheard consisted mainly of Stanley calling Banecroft every name under the sun and Banecroft responding by calling Stanley every number on his swear board.

Given that heated exchange, it was a bit of a surprise when, with Ox's assistance, Banecroft had not only sought out Stanley but also offered to buy him a drink, albeit one he almost certainly had no intention of paying for. Actually, they'd initially offered to buy Stanley an ice-cream at the Spoonful of Sugar, but had quickly left when the woman behind the dessert bar's counter had swung a baseball bat at them. Even Banecroft could pick up on that kind of subtle hint.

Ox placed the drinks down on the wobbly table and took a seat. Banecroft and Stanley were too busy eyeballing each other, and neither man acknowledged him. The place smelled of polish, which was odd because nothing looked as if it had been cleaned.

'How did you even find me?' asked Stanley.

'Simple,' said Banecroft. 'The lapel of your jacket had a stain on it that appeared to be mint chocolate-chip ice-cream. The Spoonful of Sugar is the only location in Manchester that stocks that flavour.'

'You're kidding.'

Banecroft sighed. 'Yes, Stanley. In your rather pathetic pleading speech, when you came in to beg for a job, you mentioned how you spent your days sitting at the counter of a dessert bar. There are only three such places with seating in Manchester, and I went to the most central one first.'

Stanley picked up his lemonade and grumbled something into it. Begrudgingly, Ox had to admit that was pretty good detective work. Banecroft could be smart when he wasn't concentrating his efforts on being awful.

'So, what the hell do you want now?' asked Stanley.

'I've changed my mind,' said Banecroft.

'Oh, really? And what makes you think I'd still be interested?'

'Well, it appears you are no longer welcome in the dessert bar, so you might have a bit of free time on your hands.'

Stanley paused for a moment, allowing the fruit machine to finish its periodic expulsion of random sounds, just in case anyone forgot it existed. 'How much does it pay?'

'Nothing.'

Stanley scoffed.

'Consider it a trial.'

'I've got more experience than your entire staff combined.'

'That's what worries me.'

Ox was taken aback when Banecroft looked at him. He assumed his boss had forgotten he was there.

'Stanley and I used to work together,' Banecroft explained.

'He fired me,' said Stanley.

Banecroft nodded. 'I did. I cleaned house and Stanley was the dirtiest of the dirty. He is the tabloid journalist that even other tabloid journalists find distasteful.'

'Are you here to hire me or insult me?'

'Can't I do both?'

The two men stared at one another some more. Ox, being the child of parents who refused to get divorced as they seemed to be enjoying the arguments too much, couldn't resist the urge to fill the silence. 'Are you interested in the paranormal, Stanley?'

'I wasn't. Then I was working a story and some demon creature kidnapped me and tried to have sex with me.'

'I see,' said Ox, who really didn't see at all.

'She'd probably have killed me, or worse, but my wife, Crystal, broke the door down.'

73

'That was lucky.'

The rage in Stanley's eyes caused Ox to sit back. 'Lucky? Lucky? Are you taking the mickey?'

'Ehm, no.'

Stanley shook his head and spoke to his glass of lemonade. 'Lucky, he says. My wife, the love of my life, has left me and shacked up with Maurice bastard Glenn and I'm lucky?'

Ox looked at Banecroft.

'Stanley here wants to work with us as he needs to prove to his estranged wife that the woman—'

'Creature,' interjected Stanley.

'Whatever,' continued Banecroft, 'is real.'

'And that she trapped me. People can call me a lot of things – and they have done – but I'm a faithful husband.'

Ox was taken aback by the look of sincerity in Stanley's rheumy eyes.

'Couldn't you—' started Ox before Stanley cut him off.

'I've been back there. The woman who rented the flat disappeared. It's like she never existed. No way to track her, and believe me, I tried. Even spoke to the police.'

'How did that go?' asked Banecroft.

'They tried to have me sectioned.'

'Bloody hell,' said Ox. 'That sounds awful.'

Stanley nodded, seeming slightly mollified.

'So,' said Banecroft, 'are you in or . . .'

'What's the story?'

'It's less of a story, more of an investigation. We hired some builders to redo the bathroom at the office.'

Stanley shrugged. 'Not some trading-standards thing, is it? Those are tedious.'

'Not exactly,' said Banecroft. 'The builders in question installed a trapdoor in the floor of our new shower, in order to capture a member of our staff in the cellar below and spirit them away via the Manchester sewer system.'

'What?' said Ox, beyond shocked. 'You never mentioned that.'

'I'm mentioning it now.'

'But . . .' started Ox, before heading back to, 'What?'

'And what exactly do you need me for?' asked Stanley. 'I'm assuming you know who this building firm are? You did hire them, after all.'

'Yes and assuming we didn't engage the services of the world's first serial-killer building firm, my guess is that they're being paid or coerced into doing this by a third party. I would dearly like to find out who that third party is.'

'And why can't you go to the police?'

'Remind me – how did they react when you told them about your run-in with this demon lady of yours?'

Stanley nodded, conceding the point, before leaning back in his seat. 'I do this and you'll help me with my thing?'

'You do this and I'll give you a job if you want it. That'll put you closer to the kind of people who can assist you with your enquiries.'

Stanley folded his arms and gave Banecroft an appraising look. 'How come last week I was the last man on earth you wanted to give a job to, and now you're here begging me to sign up?'

'Begging?' said Banecroft, incredulous. 'Begging?'

Stanley said nothing but raised his eyebrows.

'I am reconsidering begrudgingly because the situation has changed. It seems we are in a dirty war and we need someone with a particular set of skills. You, Stanley, are the dirtiest of the dirty.'

'I'll take that as a compliment.'

'It wasn't meant as one.' Banecroft nodded in Ox's direction. 'You'll be working with my associate here.'

'I work alone,' said Stanley.

'So do I,' agreed Ox.

Banecroft slapped the table, causing the drinks to wobble. 'Excellent, there's something you've already got in common. You're a team now – non-negotiable and you talk only to me or to my assistant editor.' He didn't wait for any kind of an answer. Banecroft stood up and held out a hand to Ox. 'Car keys?'

'I didn't think you had a licence?' asked Ox, pulling the keys out of his pocket.

'Turns out I do.'

'How am I supposed to get back to the office?'

'You're an investigative journalist – the case is out there,' Banecroft said with a vague wave of his hand, 'not back at your desk.' He snatched the keys out of Ox's hand. 'I'll leave you two lone-gun mavericks to get cracking.' He picked up his whiskey and knocked it back in one.

'What about expenses?'

'Don't incur any.' Banecroft turned and headed for the door.

Ox watched him leave before directing his attention back to the man who was apparently his new partner.

Stanley held out a hand. 'Stanley Roker.'

Ox took it. 'Ox Chen.'

As they shook hands, Ox tried to ignore how unpleasantly sticky Stanley's was, with what he fervently hoped was ice-cream.

CHAPTER 10

Reggie took a deep breath and smiled. Hannah was getting to know him well enough to realize that this was what her colleague did when he was trying not to say something that was bubbling away inside. The smile was alarmingly wide and, possibly, a fair indication of how annoyed he was. She had to admit that he had a point. They'd been wandering around for almost two hours now, and it was far too warm to be traipsing blindly up and down a canal towpath.

They'd come down here after the weekly editorial meeting. Banecroft, clearly in a hurry, had economized the normally painful two-hour slugfest by turning it into a rapid-fire demolition of most of the ideas presented to him. It had lasted a mere twenty-seven minutes and had been carnage. After that, Hannah had accompanied the still-shell-shocked Reggie down to the Bridge-water Canal.

Since then, their day had been spent trying to avoid being run over by middle-aged men in ill-judged Lycra who were cycling as if they were in the Tour de France and not on a narrow path with only just enough room for two pedestrians to pass comfortably. Interspersed with the cyclists were joggers, strollers and, inexplicably, a conga line of four drunk teenagers wearing sombreros.

The letter Banecroft had given Hannah from Mrs Harnforth, the owner of *The Stranger Times*, had wished her well on her divorce and had contained the incredibly vague instruction that if Hannah needed information regarding 'matters of an ethereal nature' she should 'look for the nail in the wall on the Bridge-water Canal'. The rest of the note read, 'You're looking for a man called Cogs. He can only speak the truth. Don't trust him.' The word 'don't' was underlined twice. Mrs H had then signed off with a postscript: 'Take a bottle of rum.' The aforementioned bottle now sat in Reggie's briefcase. Hannah had considered cracking it open more than once.

She sensed that Reggie was struggling to refrain from making the point, yet again, that they really needed more information before starting out on this 'adventure'. It had to be said, his mood probably wasn't helped by his insistence on wearing a three-piece suit during a heatwave. After an hour, in concession to the sweltering heat, he'd deigned to remove his jacket. The waistcoat remained firmly buttoned up, though – despite the rest of him resembling a six-foot wax model of Toad of Toad Hall that was melting in the heat. At least Hannah could feel less self-conscious about the fact that, given her lack of access to showering facilities, she was still in her sweaty running gear. They made quite the pair.

Hannah had to admit that this was all her fault. She'd been too excited to get going. The grim discovery of the trapdoor had shaken her and she'd wanted to spring into action, to feel as if she were doing something. If tracking down this story meant that Stella would be safer, then damn it, that was what she was going to do. Her intentions had been impeccable but yes, they should have been matched with a little more forethought.

The 'nail in the wall' wasn't a pub. They'd googled that and got nothing back of any use. In the absence of any other ideas, they'd been reduced to walking up and down the canal, looking for actual nails in actual walls. It was like searching for a needle in a haystack, if that haystack was twenty-nine miles long and frequented by Lycra lads and conga lines. They'd walked as far as Old Trafford before they'd turned around and started to head back towards central Manchester.

Hannah caught sight of Reggie's smiling, heading-for-a-meltdown face and decided some small talk was definitely needed.

'So, you're our expert on vampires, then?'

He nodded and neatly stepped around a dog turd on the path. 'Not that it is saying much, but yes. I was actually writing my thesis on the vampire in cinema.'

'I didn't know you were doing a degree.'

He shrugged. 'I was – haven't had the time to finish it. I was at the Open University.'

'What's stopped you?'

Reggie rolled his eyes. 'The pressures of work. I got a new boss.'

'Oh,' said Hannah.

'Yes. Since we've been lumbered with Ireland's answer to a question no one asked, I haven't had the time. Under our old editor, Barry, I could get out at five p.m., even do the odd bit of coursework in the office, but with Banecroft . . .'

Hannah felt bad, despite none of this being her fault. 'I'm sure we could try to make sure you've got a bit of time to . . .'

Reggie waved her away before she could finish. 'Don't worry about it. Besides, pontificating on made-up monsters seems a bit pointless now that we've come face to face with real ones.'

Hannah grunted in sympathy. It was hard to argue against such a fact.

They passed under the railway bridge where, earlier, they had spent a good thirty minutes. Hannah felt her cheeks flush with embarrassment at the memory. The problem with looking for 'a nail in the wall' wasn't finding one, more that there were quite a few items of metalwork that fitted the bill, especially if you extended the definition of 'nail' to include bolts or rivets.

Under this particular bridge, maybe twelve feet up the wall, they'd found what looked like a large nail/bolt that had a plastic bag dangling from it. They'd stood around for a bit discussing it, then spent quite a few minutes more shouting the word 'Cogs' over and over again while feeling ridiculous, before Reggie had eventually given Hannah a boost and she'd awkwardly managed to reach the carrier bag.

It had contained one shoe, two cans of lager and what Hannah was determined to believe was dog excrement, as the alternative was too grim to consider. Hannah had fallen messily from Reggie's shoulders only to realize their antics were being filmed by a couple of passing tourists. Overall, it had been something of a low point.

As they continued back towards the city centre, Reggie engaged in a thorough analysis of *The Stranger Times*' current editor. While

Banecroft came out badly, it was noticeable that Reggie couldn't bring himself to suggest that overall the newspaper wasn't anything but a much better product under the man. Banecroft was a nightmare, but he knew his way around a story. Even to a relative novice such as Hannah, that was blindingly obvious.

They were heading through Castlefield, with its inviting pubs doing a roaring trade thanks to large beer gardens, but Hannah and Reggie kept on walking. It was as if they were too committed to admit defeat. The day was starting to feel like an unhappy metaphor for her marriage.

They passed a number of houseboats, many of whose owners were sitting on the roofs, sunbathing while enjoying a cool drink. One cheery captain even had a barbecue on the go.

Hannah and Reggie carried on in amicable silence for a few moments before Hannah spoke again. 'OK, I should be honest. I don't have a clue about vampires.'

'What do you mean?'

'I mean, I don't like scary movies so I've never seen any of that stuff.'

Reggie sounded genuinely horrified. 'You mean apart from *Buffy the Vampire Slayer*?'

'Never watched it.'

This time Reggie actually gasped and clutched at his metaphorical pearls. 'Good God, what have you been doing with your life?'

'It's a fair question.'

'*Interview with the Vampire*? *Let the Right One In*? *True Blood*?'

'Are these all films?' asked Hannah.

Reggie shook his head. 'Are these all films?' he repeated, sounding scandalized. 'Actually, no, they're not, but regardless, this will not stand. As it happens, there's a season of vampire films on at the Roxy. You're coming with me – to get the education you are sorely lacking.'

'Are they scary?'

'Of course they're scary,' said Reggie. 'That is largely the point. Look at it this way, after what you've actually seen, how terrifying do you expect a film to be?'

She nodded. 'Hard to argue that one.'

'We could bring Stella,' said Reggie. 'She'd enjoy it and she definitely needs a break from the office. The poor kid looks miserable.'

'Yeah,' said Hannah non-committally, feeling awkward. At Banecroft's insistence she hadn't told anyone about the trapdoor except Grace. Taking Stella anywhere for a while might not be the cleverest of ideas. 'Seeing as we're on this story, can I get the idiot's guide to vampires?'

Reggie raised his eyebrows and gave her an arch look.

'The idiot being me,' she added quickly. 'You are the wise professor.'

'Good save. Well, the vampire is an archetype used throughout the history of cinema and long before. While Bram Stoker further popularized it, such figures have existed throughout European folklore.'

'OK.'

'In cinema, there have been many famous vampires, of course, and really, the concept is being constantly reinvented and reinvigorated by each generation of filmmakers.'

'Gotcha.'

'Having said all that, basically, it boils down to sex.'

'Excuse me?' said Hannah.

'They're a manifestation of man's obsession with the Other, and the fact that we have all these thoughts that society, religion, whatever, tells us are bad, but that doesn't stop us from having them. Vampires are a repository for all of mankind's freaky-deaky desires to be poured into. They are monsters, but they are also us. Or at least, the monster inside us that we can't admit to ourselves.'

'Right,' said Hannah. 'Wow. When you put it like that . . .'

'I know,' said Reggie. 'Kind of wish I'd written that little speech down. Would've been a good opening for my thesis if I ever get around to it.'

'So . . .' Hannah's follow-up question was cut short as a bride holding up her immense dress with both hands rushed past her.

Hannah did a double-take. She had barely finished it when an older woman in a purple dress and a hat that looked as if it had half a botanical garden growing out of it ran into her.

'I'm so sorry,' the stressed-sounding woman apologized before setting off in pursuit of the bride. 'Deirdre, sweetheart. Please, calm down. I can't run in these shoes!' Despite her words, the woman succeeded in her attempt. Not fast enough to catch up with the bride, who was already well down the towpath in front of them, but it wasn't for want of trying.

Reggie and Hannah looked at each other.

'Now, there's something you don't see every day,' said Reggie.

The bride finally came to a stop where a footbridge crossed

the canal prior to the waterway disappearing into the gloomy tunnel over which ran a busy road. A houseboat was moored about ten feet from it, although Hannah didn't know if the word 'moored' was technically correct. Every other boat they had passed was either moving or stationary beside the bank. This one, however, was anchored right in the middle of the canal. The bride strode into the centre of the footbridge. A young man in a baseball cap was already standing there. She bent over and pulled up a short length of rope that was dangling into the water. Attached to the other end was a brass bell, which she rang with all her might.

'Hey,' said the teenager in the baseball cap, 'I was here first.'

The bride turned and glared at him.

An instinct kicked in that would serve the young man well in life. He took a step back before adding meekly, 'But you can go first.'

The older woman, panting hard, finally caught up with the bride, who Hannah bet was her daughter.

'Deirdre, angel.'

The bride ignored her and continued to ring the bell.

After a moment, a middle-aged man appeared on the deck of the boat. He was short and wearing a leather waistcoat over a bare chest and ragged jeans, with a bandana tied around his head. He sported a greying Van Dyke beard – the type that combined a moustache, soul patch and chin beard. The overall effect was of a fading member of the four musketeers, the one played by Oliver Reed. Hannah had seen *some* films.

'All right, all right, all right! Didn't I tell you . . .' The man trailed off when he caught sight of the woman in the wedding dress standing on the bridge. 'Hello, hello, hello – what do we have here?'

He spoke with a growling cockney burr, although 'spoke' was probably the wrong word, as everything came out in an emphatically delivered near shout, as if all the world was a stage and he wanted to make sure those at the back still caught everything. The bride made to say something, but before she could, the man hastily pulled on a pair of industrial ear protectors and held up his hands. 'Hang on, darling, rules is rules. Before we go any further, a tribute is required. Drop it in the bucket and write your question down on a piece of paper.'

He pulled a lever and a bucket on a line made its way across the water from the boat towards the bridge.

As it did so, Reggie tapped Hannah on the arm: 'Look at the name of the boat.'

To be fair, the writing was so faded and the paint was peeling so badly that you really had to be looking for it. Hannah was only just able to make out the words '*The Nail in . . .*'

'So, that guy must be this Cogs fella, then,' said Hannah.

The presumed Cogs placed one foot on the edge of the boat and pulled a guitar from somewhere. He started to strum at the instrument despite not being able to hear his efforts because of the ear protectors. It explained, although it didn't excuse, how out of tune it was.

On the bridge, the bride seemed to be arguing with her mother, before the older woman reluctantly produced a purse. Her daughter snatched a few notes from it and, before her mother could protest, tossed them into the bucket. She turned to the young man. 'Pen. Paper.'

He sheepishly handed them over and, as she scribbled away furiously, a bulldog lolled onto the deck and joined his master.

Cogs looked down at the canine and spoke unnecessarily loudly. 'Afternoon, Zeke. I do hope we didn't disturb your fourth nap of the day.'

The dog, looking entirely nonplussed, sauntered over to a large sack and collapsed on top of it.

'Look at that,' said Cogs. 'What an athlete!'

The bride, who had now finished writing, tossed her note into the bucket and started pulling on the winch to send it back. Cogs filled in the interlude by strumming at his guitar like a troubadour.

'I wish I could write you a poem,

or capture your beauty in song,

but I'm no good at rhyming,

so the words would come out . . . shit.'

Once the bucket reached him, Cogs tossed the guitar to the deck and thrust his hand into the pail. 'Well now, normally I don't accept money as, frankly, it shows a lack of effort. Also, I'm not a big one for shopping. However' – he looked down at the dog – 'we do owe a man a little something for something, so I shall accept it this one time!' As he shoved the money in his pocket, he waved his other hand in the air. 'But nobody should see this as a cheapening of my ironclad principles!'

He then proceeded to pull the bride's note from the bucket. He scanned it and, weirdly, showed it to the dog. Odder still, the dog looked as if he were reading it too, before sitting up. Cogs took off his ear protectors, then both he and the dog gave the bride an assessing look, tilting their heads to one side. In response, the bride gave them a twirl. Cogs glanced down at the dog then spoke. 'I'm not an expert in these matters, but yes, sweetheart, I'm afraid it does make you look like a blancmange.'

Hannah registered the despair on the mother of the bride's face.

'I knew it!' screamed the bride, stomping off the bridge. 'That's it. It's off. The whole thing is off!'

Her mother jabbed an accusatory finger at the boat. 'Would it kill you to lie?'

'Actually, dear lady, it would.'

The now-tearful bride, pursued by her ashen-faced mother, pushed back past Hannah and Reggie.

'If the do is already catered, myself and the canine are partial to any finger foods you got going begging,' Cogs shouted after the departing pair. 'Or a coronation chicken or six.'

The mother of the bride turned to give Cogs the finger, something she was possibly doing for the first time in her life, judging by the fact she used the wrong digit.

'Charming,' said Cogs. He turned back to the bridge, where the young man in the baseball hat was standing nervously. 'Bloody hell, are you still here?'

The man went to speak, but before he could, Cogs held up his hands. 'Rules. You know the rules by now, surely.'

The bucket travelled back and forth as before, snagging Cogs a six-pack of a brand of beer Hannah didn't recognize. Cogs opened a can and tasted it before grimacing. 'Would it be too much effort to chill it? Young people today, I do despair!'

Baseball Cap started to say something but Cogs waved him into silence before snatching the latest piece of paper from the bucket and reading it. He looked up to the sky and huffed loudly. 'Gods give me strength!' He crumpled the paper and tossed it on the floor. 'Now, you listen carefully, son, or so help me . . .' He slapped a hand to his chest. 'I am a man cursed to speak only the truth. That's what people come here for – the truth.'

The young man nodded.

'Don't nod, sonny. Don't you nod. If you understood that, you wouldn't be asking me to tell you the winner of the three-thirty at Haydock Park. How am I supposed to know that? I don't see the future!'

'Please,' said the man, 'just give me that one.'

Cogs turned to the dog. 'Can you believe this?' He turned back to Baseball Cap. 'Here's a bit of truth for free, sonny. You've got a problem. Take your wallet and burn it – that's my advice. It'll be cheaper in the long run.'

'C'mon, I just need . . .'

'Right,' said Cogs, straining as he moved to pick up the dog. 'I'm sticking him in the bucket and if you're still there when he gets across, he's going to bite off something I guarantee you'll miss.'

The young man kicked the bridge in frustration. 'D'you know what your problem is, mate? You're an arsehole!'

'Ha!' replied Cogs. 'I've got several problems actually, but yes, that is one of them.'

Hannah and Reggie watched Baseball Cap walk off the other

end of the bridge and do his version of the storm-off. To his credit, he knew exactly which fingers to put up, and did so with vigour.

'Right,' said Reggie, handing the bottle of rum to Hannah. 'I guess that means it's our turn. You can do the talking.'

'Gee, thanks,' Hannah said as she walked up the bridge.

Before she could say anything, Cogs put on his ear protectors and shook his head. 'No, sorry. I've had enough of people for one day. Come back tomorrow.'

Hannah raised her voice. 'But it's important.'

'Are you shouting at a man wearing ear protectors? Seriously?'

'We work for *The Stranger Times*.'

Cogs looked down at the dog. 'She's still yelling, isn't she? I can see her lips moving. Gods, I hate people.'

'Please, I just . . .'

Cogs toasted her sarcastically with his can of beer. 'You keep chuntering on, sweetheart. I'm gonna go stick my head in the fridge. Can't be doing with this heat.'

'Seriously, I just . . .'

'Toodles,' he said with a wave.

Hannah cupped her hands around her mouth and shouted, 'It involves the Founders!'

Cogs didn't get to stick his head in the fridge. Before he could take another step, his own dog bit him on the leg.

CHAPTER 11

Hannah and Reggie had been waved into silence as the *Nail in the Wall* was punted to shore in order for them to come aboard. Reggie hopped down onto the deck and gallantly extended his hand to assist Hannah. She didn't need it but took it anyway.

Less gallantly, the man she was now certain was called Cogs was standing before her, apoplectic with rage. 'What the . . . Who the . . . Sweetheart, sweetheart, sweetheart, you can't just go shouting stuff out like that.'

'Yeah,' agreed Zeke.

'I'm sorry,' said Hannah, 'but . . .' Her mind caught up with her mouth. 'Did your dog just speak?'

'No,' said Cogs.

'Absolutely not,' agreed Zeke, in exactly the kind of growly accent you'd expect a bulldog to have if it could talk.

'It did it again!' yelped Reggie.

'Who you calling "it", Rupert the Bear?'

'He talked,' said Hannah, trying not to sound like she was losing it. 'Three times now.'

'He's actually done it loads more than that,' said Cogs. 'Truth be told, getting the little mongrel to shut up is the tricky part.'

'Hey,' said Zeke. 'I'm one of them purebreds. I think. I dunno.' The bulldog looked away and scrunched up his face, as if trying to recall if he'd left the gas on. 'Am I? I can't remember.'

Hannah gawped at Cogs, then at the dog, and then at Cogs again. 'You just said your dog doesn't talk.'

'I know.'

She pointed down at Zeke. 'He's talking.'

'Yeah,' said Cogs.

Reggie clicked his fingers. 'It's like the old joke – he's not your dog. Right?'

'No,' said Cogs. 'I mean, he isn't, but I was going to say that he's not really a dog. He's a man trapped in a dog's body.'

'Oh,' said Hannah.

'Well,' responded Zeke, 'I don't like to think of it like that. I was something else and now I'm this. I like this. I don't really remember being a man, although my sense is it was a lot of hard work.'

'That sounds about right,' said Reggie.

'Anyway,' said Cogs, lowering his voice and jabbing a finger in Hannah's direction, 'stop changing the bloody subject. Don't go shouting the F-word about the place. I got enough trouble in my life.' He brightened up. 'Now, is that bottle of rum for me?'

Hannah didn't respond. She was still staring down at Zeke.

The dog returned her gaze with large soulful eyes. 'Don't get attached, darling. I'll only break your heart.'

'He did it again!' said Hannah, her voice climbing an octave.

Cogs looked at Reggie. 'Is she all right? Like, in the head and that? Are you collecting to send her to swim with dolphins or summat?'

Reggie patted Hannah on the arm. 'Hannah, dear, ignore the dog.'

'But it's . . .'

'I know,' said Reggie, 'but do what I do. Store it all up and then freak out completely later on.'

'Right,' said Hannah. 'Good idea.' She looked up at Cogs. 'Hello, I'm Hannah Willis, assistant editor at *The Stranger Times*, and this is Reggie . . .'

'Reginald Fairfax the Third,' supplied Reggie.

'Fancy,' said Zeke. 'Will the First and Second be joining us?'

Cogs snapped his fingers, a look of realization spreading across his face. 'Did Mrs Harnforth send you?'

'Yes,' said Hannah.

'I always fancied her something rotten.' Cogs slammed a hand over his mouth, as if the words had escaped of their own volition.

The boat, despite sitting on still water, jolted suddenly, causing Hannah and Reggie to grab one another. Cogs, in a display of sharp if ungentlemanly instincts, grabbed the bottle of rum out of Hannah's hand, in the fear that it might fall overboard.

'How on earth?' said Reggie, looking around in bewilderment.

'Never you mind,' said Cogs quickly. 'Moving on. Moving on. What brings you to our humble abode?'

'Actually, we've been looking for you for hours. You should put up a sign.'

'Why?' asked Cogs, holding up the bottle of rum to inspect it. 'We already get far too many people bothering us as it is.'

'Really?' asked Reggie.

'I'm the world's only guaranteed one hundred per cent honest opinion, m'lad. People go crazy for that. And I mean crazy.'

'He's not wrong,' said Zeke. 'Last week we had a bloke try to ram us with his car.'

'But you're in the middle of a canal,' said Hannah.

The dog sat back and scratched himself with his paw. 'I didn't say he was successful.'

Directed by their reluctant host, they all took a seat on the deck. Hannah chose a deckchair that groaned alarmingly when she sat in it, while Reggie opted for a reasonably sturdy-looking crate. They sat in silence for a couple of minutes as Cogs used the bargepole to return the boat to its central position on the canal, before taking a seat on a stool.

'Right,' said Cogs. 'Seeing as you're here now, and I've accepted your proffered tribute' – he waggled the bottle of rum – 'what can I do for you?'

Hannah nodded. 'OK. But, just so we're clear, you promise to tell the truth?'

'Oh, here we go,' said Zeke, lying back on his sack. 'Strap in.'

Cogs stood up, in order to gesticulate freely as he spoke. 'I'm not promising nothing, darling. Fact is – I can't not tell the truth. I'm cursed, see? Cursed.' He clocked the sceptical looks on his guests' faces.

'Tell 'em the story,' said Zeke.

'I don't want to,' replied the dog's non-owner.

'Like hell you don't, you old tart. Get on with it.'

'All right, fine. Back in the day, I used to be a travelling minstrel. And before anyone says it, no, that definitely does not mean

I blacked up and sang show tunes. I mean I was a proper minstrel. Travelling far and wide, singing songs, telling stories, spreading mirth.'

'Sowing oats,' interjected Zeke, earning him a glare from Cogs. 'What? Is truth-telling only your thing now?'

Cogs ignored him. 'I was young and a tad foolish. As it happens, I had a dalliance with a fair lady and there was a . . . difference of opinion regarding expectations for the relationship.'

'He tried to hit it and quit it with a River Goddess,' clarified Zeke. 'He was whispering sweet nothings and she thought they were definitely somethings.'

'Am I telling this story or are you?' snapped Cogs.

Cogs's words were met with what would've probably been a shrug if dogs came with all the necessary shrugging equipment.

'Because of my behaviour,' continued Cogs, 'I was cursed by the aforementioned, in that I can only tell the truth.'

'I see,' said Hannah.

'And,' added Zeke, 'he has to stay on the water.'

'Yeah,' agreed Cogs. 'I've got to stay off dry land or else bad things happen. Mainly involving that land not staying very dry for very long.'

'Couldn't you just—' started Reggie.

'What?' interrupted Cogs. 'Make a run for it? Like that hasn't occurred to me. Believe me, you name it, I tried it. Once you've nearly drowned on the side of a mountain, you start to realize which way the wind is blowing.'

'We went across the road for a pint on Christmas Eve,' said Zeke. 'Thinking, y'know – it's Christmas. She flooded the place.'

'The woman has a hell of a temper,' said Cogs.

The boat started to rock vigorously.

'Justifiably, justifiably,' added Cogs quickly. 'All of this is entirely my own fault. I deserve to be punished for my callous disregard for the feelings of others.'

The boat stopped rocking and Cogs sighed deeply.

Hannah turned to Reggie. 'I think I've finally found a goddess I could properly worship.'

'Easy girl,' whispered Cogs urgently. 'Be careful what you say about things like that. Seriously.'

'Hang on,' said Reggie. 'If you're being punished, what did the dog do?'

Zeke looked up from licking one of his paws. 'I didn't do nothing. I like it here.'

'Or, to be more exact,' said Cogs, 'he's not wild about other dogs.'

'There's a lot of territorial growling and they ain't the most romantic of species,' confirmed Zeke. 'It's all a bit undignified.'

Cogs nodded. 'And he's the only creature on the planet that can live with me.'

'You don't seem that bad,' said Hannah, trying to be kind.

'Really?' said Cogs. 'People say they love the truth, but you try living with it. Your hair needs a wash and, frankly, you could do with a shower. That deodorant ain't cutting it.'

'Oh,' said Hannah, 'I see your point.' She tried to resist the urge to smell herself.

'See?' said Cogs. 'It just pops out. I can't stop it. Whereas with

Zeke here . . .' He turned to the dog. 'You spent twenty minutes licking your nether region this morning. It was disgusting.'

'Don't care,' said the dog.

'And that new dog food makes your farts smell like they could strip paint.'

Zeke nodded happily. 'Yeah.'

'You get my point?' said Cogs. 'He hasn't any shame and not much of a memory. He's pretty much your perfect flatmate, except I have to winch him ashore in a bucket a few times a day when he needs a dump.'

'Small price to pay for a lifetime of companionship,' offered Zeke.

Cogs looked as if he wanted to snap back with a retort but instead, out came the words, 'He's been a wonderful friend to me,' at which he looked exceedingly annoyed.

Zeke rolled onto his belly and wiggled about happily.

'Right,' said Hannah, as nothing else came to mind.

Cogs gave first Hannah and then Reggie a long look. 'You don't know this world, do ya?'

They both shook their heads.

'You best be careful. It ain't like the one you know. It's dangerous – in ways you probably don't even realize yet. You mark my words. Now more than ever.'

'Why now?'

Cogs looked at Zeke and they both sighed, which allowed Hannah to add being patronized by a dog to her growing list of new experiences.

'You norms,' said Cogs. 'So unaware.'

'It's unbelievable,' said Zeke. 'I'm mostly a dog, and even I can feel it.'

'Feel what?' asked Reggie.

'The Rising,' said Cogs in a dramatic whisper.

Hannah glanced at Reggie. 'Is that something to do with the Foun—' She stopped herself as her host winced. 'Sorry. The F-word?'

'No,' said Cogs, shaking his head.

'You got to explain it properly,' said Zeke.

'All right.' Cogs pulled up his stool and sat back down again. Hannah and Reggie leaned in to listen closely. 'First things first – what exactly do you know?'

Reggie looked at Hannah.

'All right,' she began. 'As far as Mrs Harnforth explained it to me, the Folk have existed since, well, for ever, and the Founders are humans who discovered that they can achieve immortality by taking the life force of the Folk. That used to mean killing them, but now there are other ways. They have to . . . Mrs Harnforth referred to it as "paying the cost". It doesn't kill them.'

'Says you,' said Zeke darkly. 'Depends what you consider living.' This earned him an agitated look from Cogs. 'What? I'm just saying,' he protested.

'What else?' asked Cogs, pointedly trying to ignore Zeke.

'There's a truce in place,' said Hannah. 'The Accord, between the two groups.'

'Basically,' said Cogs, 'that's more or less correct. Only certain

Folk have to pay the cost, though, and some of 'em more than others.'

'Wait a moment,' said Reggie, 'you just said "some of them"? Them. As in you're not one of them?'

Hannah was impressed. That was a good spot.

Cogs puffed out his cheeks. 'I realize this is an odd answer from someone who can only speak the truth, but yes and no. It's not like there's a clear definition of who is and isn't Folk. Many would consider me Folk, for example, but I don't pay the cost.'

'But you're not one of the Founders either?' asked Hannah.

Cogs looked offended by the question. 'No, I'm not. Look – you got to know how to look at this. The Founders, they're like your government, and the Folk, they're like your general population. The cost is sort of the tax they have to pay.'

'But only some of them pay it?' said Hannah.

Cogs nodded.

'Just like real taxes,' added Zeke.

'Ahhhh,' said Hannah. 'I get it. Does the Rising mean they're raising the tax?'

Hannah could now also add being laughed at by a dog to her ever-expanding list of new experiences.

'That's funny, that,' spluttered Zeke.

'No,' said Cogs. 'There's things in this world that are a lot older than us – all of us, I mean. Folk. Founders. Norms.'

'Like a River Goddess,' said Zeke.

' 'Xactly,' agreed Cogs. 'That's one example. There are lots more than that, though.'

Hannah nodded, remembering what they euphemistically

referred to as 'Manny's friend' – the terrifying spirit that protected their offices.

'The world has magic in it. You've seen that already, I expect?'

Hannah nodded, trying to keep her expression neutral. At night, she still often woke up in a cold sweat, remembering the madman who suspended her and her companions in mid-air, frozen solid as a knife danced before their eyes. And then, of course, there was also Stella.

'Good,' said Cogs. 'So it's there, and there's people what can harness it in different ways. Like water. Some people can make ice sculptures and some are good swimmers.'

'You're stretching that analogy a bit,' said Zeke.

'Shut up,' muttered Cogs, before turning back to his audience. 'The point is, the government – as in the Founders – they don't control that.'

'Not for want of trying,' grumbled Zeke.

'But more importantly,' continued Cogs, 'there's things older than them – much older. Primal things. Like, you can have as many tanks and guns as you like, but you ain't stopping a volcano erupting or a tsunami from hitting. We thought they were fading – the old forces. That's what the Folk said. That the old magic was dying.' He waved a hand about. 'We thought it was because the world was changing. All this technology and whatnot, which is just man-made magic. Electricity.'

'The internet,' offered Zeke.

'Phones.'

'Cappuccino machines,' said Zeke.

'Will you shut up about that,' said Cogs. 'We ain't getting one.'

He turned back to Hannah. 'Like I said, we all thought the old ways, the old forces, were starting to fade. Then something happened and suddenly, all of it's coming back. Nobody knows why it's happening now, but there's all kinds of theories floating about. Everyone can feel it – least everyone who's paying attention can.'

'It's like the seas rising,' said Zeke. 'Only you lot aren't noticing that either.'

'Stop trying to be Lenny Bruce,' Cogs chided his canine-like companion.

'Your references are so dated,' said Zeke. 'That's why we need to get a telly.'

'OK,' said Hannah, 'but what sort of effect would that have? This old magic rising.'

'From your perspective,' said Cogs, 'I'd imagine you'd see a big uptick in weird stuff happening to put in your paper.'

'He's right,' said Reggie.

Hannah looked at him in surprise.

'While you were away, I spent some time going through old issues. And all my notes. There's definitely been an increase in all kinds of stories coming in to us. Ghost sightings are way up. And I checked with Ox – UFOs and all manner of other weird stuff is up too. It's hard to be exact, but I'd say it started about eight months ago. It's like boiling a frog. We don't notice the increase day on day as we're smack bang in the middle of it, but when you step back and look at the numbers . . .'

Cogs clicked his fingers and pointed at Reggie. 'See? What did I tell you? All that ancient energy, it finds a way. Attaches itself to things.'

'More stories,' said Hannah. 'Banecroft will be whatever his approximation of pleased is.'

'Speaking of stories,' said Zeke, 'did a woman in Warrington really try and marry the M62?'

'Yes,' said Reggie. 'We covered it a couple of weeks ago.'

'We never miss an edition,' said Cogs.

'Yeah,' agreed Zeke. 'Only because he refuses to buy poo bags.'

'Actually,' said Hannah, remembering why they were there, 'we were hoping you could help us out with a story?'

'Right,' said Cogs, sounding slightly suspicious.

'Last night, a . . . thing got run over up on the Princess Parkway. From all we've heard, it matches the description of a vampire.'

Zeke laughed, his tongue lolling out of the side of his mouth.

'Sharp teeth, afraid of sunlight, garlic, all that?' asked Cogs.

'Yes,' said Hannah.

'Not possible.'

'Are you sure? I mean, we saw what was basically a werewolf.'

Cogs nodded. 'A Were, actually. Big difference.'

Hannah was shocked to hear him reference it.

'Really?' said Cogs. 'You think word of what happened to you lot ain't got around? A Founder breaking the Accord? It's all Folk are talking about. It might explain this, actually.'

'What?'

'Well, like I said – vampires don't exist. I don't mean any more either. They never existed. They're made up. They're one of them . . . whatchamacallits?' Cogs clicked his fingers.

'An allegory,' said Zeke.

'That's right,' agreed Cogs, clapping his hands. 'An allegory. They're made up in order to represent' – he lowered his voice – 'the Founders. It's like them *Spitting Image* puppets they used to have on TV. Those puppets aren't alive, are they?'

'No . . .' said Hannah, not looking at Reggie, 'but I was told vampires are a representation of mankind's taboo sexual desires.'

'Nah,' said Cogs. 'I mean, you made it about that – in your stories and films and whatnot – but that ain't what they were originally. You humans can make anything about sex – it's a real skill.'

'Testify,' exclaimed Zeke.

'I'd imagine the Founders think that whatever this thing is,' said Cogs, 'it's somebody trying to take a shot at them. A little payback. Someone from the Folk saying, "You break the rules, we're gonna give you the kind of stories you really hate."'

Hannah nodded. She had deliberately avoided mentioning the paper's visit from Dr Carter, but this did explain both her interest and why whoever it was she worked for needed *The Stranger Times* to look into it for them.

'But I'm telling you, the original idea is an allegory for the Founders. It's why they hate it so much. Never say the V-word to a Founder, never go all-in on two queens, and never make a joke about a Troll's mother. Them's just things you've got to know.'

'All right,' said Hannah. 'So if they don't exist, how could one be lying in a morgue right now?'

'I dunno,' said Cogs, 'but it must mean that somebody somewhere is taking the piss.'

'Who would do that?' asked Hannah.

'I've no idea, sweetheart, but whoever they are,' said Cogs, 'they're playing with fire.'

Ten minutes later, Hannah and Reggie were back on dry land, after Cogs had decided he was exhausted from all the truth-telling. Before they'd left, Hannah had asked him if he could give them a contact from the Folk to talk to.

'It's not like that, darling,' Cogs had explained. 'They ain't got a head of state. It's like asking to speak to the top ginger bloke in the country.'

Despite his words, Cogs had begrudgingly given them the name of a man, and the pub in which they could find him.

With the sun beating down on them, Hannah and Reggie walked back towards the offices of *The Stranger Times* in silence. Both were lost in their own thoughts. Hannah's mind was racing, trying to remember everything Cogs had said to them. She should have taken notes.

'That was quite something,' she said eventually.

'Indeed,' agreed Reggie.

'Going to take me a while to process that.'

'How do you think I feel?' said Reggie. 'I've got an entire thesis to rewrite.'

Earth
Cancelled!

Edgar Warwick, head of the Contentians – a religion based in Los Angeles that believes all life on the planet Earth is actually a TV show created for the entertainment of higher lifeforms – has made a shocking announcement. The self-proclaimed Grand Critic states, 'Earth has traditionally been a solid ratings-winner on the Celestial Network, but those numbers have gone soft. Focus groups tell us that the writing has hit a real slump, relying on big, badly thought-out plot twists instead of really connecting with the audience. This finding is exacerbated by the fact that all the main characters are now, to be frank, irredeemable assholes.'

He went on to say that the best anyone could hope for now is that the writers pull out a satisfying apocalypse so that Earth can end on a high: 'Let's be honest, ever since that awful millennium-bug storyline, this whole thing has been living on borrowed time.'

CHAPTER 12

DI Sturgess sat in his seat and tried not to be annoyed. He'd sent DS Wilkerson to Phillip Butler's employers earlier that morning to give them a heads-up regarding Butler's unfortunate demise and to confirm his listed next of kin. They'd established that his mother was down in Berkshire, so Wilkerson had informed the local station there and asked them to pay her a visit and do the knock with the bad news.

Sturgess was debating whether it was worth begging for the resources to send somebody down south tomorrow to talk to the mother in more detail or to just brief the locals to follow up. The odds weren't great that the woman would have known much about the 'lifestyle choices' of her son living a couple of hundred miles away. On the other hand, it would be an awkward conversation with the locals to talk them through the questions he'd need asking.

His time was limited and resources currently comprised him and DS Wilkerson. Right now, technically, he was only confirming the details of a suicide, unusual as that suicide was. Having said that, the contents of Butler's stomach gave Sturgess the uneasy feeling that there was another shoe to drop. He'd flagged it to Chief Inspector Clayborne but had not yet heard anything back. There'd been another shooting out in Salford, presumed to be related to the ongoing gang issue, and that was where the force's attention was focused.

Then there was the weather issue. People were out partying and enjoying themselves in the sunshine, which inevitably led to resources being stretched and a rise in violent crime. The job did many things to a copper, not least of which was instilling a perpetual longing for a good downpour.

He could text Concerned Citizen and ask them to have a word, but he really didn't want to do that. Not yet, at least. He'd already been 'encouraged' to talk to his source at *The Stranger Times* and share information with them. Normally, he would have dismissed the idea out of hand, but then nothing about Butler's death was normal. The idea made sense – it was literally the newspaper's mission statement to report the weird – and odds on something like this didn't come out of nowhere. However, to make contact would be horribly awkward on a personal level.

Nothing had happened between him and Hannah Willis, but it had felt that maybe . . . In any case, that had come to an abrupt end when he'd woken up on his sofa, with no idea how he'd ended up there, and the last thing he remembered was helping Hannah to find a work colleague who'd disappeared. He'd texted her but her replies had been vague and evasive. Just thinking about it caused his head to throb. Then he'd gone off to visit his sister and, well, that had been that.

He'd been staring at his phone, spending time he didn't have trying to compose another text to Hannah, when the device had vibrated in his hand. She'd texted him first. They were meeting tomorrow.

Given his lack of resources and the other lines of enquiry he had to chase up, the last thing Sturgess needed was to spend his day sitting in a meeting room, watching grown-ups behave like children. And yet that was where he found himself. To his left, on the other side of a large glass wall, a dozen supposed adults bounced up and down on space hoppers while shouting words at somebody standing at a whiteboard. Sturgess had a low opinion of the management style of the Greater Manchester Police, but at least they never did this.

He was at the offices of Fuzzy Britches Ltd. Their product was of little interest to Sturgess, but you'd have had to be living under a rock not to have heard of them. They'd started as a dating app that had been developed locally. Unusually, a brother-and-sister team were behind it; twins, in fact – Alan and Tamsin Baladin.

The plucky Manchester-based start-up that grew into a genuine tech giant. The media lapped it up – big shiny proof that Manchester was the innovative city of tomorrow they pushed in the investment brochures. Any bits of the Baladin twins' success story that didn't fit the narrative had long since been airbrushed. Like, for example, the fact that Alan never graduated from university. There had been some trouble during his time there and, while he hadn't been asked to leave – oh, heavens, no – he'd 'stepped away' from formal education. Tech giants were, after all, famously littered with people who'd never bothered to finish boring old degrees.

Tamsin had once categorized her brother's 'issue' as a bad uni romance, but there had been whispers of allegations. Sturgess read up on it on his phone while he was waiting for the meeting to start. The whole thing had the smell of serious lawyers being involved and NDAs aplenty. The last reporting of it had been three years ago. Since then, Fuzzy Britches had gone from strength to strength, and the company was about to enter the really big leagues.

Lots of companies had launched dating apps – hundreds, apparently – but Fuzzy Britches had been different. Instead of asking people for likes and dislikes, it had shared jokes, viral memes – no politics, but TV, films, books, music. It then tracked what individuals *actually* liked and disliked, as opposed to the answers they'd give if asked, and the algorithm matched them to people whom they genuinely shared interests with, and with whom they were deemed 'compatible'.

There was that and, of course, there was the 'attractiveness quotient'. Your picture was shown anonymously to ten random people who lived nowhere near you and they voted on your hotness. 'The closest thing to an honest opinion you're likely to find on the internet', as one journalist had put it. Plus, the app insisted on verified pictures taken in one of the thousands of Fuzzy Britches booths in bars, universities and nightclubs all over the world. You never knew your score but it was factored in. While a minority complained about the 'survival of the fittest' nature of the algorithm, the phenomenon was undeniable. Fuzzy Britches was the dating app of choice.

Sturgess read the long *Guardian* article in which Tamsin had given a rare one-to-one interview. Not that she wasn't in the press much – on the contrary – but it was all heavily stage-managed. She was the face of the business, the marketer who knew what people really wanted. And by 'people', they really meant women. As the article stated, if you develop a platform that women like and trust, the men will follow. The app would even track you on your date – for safety purposes. As Tamsin herself had said, 'I understand the concerns of women using this app because I am a woman using this app.'

Not any more, though. Her romance with a hunky actor had been tabloid fodder. Her brother, on the other hand, was a near recluse. Mention was made of health issues. He'd soon be able to afford some very good second opinions on that front, as Fuzzy Britches was due to be floated on the stock exchange next year. Before that, though, the company was fully joining the social media wars. Tamsin had told the *Guardian* journalist, 'Just because I'm off the market, why should I be off the app?' And so Fuzzy Britches was going toe-to-toe with the giants of social media. Some estimates valued the company at four billion pounds. Rumour had it they'd already turned down an offer from Zuckerberg.

All of this made it all the more surprising for DI Sturgess when the PA who had been offering him beverages every five minutes re-entered the meeting room and nervously showed in Tamsin Baladin herself with a quartet of serious-looking types in tow.

'DI Sturgess.' Tamsin strode towards him, hand extended. 'I'm incredibly sorry for keeping you waiting. I'm afraid there was a boo-boo on our end and I didn't realize you were actually in the building. Apologies.' She glanced at the PA, who looked like someone trying to keep a smile on her face after being informed her entire family had been accidentally fired into the sun.

Sturgess rose to shake Tamsin's hand. 'These things happen,' he said, in a tone of voice that most people would've probably taken as sincere.

'They certainly do around here at the minute, I'm afraid. It's all a bit manic.' She waved him back into his chair. 'Sit, sit, sit.'

She sat down opposite him and the backing band followed suit, taking seats beside her in such a coordinated way that Sturgess felt things weren't quite as chaotic as Tamsin would like to make out. He also noticed that she hadn't bothered to introduce herself. He guessed it was a long time since Tamsin Baladin had been in a room where someone hadn't known who she was. Admittedly, she was a particularly striking woman. A five-foot-six brunette with piercing green eyes and a charming smile. Something about her made him feel as if he were face to face with an airbrushed advert that had come to life.

Sturgess pulled out his notepad and pen. 'Do you mind?'

'No, of course not,' she said. 'Please.' Her accent was what some would consider southern but really was from nowhere. It was the kind of accent they handed out at certain private schools on admission.

He noticed that fifty per cent of the two-women-two-men entourage was also taking notes. The dark-haired man in his fifties to Tamsin's right gave Sturgess a stern look. To that man's right sat a bald guy who looked as if his only two hobbies were doing Ironman Triathlons and telling people endlessly about how he did Ironman Triathlons. Sturgess would put good money on them both being lawyers. It was something in the stares.

To Tamsin Baladin's left sat a woman who looked remarkably similar to Tamsin Baladin – like a body double she kept close by to take over if ever she got bored. To that woman's left sat a larger, nervous-looking woman whose slouched posture and anxious disposition were entirely at odds with those of her cohort. She looked like one of the before pictures for whatever product the other four were selling.

Tamsin Baladin fixed Sturgess with a sincere look. 'So, my God, Phil is dead.'

'Yes, I'm afraid so.'

She shook her head and bit her lip. 'Wow. Only twenty-six.'

'Twenty-seven,' whispered the woman who looked enough like her boss that she might actually be the voice in her head.

'So young,' said Tamsin, showing only the slightest flash of irritation at being corrected. 'Terrible. We've already reached out to his family.'

'I'm sure they'll appreciate that.'

'It's nothing. After all, he was a member of our family too.'

Sturgess nodded. 'Did you know him, Ms Baladin?'

Tamsin sat back in her seat. 'Personally? Not really. I mean, I guess you could say I knew him to see him. We hold big events every month for our staff, as you're probably aware. We're a company that likes to party.'

'I see.' Sturgess was dimly aware. A few months ago the company had all but held a parade in its own honour. The local newspapers loved that kind of story. There had been people who identified as celebrities present too. 'If you don't mind me asking, how many employees do you have?'

Tamsin puffed out her cheeks. 'It's about eight thousand now, I think.'

'Mostly based here?'

She ran her fingers through her hair. 'There's about five thousand in the three Manchester locations, with the rest scattered between the satellite offices – London, New York, LA, San Fran, Berlin, Tokyo, et cetera. Why do you ask?'

'It's just that I only came in to speak to Mr Butler's manager and presumably someone from HR – just to get some background on a man who died in circumstances we're still investigating—'

'I was of the understanding it was suicide?' asked the man to Baladin's right. Definitely a lawyer.

'There are indications pointing towards that, but you understand we have to do our due diligence.'

'Of course,' said Tamsin.

'I have to say I'm surprised to find myself sitting opposite the CEO of a multi-billion-pound company.'

Tamsin gave a tight smile. 'Well, as I said, we're a family here. News such as this and I'm sure you understand, people around here are devastated.'

Sturgess darted only the slightest glance to his left where the people on space hoppers were now shooting each other with water pistols.

To her credit, Tamsin Baladin didn't even blink. 'Obviously, the news hasn't gone around the entire company. Phil worked up on the fifth floor.'

Sturgess nodded. 'When we're done here, can I see his desk?'

Tamsin turned her head a fraction towards the man on her near right, who gave the briefest of nods. 'I'm sure we can arrange that.'

'Thank you,' said Sturgess. 'Do you know if Mr Butler was acting strangely at all in the days leading up to his death?'

'No, he wasn't.'

Sturgess nodded again. 'With respect, Ms Baladin, you just told me you hardly knew him.'

'Sorry,' she said, holding her hands up. 'I suffer from always striving to be the kid with the answer. I just meant we've been discussing it.'

'When?'

'This morning, obviously. Since we got the news. Siobhan here was Phil's line manager.'

The nervous-looking lady to Tamsin's far left nodded several times. 'Yes, yes, I am.' She winced. 'I mean, was.'

'And how was he?'

She took a deep breath. 'He was, y'know – Phil. I mean, I've worked with him for about four years now. He was the same old Phil. I'm shocked by all this. I mean . . .' She pulled out a tissue from her sleeve and held it up. 'God. Sorry.'

'That's perfectly understandable,' said Sturgess, softening his tone slightly. 'I know you have a lot going on here. Was Phil under a lot of pressure at work, would you say?'

Siobhan shook her head. 'Honestly? Nothing unusual. I mean, the whole team – none of us saw this coming.'

Tamsin nodded. 'As a company, we place a real emphasis on the mental health of our colleagues. All staff members have access to counselling, completely anonymously. We regularly promote that benefit as part of our overall wellness drive. Catherine can provide you with . . .'

She glanced at the other woman to her left, who nodded vigorously while scribbling notes.

'Thank you,' said Sturgess, turning his attention back to Siobhan. 'Did Phil have any other problems you were aware of? Personal? Financial?'

'No.'

'Was he single?'

Siobhan nodded. 'Oh, very.' She blushed. 'I mean, he was just . . . He was a guy in his twenties, you know? He was active on the dating scene.'

Tamsin gave a soft laugh. 'Hardly surprising given where he worked.'

'Had he . . .' Sturgess paused for a second, trying to find the right words. 'Had he recently changed his appearance?'

Siobhan looked down. 'Not that I— No, wait – he got a haircut a couple of weeks ago. I only remember because Neil was taking the mickey a bit, y'know? He'd gone quite tight. We were pulling his leg about male pattern baldness.' Siobhan looked suddenly horrified. 'I mean, it was just a bit of banter. Really light stuff. Nothing . . . bad.'

'But nothing outside of that?'

Siobhan shook her head, looking confused by the question. 'No.'

'Why do you ask?' said Tamsin.

Sturgess looked her in the eye. 'No reason.'

'It does seem like an odd question,' said the lawyer.

'Does it? Well, with respect, I am conducting an investigation here, so I'll ask whatever questions I deem necessary.'

'I appreciate that,' said the lawyer. 'As I'm sure you appreciate, Ms Baladin's time is valuable.'

'Which is why I didn't request a meeting with her. I actually just wanted to talk to his manager, which I assume is Miss . . .' He nodded at Siobhan.

'Regan,' she provided.

'Thank you. So, if there is anywhere any of the rest of you have to be, I don't mind.' He smiled politely.

'It's fine,' said Tamsin. 'Please, continue.'

'OK,' said Sturgess, looking down at his notes. 'And what was Phil working on?'

Before Siobhan, to whom the question was directed, could answer, the lawyer piped up. 'I'm afraid we can't discuss that.'

'I see. And who are you exactly?'

The man took a business card out of his pocket and slid it across the table in a practised motion. 'Henry Littleton. The company's head of compliance.'

Sturgess didn't touch the card. 'Right. Only, if I remember correctly, a few minutes ago Ms Baladin said you would do anything to help this investigation.'

'And we will,' said Littleton. 'But what Mr Butler was working on is not relevant.'

'As the head of the investigation, I think that's my call to make.'

'Now, now, boys,' said Tamsin, patting Littleton on the hand. 'Let's not get all alpha about this. We're happy to help DI Sturgess – of course we are. What Henry was trying to say, in his slightly bulldogish manner, is that Phil's work is nothing at all to do with this. He was a developer. One of a couple of hundred we have working on our algorithm at any given time. I could get Siobhan to explain it to you, but take it from me,' she said with a broad smile, 'she'll be the only one here who understands it. My brother has been explaining it to me since the day we started this company in a room above a kebab shop in Fallowfield, and honestly, I'm none the wiser.'

DI Sturgess nodded and left it there. In truth, he'd had absolutely no interest in Phillip Butler's work until they'd come in quite so heavy-handed. He was waiting for the . . .

'Actually,' said Tamsin. 'One thing you could possibly help us with. Phil's phone wasn't his phone. It belonged to the company.'

'I see.'

'It may have proprietary software on it,' Littleton elaborated. 'So we will need it returned to us. Security is a top priority.'

Sturgess leaned forward. 'Would it be possible that someone could have been trying to steal it from him?'

'No, no,' said Tamsin quickly.

'Is it usual for your staff to walk out of the building with things like that? I mean, if, as you say, security is a top priority?'

'Nothing like that,' said Tamsin, working her smile again. 'Sometimes developers test stuff on their own phones, that's all. The only issue is, as I'm sure you understand, we've got half the bug-eyed loons on the internet trying to hack into our systems.

Henry here loses sleep over it. We just have to be careful that any unprotected code can't be lifted off the device. That's all.'

'I see,' said Sturgess. 'That is entirely understandable.'

'Thank you.'

'You have my word that it will be returned to you once it is no longer evidence in my investigation. Until then, rest assured it is safe as houses in the possession of the Greater Manchester Police.'

Tamsin's smile remained fixed. Littleton had never managed to raise one, but his scowl told a story. Sturgess would put very good money on the phones of very senior police officers starting to ring as soon as he left the room.

'So, would it be possible to see Mr Butler's desk now?'

CHAPTER 13

The silence was unnerving. Vincent Banecroft sat there not saying a word as Hannah, with occasional interjections from Reggie, relayed everything Cogs had told them. They were back in the bullpen, and Grace and Stella were there too, listening intently. Hannah had suggested they wait for Ox to join them, but Banecroft had simply said 'the special projects team' wouldn't be returning to the office that evening, and offered no further explanation.

Hannah finished what she was saying and looked at Reggie, who nodded, satisfied that they'd covered all the salient points.

'This man's dog talks?' said Grace.

'Yes. Although it's not his dog. He doesn't actually own him.'

Grace's bracelets rattled loudly as she furiously blessed herself several times. 'Mother Mary, forgive us, this is truly the end of days.'

'And not before time,' said Banecroft. 'Did he give any more information about this ancient-powers mumbo-jumbo?'

Hannah looked at Reggie, who shrugged.

'Did you not ask further questions?'

'We tried to,' said Hannah, 'but if you remember, that wasn't what we were sent there to find out about.'

Banecroft made clear his disappointment by looking to the heavens and mumbling something under his breath. Hannah was past caring. As tasks went, trying to make Vincent Banecroft happy was right up there with holding back the sea.

'And he said it was all nonsense?' asked Banecroft.

Reggie nodded. 'To be exact, he said vampires in the forms we are familiar with – through cinema, books, et cetera – do not exist.'

'So how does he explain the thing lying in the morgue?'

'He doesn't,' said Hannah. 'Said it must be someone trying to wind up the Founders.'

'Right,' said Banecroft. 'So I can ring Dr Carter and tell her not to worry, it's all a practical joke. If I find out this is Jeremy Beadle . . .'

'He's been dead for a long time,' said Grace.

'Yes, but given recent developments, sadly that no longer rules anyone out.'

Grace blessed herself again.

Hannah caught a strange look crossing Banecroft's face as he glanced into the corner of the room. He seemed to realize that she'd noticed, and was annoyed by it. It was hard to know what to read into that – the man was annoyed by damn near everything.

'Right,' he said. 'Next steps.'

'Actually,' Hannah interrupted before Banecroft could build up a head of steam, 'Reggie had an idea.'

Reggie looked nervous but Hannah smiled at him and gave a nod of encouragement. 'Well, it might be nothing but . . .

the Roxy cinema – the lovely independent one up in Hulme – runs film festivals. Silent movies, BAME, women in cinema, Scandinavian . . .'

'Get to the point,' snapped Banecroft.

'They also screen vampire movies – every Tuesday evening and then a late show every other Thursday. Pretty popular. I go, quite often.'

'Good to know,' said Banecroft.

'Shut up,' said Hannah. 'Not you, Reggie – you keep going.'

'There's a few odd people round there. Y'know, dress up for it. Bit of harmless fun, really. I just thought, seeing as Cogs thought, that maybe we should . . .'

Banecroft nodded. 'Fine. Check it out.'

'The Roxy,' said Grace. 'Why does that ring a bell?'

'The series we did last year,' said Reggie. 'Haunted Manchester. It has that ghost.'

'Oh yes. The crying girl who runs down the hall. Pining for her lost love.' Grace clutched her hands to her chest. 'Such a sad story.'

'And now,' said Banecroft, 'the poor thing is doomed to spend every Tuesday and every other Thursday surrounded by goths for all eternity. Speaking of doomed love affairs . . .' He turned back to Hannah. 'Have you contacted your friend on the police force?'

Hannah said nothing, just glowered at him. Banecroft met it with a smile.

'You've got spinach in your teeth,' she told him.

'Ha. Not possible. I've not eaten spinach in a couple of days.'

'I don't doubt that.'

Banecroft's grin became less toothy.

'In answer to your question – yes, I have contacted DI Sturgess. I'm going to meet him tomorrow.'

'Tonight.'

'I was going to go down to that pub Cogs gave us the name of, and try and talk to the man he mentioned.'

'Not necessary,' said Banecroft. 'I'll be doing that.'

'Are you sure that's a good idea?'

'Why wouldn't it be?'

'You're not exactly a people person.'

'Nonsense.'

Grace nodded emphatically. 'That woman who came round last week, collecting for the dogs home – she called you a . . .' She glanced around nervously. 'The word that came after number ten on your awful list.'

It was odd that Grace thought not giving the exact number somehow distanced her from the system.

'Precisely my point,' said Banecroft. 'I have a way of throwing people off balance. Getting them to say things they don't want to say.'

Reggie mumbled something.

'What was that?'

'Nothing.'

'Excellent,' said Banecroft, rubbing his hands together. 'I also just remembered that I'm the boss, so this is no longer up for discussion. I will meet this . . .' He looked at Hannah expectantly.

'John Mor,' said Hannah, filling in the gap.

'. . . and discuss this sensitive issue with him. Meanwhile, our assistant editor can meet up with her source tonight.'

Hannah sighed. 'Fine. I'll text and see if he's available.' It probably did make sense to get it over with.

'Lovely. And if you have to "bump uglies", as I believe the kids say, in order to get information, you have my approval.'

Grace gasped, scandalized.

'I'll be honest,' said Hannah, 'the memory of you saying those words might stop that from ever happening with anyone ever again.'

'Speaking of which, how did your divorce go?' asked Banecroft.

'Wonderfully. Now I only have one one-ing six in my life.'

'See?' said Banecroft, with a wolfish grin that still featured two-day-old spinach. 'The Banecroftian swearing system is really taking off.'

Hannah knocked on the door to Stella's room.

'Go away.'

'It's me.'

'Oh,' came a voice from inside. 'Hang on.'

Stella appeared from behind the door, her purple hair hanging down over her eyes and clashing with her green T-shirt proclaiming 'Punk Is Dead, Long Live Punk'. Combat trousers and Doc Martens rounded off the outfit. Her room wasn't really a room as such. It was actually the steeple of the church. She had two landings and a winding staircase – the bed had barely fitted in. It didn't even have a proper door, but rather a large length of plywood Ox had sourced from somewhere, which Stella could move into place for a bit of privacy. As she slid it aside to let Hannah in, Hannah noticed that her young colleague had made minimal changes to the room.

'Hey, I thought you were going to zhuzh this place up a bit?'

'Zhuzh?' asked Stella.

'It means . . . Y'know, I'm not exactly sure what it means, come to think of it. Decorate? Do up?'

'Nah. That'd mean I'm staying. Got my bag packed.'

'Right,' said Hannah, looking at the rucksack in the corner. 'About that.'

She felt like a prize shit as she watched Stella's face drop at the realization of what was coming.

'Look, I know we said you could move into mine as soon as I got back, but while I was away . . . it flooded.'

'How'd that happen in the middle of a heatwave?'

'Exactly,' said Hannah. 'That's what I've got to find out.'

'I don't mind.'

'No – honestly, it reeks.'

'This place hasn't even got a loo.'

'Grace said she's getting that sorted tomorrow. Some guy in her church can get us a Portaloo.'

'Great.'

'It'll be like being at a festival,' said Hannah, instantly regretting her words.

'Whoopee. I'm pretty sure the crapping into a fancy bucket part is the best bit of the Glastonbury experience.'

'Look . . .'

'Nah, forget it. Doesn't matter. If you changed your mind, just say.'

'No, really. It's not that.'

Stella hopped onto her bed, pulled up her knees and hugged them to her. 'Just get out of my room that isn't a room, please.'

'I promise—'

'You already promised,' snapped Stella. 'Don't double down on that nonsense. Now, can you please leave? I don't have a proper door I can slam, so you'll just have to politely bugger off.'

'It's only for a little while.'

'Yeah. Don't do me no favours. Anyway, I'm thinking of growing my hair real long. Hopefully some passing prince will climb up it and save the freak in the tower.'

'You're not a . . .'

A blue flash appeared in Stella's eyes. She quickly turned around and lay down facing the stone wall.

'Please leave.'

Hannah tried to think of something to say but nothing would come.

Feeling dreadful, she turned and walked away.

That went well.

CHAPTER 14

He sat there. Motionless.

It was all about control. Control of oneself and of one's environment.

The hunger was new but it was just something else to be controlled.

He'd realized almost immediately that something was happening to him, and he'd observed the changes with great interest. He knew the 'normal' reaction should have been one of terror but he'd never been normal. Even as a child he'd had impulses that others not only didn't share, but also found repulsive. There had been incidents. He'd been sent to see people. They hadn't changed him, at least not in the way they'd intended. He'd merely learned what he needed to conceal in order to fit in.

He prided himself on the fact he'd grown very good at it. He was popular at work, had a healthy social life, and was considered quite the ladies' man. He'd known long ago that a long-term relationship wasn't something he could ever have, the mask would always slip, but he did enjoy playing the dating game. He was already very good at lying, and sex was an excellent way of keeping score.

Now, of course, with the changes, the game had been altered considerably. He'd called in to work and told them he was going home for a few days because of a family emergency. As it was, his mother insisted on ringing every now and then, but he hadn't been home in years. He had the distinct impression that his father was the one person on the planet he hadn't fooled.

His current predicament was certainly interesting, but it had one considerable upside: power. He was physically stronger and faster. He could feel it. He'd always been athletic, but this was something else. And then there were his senses. He'd noticed them last night. Sitting in his apartment, he'd heard the couple two doors down arguing, then screwing, then arguing again – all of it at a low volume. The woman in the flat opposite had been testing a few bottles of perfume she'd stolen from work. He'd been able to smell the scents. When he'd concentrated, he'd fancied he'd even smelled her excitement. Amusingly, the cat upstairs had scratched her idiot of an owner. He'd smelled the blood and his reaction to it had confirmed his suspicion. Not that it had been much of a leap of reasoning – the teeth had been a rather big clue.

His plan had been to wait until sunset before taking some form of action. Sitting there now, though, he knew the plan was about to change.

He sensed the man as soon as he got out of the lift. Most animals had it – the ability to sense when a predator had entered their sphere – even if they didn't know quite what it was. Either it was present in all lifeforms, or else the ones that didn't have it had been naturally selected out of existence. In human beings the sense had all but died out. They lived in the mistaken belief that they had no predators left. He knew differently. He'd already killed three people.

The killings had happened over the course of several years, and a careful, meticulous approach had meant that nobody but he knew about them. Each experience had been very instructive in its own way. People who had taken the life of another were different. It was there to see in how they carried themselves. Understanding you possessed that lethal power changed you on a fundamental level. He and Angus from Accounts, for example, had hardly spoken, but he sensed it in his colleague. He'd long theorized that it was far more common than people thought. If you knew what you were doing, it was so easy to make it look like natural causes, and if you knew where to look, there was a whole layer of society nobody paid attention to.

He was a killer and so was the man who was about to knock on his door.

'Who is it?' He smiled to himself, sensing the man's confusion as he had not knocked on the door yet.

'Is that Mr Campbell?' The voice was almost accentless, but contained the merest hint of Israeli.

'Yes.'

'Andrew Campbell?'

'That's me.' He stood and zipped up his red hoodie. Red had always been his favourite colour.

'Can I have a word?'

'What about?'

He recognized the smell now, from when he'd gone to that

shooting range in Florida. Gun oil. With a thrill of excitement he realized the man was armed.

'This is a chat we'd need to have face to face.'

'Now isn't a great time.' He smiled again. 'I'm not quite myself.'

The visitor lowered his voice, aiming for a well-practised threatening undertone. 'I need to speak to Mr Red.'

Ahhhh, so that was what this was about. How interesting. Just a bit of fun and now there was a man at his door with a gun.

He began to salivate.

Technically, this probably wasn't even murder. In court, he could certainly make the case for self-defence.

He licked his lips. 'Just a second.'

He was so very hungry, though.

CHAPTER 15

Ox blinked to try to keep the sweat out of his eyes. He was sitting in a van parked on a fairly quiet road in the Manchester suburb of Worsley. He was in the driver's seat. He wasn't allowed to drive but the van's owner – and, judging by the sleeping bag and cooking stove in the back, occupier – had called dibs on the passenger seat as he said it was more comfortable.

'Can we not—' started Ox.

'No,' replied Stanley. 'You cannot open a window.'

'But—'

'The pollen in the air plays havoc with my allergies.'

'OK. How about—'

'The air-con runs down the battery.'

'But it's so—'

'The door is there if you want to leave. I didn't ask for your help.'

Ox huffed. 'The planet Mars is about half the size of Earth.'

Stanley turned in his seat, temporarily taking his eyes off the property they were staking out. 'What are you on about?'

'I just wanted to remember what it was like to finish a whole sentence.'

Stanley sneered and looked back across the road. The property was a large five-bedroomed house, although a sizeable chunk of it was being knocked down to make it even larger. The company carrying out the work was Echelon Construction Ltd – the same outfit that had been doing *The Stranger Times*' bathroom until Banecroft had fired them for no apparent reason, although Ox had since been brought up to speed on that. He couldn't help but think that most people would've extended him that courtesy before telling Stanley about it, but that was Banecroft all over.

Ox hadn't been consulted before Banecroft had announced that he and Stanley were a team either. Since being thrown together, there hadn't been a great deal of chat between the pair, given the only thing they had in common was that they both resented Ox having to be there. Stanley clearly worked alone, and Ox, well, he needed to work on a solution to his other problem. Nevertheless, here they both were.

The van was an ordinary panel van, like one of thousands you see making deliveries every day, being used on building sites, and so on, which Ox guessed was the point. That, and it offered a bit more room than a car, if you had to live in the thing.

He had to admit, albeit begrudgingly, that Stanley did seem to know what he was doing. As soon as they'd left the pub, and without speaking a word to Ox, he'd started making calls. From what Ox could gather, Stanley was contacting various people and asking them to look into Echelon Construction. Although he could hear only one side of the conversations, it was pretty clear that nobody was very happy to hear from Stanley. However, his new partner seemed to have something on everyone he spoke to, as they all reluctantly acceded to his requests.

The next thing Stanley had done was look up the number for Echelon Construction. He'd called it and, much to Ox's surprise, started screaming down the phone.

'Don't you hello me! I've got a delivery of timber here and where the hell are your boys? I've got my boss screaming at me and I've not got the right address . . . What? I'm out in Sale . . . Don't mess me around . . . Where *do* you have jobs on the go, then?' Stanley had listened for a few seconds then said, 'Oh, wait a minute, this is the wrong company.' He'd promptly hung up the phone without any apology. 'Right, they got jobs on in Prestwich, Knutsford and Worsley. We'll go to Worsley first – smallest area, easiest to find 'em.'

Just under an hour later, after driving about, looking for any builders at work, they had indeed found them. These days, every building firm worth their salt had signs pitched outside whatever site they were working on – free advertising.

Since then, for the best part of three hours, the two men had sat in near silence watching a team of builders go about their business. Ox's phone was running out of battery. His request to charge it had already been firmly rebuffed – for much the same reason as the air-con was a no-go. This van's battery was apparently saving itself for its wedding night.

'What are we waiting for?' asked Ox, making no attempt to keep the annoyance from his voice.

Stanley tutted without taking his eyes off the house.

'What?' Ox resisted the urge to scream the word.

'What do you see?'

'Same thing you do. Some builders working on a bloody house. Big deal.'

Stanley tutted again.

'So help me, you tut at me one more time . . .'

Stanley ignored the remark. 'That house – gotta be worth not much less than three-quarters of a million, wouldn't you say?'

'I guess,' said Ox.

'Look up and down the street. Beemers and Mercs on the drives, and two- or three-car households. All detached. I happen to know for a fact, Ryan Giggs used to live just up that way. His ex still does or . . . No, she sold up, I think. Yeah.'

Ox waited but Stanley didn't speak for a few seconds. 'And?'

'Look at this job. Look at the vans parked outside. They're high spec and in good nick. These boys are working the lucrative end of the market. So why is this company doing your raggedy cheap bathroom?'

'Oh,' said Ox.

'Yeah. Not their normal kinda job at all. My guess is that somebody pressured them into doing it. We need to find out how and who it was.' He nodded. 'And that's why I'm an investigative journalist and you're some bloke who chases UFOs.'

'Banecroft seemed to hold you in high esteem.'

'Me and him got a history.'

'He mentioned. Something about firing you.'

Stanley stiffened. 'Thought he was better than me, didn't he? He needs me now, though – don't he? Not so clever now.'

Ox glanced over his shoulder at the sleeping bag in the back but decided that continuing the argument wouldn't be the smartest of ideas.

Just then, a shiny white SUV pulled up and a well-groomed, heavily tanned man in his early forties hopped out. Instantly, the workmen picked up the tempo of whatever they were doing.

'This'll be the boss,' said Stanley.

'Could be the homeowner.' Ox watched as the man rang the doorbell. 'Or not.'

The man who clearly was the boss disappeared inside as soon as a blonde woman answered the door, but not before Stanley had picked up his camera and surreptitiously taken a few snaps of him. Stanley looked at the small display on the back of the camera before nodding. 'The man in charge. Sure, we can check Companies House and permits, all that, and they'll tell us who's supposed to be in charge, but nothing beats seeing who's actually giving commands, boots on the ground. You can't trust technology. All them beepy-boo-boop boxes.'

'Beepy-boop-what?' asked Ox.

'I'm telling ya, computers lie. So do people, of course, but not in the same way. We need to follow that geezer when he comes out.'

'OK.'

'So you're going to have to climb over me so I can get into the driving seat.'

'Can I not just get out and walk around?'

'No, I've—'

'Got allergies,' finished Ox. 'Super.'

CHAPTER 16

Vincent Banecroft slipped through the doors of the Kanky's Rest pub and looked around him. He'd never been here before and yet he knew the place well. It was a proper old fellas pub. Everything was made out of hardened wood or worn leather, including the clientele. There were no big-screen TVs, yammering quiz machines or loud music. There was a dartboard, a pool table and a hushed reverence enjoyed by those who took their drinking seriously.

A red-headed woman was tossing darts at the dartboard. Banecroft noticed that she was hitting the bullseye time after time, and seemed thoroughly bored of doing so. In one corner, a couple of old women sat knitting. Unusually, they were working on the same garment, although judging by the number of superfluous arms and legs it had, they might not have discussed beforehand exactly what it was going to be.

In another corner, a spirited argument appeared to be taking place, despite there being only one man seated at the table. In outright defiance of the evening temperature, which was touching nearly thirty degrees outside, the man was wearing a thick overcoat. It was possible his sartorial choice was the subject of the debate between him and his imaginary friend. He was also speaking in a language Banecroft had never heard before. A few months ago Banecroft would have dismissed such a scene as a madman rambling to himself, but recent events had forced him to broaden his horizons.

What the pub was short on was natural light. When all the world and its boozehound work colleague was out looking for a beer garden, not only did it lack that, it was also fitted with the kind of opaque windows designed to fulfil the window requirement without providing any of the window benefit. Despite the blazing sun outside, the Kanky's Rest had the lights on and candles on the table. It was sort of like a Las Vegas casino. You could find yourself sitting there with no idea what time of day or night it was. Helpfully, the clock on the wall showed it to be five to eleven, forever last orders.

Another thing it lacked was staff. Two people stood at the bar, waiting for someone to appear on the other side to take their order. On the left was a woman with long black hair that matched her outfit. She was standing completely still – statuesque – with one hand, sporting alarmingly long nails filed to a sharp point, resting on the bar top. In contrast, a man in his thirties stood to her right, drumming his fingers irritably on the counter. He was wearing a nice grey suit and a pissed-off expression. Banecroft guessed this wasn't his local. In a room full of people who looked odd, he was the odd one out because he looked normal. Banecroft took up position between them.

As he did so, a broad-shouldered man ducked through the door behind the bar and straightened up his six-foot-eight frame. He was powerfully built in a way given by God and hard physical labour rather than by means of a well-used gym membership. Banecroft felt it highly unlikely the man had ever worked out, given the salt-and-pepper beard that extended down to his navel would undoubtedly get trapped in the various machines of torture. Or if it didn't, then the ponytail of the same length that snaked down his back certainly would. From what was visible around the man's sweat-stained vest, masses of intricate tattoos covered most of his body.

He pointed at the woman. 'Same again, Margo?'

The woman didn't appear to move or say anything, but the barman poured her a half-pint of ale anyway. Once he'd placed it in front of her, he looked at Banecroft. 'And for yourself?'

'I was here first,' snapped the other customer irritably.

'Is that right?' asked the barman.

'Yes.'

Banecroft nodded. The first-come-first-served rule was one of the few in life he held sacrosanct.

The barman moved over to stand in front of the other customer. 'How long have you been waiting?'

'At least five minutes.'

'Right,' said the barman, his calm tone a sharp contrast to the other man's irritable edge. 'How long before that, though?'

'Excuse me?'

'Has it been a while since you've had a drink?'

The man ignored the question. 'I want a vodka and Coke.'

The barman's voice softened as he leaned on the bar and reduced the height difference between himself and his customer. 'Do you, though? Are you sure that's a good idea?'

'What?'

As he spoke, the big man casually slid his finger along and around the finely polished bar top, as if he were drawing out a series of symbols or just amusing himself. His voice was a deep sonorous burr. 'How's about I give you just the Coke and then you go and ring your sponsor?'

'I don't . . . It's none of your business. Do you serve booze or not?'

'We do, of course, sir. I'm afraid you'll have to wait a few minutes, though, as I need to change the bottle.'

The man swore, tears in his eyes. He turned sharply and left, loudly slamming the door behind him.

Banecroft watched him go then turned back to the bar, where the large man was now leaning on the bar across from him. He gave off an air of relaxed power – like trouble wasn't an issue because it would be a terrible waste of everyone's time.

'Do you normally put such effort into not serving people?' enquired Banecroft.

'Not as a rule, Mr Banecroft.'

'And why is that, Mr Mor?'

The other man nodded and smiled. 'It's not Mr Mor, it's John Mór. As in . . .'

'Big John,' finished Banecroft. 'I'm not that far removed from my education in Irish that I don't remember the basics. You're not Irish, though.'

'Languages don't know geography.'

'That mind-reading trick with the names must come in handy.'

The big man shook his head. 'No trick to it, Mr Banecroft. My people know who you are. I knew before that nasty business a few months ago, but since then the wider community has taken an interest.'

'Is that right? Let's hope they all take out a subscription too. I could use a nice holiday.'

'Really? You don't strike me as the kind of man who ever takes one.' As he spoke, John Mór leaned back, raised a glass to an optic and set an unasked-for double whiskey on the bar in front of Banecroft.

'Not going to try and talk me out of drinking, then, I see?'

John Mór shook his head and smiled. 'That man – the drink was causing his pain. With you, the drink is how you cope with it.'

Banecroft shifted. 'Do you charge by the hour for this?'

John Mór held up his hands. 'Sorry, no offence meant. You asked.'

Banecroft picked up his drink and looked at it. Then he glanced at the woman still standing utterly still beside him. 'Can we talk somewhere in private?'

The big man ran a hand down his beard, twisting its point as he spoke. 'I doubt you're going to ask anything that anyone in this bar would be shocked by.'

'Really?' Banecroft scanned the room. 'They look like they'd be shocked to find out it was sunny outside.'

'Oh no, they know that. Some people just get very used to sticking to the shadows. Call it a survival instinct.'

Banecroft nodded. 'Who are you exactly?'

'John Mór.'

'Yes, we covered that. I mean – what role do you have?'

'Landlord.'

'I mean . . .'

John Mór gave a soft laugh and took out a rag from some-where to give the bar top a polish it didn't need. 'We're not like you. I don't have a title. I'm not in charge of anything. I'm just somebody who knows people and somebody those people talk to.'

'How enigmatic.'

'That's what it says on my business cards. Now, did you just come here for a free drink or do you have something to ask?'

Banecroft lifted his glass. 'Free?'

The big man nodded. 'As a thank-you for that thing a few months ago.'

Banecroft tilted his head. 'If I'd have known it came with a free bar tab, I'd have tried to find you a long time before now.'

'Not a tab. One drink. I'm grateful, not attempting to commit commercial suicide.'

Banecroft nodded at the unmoving Margo. 'I hope she's pay-ing, seeing as so far you've failed to sell a drink to two customers in a row. She . . .' He trailed off. The glass in front of Margo was now empty, even though he hadn't seen her move. 'How did she do that?'

'Now,' said John Mór, 'that really is a personal question.' He nodded at the woman. 'Same again, Margo?' He took her glass and started to pull another half of bitter into it. 'I'm going to have to change a barrel in a minute, Mr Banecroft, so do you mind asking the question they sent you to ask?'

'Nobody sent me.'

John Mór raised an eyebrow as he placed the now-full glass back in front of the still-unmoving Margo.

'I'm following up on a story of interest to the paper.'

'I see. By the way, did a woman in Germany really get chased by the ghost of a dinosaur?'

'She claimed to.'

John Mór scratched his beard and smiled. 'Now that's a thing I'd like to see.'

'I'll let you know if we get any stories about it going on tour.'

He laughed. 'Anyway, I must crack on, so . . . no, we didn't.'

'Excuse me?'

'Your story of interest. Whatever went on there, nobody I know had anything to do with it.'

'I see. And you've checked with everybody?'

'No. We don't work like that. It's not like we have a . . .' He looked at Margo. 'What do they call them?'

'WhatsApp group,' supplied Margo in a surprisingly cheery-sounding West Country accent.

'Yeah,' said John Mór, 'one of them. But I asked around when I knew you were coming.'

'Psychic powers again?'

'Oh no. Cogs might be a great man for the truth, but nobody has ever accused him of being discreet. Still, whatever that thing is, it's nothing to do with us. You can tell your employers that.'

Banecroft bristled. 'They're not my employers.'

'Aren't they? That's good to hear. I hope you sort it out, though. We don't want trouble any more than they do.'

'What kind of trouble would that be?' asked Banecroft.

'When them lot get annoyed, it's trouble for everybody. Best of luck.' And with that, John Mór turned and, crouching, headed out of the door at the back of the bar.

Banecroft stood there, listening to the big man's feet reverberate on the steps heading down to the cellar. He glanced at Margo beside him but she was no longer there. He turned around to see her now sitting beside the man in the corner who was still chatting away.

Banecroft finished his drink and left, but not before leaving a ten-pound note on the counter, for reasons he couldn't articulate to himself. He had to shield his eyes as he emerged into the painfully bright evening sunlight after the darkness of the Kanky's Rest. As he walked away, he passed the man in the grey suit, sitting on a bench, talking tearfully to someone on the phone.

Morrissey Is Possessed!

Good news this week for music fans as demonologist and part-time wedding DJ Michael Legge confirmed a suspicion that many have had for years – musical icon Morrissey is possessed.

According to Mr Legge, 'Our research has shown that Morrissey became possessed by a hate-filled entity some time in 2017 after recording the album *Low in High School*, which was pretty good. So basically, you're fine still loving all the Smiths stuff, and most of the good solo stuff – like, for example, *Viva Hate*, which, yes, does seem a tad ironic as a title now. Having said that, I reckon he might have been a bit possessed when he made *Kill Uncle*, as that was largely pants.'

CHAPTER 17

As DI Tom Sturgess held the phone to his ear, he looked down at the meal in front of him going cold.

'Right,' he said, running a hand across his eyes wearily.

DS Wilkerson's report wasn't telling him anything unduly surprising, just confirming steps she had taken. Normally, when working an investigation, action points would be generated and assigned via the HOLMES computer system, but senior management had politely requested that Sturgess keep separate, unofficial records. They hadn't even been able to come up with a reason for their request, at least not something they were prepared to admit to. It was obvious. They didn't want any of Sturgess's woo-woo nonsense officially input into police records because these days, with freedom of information requests and all that, no records were truly sealed, and such things becoming public would be spectacularly embarrassing.

So Sturgess was essentially running an investigation from notes in his phone. He didn't mind, though – he was the only police officer in the country not complaining about the amount of paperwork they had to do. He had a sneaking suspicion they'd happily pay him under the table too, if they could. He'd gone from a rising star to the invisible man. That said, he couldn't bring himself to care much. All he wanted to know was what the hell was going on – in general, and in this case in particular.

He now decided that ordering food had been a terrible idea, even if his logic had been sound. He was meeting Hannah Willis for an exchange of information at 8 p.m. He wanted to make clear that was all it was – all he thought it was, at least. He'd arrived forty minutes early because he hadn't had time to go home first, so it had made sense to eat while he was waiting. In any case, there wasn't anything in his fridge bar condiments and rotting good intentions. Now, though, seeing as it was almost eight and he'd managed to consume the sum total of one cheesy fry, it would just seem like he was being rude. He definitely didn't want to be that either.

The reason his genuinely appetizing-looking hot dog and cheesy fries had been sitting in front of him for almost half an hour now was that his phone hadn't stopped ringing since he'd sat down. First it had been Dr Charlie Mason from the morgue, informing him that Butler's dental records didn't offer any explanation for his messed-up mouth. They also offered no other details on the emergency appointment that Butler made hours before he died but didn't attend. The pathologist had been abrupt, still off with Sturgess for the embarrassing phantom phone-call incident earlier that day. He'd confirmed that the blood in Butler's stomach had been analysed and it was definitely human and definitely didn't belong to Butler. He'd offered no explanation for either finding.

Then Manesh Patel from Tech had called, informing him that

he couldn't get into the late Phillip Butler's phone. Sturgess had then rung Dr Mason back and told him that Patel was on his way over to try to use fingerprint recognition to open the device. He'd been expecting more pushback from Mason – first, because he'd been on his way out the door when Sturgess had called, and second, because using a dead man's fingerprint to unlock a phone was, at best, murky legal territory. Surprisingly, the pathologist acceded to the request with the bare minimum of fuss.

After that, Sturgess had received the call he'd been expecting from Chief Inspector Clayborne, telling him that Butler's phone should be returned to his employers at Fuzzy Britches as soon as possible. Sturgess was surprised it had taken this long for Clayborne to get in touch – she must've been out on the golf course or in a meeting when whoever the company's lawyer was had rung her to demand it get sorted out. Sturgess had made the case that this wasn't a simple suicide but had been overruled.

His final communication had been a reluctant text to Concerned Citizen, his mysterious benefactor, explaining the situation. He'd been simultaneously impressed and horrified when Clayborne rang back five minutes later to tell him she'd reconsidered his case and that he could hold on to the phone until he was satisfied it didn't have an evidentiary value. Who the hell had the level of influence that could make a chief inspector flip like that? Having spent so long as a lone voice on the force, being dismissed as a crank, maybe Sturgess should have felt some vindication or vicarious joy at suddenly having the invisible powers that be working in his favour, but he didn't. It just added to his growing unease that he had been compromised.

He was sitting in a booth in the bar-cum-restaurant of the Roxy cinema. The venue had been Hannah's suggestion. The main entrance was down an alleyway but the large windows in the bar offered a good view of the comings and goings of the city. It was nice – the decor was all chrome and red leather, like one of those old American diners. The walls were covered in posters for old movies – the Marx Brothers and Three Stooges randomly mixed in with garish playbills for old-school horror flicks showing scantily clad ladies holding their cheeks and screaming as terrifying monsters ambled towards them. Despite it being a Monday evening in the middle of a heatwave the place was doing a steady trade.

It was only after he'd ordered his food that Sturgess noticed he'd sat in a booth with a poster for *Blood of the Vampire* on the wall above it. The poster was notable for the fact that the vampire, shown in terrifying close-up over the inevitable screaming buxom blonde strapped to a table, had his eyebrows fashioned to look like bats. The other notable feature was the tagline of 'No woman is safe from the most frightening fiend in the history of horror'. He seriously considered moving. For several reasons, the poster wasn't setting the right vibe.

On the other end of the line, DS Wilkerson was now finishing delivering her report: she'd requested Butler's phone and bank records, her earlier examination of his apartment had yielded nothing out of the ordinary, and the tox screens on the HGV driver had, as expected, come back showing nothing. As Sturgess had suspected, the guy had just been the unlucky sod in the wrong place at the wrong time.

'And lastly,' concluded Wilkerson, 'I just double-checked with our lot – no unexplained bodies have shown up. I also ran it by Merseyside, Cheshire, Yorkshire and Derbyshire – nothing out of the ordinary in any of their locations that could explain the blood discovered in Butler's stomach, but they'll keep me informed. I also contacted the blood transfusion service and the local hospitals – nothing missing.'

'Right,' said Sturgess. Wilkerson was good. He hadn't thought of the blood transfusion thing, but it had been worth checking. 'OK. Well, we'll pick this up tomorrow.'

'Sure, guv.'

'And ehm, good work today, Andrea.'

Wilkerson sounded surprised. 'Oh, er – thanks. See you tomorrow . . . Tom.' He could hear her cringe as she added the 'Tom'. It was quite possibly the first time she'd ever used it.

'Bye.'

Sturgess had to admit that his new drive to be a bit better on the people side of things was, so far, really just highlighting what a cantankerous sod he was perceived as being. He might have to reconsider his previously rejected idea of buying a box of dough-nuts for the station.

He looked down at his food. The previously mouth-watering cheese had now cooled and congealed into unhappy stodge. Still, if he got a move on, he might just finish it before—

'Hi.'

He actually jumped.

'Sorry,' said Hannah. 'Didn't mean to startle you.'

'Oh no,' said Sturgess, embarrassed. He tried to slip out of the booth and get to his feet.

'I'm a little early. Relax. Finish your meal.'

'Don't worry about it. It's gone cold.'

An awkward moment ensued, during which each side considered the handshake, hug, and kiss on the cheek as greeting options but, crucially, never at the same time. The result was an embarrassed little dance before Sturgess opted for a convivial, platonic pat on the upper arm and they both sat down, keen to move on.

'So,' said Sturgess, 'how've you been?'

'Good. Just got back from getting divorced.' Hannah winced. 'I mean, not yet – its wheels are in motion.' She turned bright red and Sturgess guessed that was not the opening she'd had planned.

'Well, you look well. Clearly it suits you.'

'Thanks.'

She genuinely did. He suddenly felt very aware that he was on day three with his suit and was sporting a mustard stain on the tie he'd forgot to change. He silently cursed himself for not leaving enough time to make it home and back again.

'How are your headaches?' asked Hannah.

'Better, thanks. I've been cutting back on caffeine and, y'know, generally trying to take a bit better care of myself.'

'That's excellent,' said Hannah, who was looking distractedly at the top of Sturgess's head rather than at his face. 'Really good.'

'Do I have something in my hair?'

It was Hannah's turn to jump. 'No, oh no. God, no. Sorry. I was . . . looking at that poster on the wall.'

'I see,' said Sturgess, peering over his shoulder. 'The one for *And Now the Screaming Starts*?'

'Yes,' said Hannah. 'Looks good. Actually, no, it doesn't. I don't know why I said that. I hate horror movies.'

Just then, a waitress with dyed blue hair appeared beside them. 'Hi, can I get you guys a drink?'

'God, yes,' said Hannah. 'Large white wine.'

'And yourself, sir?'

'I'll just have a water, please.'

The waitress looked down at the table. 'Is there something wrong with your food?'

'No, no,' said Sturgess. 'Sorry, I just . . . lost my appetite.'

'Oh,' said the waitress, looking unsure. 'If you like, I can heat it up for you?'

'No, thanks,' said Sturgess. He held up the plate. 'You can take it away, though. Thanks very much.'

'Are you sure about that?'

'Yes. Thanks.'

The waitress puffed out her cheeks. 'Well, OK, then, I guess.' She departed, eyeing the plate of untouched food suspiciously as she did so.

Hannah and Sturgess looked at each other awkwardly. There didn't seem to be an obvious conversational segue from here.

'So . . .'

'So . . .'

Sturgess threw a jovial thumb up at the poster on the wall. 'Vampires, then.'

'Don't exist,' said Hannah.

'Right.'

'I mean . . .' She looked uncomfortable before giving a shrug. 'Well, they don't.'

'That's good to know. I've got a dead guy sitting in the morgue who is trying to argue otherwise.'

'I know. I saw the report.'

Sturgess's smile dropped. 'Excuse me?'

Hannah looked alarmed, having realized what she'd said. 'Well, somebody tipped us off.'

'Right. I don't suppose we could kick off this information-sharing meeting with you giving me that name, could we?'

'Probably best not.'

'Good start.'

'It can only go up from here,' replied Hannah with a nervous smile. 'I mean . . . When I said vampires don't exist – I've been talking to the kind of people who think lots of things exist and even they say they don't.'

'Right.'

'That sounded better in my head.'

'I can imagine.'

Hannah cleared her throat. 'What I'm trying to say is, we – *The Stranger Times* – have contacted our sources in the community and they've told us that whatever this is, it's somebody pretending somehow.'

'Speaking as someone who has seen the body, it is a very, very good fake, then.'

'Really?'

He nodded. 'The teeth were, well, real, and we've checked dental records. He didn't have them five weeks ago . . .'

'Oh,' said Hannah, 'that *is* odd.'

'That isn't even the oddest bit.' Sturgess hesitated, but then again, he'd been told to share information. 'The victim had blood in his stomach.'

'Right. Well, it was a horrible crash.'

'No, you've misunderstood me. He had someone else's blood in his stomach.'

Hannah put her hand to her mouth. 'Oh my God, that is the most disgusting thing.'

At that precise moment the waitress turned up with their drinks. She'd clearly heard Hannah's last words. She placed the drinks down before asking, 'Can I just check there was definitely nothing wrong with the food?'

Sturgess tried to smile. 'Honestly, it looked great.'

'Right. I can get you another if you'd like?'

'There's no need. Thanks.'

The waitress nodded and departed.

'*Was* there something wrong with the food?'

'No,' said Sturgess. 'I just – I kept getting phone calls and it went cold.'

'Well, somebody's popular!' Hannah gave a slightly forced laugh, then instantly looked like she regretted it.

'Speaking of which, are you familiar with Fuzzy Britches?'

'Yeah,' said Hannah. 'My friend Maggie tried to get me to set up a profile, but I didn't want to.' She looked suddenly horrified. 'Oh God, she didn't set one up for me, did she?'

Sturgess took a sip of his water. 'Ehm, no. I meant Phillip Butler – the dead guy – worked for them.'

'Right. You meant . . . Yeah, I knew that. I just . . . So, he worked for them?'

'He did. I met Tamsin Baladin this afternoon.'

'Really?'

'Which is a bit unusual. I mean, the CEO of a massive company taking an interest in the apparent suicide of one of their employees.'

'I suppose so. Did she know him?'

'Not really. To be honest, they're mainly concerned about getting his phone back and . . .' Sturgess's own phone, which he'd placed on the table, beeped. 'Speaking of which . . .' He picked it up and read the text. 'Damn.'

Hannah looked interested but was polite enough not to enquire. Sturgess held up the handset. 'We just tried to open the victim's phone using facial recognition. No dice.'

'Oh.'

'Probably because of the . . .' Sturgess pointed at his teeth.

'Actually,' said Hannah, leaning in, 'that's why I suggested meeting here. Reggie, who works with me – I think you met him?'

'Is he the guy I arrested?'

Hannah smiled. 'No, that was Ox.'

'Of course. Do tell him the jack-booted thug of the authoritarian state sends his regards.'

Hannah smiled. 'He calls everybody that.'

'Really?'

'Nah. Just you.'

'Fair enough.'

'Back to Reggie. He's a regular here – they have a weekly vampire movie night. Like a sort of ongoing festival. He says there's lots of people who come dressed up for it, in the whole, well . . .' She pointed up at the poster. 'I mean, I'm sure most of them are just having a bit of fun, but . . .'

Sturgess nodded. 'Might be worth looking into. Frankly, we're drawing a blank on that side of things. Thanks.'

Hannah smiled again and Sturgess could see she was pleased with herself.

He took another sip of water. 'Actually, I wanted to ask you about—' He grimaced as his phone rang. 'Excuse me.' He answered it.

'Boss,' said DS Wilkerson.

'I thought I told you to go home?'

'Yeah, they've found a body. Building site off Cambridge Street. There are teeth marks.'

Sturgess stood up abruptly. 'I'm on my way, text me the address.'

Hannah looked up at him.

'Sorry, I've got to go.'

'No problem. I . . .'

Sturgess didn't hear the rest of what she said. He was already halfway out the door.

★

Hannah sat there for a minute, looking at her glass of wine. 'That went well,' she said to it.

It was her turn to jump as someone sat down opposite her. Reggie.

'Bloody hell, you came out of nowhere.'

Reggie smiled. 'I decided I might as well pop in. Y'know, do a bit of investigating. So, how did that go?'

'What?'

Reggie wiggled his eyebrows. 'Oh, come on. You know well what I mean.'

'Let me put it this way – you know the opening scene of *Saving Private Ryan*?'

'That bad?'

'No. Worse.'

'Oh dear.'

'So,' said Hannah, 'you're here investigating?'

'I am. I know the manager, Ronnie. I thought she might be able to point us in the direction of anyone taking the vampire thing a bit too seriously.' He looked over Hannah's right shoulder. 'Oh, here she is now. Hello, Veronica.'

A woman with a shaved head stopped beside their table. In her hand was a plate that looked very familiar.

'Don't you hello me.' She spoke with a strong Yorkshire accent. 'I told ya – you send one more meal back here and you're barred!'

Reggie looked all wounded pride. 'I didn't!'

CHAPTER 18

Hannah moved over in the booth to allow Ronnie to slide in next to her. It was a bit of a tight squeeze. The manager was a stout woman with a shaved head and a tattoo of the Golden Girls on one forearm.

Reggie, sitting opposite, clutched his chest. 'I promise you, Ronnie – hand on heart – I did not send any food back.'

'He really didn't,' said Hannah. 'The guy who was sitting there before him – DI Sturgess – sent it back, but only because it went cold while he was on the phone. Entirely his fault.'

'What's a copper doing here?' asked Ronnie, now alarmed for a whole bunch of other reasons.

'We were just having a social drink.'

'Come to that, who are you?'

Hannah extended her hand awkwardly into the tight space between them. 'I'm Hannah. I work with Reggie at *The Stranger Times*.'

Ronnie studied Hannah's hand for a moment then shook it. 'All right. Hiya. Sorry. So, a detective inspector? Did you meet on that uniform dating site or summat?'

'No. We're just friends.'

'The lady doth protest too much, methinks.'

'Is everything all right, Ronnie?' asked Reggie. 'You do seem rather tense.'

Ronnie let out a deep sigh. 'Sorry. I've got a new chef and she's a little temperamental. Someone sent back a pizza last week and she hit the roof. I'm keen not to have a repeat of that particular Monty Python sketch, thank you very much.'

'What happened to Sam?'

'That,' said Ronnie, 'is another of my problems.' She looked around to check who might be within earshot. 'Stevo, the projectionist who used to work here, left a few months ago – claimed he was being harassed in the workplace. Said people were constantly messing with his stuff. He said we were whispering insults at him.'

'Whispering insults?' asked Hannah.

'Don't ask. I haven't a clue where he got that from. Then Sam, the chef, has a falling-out with a waitress. Claims she stabbed him in the hand with a paring knife. She says she was nowhere near him. Like, not even in the room at the time – and I believe her. She's not the sort to do that over a missed nachos order. Anyway, long story short – they got themselves a solicitor. A couple of other ex-staff have hopped aboard the free-money express and they're all suing us. I'm now the psycho, man-hating lesbian who made any man who worked here's life a misery.'

'Oh, for . . .' said Reggie.

'Yeah, so the last thing I need right now is any more hassle.'

Reggie nodded. 'I can see that. I remember Sam from when I was here doing the story. I thought you and him were great mates?'

'We are. Or at least we used to be. Me and him were the two longest-serving members of staff. Now, the trust that runs this place is up in arms. I tried to reason with him. He's pissed that I don't believe him, but the thing is, the CCTV shows Fiona – the waitress – out having a cigarette, and then one of the other girls rushes out to tell her Sam had an accident. If Fiona did it, then she's a bloody wizard.'

Hannah and Reggie shared a brief but pointed look.

'So now,' continued Ronnie, 'my oldest mate is suing me. I've got to go and get a lawyer, and the trust needs one too. This place doesn't make much money – not when you factor in the repayments on the loans we took out to buy and restore the building. We can't afford a big payout.'

'That is rough,' sympathized Reggie.

'Between that and my massive organ.'

'Excuse me?' asked Hannah.

Reggie waved his hand. 'The Roxy used to be a music hall and, at great expense, they got the original organ restored last year.'

'It sounds great,' said Ronnie. 'You should be here for the one week in four that it's working. We've got all these silent movies with organ accompaniment scheduled and we keep having to cancel.'

'Oh dear,' said Hannah with a wince.

'Anyway. I shouldn't be dumping all my woes on you. You just here for a drink or are you catching a flick? We got *The Apartment* with Jack Lemmon and Shirley MacLaine on tonight. All-time classic.'

'Actually,' said Reggie, 'I was hoping we could have a chat about your Tuesday-night crowd?'

'If you ask me about those bloody students, I'm going to punch you right in the mush, Reginald. I mean it.'

'Not about that,' said Reggie. 'I promise.'

Reggie caught Hannah's quizzical look. 'A few months ago, some students thought it would be a good idea to drop acid and go watch a movie.'

'Yeah,' said Ronnie. 'And they thought a screening of *The Exorcist* was the best place to do it.'

'I haven't seen it,' said Hannah.

'Neither have they. They ran out screaming at the "your mother sucks cocks in hell" bit. One of them ran into the gospel church over the road, right in the middle of a service, and started hollering about Satan. Things got a bit insane after that. We had a minister outside throwing holy water on everyone going in and out for a week. The *Evening News* ran a two-page spread on it.' Ronnie shook her head. 'Bloody students.'

'It's not about that,' promised Reggie. 'We're interested in the vampire crowd.'

Ronnie laughed. 'Let me guess – has one of them started biting people?'

Reggie shifted awkwardly in his seat.

'Fuck a duck,' said Ronnie as her face dropped. 'Please tell me they haven't?'

'No, no, no,' said Reggie. 'Nothing like that.'

'Yeah,' Hannah chimed in. 'We're just looking to do a feature on the subculture. It's part of a series we're pitching. Ufologists, ghost hunters, furries.'

'Ah, right. Gotcha. Yeah, we get them all right.'

'Really?' asked Hannah.

'The vampire lot, I mean. Not the furries. They're the people who dress up as animals and get jiggy with it, right?'

'Yes,' said Hannah.

'Nah, we don't get them. Not that I'd mind if we did. Anyone who can keep this place busy on a weeknight, I'm open to offers.' Ronnie drummed her hands on the table. 'Within reason, obviously. The National Front can do one. Soz – I'm rambling. Yeah – the vampire lot. I mean, it's mostly dressing up. Y'know, people just having a laugh. A lot of them come to the *Rocky Horror Picture Show* screening on the last Friday of every month too. Some folks just love doing anything involving fancy dress. When we did the *Close Encounters* festival last year, we were wall to wall with all kinds of aliens. We had someone come down from Glasgow for it every week. That lady didn't even go into the films, she just stood out here, dressed as the creature from *Predator*, knocking back sambucas. You've not lived until you've seen someone try to use the bathroom dressed like that. We had to let her use the disabled loo in the end, after she got stuck. Then Chewbacca in a wheelchair kicked off.'

'Sounds mad,' said Hannah.

Ronnie shrugged. 'Same old, same old, really. You've got to understand – we're not trying to compete with the multiplexes, because we can't. And if you want to go watch serious arthouse films, there's HOME, with their big grants and patrons. I'm not having a go – they do good stuff, if that's what floats your boat. This place, though – we're the trashy misfit. We get by on catering to the freaks and weirdos, and I proudly count myself in their number.

'We make our money on the food and drink – plus, we've got that meeting room that we rent out. We get the odd corporate thing looking for somewhere different, but it's mostly board-gamers, who aren't the biggest drinkers but they do go mental for nachos, and there's the communist collective who bring their own sandwiches made from their allotment produce but drink the place dry, bless their little Bolshevik hearts. Them and a couple of book clubs.'

'Whatever works,' said Reggie.

'Exactly. The vampire lot are all right. We even do cocktails for them. Bloody Marys, that kind of thing. Anything red, basically. Marsha also does this thing with dry ice – it does look pretty cool. We sell a ton of those bad boys. We do all these things for the Rocky Horror bunch too – I tell you, that lot are a dream come true! Anybody in that film gets cancelled and this place would fold.'

'The vampires,' said Reggie, trying to steer the conversation. 'Whenever I've been here, I've seen a few of them who look pretty hardcore.'

Ronnie laughed. 'I imagine you're referring to Victor and his acolytes. Victor the vampire – sounds like a cartoon, doesn't it? He's pretty full-on. He petitioned to change the time of the films a few weeks ago – said he couldn't turn up until after dark. I told him he could have an umbrella if he liked, but come hell or high water, the film starts at eight p.m. That way we can sell food on the way in and booze on the way out, plus popcorn and ice-cream during the interval.'

'Sounds sensible,' said Hannah.

'Which is more than can be said for Victor. He's had his teeth done – y'know, to have the permanent fangs. I mean, don't get me wrong, I'm firmly "your body, your choice". I've got a few piercings and tats myself, but the teeth – personally, that's a bit much for my tastes.'

'And there are others with him?'

'Oh yeah,' said Ronnie. 'There's a group of them. They're like a subsection of goths, I guess. The kind of bloke who wears leather trousers and frilly shirts, and the kind of silly girls who go for that. Y'know – the "not actually a bad boy" bad boy and the kind of women who are afraid to walk the streets at night but are pen pals with serial killers in prison.'

'Right,' said Hannah.

'Sorry,' said Ronnie. 'I'm probably being really unfair. It's been a long week and it's only Monday. I'm normally a very tolerant sort – honest.'

'Relax, Veronica,' said Reggie. 'Your status as house mother for the freak show is secure.'

'Oh, Reggie, you smooth-talking dog, you.'

'So, Victor?' he continued, attempting to redirect her.

'Yeah. I heard him explain to someone how he lives his life as a real-life vampire.'

Reggie nodded. 'There are groups around the world that do that.'

'You're kidding?' said Hannah.

'No. They call themselves sanguinarians and they feed on animal and, occasionally, human blood.' Reggie saw Hannah's eyes widen. 'Blood that's given by donors or significant others, or whatever.'

'Wow,' said Hannah. 'Well, that's . . . disturbing.'

'I tend to agree,' said Ronnie, 'and I'm the most snowflake liberal you're likely to find.' She looked over her shoulder towards the bar. 'I'd better get back. Marsha is due a break.'

'Would you happen to know where this Victor guy lives?' asked Reggie.

'Y'know,' said Ronnie, 'as almost impossible as this must be to believe, I've never gone back to his. What with him being a wannabe vampire and me being a hardcore lesbian who makes the lives of hardworking men a living nightmare.'

'Veronica, dear,' said Reggie with a smile, 'sarcasm is beneath you.'

'Reginald, dearest,' she responded, aping his tone, 'would you be kind enough to blow it out your arse?'

Hannah laughed.

Ronnie gave her an appraising look. 'You've got a nice laugh, I'll give you that. I can see what Inspector Do-dah sees in you.'

'It was just a business thing.'

'Yeah, right,' said Ronnie. 'And Angelina Jolie keeps ringing me but I'm playing hard to get.'

'She'd be lucky to have you,' said Reggie. 'Is there any chance you know Victor's address?'

'Victor isn't even his real name,' said Ronnie. 'I only know that because he's paid by card a couple of times.'

Reggie gave his best attempt at a winning smile. 'Could you maybe check for us?'

Ronnie nodded. 'Hallowe'en is coming up at the end of October.'

Reggie sat there looking bamboozled by this apparent non-sequitur.

'It is,' agreed Hannah. 'And, as assistant editor of *The Stranger Times*, I was thinking we should run another special on the most haunted locations in Manchester.'

Ronnie patted her on the arm. 'I knew I was going to like you.'

CHAPTER 19

DI Sturgess stood in silence and looked down at the body covered in a white sheet as DS Wilkerson brought him up to speed. The sound from the apartment building across the road of a party in full swing was a sharp contrast to the sight before him. Forensic tents were rarely happy places.

'They found it an hour ago, when everybody was leaving for the day,' Wilkerson explained in a low voice. 'The new night watchman had just started. The old one was nowhere to be seen when the site manager got in this morning, and he wasn't answering any calls. He – the site manager – had been showing the new guy around when they found the body. Said he thought the old night watchman, Mr Alashev here, had just buggered off. Apparently, that kind of thing happens a fair bit. Agency workers and all that.'

'And on a busy building site nobody noticed the body all day?' asked Sturgess. He'd driven by here only yesterday and had noted how quickly the latest development of apartment buildings was going up. Fifty feet from where they were standing, the metal skeleton of yet another block of 'executive' apartments stood awaiting its flesh.

'That storage container outside blocked it from view. Nobody comes over here because they're working at the far end of the site. Site manager says the lads usually eat their lunch here to shelter from the rain, but seeing as it's been sunny, they've all been heading down to the canal for their breaks. To quote him exactly, "That's where the girls go by."'

'Good to see some lazy stereotypes are alive and well.'

'The site manager is outside. He's waiting to talk to you.'

'Where's the new night watchman?'

'He's at the hospital, guv.' Wilkerson caught Sturgess's look. 'They say he took it really badly. Started screaming the place down. Somebody ended up calling for an ambulance. Had to sedate him. Very religious fella, apparently.'

'And the body hasn't been moved?'

'Nope. Provisionally, Forensics reckon this is the kill site. Signs of a struggle, lots of blood on the ground.'

'Right,' said Sturgess. He checked the latex gloves he'd put on and pulled up his face mask. As he kneeled down, the sickly stench of a body that had been lying in the heat all day rose to meet him.

Wilkerson cleared her throat. 'Fair warning, guv. It's a nasty one.'

'OK. Well . . .' Sturgess pulled away the sheet. Despite the warning, he found himself jerking his head back. 'Christ.'

'Yeah.'

'Are those teeth marks?'

'Fransen says, unofficially, yes . . .'

'That man wouldn't officially confirm his own death until he got a second opinion. How long . . .'

Sturgess trailed off as he heard the tent flap open and close behind him.

He couldn't blame her. He'd long since lost count of the number of dead bodies he'd seen in the job, but as much as they all pretended otherwise, it didn't ever become a mundanity. Certainly not something like this – not that he'd ever seen anything quite like this.

The neck was a ragged, bloody mess. If the trauma really had been inflicted by teeth, then it was with a level of power and ferocity that simply wasn't natural. The throat was bad, but what would wake Sturgess in the middle of the night was the look of terror in the victim's wide eyes. Some cultures believe that the iris retains an image of a victim's killer captured at the moment of death. Sturgess didn't need to look any closer, though – he knew there was nothing there.

That wasn't to say that the eyes didn't tell any tales. That level of fear is experienced only by someone who doesn't understand what they're looking at but knows what it means. If this was the handiwork of the late Phillip Butler, then whatever he was or thought he was, he was possessed of a rare brutality.

The words of one of Sturgess's old lecturers came back to him – murders are moments defined by one of two things: rage or calculated judgement. The perpetrator either couldn't stop themselves from doing it or decided to do it. However, this looked like neither of those things. This was hunger. Real or imagined. Hunger.

When Sturgess stepped into the fresh air, he nodded at Forensics, who headed back into the tent to finish their work. He took off his mask and gloves, and tossed them into the medical waste bag. Wilkerson appeared from behind the shipping container, wiping her mouth and looking sheepish. Two uniforms stood to the side, guarding the scene. One of them smirked at the other.

'Sorry, boss,' said Wilkerson.

'Nothing to be sorry for. I was about to eat when I got the call. Glad I didn't or I'd have ended up joining you.'

Wilkerson nodded awkwardly, appreciating the attempt to assuage her embarrassment.

'So,' said Sturgess, lowering his voice, 'I'll be the one to say it out loud – are you willing to bet against Mr Alashev's blood matching the blood we found in Butler's stomach?'

'I know you don't like guessing, but no, I'm not.'

'So, what do you think?'

'Our boy wants to fulfil some messed-up fantasy.' She jutted her chin towards the tent. 'He does that, then quickly realizes he can't live with the reality.'

Sturgess scratched at his beard and nodded. 'Makes sense.'

He could tell he and his DS both shared the same thought. It made sense only if you could square a human being actually being capable of such an atrocity.

'All right,' he said. 'I'm going to make a quick call. Can you prep the site manager for a chat?'

'Sure, guv.'

The first clue PC Roberts had that he was in trouble was the appearance of DI Sturgess's face six inches in front of him.

'Don't stop smirking on my account, officer.'

'Sir. Sorry, sir.'

'What are you sorry about, officer?' Sturgess used his phone to snap a picture of the constable's name badge. 'Roberts. PC Roberts. Excellent, I shall remember you.'

'Sir?'

'Forgive me, Roberts. I interrupted you explaining what you were sorry for?'

Roberts kept schtum.

After a moment, Sturgess leaned in. 'So tell me, Roberts, do you one day hope to make detective?'

'Yes, sir.'

'Good man. Nothing wrong with a bit of ambition. Let me give you some friendly advice, officer to officer. If, one day, you find yourself inside the tent, as opposed to guarding the tent, and, when confronted with a human life ended in the most horrific and repugnant way imaginable it doesn't turn your stomach, then get the hell out of the tent, because at that point you're no good to anybody, since you're closer in mentality to those you are chasing than to those you are sworn to protect. Do you understand me?'

Roberts nodded. 'Yes, sir.'

Sturgess patted him on the arm. 'Don't worry, though – I don't think you'll ever have that problem. I mean, if you're dumb enough to take the piss out of a senior officer and get caught doing it by an even more senior officer, then, well, I'm not sure high-ranking police work is likely to be your calling in life.'

'Sorry, sir.'

'Stop saying sorry if you don't know what you're sorry for,' snapped Sturgess.

Roberts glanced at the other PC.

'I wouldn't look over there, Roberts. Right now Officer Kilcoyne is hoping and praying that I haven't taken note of his name too, because deep down he's always considered you a bit of an idiot and the last thing he wants is for the stink of your stupidity to stick to him. Am I right, Kilcoyne?'

'Yes, sir.'

'Well judged, Kilcoyne. Anyway, I'll let you boys get back to work. Do me a favour, though, Roberts. Every time you smirk from now on, think of me and remember that I'm a man with an excellent long-term memory.'

Before Roberts could attempt to form a sentence, Sturgess turned and departed. He kept his eyes fixed ahead of him, which was why, if compelled to do so, he would not have been able to attest to the fact that Kilcoyne slapped Roberts roundly on the back of the head.

CHAPTER 20

Ox rolled his head in slow circles and listened to the unhappy crackle of muscle and cartilage that was his neck making clear how much it disliked sitting in a cramped van for ten hours solid. He'd been surprised when Stanley had offered to drive him home. At least, he had up until Stanley had invited himself in to use the shower when they got there. Ox didn't mind. While he wasn't wild about the idea of Stanley coming to the flat that he and Reggie shared, he was considerably keener on having a fresher-smelling Stanley in the van it seemed they were destined to share for the next few days.

By the time the tanned man they'd seen entering the house in Worsley had re-emerged, they'd been able to identify him as one Darius Williams, owner of Echelon Construction Ltd. In spite of himself, Ox had been a little bit impressed as he'd sat there and watched Stanley typing furiously on his laptop. Stanley had called up the Companies House records for Echelon, confirmed Williams as the majority stakeholder, and verified the man they had seen was indeed Williams by finding a picture from some local construction industry awards dinner. He also had both Williams's and Echelon Construction's bank records, which even Ox knew weren't supposed to be readily accessible to just anyone.

One of the people who had been unhappy to hear from Stanley earlier in the day clearly worked in banking.

'Hmmm,' Stanley had said as he'd scanned the records. 'No obvious financial difficulties here that I can see. Big payments coming in, but then the company does some pretty big jobs. 'Course, could be off-the-books stuff. I'll put some feelers out, see if anyone on the more unregulated end of the financial markets knows Mr Williams.' He opened another email that contained just an attachment. 'Mr Williams engaged in some vehicular larceny when he was younger, but nothing too heavy. What's not clear is how a kid from Salford who didn't finish school got the money together to set up his own company.'

'Hard work and clean living?' Ox had said, earning a snort of derision from Stanley. 'You reckon somebody's definitely blackmailing him, then?'

'Works his way up to being a respectable builder doing high-end jobs and suddenly he risks it all by going into your offices and fitting a trapdoor in your shower? Yeah, I'd imagine somebody has got some heavy pressure on Mr Williams.'

Ox had studied the picture on the screen. The tanned man in a sharp suit, holding a glass award and looking like king of the world, beamed out at them. 'He looks like he has it all.'

'Two things you learn in this business: having it all doesn't stop people wanting more and, if you look hard enough, everybody has a point of weakness.'

'You really should do your own line in inspirational posters, Stanley. Stick some of these pearls of wisdom over some cat pictures and you could make your fortune.'

Stanley had slammed the laptop closed and shrugged. 'Say what you like, doesn't make me wrong, does it? 'Course, he could be an alien from another planet or that.'

'You read *The Stranger Times*,' Ox had said.

'As if.'

'You do. How else would you know my area of expertise?'

Stanley had shifted uncomfortably. 'I've started skimming it recently, given the crap I've been going through.'

'You shagging some demon, you mean?'

Ox had pulled back in shock at the ferocity on Stanley's face as he'd turned and jabbed a finger at him.

'I didn't shag anybody!'

Ox had held up his hands. 'Jesus. All right. All right.'

They'd sat there in an even frostier silence until Williams re-emerged. The frost had been in name only, given the rolled-up windows and air-con ban. In reality, Ox was starting to feel like a slow-roasting chicken.

After Williams had emerged, they'd followed him from a distance as he'd headed back to the home address they had for him out near Knutsford. The house was a fancy-looking modern design, all glass walls and hard right angles, out of place alongside the more conventional houses surrounding it. Williams had buzzed himself through a set of electric gates and, as Stanley drove past slowly, Ox had watched as Williams was greeted by two enthusiastic Dalmatians and a rather more reserved wife.

Stanley had parked up the street and instructed Ox to do a walk-by. Happy for the fresh air, Ox had complied. Thanks to the property's massive windows, he'd been able to observe Williams settling down in front of the TV to watch a football match while the missus busied herself in the kitchen cooking up a storm. Williams sure didn't look like a man with an awful lot to hide.

Then, afterwards, Stanley had made his offer to drop Ox back to his flat in Trafford – the one with the shower.

'I know this area,' Stanley commented as they turned on to Talbot Road and passed the nearest bookies to Ox's flat – not that they let Ox in there any more. 'There used to be a brothel down the end there. Specialized in men dressing up as babies.'

'Really?'

'Yeah. I sold pics of a cricketer coming out of it. Stevie Wilkes beat me to the interview with the hooker, though. Sneaky little sod.'

'Some people have no morals, do they?' Ox regretted his words as soon as they left his mouth. Stanley may be reprehensible but he was also giving him a lift home. 'Take a right up here, please.'

'So, tomorrow,' said Stanley, 'we need to—'

His train of thought was interrupted as Ox hurled himself onto the floor of the van.

'What?'

'Keep driving,' pleaded Ox. 'Don't stop. Don't stop.'

Stanley did as he was asked, drove down the street and pulled up around the corner.

Ox looked up tentatively. 'Right, sorry about that. I . . . Some friends of mine are outside the flat. I forgot it's my birthday today and I'm not supposed to be home until later. They're waiting for my flatmate.' He laughed. 'Nearly ruined my own surprise party. I mean, obviously I know about it, but Reggie's put a lot of work into it and I'd hate him to know that I know. So yeah.'

'Right,' said Stanley. 'That makes total sense. So, how long have you been best buddies with the notorious Fenton brothers, loan sharks, bookies and inveterate leg-breakers?'

'Are they?' said Ox, painfully aware of how unconvincing his feigned disbelief sounded. 'I just know them from our book club.'

'Did you really think I wouldn't know who they are? After all, I'm a – what was it you called me? Oh yeah – a bottom-feeding tabloid hack. Knowing who people like them are is all part of the job.' Stanley shook his head. 'Anyway, out you pop. You need to head home where you can feel all morally superior to silly old Stanley.'

'I'm just going to wait a couple of minutes,' said Ox. 'They won't stay there long.'

'You mean before they go inside so they can pop out from behind the sofa and yell, "Surprise" and then you can all settle down to give your opinions on *Pride and Prejudice*?'

Ox kept quiet.

'Happy birthday, by the way.'

'Thanks,' said Ox. Despite being aware how pathetically see-through his lies were, somehow he couldn't bring himself to abandon them.

'What star sign are you?' asked Stanley.

'Virgo?'

Stanley shook his head.

'Ehm, Sagittarius?'

'Take it from one who knows, you're a truly awful liar. So . . .' Stanley looked Ox up and down appraisingly. 'Horses?'

'I don't know what you're talking about.'

'Of course you don't,' said Stanley. 'Well, unless I'm way off, it isn't drugs. I'd have noticed. I reckon it probably isn't cards either. I mean, I hope it isn't, given how bad a liar you are. You do not have a poker face. There's only so many ways a bloke like you could end up in over his head with the Fentons. I'm guessing horses. Maybe dogs?'

Ox sighed. 'Both.'

'How much?'

'Twenty grand.' Weirdly, mixed with his shame was a sense of relief. Ox hadn't told anyone about his debts. Months ago, Reggie had made him promise that he'd given up gambling entirely. He wanted to quit, he really did. He just needed to get even.

Stanley whistled. 'Have you got a plan to get yourself out of it?'

'Well,' said Ox, 'I've got . . .'

Stanley held up a hand. 'Fair warning: if this sentence features the words "hot tip", I'm going to punch you in the nuts. Hard.'

Ox hung his head. 'I'm screwed.'

'Who can they get to?'

'What?'

'The Fentons,' said Stanley. 'You got family? Friends?'

'Just Reggie, my flatmate.'

'Ring him,' said Stanley.

'But why would—'

'Because,' interrupted Stanley, 'if you owe them that kind of money, they're going to go looking for pressure points. If he's home, tell him to keep his head down, and if he isn't, tell him to go sleep somewhere else tonight. For that kind of cash, those boys aren't leaving here without sending a message.'

'Oh God,' said Ox, 'I think I'm going to be sick.'

Stanley grabbed Ox's mobile from his hand and shoved the charger dangling out of the cigarette lighter into it. 'Ring him.' He restarted the engine. 'You're sleeping in the front seat, and before you say it, no – we cannot open a window.'

CHAPTER 21

Hannah was, in a word, drunk.

In two words, very drunk.

In three words, very, very drunk.

In two words again, but this time with one of them being a big score in Scrabble – paralytically drunk.

The problem, thought Reggie, was one of capacity. He had matched Hannah drink for drink, but he was twice her size and, as he'd realized far too late, he had eaten whereas she had not.

What Hannah did have, it turned out, was the kind of raging thirst that only going through a tortuous divorce, returning to work and being thrown straight into a crisis, and then having an awkward meeting with a man you sort of had an almost-thing with could give you.

At this moment in time, Hannah was in what Reggie considered to be the 'danger zone'. She was simultaneously too drunk and not drunk enough. Too drunk in that her decision-making was off, as was her ability to walk in a particularly straight line. Not drunk enough in that she was still able to make decisions and walk in an approximate direction well enough to act on those decisions. She was also cursed with the kind of terrifying certainty found only in drunks, religious zealots and people who used the word 'sheeple' on social media.

They had been the last to leave the Roxy and, despite Reggie's less than subtle hints, Hannah had not wanted to go home. She had an idea. Reggie didn't understand it, but he felt compelled to follow her, because that's what friends were for. Also, for purely selfish reasons, Hannah was also his best chance at a bed for the night. A spare bed, that is. The phone call from Ox had been both brief and infuriatingly short on detail, but from what Reggie could gather, the Fenton brothers were staking out their flat.

As it happened, Reggie had dealt with this particular grue-some twosome before, but this time around he wouldn't have the element of surprise on his side. Also, back when he reinvented himself, Reggie had sworn off ever committing an act of violence again. Self-defence was self-defence, but it was better to avoid it altogether than have to justify it to himself or to the police after the fact. As a result, he now found himself following in the wake of a determined drunken woman while also trying to prevent her from falling into a canal.

The pair finally managed to reach the footbridge they'd stood on earlier that day, which already felt like a long time ago.

'For the record,' said Reggie for the umpteenth time, in the forlorn hope that it might hit home on this occasion, 'I think this is a terrible idea.'

'Stop repeating yourself, Reginald,' said Hannah. 'It's a sign of an enfeebled mind. That's what my grandma used to say, and she was a badass. I need to be more like my grandma. I really miss her.'

Reggie bit his tongue. Hannah had already recapped her bad day six times for Reggie, and once for a homeless man who'd just been looking for change. Prior to that, she'd spent quite a lot of the evening at their table in the Roxy discussing her almost ex-husband in less than glowing terms.

'When did your grandmother die?' asked Reggie.

'Oh,' said Hannah, 'ages ago now.' She grabbed the towrope and fished the bell out of the water. She slapped Reggie on the shoulder drunkenly. 'No, wait. She's still alive. Why did I . . . That was weird.'

'It might be explained by the fact that you are very, very drunk.'

'Nope. I've been drinking, but my mind is clear.' She went to tap her temple to emphasize her point but did so with the hand holding the bell, and simply managed to wallop herself with it. 'Ouch!'

'Oh dear,' said Reggie – at the whole situation, really.

'Right,' said Hannah, demonstrating a level of imperviousness to pain normally associated with religious zealots, drunks or someone who had got the chance to punch the kind of person who used the word 'sheeple' on social media. 'Here goes nothing.'

She gripped the bell in both hands and rang it.

'Bugger off,' came the voice of Cogs from inside the houseboat moored in the middle of the water.

'No,' shouted Hannah, ringing the bell harder.

A light came on inside the boat. 'Give it up. Come back in the morning – or never. Either of those is a better time.'

'I. Have. A. Question.' Hannah rang the bell as hard as she

could, which was doing nothing for the headache Reggie could feel building. Thankfully, the ringing stopped, but only because the tongue of the bell, deciding enough was enough, detached itself and fell into the water with a splash.

'Oops,' said Hannah.

'Oh dear,' said Reggie, who was in danger of developing a catchphrase.

Cogs appeared on the deck, naked bar a bowler hat he was holding to protect his modesty. 'What in the . . . Oh, it's you.'

'Yes, it is,' said Hannah, defiant.

'Did you just break my bell?'

'It broke,' conceded Hannah, 'but I do not believe I can be held responsible.'

'I disagree.'

Zeke, the dog that was not a dog, leaned his front paws on the side of the boat to look over. 'I told you to bring that bell in at night.'

'And I,' said Cogs, 'told you to remind me to do it.'

'I'm a dog. Got no concept of time.'

'Really?' asked Cogs. 'I missed your dinner by five minutes yesterday and you shat in my slipper.'

The dog that wasn't a dog laughed. 'Lucky guess.'

'Excuse me,' said Hannah, 'but I have a question.'

'We're closed,' said Cogs.

Hannah stamped her foot. 'It's important.'

'Not to me.'

'Right,' said Hannah, attempting to climb the iron railing at the side of the bridge. 'I'm swimming over.'

Reggie grabbed her arm and attempted to restrain her as she flailed about. He looked at Cogs with pleading eyes. 'Perhaps it'd just be easier if you answered the lady's question.'

'Nope. And besides, she's not given an offering. Rules is rules.'

'I'll offer you something in a minute.'

'Offer a song,' shouted Zeke.

Cogs threw down the bowler hat in frustration. 'Why do you keep telling people that?'

'Because you forgot my dinner.'

'What?' shouted Reggie.

'She can sing a song,' shouted Zeke back. 'As an offering. He's a minstrel, you see. Has to accept it as payment.'

Cogs glared at Zeke, appalled at this betrayal. 'You know what your problem is?'

'Do you mean other than the view?'

'What? Oh.' Cogs picked up the bowler hat and re-covered himself.

Hannah stopped struggling. 'OK, I'm gonna sing the song. I'll sing the song.'

Reggie released her, but stood ready to pounce if she looked as if she were going to attempt to swim across again.

'Wonderful,' said Zeke. 'What song will you be performing?'

'"I Will Survive",' said Hannah.

'Classic,' said Zeke. 'I'll count you in.'

The next three minutes were memorable. At least they were in the sense that Reggie doubted he would ever be able to hear that song again without getting flashbacks.

Finally, Hannah finished and threw out her arms in a Celine Dion-like flourish that nothing about her performance warranted.

Cogs and Zeke looked at one another.

'You know how I can only speak the truth?' asked Cogs.

'Yes,' said Hannah.

'That was the worst performance I have ever heard.'

'Oh.' She looked crestfallen.

'I liked it,' said Zeke.

'Really?'

'Ignore him,' responded Cogs. 'He likes to annoy me by showing off how he can lie.'

'Oh.'

'Right,' said Cogs. 'Let's get this over with. What's the question?'

'OK.' Hannah glanced nervously in Reggie's direction. 'Say someone has a . . . y'know . . .' She dangled one of her arms over her head.

'A what?' said Cogs.

'One of these.' She repeated the mime.

'I love this game,' said Zeke. 'Elvis hairdo? Pointy hat? Penis? Is it penis? I think it's penis.'

'No,' said Hannah, taking her hand down. 'It's not a penis.'

'Looked like a penis.'

'What are you on about?' asked Cogs, thoroughly bewildered.

'I don't want to say it,' said Hannah.

'Can you sing it?' asked Zeke.

'No,' said Reggie quickly, which earned him a glare from Hannah. 'Look, I'm tired. Let's just go home.'

'To my home,' said Hannah.

'Yes.'

'I think I know what your question is,' said Cogs. He waved a finger between Hannah and Reggie. 'I don't see this working out.'

'No!' said Hannah. 'We're just good friends.'

'And to be honest,' said Reggie, 'if this goes on much longer, we may not even be that.'

'OK. Fine,' said Hannah. 'Is there any way to get an eyeball out of somebody's head?'

'Wow,' said Zeke. 'This has taken an unexpected turn.'

'No. I don't mean like that. This . . . My . . . A friend of mine . . . He's got an eyeball that pops out of the top of his head.'

'OK,' said Reggie, trying to guide Hannah away. 'You really need a pint of water and a bed.'

'Like, on a stalk?' asked Cogs.

'Yes!' Hannah clapped her hands together.

Reggie looked back in Cogs's direction. 'You're kidding?'

Cogs shrugged. 'It's a thing.'

'I'm a talking dog – sort of,' said the sort-of talking dog.

'Good point,' said Reggie. He sat down on the ground. 'I might have reached maximum weird.'

'Anyway,' said Cogs. 'This third eyeball – how long has the person had it?'

'I don't know,' said Hannah. 'Oh, but he doesn't know he has it.'

'Ahhhh,' said Cogs. 'It's one of them whatchamacallits?'

'A parapsyche,' stated the lifeform that, of those present, was closest to being a dog.

'A parasite?' asked Hannah.

'No. A para-psyche,' said Zeke.

'Yeah,' agreed his non-owner. 'It attaches to the brain, only the brain don't know it's there. The person in control of it can see what they see, all of that. That's some powerful magic to get one of them into somebody.'

'That's the one,' said Zeke. 'And if the host finds out it's there, the parapsyche kills it as, like, a defence mechanism.'

'Right,' said Hannah. 'Can I get it out of him?'

'Absolutely,' said Cogs.

'Great.'

'Do you want the host to be alive afterwards?'

'Yes!' shouted Hannah, exasperated. 'Of course.'

'Ah, right,' said Cogs. 'In that case, no. I mean . . .' He looked at Zeke.

'The person who put it in there could probably take it out,' offered Zeke.

'Yeah,' agreed Cogs. 'Probably. Other than that, though . . .'

'You'd need somebody with serious skills.'

'And even then . . .'

'Yeah,' said Zeke. 'Tough gig.'

'Yep.'

Hannah leaned against the bridge. 'Really?'

'Really,' said Zeke.

She kicked the bridge, then yelped in pain. 'Damn it, I thought you were supposed to be helpful?'

'For the last time,' said Cogs, 'how hard is it for people to understand this? I'm not helpful, I don't see the future and I can't tell you what to do. All I do is tell the bloody truth!' With that, he tossed the bowler hat up in the air and caught it on his head. 'Good evening to you, *madame*. And you owe me a new bell!'

He and Zeke disappeared below deck.

Reggie got to his feet and guided Hannah down off the bridge. They walked in silence for a few minutes, heading towards Hannah's flat, each of them lost in thought. Around them, young people high on life, booze and who knew what else spilled out of pubs or taxis, having had pre-drinks at home. They passed Deansgate Locks, where queues formed on the bridges that extended over the canal from the road, in front of the various neon-lit nightclubs pumping decibels into the night. Second from the end, the wide grin of the Comedy Store stood out, disgorging at regular intervals couples who passed their younger selves queuing up on the other side of the bridge.

Eventually, Reggie broke the silence. 'Can I just ask . . .'

'What?'

'It's not me who has that eyeball thing in my head, is it?'

'No.'

'Right. Would you tell me if it was?'

'No. If you had it, me telling you would kill you.'

'Right,' said Reggie.

'But you don't.'

'Thanks. That's really reassuring.'

CHAPTER 22

Banecroft jerked up his head and looked around, confused. After he rubbed his eyes and realized what the noise was, he slapped his beeping alarm clock into silence before picking up a half-finished glass of whiskey and knocking it back. It didn't get rid of the sour taste in his mouth so much as refresh it.

He stood up and stretched out his back. Hope was a dangerous thing, and nobody knew that more than he did. He tried to keep any from infecting his mind as he headed for the office door. More often than not, there would be nothing. There'd been a brief appearance last week, and three the week before that. There didn't seem to be a pattern to it, other than when the paper was working on a particularly interesting story. That was why, in spite of his best efforts, hope was sneaking into Banecroft's mind. The day he'd had could be described in many ways, 'interesting' being one of the mildest adjectives.

He gently opened the door and looked out into the corridor. There, in the soft moonlight falling through the stained-glass windows, was the ghost of Simon Brush, seated at the same desk as always. He was looking through the reading materials that

Banecroft had left out for him. Banecroft tried not to think of them as bait, but that's what they were.

Banecroft moved slowly towards Simon's form. Over the past few months, he had been quietly reading all he could about ghosts. There were numerous theories: they were living memories; spirits of the dead that couldn't move on until they had completed some task; echoes of a life that hadn't faded away. The more he read, the less he understood. There were some things he did know, though. Whenever Simon appeared, he was always sitting at that desk, despite never having had one in *The Stranger Times* offices when he was alive. Banecroft knew it was some indication of Simon's unfulfilled dreams and potential, but he was electing to ignore it. He was blocking it from his mind, because what he saw in Simon, more than anything, was an opportunity. A last hope.

'Hello, Mr Banecroft.'

'Hello, Simon. How are you?'

Banecroft leaned on the next desk over from where Simon sat, keen to give him room. Once before, in his eagerness to try to make his point, he'd come too close and Simon had just disappeared.

'What are you reading?'

'This report on the ghost in Manchester Town Hall. It's quite interesting.'

'Yes,' said Banecroft, 'it is. Friend of yours?'

He winced. The weak attempt at a joke sounded forced. Simon ignored it and turned the page.

It had been odd, the first few times – talking to someone you could see through. Having said that, Banecroft had noticed that on some nights Simon seemed more substantial than on others. Tonight, he was barely see-through at all.

'So,' said Banecroft, 'we had something very interesting come in today.'

'Did you?'

'Yes. Vampires – in a manner of speaking.'

'They don't exist.'

Banecroft was slightly taken aback. 'What makes you say that?'

Simon didn't reply. This happened a lot. It was as if he faded in and out of the conversation.

Banecroft left a gap then continued, 'A man died last night – up on the Princess Parkway. Jumped in front of a truck. Had the teeth. Witnesses said he ran very fast too. Inhumanly fast.'

Simon turned another page.

'What's really interesting is that Dr Carter – you know, the woman who seems to represent the Founders – came in to ask us to look into it. That . . . is very peculiar, isn't it?'

Simon nodded. 'It is. Have you found out much about them?'

'Not yet. But I had a meeting today with a man called John Mór. He's one of the leaders of the Folk. That was very interesting too.'

'Was it?'

'Yes,' said Banecroft, licking his lips. 'And I'll tell you all about it. But first, did you get a chance to ask about my wife?'

Simon turned the page again. 'This report about the UFO sighting in Devon has a spelling mistake in it.'

'Does it?' Banecroft clutched his hands together, trying to

keep his cool. When he'd lost it before, Simon hadn't appeared for nearly two weeks. Banecroft had been worried he was gone for good. This could be his last chance.

Simon turned the page again. 'I did ask.'

'What did they say?'

'It didn't make much sense.'

'What didn't?'

Simon closed the newspaper and studied the back page. 'Mrs Wilkes is the newspaper's longest-running advertiser, isn't she? What is an "implement of romance"?'

'I'll explain it some other time.' In spite of the promise he'd made to himself, Banecroft moved forward a couple of steps and bent down to position himself in Simon's eyeline.

'Simon, what didn't make sense? Was it something about my wife? Charlotte? Was it something about her?'

Simon started to fade away. Banecroft stepped back quickly. 'No, sorry. I'm sorry, Simon. Stay . . . Don't go . . . I've not told you about the shower yet. Stay, please . . . I . . .'

Banecroft trailed off. He was pleading with an empty chair.

CHAPTER 23

Georgina Grant punched her pillow as if her lack of sleep were all its fault. She found herself like this every time she was in the midst of an investigation. Her bloody mind – just because it was the middle of the night and she didn't have access to the data required to find answers didn't mean her brain wouldn't pester her with questions.

She was a forensic accountant, and a good one. That was why she was in Manchester and not at home in Bristol punching her own pillow. She was in town to do a thorough audit of the accounts of Jester Mirth Ltd, a company that owned the kind of bars whose business relied on Christmas dos, stag nights and any other kind of event where the important thing was to get smashed as quickly as possible. Georgina was a professional, which was why she was not allowing the fact that three of the worst nights of her life had all been in establishments owned by Jester Mirth Ltd to impinge on her impartiality in any way, shape or form.

Her mind, being her mind, had ranked those three nightmare nights in reverse order of awfulness. Third – old company's Christmas do, Carol from Accounts threw up, both on and down

Georgina's dress. Second – Riona's hen do, bride and maid of honour had a fist fight, Georgina got headbutted while trying to break it up. First – Uncle Terry's fiftieth, Mum revealed she and Terry had been having an affair for fifteen years. That one could've been worse, only by that point, everyone already knew. It was more embarrassing to see her mother's disappointment at not eliciting the scene she'd hoped for.

Georgina's company had been called in by a couple of shareholders who'd become suspicious about Jester Mirth's accounts. The CEO, a slimy toad of a man called Marios, had welcomed her with open arms and offered to be helpful in any way he could. Georgina found him particularly grating. You met his kind of man a lot in this job. Convinced he was smarter than the diminutive bookish girl with glasses; that he was too smart to get caught by her and, even if he was proved wrong in that belief, confident he could 'charm' his way out of it. She was going to conduct a thorough investigation and then nail the condescending asshat to the wall by the scrotum, metaphorically speaking.

She kicked off the duvet and rolled over again. The other problem was the apartment she'd been put up in. It was a short let and, actually, it had been meant as a perk. Georgina was coming off a big case involving a certain car-leasing firm in which her above-and-beyond investigative work had prevented a multi-million-pound fraud. Having missed out on a promotion last year, her boss all but admitted that he'd been wrong and there were now rumblings of a greatly improved package on the cards. Rival companies interested in her services were also putting out feelers. In the forensic accounting world, Georgina was a rock star. In acknowledgement of this, the company had put her in an apartment on the fourteenth floor of Skyline Central, where there was also a gym and a swimming pool on the top floor. She'd not used either yet but she'd nipped up quickly just before they closed one evening last week, and they looked lovely.

The problem with the apartment was that while it did indeed look lovely – especially the thick glass exterior wall that was the defining feature of the main room – unfortunately, nobody had considered how that would work if Manchester actually experienced a heatwave. For the duration of her stay, every time she returned to the apartment at the end of the day, it was like stepping into an oven. Invariably, she ended up opening the door to the balcony and sitting there naked to eat her microwave meal. As daring as it felt, there was zero chance of anyone seeing her, given the fact she was fourteen storeys up and the absence of overlooking buildings.

Try as she might, Georgina hadn't been able to cool down the place before going to bed that evening. She'd attempted to order a fan but everywhere had sold out. Instead, she'd have to lie there, sweating the night away while listening to noise from the street below. It was amazing how, despite being so high up, the sound still travelled. She'd been able to hear snatches of conversation as people passed, couples argued and, in one memorable exchange, a girl described to her shrieking friend a regrettable sexual experiment with a feather duster and a boyfriend with allergies.

She stared up at the ceiling. She couldn't look at her phone because if she looked at her phone then she'd know what time it was, and then she'd start obsessing about how little time was left before she had to get up. Marios had taken to buying her a muffin and leaving it on her desk, which she hated, not only because it was highly inappropriate but also because she was on a diet and she bloody loved muffins.

She closed her eyes and tried to steady her breathing. She'd read every book available on the subject of insomnia, and every last one recommended focusing on taking slow and steady breaths. She tried to do that while counting backwards from three hundred, which had also been recommended by some author or another.

In.

Out.

In.

Out.

She could feel herself starting to relax a little as the slow, deep breaths moved through her.

Something sounded odd, though. As if her breathing wasn't quite right.

A jolt of panic passed through her. Her breathing sounded wrong because it wasn't just her who was breathing. There was someone else in the room.

The sensible part of her mind tried to dismiss the idea. She was fourteen storeys up, the door to the apartment was locked and the building had a 24-hour concierge. He was an older gentleman with a reassuringly friendly face, who was reading a Brandon Sanderson novel. He wouldn't let anything happen to her.

Despite the application of logic, the other breaths continued.

OK. She was just freaking herself out here, that was all. Lack of sleep can do funny things to the mind.

Georgina slowly turned her head to the left, in the direction of the built-in wardrobe and its ludicrous mirrored doors. Designed by the kind of person who apparently wanted to be able to see themselves up close and personal first thing in the morning. Georgina hated the mirrors but was glad of them at this moment. She carefully opened her left eye. The moonlight coming through the window was enough to show the whole room was empty, save for the reflection of one paranoid woman who really needed to get to sleep.

She let out a deep sigh as her whole body relaxed. That was it – she was taking a holiday and, possibly, going back on those pills. At this rate she'd not sleep herself into an early grave.

She sat up to reposition herself in the bed for the thousandth time and froze. At the end of her bed stood an impossible man in, of all things, a green anorak.

As her mouth dropped open in terror, she glanced back at the lying bastard of a mirror that still showed her alone in the room.

She screamed.

CHAPTER 24

Hannah felt utterly wretched. It was hard to nail down the exact reason behind this, simply because there were so many pegs on which to hang that particular hat. First, her 'new me' healthy-living initiative had lasted all the way until the end of day one, when she'd got smashed. True, she'd cut back on the calories – by not eating and by throwing up all the wine she'd consumed – but it was still a terrible start. She fully deserved the horrendous headache she'd acquired. The one that made her want to break into tears every time she inhaled.

Then, memories started to flood back. She'd spent quite a lot of time in a booth in the Roxy talking about her soon-to-be ex-husband in less than glowing terms. Then, she'd woken up Cogs in the middle of the night to drunkenly ask about DI Sturgess's 'issue'. Previously, she and Banecroft had agreed that the fact the detective inspector had a parasitic eyeball living inside his head, spying on him from within, should be their little secret – given how they'd been told that if Sturgess found out, that news would literally kill him.

Last night had been the first time Hannah had met Sturgess since she had found out about it – a revelation in a night full of them, as she, Sturgess and Banecroft had been rescuing Stella from the psychopath that had kidnapped her. It was hard to look him in the eyes now, knowing that thing was lurking behind them, the creepy little voyeur. It had clearly been on her mind and prompted her ill-judged drunken hunt for answers. Mostly, her exchange with Cogs had confirmed what she'd been told previously by the odious Dr Carter.

She found some assurance in the fact that she hadn't ever mentioned Sturgess's name last night. She knew she'd kept quiet on that front, at least, because when she'd woken up in the morning, she'd had to reveal to Reggie the identity of the unfortunate soul. Apparently, he'd been awake for half the night, convinced it was he himself who was harbouring the brain-dwelling parasite.

Hannah hugged the loo for a bit, stood in the shower for a while longer and then did her best to make herself presentable. She and Reggie walked into the office together in near silence. Not only was Hannah feeling horrendously embarrassed but she was also incapable of walking and talking at the same time.

The relief when she reached her desk had been something else. She was OK now, OK as long as . . .

The door to Banecroft's office slammed open and the man himself stomped through, his blunderbuss resting on his shoulder. 'Right, time for a meeting.'

Hannah closed her eyes. He was like an inverse fairy godmother – every time you didn't want Banecroft, he magically appeared.

'OK,' he continued, 'I'm a very busy man, so let's keep this brief. Every time I point the gun at you, you speak.'

'That doesn't sound—' started Hannah.

'Too late.' Banecroft whirled round and pointed the blunderbuss at Reggie, who gave an involuntary yelp. 'Well?'

'I . . . went to the Roxy cinema last night, where they have an ongoing festival of sorts featuring vampire films. We spoke to the manager, who I know from that feature we did last year on their weeping girl ghost. She gave us the name of one particular individual who takes the whole vampire thing very seriously, and we're chasing him up.'

'Right.' Banecroft spun round to point the gun at Stella. 'You?'

'What, me? I'm stuck here twenty-four-seven, I got nothing to report.'

'I told you to go through our archives and dig up anything and everything we've ever reported about vampires in this city.'

'No, you didn't.'

'Didn't I? Right, well I'm telling you now. Get cracking, you're already a day late. Next.'

Hannah winced as Banecroft twirled in her direction and set her in his metaphorical and literal sights. 'How'd it go with lover boy?'

Hannah put her hand to her brow. 'Could you just tone it down for once? I'm not in the mood.'

Banecroft raised the gun and grinned at her. 'Are you hungover?'

'A little.'

Banecroft looked genuinely appalled. 'This is entirely unacceptable. We have very strict rules about working here while under the influence of alcohol.'

'Actually, we have two rules,' said Hannah. 'The one you're about to make up, and the one that says none of it applies to you.'

'Alcohol makes you so cynical.'

'I know, I'm turning into you. The realization of that is the best intervention imaginable. I'll never drink again.'

'And?'

'What?'

'Lover boy?'

'I'm assuming you mean DI Sturgess. The big news is this Phillip Butler guy had blood in his stomach.'

'I'd imagine trying to tango with a heavy goods vehicle will do that to you.'

'Someone else's blood.' Hannah regretted saying the words out loud. She hadn't thought about that horrible detail so far this morning, and now she had, she could feel bile starting to rise in her throat. She eyed the wastepaper bin beside her desk. Please God, don't let her throw up in a meeting – she'd never hear the end of it.

'Right,' said Banecroft. 'Well, that does rather put a different perspective on things. Where did it come from?'

'They don't know.'

'They don't know?' repeated Banecroft, at an unnecessary volume.

'I'd imagine they're investigating it.'

'I wouldn't bank on it. Anyway, next moves?'

'For the police?'

'No,' said Banecroft. 'You! You!'

Hannah couldn't come up with anything.

'Victor,' interjected Reggie.

'Who asked you?' said Banecroft.

'You threw it out like a general question.'

'I made it very clear that only the person at whom I am point-ing the gun may speak. Simon says, you're out.' He turned back to Hannah. 'So, what are you doing here, then?'

'I came in to check the Loon Line. See if there's anything inter-esting.' Hannah was very pleased with the lie, first because it fended off Banecroft and second because it was actually a good idea. She picked up the phone on her desk. 'So, unless there's anything else?'

'There is, actually. I met with John Mór yesterday. The gentle-man our new source pointed us in the direction of. One of the senior figures in the Folk community. He assured me he knows nothing about any pointed-toothed blood-suckers doing the rounds but he'll let us know if that changes.'

'Right,' said Hannah, in the absence of anything else to say.

'Good meeting,' said Banecroft. 'Go team, et cetera.' He raised his voice. 'Grace! Tea!'

'Make your own!' came the shouted response from reception.

Banecroft pulled a face. 'What's up with you?'

'Seriously?'

Banecroft nodded. 'Ah, yes. I remember now. Fine, but you've just lost five points towards being employee of the month.'

'We have no such award,' hollered Grace.

'Ha!' barked Banecroft. 'We do, actually. It's just none of you has ever achieved a positive score so I haven't given it out.'

'Is there any chance,' said Hannah, rubbing her scalp, which was inexplicably hurting too, 'that the two of you could have this conversation while you're both in the same room?'

'WHY?' bellowed Banecroft. 'IS THE NOISE BOTHERING YOU?'

With that, he marched back into his office and slammed the door shut behind him.

Hannah shook her head. 'How has he got this far in life without anyone stabbing him?'

'I heard that,' roared Banecroft from the other room. 'Shows what you know. I've been stabbed twice!'

Hannah looked at Reggie and held up her hand to signal five minutes. He nodded and then she crawled under her desk.

CHAPTER 25

For the second time in twelve hours, DI Tom Sturgess found himself sitting at a table in a restaurant and waiting for a woman to turn up while he watched the food in front of him go cold. The breakfast burrito smelled delicious. His mouth had been salivating, ready to devour it before his 'guest' turned up, when he'd received the call from Dr Charlie Mason, pathologist and barbecue enthusiast.

Mason had explained that the blood in Phillip Butler's stomach had been one hundred per cent confirmed as belonging to Andre Alashev, the night watchman whose body they'd found the day before. The findings didn't come as a shock to Sturgess, but still, the reality of the news was enough to mean his burrito went untouched.

The restaurant was made up of a serving counter and half a dozen long wooden tables with benches on either side of them. The walls were festooned with pictures of colourful masked wrestlers glowering at each other. Sturgess hypothesized that the benches – the most uncomfortable thing to sit on that was supposedly designed for the purpose – had been a deliberate choice. In the entire establishment, he was the only patron who, at that moment, didn't have a laptop out and headphones in.

The 'hot-desking, locationally fluid remote-working' economy had descended on the place like a plague of apathetic locusts. As the exasperated woman behind the counter had taken his order, she'd made pointed remarks for the benefit of everyone in ear-shot about the requirement for customers to actually purchase food. Reluctantly, two patrons had formed a queue behind him. Sturgess guessed they were a web designer and, judging by the phone call he'd just overheard, either an HR consultant or an office gossip without an office.

For the ten minutes he'd been sitting there uncomfortably, waiting for his food, Sturgess had occupied himself trying to determine what everyone in the room did for a living while they were sending a burrito restaurant out of business. He was stumped by the guy in the corner who was hogging the power point while charging his laptop, phone, mobile fan, Kindle and headphones, and sipping on the bottle of water he'd reluctantly bought for himself, but given his shamelessness, politics would be a distinct possibility in his future.

The guy in the green shirt, who'd informed Sturgess earlier that you couldn't hold seats for other people, turned and shot him a dirty look. Apparently, it was an unwritten rule. Sturgess had politely suggested the guy got somebody to write it down and then come back to him. The guy had huffed off to one of the window seats where he'd sat in the sun's glare. Sturgess had watched him use the time since their chat to pick his nose with nowhere near enough subtlety while updating his Fuzzy Britches dating profile. He knew it was that particular app because he'd taken a look at the website last night and now recognized the distinctive purple-and-green colour scheme on the guy's screen. He'd never managed to get as much information out of a suspect as users were seemingly happy to give up on creating an account.

First thing that morning he had updated CI Clayborne about his suspicions concerning Messers Butler and Alashev. It was a bit of a mixed bag for the chief inspector, this one. On one hand, the case counted as a solved murder, which was important when it came to the stats, given the recent press exposure on that front. On the other hand, Clayborne would rather chew her own arm off than have to answer questions about this particular murder at that public-forum thing the mayor had recently decided was a good idea.

The confirmation of Butler's attack on Alashev didn't add much weight to Sturgess's so far unanswered request for additional resources either. A murder-suicide was a horrible thing, but in policing terms, it was a neatly wrapped-up horrible thing. Policing might be about answering questions, but ultimately, the 'why' wasn't something to which they were going to commit a huge amount of resources, when the 'who' had been conclusively nailed down. Bigger fish to fry and all that. Manchester's latest gangland war had made the national news last night, and to say the Greater Manchester Police hadn't come out of it smelling of roses was an understatement.

Clayborne had sounded stressed and distracted during the call. All of Sturgess's reports were delivered over the phone now, given the previously stated desire of the GMP for him to follow the principle of the paperless office to the extreme. He got the impression that they'd rather not know what he was up to at all, but were too worried about it coming back to bite them in the arse not to pay attention begrudgingly.

Siobhan Regan entered the restaurant and looked around nervously. She spotted him and went to wave, before she remembered herself. Instead, she hurried towards him. Sturgess was all too familiar with her behaviour – that of an ordinary person doing something they shouldn't and trying to 'act casual', only they did so in such a way that attracted far more attention than they'd otherwise get.

Sturgess indicated the space on the bench opposite he'd been holding for her. It was rather too far away for a private conversation, but it was better than having her sit beside him, which would have been uncomfortably close.

'Thanks for coming,' he said.

Siobhan sat down opposite him and spoke in a hushed voice. 'I can't stay long.'

Yesterday, while inspecting Phillip Butler's desk at Fuzzy Britches (an entirely pointless exercise in and of itself, as he had known it would be), Sturgess had managed to slip Siobhan Regan his card with a note written on the back asking her to ring him. He was, of course, well within his rights just to interview her, but he wanted to talk to her out of sight of her employers, when she might be more forthcoming. Understandably, she'd been apprehensive but had agreed to meet him this morning while she was in town for a dental appointment.

'So, is it just a check-up?'

Siobhan looked confused. 'What?'

'The dentist.'

'Oh right,' she said. 'Afraid not. I've got a pain in the back there.' She opened her mouth and pointed inside with her little finger. 'I've been avoiding googling it for fear of what it might be – like, a root canal or something. I don't even know what one of those is, but I've heard about them on TV shows and they seem to be really bad. Are they really bad? Don't answer that. Sorry, I'm rambling.'

'No problem.' Sturgess smiled. 'Hope it isn't too serious.'

'Knowing my luck . . . Well, we'll see.'

'Can I get you anything to eat?'

'No,' she said. 'I can't be going in with burrito breath. And besides, I'm in a hurry.'

'Of course.' Sturgess decided to move on from attempting to relax the witness. 'Speaking of dentists, did Phillip ever mention getting any cosmetic dental work done? Anything like that?'

Siobhan shrugged. 'I don't recall. He might have got his teeth whitened or something. He was definitely the type for that.'

'What makes you say that?'

'Oh, nothing. Only . . . I'd be pretty sure he went on a sunbed. Y'know. He paid a lot of attention to his appearance.'

'You didn't like him, did you?'

Siobhan sat back, looking surprised. 'I wouldn't say that. He was all right. I was his boss, y'know – I'm sure he'd say worse about me.' She laughed nervously. 'We are . . . were . . . are . . . no, were . . . Sorry, we were very different people. I mean . . . I wouldn't speak ill of the dead.'

Sturgess nodded. 'I wouldn't normally ask you to, only that rule doesn't really apply when you're talking to the guy whose job it is to find out how Phillip ended up being dead.'

Siobhan pulled a face. 'I suppose. I mean, he was an OK fella. We were just very different people, y'know?'

'So you said. How so?'

'He was fine in work but, well . . . When we went out – the team, I mean . . . As my old ma would say, he was like a dog in heat.'

'Bit of a ladies' man?'

'Thought he was.' She drummed her fingers on the table nervously. 'He was at my birthday a couple of years ago – I invited everybody. Thirtieth. Upstairs at the Rain Bar, just around the corner. Phil had a one-night stand with a friend of mine. Then he ghosted her.'

'Right.'

'I mean, I guess that kind of thing happens all the time, but . . . Trish is a bit sensitive and he was, frankly, a prick. That's the way these things go, though, I suppose.'

'Was Trish upset?' Sturgess caught Siobhan's horrified expression and moved quickly to head her off at the pass. 'Relax. I didn't mean . . . I'm not looking for any suspects in relation to his death.'

'I'm glad to hear it. Trish doesn't need any hassle in her life.'

'So, Phil wasn't a nice guy?'

'Look,' said Siobhan, 'that was one incident. Not really fair to judge the fella on that alone, is it? We all do stupid things when we're drunk. I bumped into him while I was out another night – by accident. He looked embarrassed, said he was going to his book group meeting. I remember thinking I'd have never picked him out as a reader. I guess . . . I'm just saying, there are lots of sides to all of us, aren't there? Hard to really know anyone. I mean, I'd have never thought in a million years that he might be' – she lowered her voice to a whisper – 'suicidal. I've been thinking about it constantly. Honestly, I can't piece it together. I shouldn't say this, but if you asked me to rank the whole team in order of suicidal tendencies, he'd have been last.' She looked down. 'Sorry, I know that's a terrible thing to say, but it's the kind of thing your mind goes to at four in the morning when you can't sleep.'

'I completely understand. I was wondering – could you give me an idea of what he was working on?'

She looked around nervously. 'I shouldn't even be talking to you. They'd kill me if they found out.'

'Relax,' said Sturgess. 'We're just two people chatting, nobody will find out. And even if they did, which they won't, nobody can say anything to you about helping a police officer with his enquiries about the tragic death of a colleague, can they? Trust me, you're fine.'

Siobhan looked slightly mollified by this. Sturgess watched her debating her options internally before nodding, her decision made.

'I mean . . . Look, he wasn't doing anything exciting – it was just work on a part of the algorithm we're rolling out for locations. Restaurants – that kind of thing. Users can leave ratings and, if they like, venues can pay us to show people their rating. It's basically a bit of stealth advertising. It's how most platforms make their money. Not something the company would want highlighted but not illegal or dodgy.'

'And that's it?'

'Yes,' said Siobhan.

'And that's all he did?'

'Recently, yes. I mean, there's the pick-up teams, too – obviously.'

Whatever the pick-up teams were wasn't obvious to Sturgess at all. 'The what?'

'It's a company thing. A form of brainstorming. At random, every now and then, people get selected from all over the company to go to a meeting where they talk about a certain idea, or problem, or whatever. It's based on some research – wisdom of crowds, or something like that. Honestly, as a line manager, it's more of a pain in the arse than anything. Your team members just disappearing like that – sometimes for five minutes, sometimes for a week.'

'And Phillip took part in these?'

'Everybody does,' said Siobhan. 'But yeah, I remember he was on more than his fair share.'

'And what were they about?'

Siobhan shrugged. 'Anything. Nothing. I don't know. I was in one last week about pictures of cats.'

'Really?'

'Yeah. For a whole day we discussed how best to present pictures of cats.'

'Why?' asked Sturgess, which earned him a quizzical look from Siobhan.

'You don't use social media much, do you?'

'No.'

'You can tell.'

'Could you find out what groups he was in?'

'No,' said Siobhan, 'I could not. I'm sure somebody some-where is tracking that, but I don't have access to that kind of data.'

'Could this be why the company wants his phone back so badly?'

Siobhan puffed out her cheeks in exasperation. 'Listen – you need to understand, tech companies are incredibly paranoid. It's the nature of the beast. They're worth billions, and they don't make anything tangible, like cars or hoovers or' – she looked down at the table for inspiration – 'burritos. All they have is data and code, so yeah, they get crazy paranoid. Fuzzy Britches is a nice place to work, and they might be a little odd from time to time, but they treat people well. Do you know how many tech companies are run by a woman?'

'No,' said Sturgess.

'Neither do I, but "not nearly enough" is a solid answer.' She looked at her watch. 'I'm sorry that Phil is dead, and good luck figuring out whatever the hell you're trying to figure out, but if you'll excuse me, I need to get going.'

Before Sturgess could say anything, Siobhan was up and out into the bright sunlight of the morning, hurrying across the street.

Sturgess grabbed his tray and got up to leave. He stepped the wrong way, allowing enough time for a short guy with a ludicrously long beard and a tall woman with dangly earrings to grab his now-vacant table ahead of the green-shirted nose-picker.

As he emptied his tray into the bin, he basked momentarily in the warm glow of the morning sun and a complete stranger's hatred.

CHAPTER 26

Hannah and Reggie were sitting in Banecroft's Jag, which they had borrowed only after its owner had administered an impromptu rules-of-the-road quiz. Hannah hadn't passed, as such, but only because it had quickly become obvious that Banecroft himself had no idea of the rules of the road.

It was unpleasantly warm as the noonday sun beat down outside. The Jag was a 'classic', which meant it looked good but had none of the fixtures and fittings, such as air-con, that actually made a car comfortable. Ronnie, the manager at the Roxy, had given Hannah and Reggie an address for Victor, the 'vampire' who frequented her establishment, and the pair were currently parked up opposite it.

After sitting there for an hour, it had become clear that Reggie was an inveterate and highly annoying fidgeter, and Hannah was trying hard not to lose her temper. Right now, despite her having mentioned it a couple of times already, he was finger-tapping a seemingly never-ending drum solo on his knees. Loudly. She was still feeling the effects of her hangover, which had been only slightly assuaged by the coffee and bagels they'd stopped to get on their way over here, and she was trying not to take out her bad mood on the person who'd been kind enough to make sure she'd got home safely after making a bit of a spectacle of herself.

The idea was to watch the place, and wait to follow Victor when he emerged. Assuming he was even in there. And that this was definitely the right place.

'Are we sure this is the right place?' asked Hannah.

'It's the address Veronica gave us, so one would presume so. She hasn't got any reason to lie.'

'Right.'

'I still think we're parked too close.'

'It's on a bend in the road,' said Hannah, repeating the earlier 'discussion' they'd had on this topic. 'If we move any further back, we won't be able to see it.'

'This Victor chap wears leather trousers, a long black coat, a wide-brimmed hat and the kind of frilly black shirts you won't see anywhere else – unless The Cult are back on tour. We're unlikely to miss him. And this car sticks out like a sore thumb. While an old green Jag gains points for style, it isn't exactly inconspicuous, is it?'

'All right, but think about it this way – nobody would use such a vehicle to stake out a place, would they? So, in a weird way, we're hiding in plain sight.'

'That feels like one of those sentences that sounds like logic but really isn't. Also, don't use the word "stake" around Victor. I imagine it'd upset him.'

Hannah laughed. 'Good point.' She looked back across the road at the house, which was a disappointingly ordinary semi-detached house in the suburbs. 'What happens if he doesn't come out?'

'Nothing, I guess,' shrugged Reggie.

'How come you never learned to drive?'

'Ah, that, my dear, is but one of the many regrets I have in my life.'

'Is it?' She'd increasingly become aware of how Reggie avoided talking about his past and always deflected the conversation in a different direction.

'Can I ask— AARGH!'

Hannah's scream was induced by the middle-aged man with tightly cropped hair who had tapped on the car window, right beside her head. She smiled apologetically as she wound down the window.

'Sorry, are we blocking your space or . . .'

'No,' said the man, in a strong Glaswegian accent. He was wearing an open checked shirt over a plain black T-shirt, and blue jeans. 'Youse are watching my house, though.' He indicated the house across the street they were indeed supposed to be watching.

'Oh, no, we're just . . .' Hannah stopped as she realized they hadn't even come up with a cover story should this eventuality arise.

'Aye,' the man said. 'No offence, but you're parked way too close and this motor sticks out like a sore thumb. You're from *The Stranger Times* and you're here about my son, Victor.'

'How do you know that?' asked Reggie.

'I'm former polis, and I ran your plates. By the way, you do know this vehicle isn't taxed?'

'Oh,' said Hannah. 'Sorry.'

'Relax,' said the man, 'I said former polis. I'm Gregory Tombs. Ye better come in.'

And without another word, he walked across the road and headed into his house.

'Well,' said Hannah, 'that was embarrassing.'

'Yes,' agreed Reggie, 'it was rather. Where did he even come from?'

'He must have gone out the back and walked around,' said Hannah. 'Christ – the back door. We never even thought of that. We really are rubbish at this.'

Given that he'd discovered them watching his house, Gregory Tombs was a very considerate host. He invited them to sit down in his kitchen, and offered tea and biscuits.

'Can I ask,' said Hannah, 'how soon did you realize we were out there?'

'How long were you there?'

'About an hour.'

Tombs set down a plate of chocolate Hobnobs. 'Pretty much straight away, then. I'm a security consultant now but . . . Well, let's just say back in ma days on the force, I may've pissed off some of the kind of people who have long memories and bear grudges. Help yourself to milk and sugar.'

They did.

'It took me a little time to ring my mate and get your plates run. Unless I'm very much mistaken, though, neither of the two of youse is Vincent Banecroft.'

'Sorry,' said Hannah, 'we should introduce ourselves properly. I'm Hannah Willis and this is my colleague Reginald Fairfax.'

'Gregory Tombs,' said their host in turn, 'and yes, given that you're here about Victor, you'll have no doubt noted the irony of the surname. Entirely coincidental, I assure you.' He shifted awkwardly. 'Although, I have wondered about that meself at times.'

'Is Victor here?'

Gregory nodded. 'He's downstairs. He lives mostly in the basement. Calls it his crypt.' He looked embarrassed by his words. 'It's soundproof – because it's also where his band practises and, y'know, he sleeps during the day.'

'Right,' said Hannah. 'Are they any good?'

'The band?' Gregory gave a bark of nervous laughter. 'No. Pure shite, to be honest with ye. Spend most of the time arguing about their name. I've lost track it's changed that much.'

'OK.' Hannah tried to give him a warm smile.

Gregory rubbed a hand over his neatly cropped hair. He was a stocky man in his late forties. Attractive, but his eyes had a tiredness to them. Something about him felt weighted down, as if he were carrying the world on his shoulders. He rotated his mug of tea and set the handle at an angle that seemed to please him. Hannah glanced around the kitchen again. On second look, it wasn't just neat, it was precise.

'OK,' said Gregory, clearly having made some kind of decision on how to proceed. 'Look, I know you're interested in Victor. I always knew this was coming, I guess, but . . . I just want to give ye a bit of background first. OK?'

'OK,' said Hannah.

Gregory nodded and studied the back of his hand as he spoke. 'If there's one thing me and the doctors agree on, it's that it all started with his mother. She died when he was young – eight. Leukaemia.' He looked up. 'Yeah, blood disorder. Psychiatrists love that wee detail. Her illness was pretty short and brutal.' Gregory lowered his gaze again. 'She was . . . She was a great mother and I guess I'd let her get on with it. I mean, it wasn't that I didn't love my son, I just . . . I was dedicated to the job, ye know? And Lucy had it all handled. She didn't mind. We were good together. She understood the job the way many don't. And besides, she'd loads of other interests. She was an artist and . . . She was something else.'

Hannah felt a lump form in her throat as she listened to the man describe the woman he had clearly adored and lost.

'So, ye know – after she went, I guess I threw myself into the work. Even more than I ever had. I wasn't paying enough attention. Hands up – that was my fault. Being a parent doesn't come with a manual, but I should've known.' He moved his teaspoon a fraction of an inch. 'He was, is, the spit of her. Even now. I guess I wasn't coping too well with the loss and he suffered for it. Maybe if I'd have been paying more attention . . .' He looked up as if suddenly pulled back into the present. 'Is the tea all right?'

Hannah nodded.

'Yes,' said Reggie in a soft voice. 'Lovely. Thank you.'

'Good. Good, good.' Gregory cracked his knuckles. 'So anyway, yeah – he got into it, ye know? It was sort of a goth thing and then, well, it developed. A fascination, I guess you'd call it.

I had an idea. I mean, I thought I did, but then there was that article in the paper I'm sure you've seen.'

They hadn't, but Hannah decided it was better not to correct him.

'After that, well, I was encouraged to leave the force. It was felt I might be "compromised". Like I'm the first officer ever to have a kid with some issues to work through.' He shrugged. 'By then I didn't care. I was belatedly trying to catch up with who my son was. Took him to see doctors. We argued. A lot.' He laughed a sad laugh. 'A lot,' he repeated. 'Then I started reading up on it. Met this one therapist who took a different tack. Instead of trying to "cure" him, she suggested I listen and try to understand. So I did. You shouldn't need to be told to do that, but, well.'

Gregory looked up. 'I ken it's weird, and I'm sure from the outside it might seem like a funny story and all that.' He darted his eyes around and lowered his voice. 'With the way he dresses and all, my son might appear ridiculous, but he's a good lad and he'd never hurt anybody.' He looked Hannah then Reggie directly in the eye, and Hannah could see his fierce parental instinct. 'He's a harmless eccentric.'

'I'm sure,' said Reggie. 'So he lives as a vampire?'

Gregory pursed his lips. 'Yes and no. It's true – he stays out of the sunlight, sleeps days, works nights. He actually works in the business with me. He's really good at the computer end of stuff.'

'Sorry,' said Hannah, ' "the business"?'

'I'm a security consultant. Say you're a Premiership footballer, or whatever, and you've got somebody trying to put the squeeze on you. More often than not, I'm the number somebody will give you.' He sat back. 'Nothing illegal, mind. I'm not covering up crimes or anything like that.'

'Of course,' said Reggie.

'And it turns out Victor is a bit of a dab hand on the tech side of things. Got a nose for it. That, at least, I guess he did get from me.'

'So does Victor . . .' started Hannah. She found herself liking Gregory Tombs, and she didn't want to embarrass him, but they needed to know what they were dealing with.

Gregory ran his hand over his hair again and looked at the table as he spoke. 'He lives as a sanguinarian. That's what they call themselves. It means he gets some of his nourishment from blood. There's actually quite a lot of people around the world like that.'

'He drinks blood?' said Reggie, trying and failing to keep a hint of revulsion from his voice. Gregory's eyes flicked up to meet his.

'Where does he get it?' asked Hannah.

In response, Gregory slipped his shirt down off his shoulders and pulled up the sleeve of his T-shirt to reveal his upper right arm. In spite of herself, Hannah let out a gasp as she saw the neat row of needle marks.

Gregory held up a finger. 'All right, just hang on. It's important ye understand. He only ever has my blood, and just a small amount, diluted. That's part of our deal – only ever my blood. To be honest, he'd be too nervous to take anyone else's. Others use animal blood but Victor doesn't.' He pulled his shirt back up and puffed out his cheeks. 'I realize I'm giving ye your easy angle here, but Victor is a vegan.'

'Excuse me?' said Reggie.

'Yeah. He doesnae eat meat, or any of the rest of it. I know – seems ridiculous, right? Well, not to my son. He loves animals. Our cat died last year. Honestly, poor lad – couldn't cope with it.'

Hannah nodded.

'Can I ask, why now?' said Gregory. 'I mean, why come knocking on our door now?'

'There was an incident,' began Hannah. 'Involving somebody who was, well, y'know, fangs and all that.'

'OK,' said Gregory, sounding like a man waiting for the other shoe to drop. 'First things first, when was this?'

'Sunday night,' answered Hannah.

'Right. Victor and I had dinner – an ordinary meal – at eight p.m. He was downstairs practising with the lads from nine until three in the morning. They left and I locked up the place. We've got cameras on all exits that'll confirm that, and I'll give ye the contact details for Terence and Ricardo from the band so you can verify.'

'OK,' said Hannah, quite taken aback. As interviews went, this one really felt like Gregory Tombs was asking and answering most of the questions. Probably just as well – he was better at it than they were.

'This incident,' said Hannah in an attempt to steer the conversation. 'The individual involved was called Phillip Butler.'

Gregory shook his head. 'Never heard of him.'

'Do you think we could ask Victor?'

'No.'

'I understand your concern. We don't have to mention Victor or you in any article. We're just trying to understand.'

Gregory placed his left hand down on the table in front of Hannah. 'Here's what ye need to understand. My son, odd though he may be, is a good lad. He also hardly ever leaves the house. He goes to the very occasional gig, in three years he's played the grand total of one of them himself, and he goes to the Roxy for the films once a week. That's it. I know that because I drive him to and pick him up from all of those places.'

'But . . .' started Reggie.

'Have ye met my son?'

'No, but I've seen him from a distance. At the Roxy.'

Gregory jutted his chin. 'How long do ye think he'd last walking around the streets of Manchester – or anywhere, for that matter – dressed like that? I take him everywhere he goes and then I bring him home again. I also know everyone he knows and I'm telling ye, he doesnae know this Phillip Butler. You start asking him about this stuff and he'll get all stressed out, and then all the work he's been doing with his therapist, and me, and . . . all of that. You'll set him back years.'

Hannah and Reggie glanced at each other before Hannah spoke. 'With respect, Mr Tombs, we're not trying to upset anyone, but your son is a grown man. You can't know everyone he does or doesn't know.'

Gregory slammed his hand on the table and Hannah sat back in shock.

'Sorry, sorry,' he said quickly. 'I didn't mean to . . .' He rubbed his hands up and down his face for a few seconds before fixing Hannah with a long stare. 'Can I trust ye?'

'Well . . .'

He waved it away. 'Don't bother answering that. It's a daft question. Whether I can or I cannae, you'd answer the same. I'll say this, though – I've explained our lives to ye and how we ended up here, so maybe on a basic human level you'll take that into consideration. God forgive an old copper for saying this, but you've got a trustworthy face, daft as that sounds. I'm going to put my whole relationship with my son in your hands.'

He stood up, walked across the kitchen, took a folder from a cupboard and placed it down on the table in front of Hannah.

'This,' said Gregory, 'is a dossier on every known associate my son has. I want to emphasize that most of them are harmless eccentrics with an odd hobby. Some take it more seriously than others, but they aren't doing anything illegal. There's the occa- sional concerning person who – honestly? – the group is actually pretty good at sussing out and removing by themselves. Neither my son nor his friends are stupid. Still, there's an index in there, at the back, with a few people ye could look at if some strange stuff is going down.'

Hannah stared down at the folder and then up at Gregory in disbelief.

He sighed. 'Yes. I've been running surveillance on my own son for about six years now. What you've got there is the results. Printing it out was the other thing I did while you were sitting outside my house for an hour. And if he ever finds out, I've no doubt that he'll never speak to me again. That's entirely on ye. Now, unless there's anything else, I've got a job to get to.'

★

Two minutes later, Hannah and Reggie were back in the Jag. In Hannah's hands was the dossier Gregory Tombs had just provided them with.

'Bloody hell,' said Reggie.

'Yeah,' said Hannah, 'I know.' She handed Reggie the folder. 'Nobody ever finds out where we got this.'

'Agreed.'

Corrections and Clarifications

We at *The Stranger Times* always endeavour to provide you, our readers, with the most accurate and even-handed reporting. It is with this in mind that, in the rare event that an error occurs, we go out of our way to correct it.

On this occasion, Mr Jonathan Fairburn, self-professed medium and gateway to the great beyond, has been in contact with us and demanded that I withdraw the editorial in which I refer to him as a 'charlatan'. On mature reflection, I am happy to do so. Mr Fairburn is not a charlatan, and referring to him as such was grossly unfair to charlatans everywhere. He can be more accurately described as a money-grabbing, parasitic, pennies-off-a-dead-man's-eyes lowlife with the moral rectitude of bacillary dysentery, who shamelessly milks money from the grieving with cheap parlour tricks and a level of dishonesty not to be found outside of the political realm. I hope this clarifies matters.

Yours sincerely,
Vincent Banecroft

CHAPTER 27

After spending a full twenty-four hours in Stanley Roker's company, the man – in Ox's opinion – was a medical miracle. No, miracle wasn't the right word. Phenomenon? Cautionary tale? Car crash? Whatever he was, he definitely deserved to be the subject of further study and, possibly, an intervention. Ox had never considered himself to be a healthy eater, but Stanley seemed committed to the kind of diet an obese eight-year-old being force-fed celery might fantasize about eating when he was a grown-up and nobody could stop him. Stanley Roker was a grown-up and somebody needed to stop him. It wasn't going to be Ox. Ultimately, one way or the other, it would be Stanley Roker.

The night spent in Stanley's van had been neither fun nor restful. Between Ox's trepidation regarding his crushing debt to the crushing Fenton brothers and trying to sleep in the front seat of a van while the back contained the snoring, farting and, most distressingly, sleep-talking Stanley, it meant little sleeping was actually done. Stanley had woken Ox at 7 a.m., which wasn't long after he'd finally nodded off.

Ox didn't mention the sleep-talking. It had been pretty

intense. They hadn't discussed Stanley's apparent run-in with what he himself described as a marriage-wrecking demon again, but from his desperate pleas for someone to get off him, leave him alone or, somehow saddest of all, to please just listen to him, it became very clear that Stanley not only believed it absolutely, but was reliving it again and again. In the past, Ox would have dismissed the idea entirely, but once you've witnessed a terrifying angel emerge from the body of the nice bloke who works downstairs, and with whom you occasionally share a joint, well, your days of dismissing things out of hand have come to an end.

Stanley had stopped the van outside the dessert shop where Ox and Banecroft had found him yesterday. He'd given Ox a twenty-pound note and instructed him to buy a dozen doughnuts, two slices of coffee cake and a milkshake. Stanley had then spent the day steadily munching his way through the haul of food without offering Ox any. In truth, Ox didn't mind – watching Stanley eat would cause anyone to lose their appetite. It was like witnessing a form of self-harm.

The man did not appear to be likeable in any way, but Ox found himself feeling a bit sorry for him. That feeling came and went, in line with Stanley's insistence not only on keeping the windows closed, but also on announcing and rating his own farts. It was hard to believe the man had ever been married.

For most of the day they'd followed Darius Williams, the builder, as he'd visited three different sites on which he had guys working. They'd all looked like high-end jobs. He'd spent a while at the one in Stockport, having what looked like a quite heated discussion with his foreman, before he'd changed out of his smart suit into a pair of jeans he had in his car, climbed up on the scaffolding and got stuck in himself. It was noticeable that as he did so, everyone else started working flat out too.

Williams worked with his shirt off, which revealed several tattoos on his torso. Stanley had taken a lot of pictures. When he'd noticed Ox leaning in to look at the display on the back of the camera, Stanley had held it up.

'Unusual tats. Never seen stuff like that. Might be nothing but I know a guy who can tell us. Once found out that a United youth team player had Russian mafia insignias. Nice little earner that one turned out to be.'

They were now sitting outside a rather upmarket gym where, after a couple of hours of work on an actual building site, Darius Williams was now paying someone else for the privilege of lifting stuff.

'This seems pointless,' muttered Ox.

Stanley spoke around a mouthful of doughnut. 'It's the job.'

'Just following him?'

'Yeah. And the other stuff. I still got my contacts digging around, trying to find out how a bloke from Salford with a couple of convictions for nicking cars got himself set up as a high-end builder. Something about all this smells fishy.'

'All right,' conceded Ox, 'but is any of that going to help us find out why his firm took the gig doing our bathroom and then installed a . . . I don't even know what you'd call it? A kidnap trap? I mean, come on!'

'If you've got a better idea, I'm all ears.'

Ox went back to staring out the window. His eyes fell on two blokes in the middle of an argument. In the nearly full car park, one of them had parked his Merc diagonally across two spaces to safeguard it from scratches.

Ox nodded. 'Fiver says the bloke in the Golf swings for him.'

Stanley belched. 'A, I'm not betting with you because I know you're not good for it. And B, you're wrong. He'll get back in his car and drive off . . .'

They watched as, after a further minute of heated exchange, the man in the Golf did exactly as Stanley had predicted.

'Now, give it a few minutes and he'll be back to run a coin up the side of that muppet's shiny new car – you see if he doesn't.'

A sullen silence fell in the van, punctuated only by Stanley releasing what he rated as a couple of sixes and a seven. So far, nothing had exceeded a seven on the Stanley scale, and Ox feared for his life if it did.

'Do you believe in karma?'

The question came so completely out of nowhere that Ox gawped at Stanley in confusion.

'What?'

'Karma,' repeated Stanley without taking his eyes off the main entrance to the gym. 'Do you believe in it? The idea that we get punished for all the shitty things we've done?'

'I dunno. I've never really thought about it.'

'Neither had I, until recently. Every day I try and ring my Crystal, and every day, no answer. She had one rule, see – one rule. She made it clear on the day I proposed. She said to me, "You ever cheat on me, Stanley Roker, and we're done." She had a lot of stuff in her past – family and that.'

'Right.'

'God as my witness, though,' continued Stanley, 'I didn't. I was working a story and I got jumped by these three guys. It happens. We're not popular people, us journalists. I got knocked silly by a hipster roller-skate.'

'Is that, like, rhyming slang?'

Stanley looked at Ox briefly, the annoyance on his face mingled with a sad wetness in his eyes. 'What? No. A hipster wearing roller-skates kicked me in the head.'

'Oh, OK.'

Stanley went back to staring at the doors of the gym. 'This girl helps me out. Said she was a nurse. Least I thought she was. I couldn't go home in the state I was in and she said I could sleep on her sofa. I had no phone, no money, nothing. Thought she was one of them whatchamacallits – Good Samaritans. Should've known. All I've seen of life. Nobody does nothing for free – not in this world.' He coughed to clear his throat before continuing. 'So, it all seems fine, only she gets me in her flat and I pass out. I wake up and I'm on this bed – only it's not a bed. It's holding me in place, I can't move.'

Ox noticed Stanley judder slightly as the memory passed through him.

'And she's on top of me. Only it isn't her. She's now this . . . I don't know what you call it. Demon. And she's laughing. She's going to kill me afterwards too. I know that for certain. But my

Crystal – I found out later she'd been having me followed because she was suspicious. I was only working but, well, like I said, she's got stuff in her past. Anyway, the guy she's got following me – Maurice bastard Glenn – he's gone to get her. Luckily and unluckily for me, Crystal bursts in and twats this whatever it is with a statue, knocks it out cold. Only to her, it must just look like a woman. She then tells me it's over and leaves.'

Stanley's voice cracked as he stared off into the distance. 'I can't follow her immediately – not until that bloody bed thing sets me free – and then she's gone. Won't talk to me. Not over the phone. Not in person. Nothing.' He stopped to rub his sleeve across his eyes. 'Went back to that flat the next day, brought the cops with me. Took a while to get them to listen to me too, seeing as I got picked up running about the streets naked. Anyway, the woman – or whatever she was – was gone by then. The whole place was cleared out. Chased it up – complete dead end. And believe me, I looked.'

'Wow,' said Ox, in honest astonishment.

'Yeah,' replied Stanley. 'Been over it in my head again and again. Y'know what I reckon? I'm certain I didn't do anything wrong that night. I never even looked at another woman since I laid eyes on my Crystal neither. So I reckon it's karma. All those stories I did over the years? All that damage I caused? This is the payback. Tell you what, they got me good too. Right in my point of weakness. They know the game, whoever's in charge of karma – I'll give 'em that.' He looked down at the steering wheel and repeated in a near whisper, 'They know the game.'

Ox opened his mouth to speak. He wanted to put together

some coherent words of sympathy, but before he could gather his thoughts, Stanley jabbed a finger at the windscreen.

'Why the hell is that little girl on a skateboard waving at us?'

'What? Oh, that's my mate T-Bone's little sister, KK. He owes me a favour and he's lending me something.'

'You say that like it's some kind of explanation. We're under-cover following somebody here. We ain't got time to babysit.'

Ox fished his phone out of his pocket and started texting. 'She's actually thirteen, so she doesn't need babysitting. She's small for her age. Sharp as a tack, though.' He watched as KK took out her phone, read a message from it and then gave a subtle thumbs-up.

'What is going on?'

'Relax. She knows what she's doing.'

'Yeah,' said Stanley, 'but my point is, I want to know *what* she's doing.'

KK began to scoot around the car park on her skateboard. She attempted an ollie and failed, ending up sprawled on the ground right beside Darius Williams's SUV.

'What is she . . .'

Before Stanley could finish his thought, KK rolled under the SUV and back out again, then picked herself up and skated off.

Ox held up his phone and showed Stanley a map on which there was now a flashing red dot. 'There you go. For the next seventy-two hours we'll know where Darius Williams's vehicle is without following it about. Beep boop beep.'

'He could have rumbled us!'

'How? We didn't go near it. This way we can hang back and know where he is.'

'But . . .'

'You're welcome,' said Ox. 'Turns out you pick up the odd trick when you're out chasing UFOs too.'

Stanley mumbled something under his breath.

Silence descended on the van once again, punctuated only by a couple of Stanley's pungent fives and the sight of a VW Golf driver coming back to key the side of a badly parked Merc.

CHAPTER 28

Banecroft lit a fresh cigarette off the butt of his last one and picked up the folder that was sitting on top of the most recent layer of detritus that made up the surface of his desk. He leaned back in his chair, put up his feet and flicked open the file. He'd asked Stella to assemble everything she could find about vampires in the newspaper's archives. Earlier that morning she had presented him with her findings before stomping off sullenly.

The kid was pissed off, and rightly so – it was the middle of a heatwave and she was being forced to stay inside this festering old heap of a building. That it was for her own safety was of no comfort. Teenagers don't think about death as a real thing. Unless they're very unlucky, they don't have to. On the other hand, Stella was a long way from ordinary. The fact they didn't know exactly how far was one of their many worries. He'd seen only one flash of her abilities, but he knew they'd been enough to tear down half of Grace's house when she'd been threatened. He'd essentially given an apprenticeship to an unstable nuclear bomb.

She was thorough, though – he'd give her that. As he read through the file, he could tell, even by the way she'd assembled it, that she had an eye for an interesting angle when it came to stories. Whatever else happened, she might just make a journalist.

The clippings themselves were mostly what he'd been expecting. Numerous claims of vampire sightings and experiences from across the world, and individuals like the one Hannah and Reggie were chasing up who were living as sanguinarians. There was also a piece on how, in 2013, some ancient graves in Bulgaria were dug up and two bodies with metal rods through the heart were exhumed.

There was no end of the stuff. Vampire goats in South America, vampire carnivals, whole communities living as vampires. Stella had also included a piece from the *Evening News* about the Roxy's vampire festival. It read like a regurgitated press release, complete with a rather superfluous reference to the weeping girl ghost that apparently haunted the venue. *The Stranger Times* article on the ghost was in there too, written by Reggie before Banecroft's time as editor, as evidenced by Reggie's adjective addiction being given free rein. The hypothesis was that the ghost was a girl – one who had been jilted at the altar and who used to play the organ back in the day when the Roxy was a music hall. Banecroft had a sneaking suspicion that angle was being worked by the Roxy as they'd been doing a fundraiser to restore the old organ at the time. Lucky they weren't trying to install a new condom machine or heaven knows what kind of ghost they'd have come up with.

In all of the many references to vampires in stories from all over the world, there was nothing that gave a plausible explanation as to how Phillip Butler had gone from IT geek to bloodsucking freak seemingly overnight. Banecroft could see why Dr Carter and the shadowy figures she represented were nervous – this story felt as if it had legs and, more worryingly, teeth.

His thoughts were disturbed as the office doors flew open. Grace barged into the room while simultaneously banging on the woodwork as a token gesture towards following his oft-expressed wish for people to knock before entering.

'He is on the phone,' she said breathlessly.

'Come in.'

'What?'

'Never mind,' said Banecroft.

'He is on the phone,' repeated Grace, pointing urgently back towards reception.

'I'm afraid you're going to have to narrow that down for me slightly, Grace.'

'Mr Williams, the builder.'

'Right.'

She lowered her voice. 'The one who was doing our bathroom. Y'know . . .'

'Ironically, you've now narrowed that down too much.'

'What are we going to do? He's waiting to speak to you.'

Banecroft casually booted some books off his desk to reveal the phone. 'I knew it was around here somewhere.' He leaned forward to grab the handset. 'What line?'

'We only have one line.'

'Well say "line one", then.' Banecroft hit the button to accept the call. 'Hello!'

'Hi, is that Mr Banecroft?' Darius Williams sounded like a man determined to be reasonable.

'Yes, it is, Mr Williams. More importantly, when is your birthday?'

'What?'

'Birthday – quickly, quickly, quickly.'

'August twenty-fourth.'

'Yes, that explains a lot.'

'Does it?' asked Williams, sounding as if this conversation was heading in a direction he didn't expect.

'Virgo. Do you have any understanding of the fundamentals of feng shui?'

'Ehm, I know a bit.'

'Excellent. Do you know what the consequences would be if a dragon entered a room and the first thing he saw was a toilet?'

'Not exactly, but—'

'Neither do I,' said Banecroft, 'but I'm pretty sure it'd be bad. Very bad. I'm sorry, but I hired your company on the understanding that you were culturally sensitive.'

'What?'

'One of my staff is a bit Asian.'

'What?' repeated Williams.

'I do apologize, but I have no choice but to engage another firm of builders to redo the entire job.'

'No,' said Williams, suddenly sounding desperate. 'Look, hang on. Seeing as there's been this misunderstanding, we'll redo the whole job and we'll do it for free.'

'Free?'

'Yes, free.'

'How dare you? Are you suggesting I'm in need of your charity?'

'What? No, I—'

Banecroft slammed down the phone and looked at Grace. 'That's that done.'

'"One of my staff is a bit Asian"?' repeated Grace.

'And he is. You really should notice these things, Grace.'

'You can't remember his name, can you?'

'Of course I can.'

Grace folded her arms, raised her eyebrows and waited. 'Go on, then.'

Outside, a phone rang.

'I'm guessing,' said Banecroft, 'that will be Mr Williams. Tell him I am in a meeting for the rest of the day and that you'll try to talk me round later on.'

'Ha,' said Grace. 'He doesn't know you at all if he falls for that.'

'And inform the aforementioned that Mr Williams is desperate now. If I'm any judge, and I am, whoever Williams is working for will want a word.'

'The aforementioned?'

'The one who is a bit Asian.'

'You have now managed to make this offensive on almost every level.'

Banecroft pointed towards reception. 'Do you not hear that phone ringing?'

Grace shook her head and exited the room.

Banecroft leaned back in his chair again and returned to

perusing the folder. 'Bloody woman, suggesting I don't know the names of my own staff.'

He skimmed the article *The Stranger Times* had published late last year on the 'attacks' at a Welsh waxworks museum, when someone appeared to have broken in and bit the necks of some of their famous exhibits, but only the English ones, which had led to speculation about a Welsh nationalist vampire cult.

He was just getting himself a drink from his desk drawer when the door to his office flew open again. There was no knock this time as Grace came barrelling through.

'Bloody hell, woman!'

'It's Stella. She's gone.'

Banecroft jumped to his feet. 'What? What do you mean "she's gone"?'

'She's run off. While I was in here, she must've slipped out. I saw her out the window and when I called after her she started running.'

'Ah,' said Banecroft. 'Right.' He sat back down.

'What are you doing? We need to get after her.'

'No, we don't. This isn't a kidnap, it's a teenage rebellion. We come down on it like a ton of bricks and it'll just make it worse.'

'But she could go anywhere.'

'Did she have a bag with her?'

'I'm going to ring Hannah.'

'You will do no such thing. Listen to me, Grace – did she have a bag with her?'

'No.'

'Good. Then this is just a day trip. I will handle this.'

Grace's eyebrows shot up so fast they looked in danger of achieving escape velocity and clearing the atmosphere. 'You?'

'Yes. To be honest, I thought this would happen before now.'

'But?'

'I am the boss and I have spoken. It is my job to care for my staff.'

'Really? In all the time I have known you, you have done nothing to indicate that is the case.'

'I'm all about tough love.'

'You don't even know all their names.'

'I have spoken,' repeated Banecroft.

'Stop saying that!' Grace slammed the door behind her.

Banecroft picked up the folder once more and continued to flick through. 'Bloody insufferable woman. "You don't know the names of your staff. You don't know the names of your staff."' Course I know . . .' He nearly fell off his chair as he shouted after her, 'Ox! It's Ox!'

'Too late.'

CHAPTER 29

Hannah looked up at the Skyline One building, eighteen storeys of executive apartments gleaming in the afternoon sun. Behind her, the Skyline Two building, several storeys shorter, was basking in a similar fashion and throwing sheets of reflected light into the valley between the two structures. Beside her, Reggie was finishing the bottle of cold water she'd insisted on buying him. The man was not designed for a warm climate.

'Perhaps,' said Hannah, 'you should consider not wearing a waistcoat for a few days?'

Reggie looked appalled. 'There's such a thing as standards, you know?'

'There's also such a thing as heatstroke. It's a toss-up to see what's going to last until Friday – your standards or you. Have you considered a short-sleeved shirt? Maybe some light chinos?'

'I'd rather die,' said Reggie, without a hint of sarcasm.

Hannah patted her pockets. 'Damn it, I left my notebook in the car. I thought I should take down what you just said so I can repeat it at your funeral.'

Reggie placed his empty bottle in his briefcase. 'How presumptuous of you to assume you're making that guest list.'

Hannah noticed an older man with short silver hair waving at them from the building's reception area. Reggie waved back.

'So this guy is a security guard here. How do you know him?'

'He's Too Dead Tony. We've appeared in many amateur dramatic productions together.'

'Do I want to know?'

'The name comes from the fact that Antony does an incredible corpse.'

'Excuse me?'

'Plays dead like nobody's business. Unbelievably convincing. We did a production of *Hamlet* with him as the late king. Left him on stage the entire time – even the interval. He was the best thing in it. Extraordinary.'

'Right.'

'*Pirates of Penzance* is a musical with no dead bodies in it, but our director wrote one in. People come just to see Tony. It's quite something.'

'Sounds it.'

'He gets offers from TV all the time, but he did a stint on *Casualty* a few years back and hated it. Says it cheapens the art. Now he just does am-dram.'

'Doesn't he ever . . .'

'What?' asked Reggie.

'Fancy speaking?'

'Speaking?' scoffed Reggie. 'Asking Too Dead to speak is like asking Mozart to rap. Only a philistine—'

Thankfully, Reggie's rant was cut off by the ironically lively-looking Tony opening the door for them with a nervous smile.

'Reginald, thanks so much for coming.'

'No problem at all, Tony. This is Hannah Willis. She is the assistant editor.'

Tony nodded. 'I never miss an issue!'

'Oh,' said Hannah. 'Thank you.'

'So, take me through this again?' asked Reggie.

Tony waved the pair towards the lifts, giving a nod to the man reading a thick book behind the reception desk as he went. 'I'll explain as we go.'

They entered the open lift and Tony hit the button for the fourteenth floor. He spoke again only once the doors had closed.

'Sorry, but Michael thinks I shouldn't have called you. He didn't see her, though – I mean, when it happened. I did. I was on nights last night.'

'See who?' asked Hannah.

'A lady called Georgina Grant. She's here on a short-term let. Woke up in the middle of the night with a strange man standing in her room.'

'Isn't this something for the police?'

'Oh, they've been,' said Tony. 'But—'

He was interrupted by a *ding* as the lift reached the fourteenth floor. The trio stepped out onto the landing and Tony made his way over to one of the apartment doors.

'It's best you hear it from her,' he finished. He knocked loudly and raised his voice. 'Ms Grant – it's Tony. I'm here with those people I mentioned.'

After a minute or so, a very pale woman wearing glasses

opened the door. She looked at them nervously for a moment then stepped back, leaving the door open, and hurried down the hall.

Reggie and Hannah exchanged a look as Tony walked in first and led them down the corridor. Wooden floors, freshly painted walls – the place smelled high-end. The corridor took them into an open-plan kitchen and living room that usually had a nice view of the city. The reason it didn't today was that the sofa, and most of the other furniture in the room, had been moved to form a makeshift barrier in front of the door to the balcony.

At the far end of the room sat Georgina Grant in an armchair, with her knees pulled up to her chest.

'Georgina,' said Tony softly. 'Like I was saying, these people are from that newspaper.'

Reggie and Hannah introduced themselves and Georgina nodded before blurting out, 'Look, I don't believe in this stuff.'

Reggie looked at Hannah to take the lead.

'OK,' she said. 'No problem. Well, why don't you tell us what happened, and we'll take it from there.'

'It's simple,' said Georgina as she pulled at her hair absent-mindedly. 'In the middle of the night, I sense somebody is in the room. I open my eyes and . . .'

'It's OK,' said Hannah in her best soothing voice. 'You're safe now.'

'Ha,' said Georgina bitterly before she looked down and took a deep breath. 'Sorry. I know you're only trying to help. I was in bed – down there, at the end of the hall. I open my eyes and there's this . . . man standing there, at the end of my bed. He's got' – she pointed at her mouth – 'y'know, vampire teeth. His eyes are red and he's staring at me. It was really good make-up.'

'And you're sure it was make-up?'

'Well, what else would it be?'

'Right,' said Hannah. 'And did he . . .' She left her question hanging.

Georgina reached down, picked up a large glass of milk and held it in her shaking hands. 'He moved towards me and I screamed, and then he turned and ran off.'

'I see.'

'He came this way – into this room. I followed him because . . .' She went to take a sip of her drink but then didn't. 'I don't know why. I ran after him, but when I get in here, he's gone. And the door is open.'

'The one to the balcony?' asked Hannah, which just elicited a nod from Georgina.

'I grabbed a knife and went round the apartment checking every room – just in case. I looked outside on the balcony. Up. Down. Nothing.'

Hannah noticed the large kitchen knife on the floor near to where the glass of milk had been. 'The front door was locked. I know because I had to unlock the bloody thing to get out. He couldn't have left that way.'

'OK,' said Hannah, trying to sound calmer than she felt. 'That sounds like an absolute nightmare.'

'That's what the bloody police said – that I'd had a nightmare.' Georgina was gripping the glass so tightly her knuckles had turned white.

Tony cleared his throat. 'I called them as soon as Ms Grant came down to reception. A couple of uniforms came over straight away. They checked the apartment – again. Then we looked at the CCTV. This place has a lot of cameras – the lobby, the lifts, the stairwells, outside the building. This guy didn't show up anywhere.'

'That's because he didn't come in that way,' said Georgina. 'I told them that.'

'She did,' confirmed Tony.

Georgina pointed at the balcony door. 'That was open because of the heat. He came in that way. Only the police said nobody could possibly climb up from below – it's way too far. So basically, it was a really vivid nightmare and I made it all up.'

Tony winced and nodded. 'That's what they said. That's why I called you.'

'I know what I saw.' Georgina banged her free hand on the arm of the chair. 'I'm not crazy.'

'We believe you,' said Hannah.

'Great. No offence, but the people from the loony paper believing me doesn't reassure me.' She nodded towards the table where Hannah could see what looked like last week's edition of *The Stranger Times* lying open. 'Next week it'll be me in there along-side the woman who married the M62.' Georgina looked up, her eyes wide. 'Oh God, don't put me in the paper.'

'Relax. I promise we won't do that.'

'OK. Thanks. Just, my job and all . . .'

'Sure.' Hannah tried to pick her next words carefully. 'Can I ask . . . Do you think he got scared when you screamed?'

Georgina drummed her fingers on her forehead for a few seconds and then looked back up at Hannah. 'It was weird. I mean – well, weirder. It was as if he came out of a trance. I screamed and he looked horrified. Like he'd just realized what he was doing.'

A silence descended on the room for a minute before Reggie spoke up. 'Apart from the teeth and the eyes, do you remember anything else about his appearance?'

Georgina let out a deep sigh. 'You'll laugh.'

'I promise,' said Reggie, 'we will not.'

She looked up at the ceiling. 'He was wearing a green anorak.' She glared at Reggie and Hannah then looked away. 'Congratulations. One of the police officers actually laughed at me at that point. At least you two kept a straight face.'

'Like I said, Georgina,' assured Hannah, 'we believe you. We hear about things that defy rational explanation all the time. It doesn't mean they aren't true. If it makes you feel better, you're not the first person to mention something like this.'

She looked up. 'Really?'

'Really,' said Hannah. 'I promise you, you're not losing your mind.'

Georgina laughed. 'Well, let's not rule that out entirely.'

Hannah smiled. 'OK. Is there anything else you can remember?'

'He . . .' Georgina trailed off.

'What?' asked Hannah. 'It's OK, you can tell us.'

'The . . . Oh, for— The vampire. Let's just say it – the vampire. When I screamed and he . . .'

'Realized what he was doing?' prompted Hannah.

'Yeah. Before he ran off . . . he said he was sorry.'

CHAPTER 30

Stella liked books. She loved them, in fact. They had a very calming quality to them – as if nothing could be that bad if you were holding one. Life had shown her that was definitely not true, but still. Given her feelings towards books, a library should have been a tremendously relaxing place for her, but it wasn't.

She had come here seeking answers, and the woman working behind the counter at the far end of the library was her best chance at getting some. Stella didn't know her. They had met before, but only once, and that had not been in the best of circumstances. They had both been kidnapped by a madman who had wanted to use them as sacrifices in a ritual he was trying to carry out. In the process of making good their escape, Stella had seen this woman perform magic – actual magic – which meant that in some way she was like Stella and therefore she could hopefully tell Stella what the hell was happening to her.

The urge to talk to her had been bubbling away in Stella for a while, but the last few days had brought things to a head. Stella was sick of being hidden away, sick of being scared all the time and, most of all, sick of not knowing who or what she was.

To start with, Stella had gone round to a house in Chorlton. It

247

was where she and Hannah had dropped off the woman once Hannah and Banecroft had rescued them. She'd rung the doorbell a couple of times and waited, but there had been no response. A kindly-looking old man who'd been doing some weeding in the next-door garden had popped his head over the fence.

'Hello there – are you looking for the girls? Keira and Siobhan?'

'Actually,' said Stella, 'I'm looking for Vera.'

'Oh, right,' said the man, looking slightly taken aback.

'She's a friend of my mum's.'

'It's a Tuesday, so I'd imagine she's at work.'

'Oh,' said Stella, clearly looking disappointed.

'It's just the library up the road there. I'm sure you could drop in and say hello, as long as you whisper.' The man laughed heartily at his own joke.

Stella had thanked him, and hurried off.

She'd found the library easily enough and as soon as she walked in, she spotted Vera working behind the counter. Stella hung back but kept throwing furtive glances at the desk as she waited for Vera to become free. Unfortunately, the library was surprisingly busy. As it was the summer holidays, it was also pretty loud. The kids might have been mostly corralled in the children's section – with the exception of the occasional bolter – but their noise carried across the whole library. Stella noticed an old man sitting at one of the reading tables in the corner. He looked irritated by the whole thing.

After a while, she plucked up her courage, grabbed a book at random from one of the nearby shelves and joined the queue. A mother and her three children finished getting their newly borrowed books stamped and headed for the exit, the children chattering excitedly as they went. Stella couldn't help but feel a tiny pang of jealousy as she wondered what it must be like to be part of a family.

As she stood in the queue she kept her eyes down, but when the elderly woman in front of her pushed her stack of five books onto the counter, Stella looked up and caught a flash of something in Vera's face.

'Hello again, Mrs Corry.'

'Yes, hello, Vera. I have to say, I'm still reeling from the shock of discovering that this library stocks such filth.'

Vera attempted a smile but it didn't reach her eyes. 'And as we discussed earlier, these are books written by adults for adults. I appreciate that the scene you pointed out might be too racy for your tastes, but it is fairly commonplace in the genre.'

'Filth it was – pure filth!' Mrs Corry's accent was distinctly Irish and she screwed up her face between sentences as if she were in an invisible sandstorm. 'Heaving bosoms. I ask you. And references to hands grabbing things roughly and, while I'd never heard the like before, what I can only assume was a reference to the male penis.'

'As opposed to the female one?'

'What?' barked Mrs Corry.

'I was just . . . Never mind. As I said, if you avoid books with the kind of cover like' – Vera regarded the pile of well-worn paperbacks in front of her – 'the ones you've selected several more of.'

'That's right. I've decided to see just how much depravity this library is pushing on the unsuspecting public.'

'I see.' Vera held up one of the books. 'I think this is the same title you came in to complain about.' She flicked through a few of the pages. 'Yes, look – here are the passages you've underlined.'

'That's right,' said Mrs Corry. 'I'm taking it out again. My son Darren will be ringing me from South Africa tonight. I'm going to read it to him over the phone, so he can hear it for himself. I'm sure he'll be horrified.'

'Of that I have no doubt,' said Vera. 'He'll quite probably be scarred for life.'

Mrs Corry nodded as the sarcasm sailed over her tiny angry head. 'Good, respectable married people come into this library. They don't want to be reading about this kind of carry-on.'

'I'm sure you're right,' said Vera, holding up another of the tattered paperbacks. 'No doubt these books are all so worn out from people throwing them across the room in disgust.' She finished stamping the last one and pushed the stack back across the counter. 'Enjoy.'

'I will not,' said Mrs Corry. 'How dare you! The very idea.'

She snatched up the books and stomped towards the exit. A teenaged boy, who had the misfortune to be walking in the other direction with an armful of books, leaped in the air and distributed them across a wide area when the elderly woman barked the word 'filth' in his direction. She proceeded to march on undaunted, no doubt into several enraptured evenings of horrified outrage.

Vera turned back to her next customer, Stella, with a smile.

There was a momentary flicker of recognition before it was her turn to look horrified as she realized who was standing in front of her.

'Hi,' said Stella.

Vera glanced round furtively. 'You can't be here.'

'Sorry, I . . . I just wanted to have a quick chat with you.'

'About what?' Vera's eyes flicked up to some movement behind Stella. 'Sorry, I can't.'

'Please? I don't have anyone else to talk to.'

Vera bit her lip for a second. 'It's my break in half an hour. I'll meet you down the road at the water park.'

Thirty minutes later, Stella was seated on a bench in Chorlton Water Park as she watched Vera Doyle approach the main gates. The woman looked remarkably unremarkable: shoulder-length brown hair tied into a ponytail, a plain summer dress with sensible shoes. Her eyes were kind with laughter lines around them, but something about her said she could also be stern, if required. A woman infinitely capable of delivering the mother of all shushings.

Stella raised her hand in a tentative wave, which was met with the faintest of nods from Vera. The librarian stopped at the ice-cream van that was doing a roaring trade. Two minutes later, she handed Stella a 99 ice-cream.

'Sorry,' she said.

'For what?' asked Stella.

'On reflection, you saved my life and I acted like a bit of a shit when you turned up just now. I apologize. You just caught me by surprise.' She looked at the posse of mothers pushing prams that were heading in their direction, and nodded towards the path that went round the park. 'Do you mind if we walk? I need the steps.' She held up her ice-cream cone and laughed. 'Hard as it is to believe, I'm on a bit of a fitness kick.'

They walked in silence for a minute as they each got stuck into their ice-cream.

'God, that's good,' said Vera, before dropping the remnants of her cone into a dustbin. 'Too good.'

Stella still had half of hers left. It did indeed taste glorious, all the more so because she'd spent the previous half-hour longing for one, when she wasn't feeling mortified by Vera's reaction at seeing her. Treats had been such a rarity when she was growing up that she had learned to draw them out, to maximize her enjoyment.

'So,' said Vera, 'are you OK? Nothing's happened, has it?'

'No,' said Stella. 'Well, kinda.'

'Having two of my own, I speak fluent teenager. What happened?'

'You know I'm staying at *The Stranger Times*?'

'I do. Their offices are in that old church, aren't they?'

Stella nodded.

'That's good. They're protected.'

'Yes. Manny, who works there, he . . . He's sort of possessed by this demon, but it's a good one.'

Vera held up a hand and tilted her head. 'No offence, and, I'm sorry for how this will sound, but I don't want to know things like that.'

'Oh,' said Stella, taken aback by Vera's tone.

'Sorry, kiddo. It's . . . You have to understand – I'm under the radar. My husband, my kids – they don't know what I am, and I'd like to keep it that way for as long as possible. That's why I stay well away from everything. I've been out of that circle entirely. At least, I had been until – well, until that maniac took me.' She grabbed Stella's arm. 'And, sorry again, but I . . . I don't think I ever had the chance to say properly, thank you. If you hadn't . . .'

Stella was shocked when the older woman hugged her briefly then pulled away abruptly.

'Sorry.'

'You can stop saying that,' said Stella awkwardly. 'And I'm sorry I kind of ambushed you. It's just . . . I'm so sick of being confused and scared all the time.'

'I understand,' said Vera as they continued walking. 'I don't know if I'll be able to be much help, though.'

'What are we?' Stella could feel her own pulse quicken as she asked.

'Well, now, that's quite the question. What I am is – to put it in simple terms – a witch. We don't actually like that word much. "Practitioner" is the preferred term these days. "Witch" has a lot of negative connotations. Plus, a lot of people who read palms and bang on about sprinkling sage around your toilet have adopted it. But, er . . . I'm afraid that isn't what you are.'

Vera slowed beside the pond and Stella came to a stop next to her. They watched a few ducks fight over the pieces of bread a small boy was tossing into the water, as his mother stood behind him, ready in case the child lost his balance.

'So . . . what am I?'

Vera turned to look at Stella. 'I'm afraid I don't know. When you . . . When your power kicked in, back in that horrible place, I'd never felt anything like it. The best I can explain it – people like me, or, well, any form of practitioner, we harness power in some form. You – *you* are power.'

'So who would know what I am?'

Vera winced. 'I understand why you want to know, I really do, but if you want my honest advice, don't go looking. Whatever you are, you're powerful. How this world is, people will try and use that.'

'But I need to learn how to control it or I could hurt somebody.'

'I know. And that's scary for you, but the thing is, right now, nobody knows who or what you are. If I were you, I'd keep it that way.'

'That's the thing, though – somebody must know already. They built a trapdoor thing to try and kidnap me.'

'What?' said Vera, doing nothing to hide her shock.

'Yeah. The people who raised me . . .'

Vera held up a hand. 'I'm . . . I'm sorry, but don't tell me any more.'

'But . . .'

'You have to understand – if I know too much, I become a danger to you.'

'I trust you,' said Stella in a soft, almost pleading voice.

'You shouldn't,' said Vera, turning away. 'Don't get me wrong, I'd love to help you, I really really would, but I'm a mother. All anyone has to do is threaten my daughters and I'd tell them everything. It's . . . I wouldn't have a choice.'

'Right,' said Stella, trying to look stronger than she felt as she quickly wiped a sleeve across her eyes. 'I get it.'

'This is why I told that Mr Banecroft I wouldn't speak to you. That I couldn't help.'

Stella was taken aback. 'Banecroft talked to you?'

'Yes,' said Vera, sounding surprised. 'Sorry, I thought you knew. A couple of times.'

'Oh.'

'I'll tell you what I told him: don't go looking. You might not like what you find.'

'That's easy for you to say,' said Stella. 'Thanks for your time.'

And she walked away.

CHAPTER 31

DI Sturgess was starting to really dislike meeting rooms. He hadn't much liked meetings back in the days when the Greater Manchester Police had him attending them, but now he was released from that burden he realized that he found the rooms in which they were held almost as annoying.

He wasn't sure what it was about them. Part of it was the art invariably hung on the walls. There seemed to be an entire school of it where the goal was to be so undeniably bland that what you produced was not only universally inoffensive, but also so dull that it failed to distract anyone in a meeting, no matter how bored they were. Usually, it involved a boat on an expanse of water. Occasionally, a tree. Sometimes, a bird but, crucially, not one detailed or realistic enough to allow the imagination of the person detained in the meeting against their will to daydream of freedom or nature or being outdoors, liberated from suits, ties, action points or PowerPoint presentations.

In this particular meeting room, the artwork was a crudely drawn bird in a tree, looking out at a boat on a distant sea. Sturgess had an irrational urge to rip it off the wall and smash it to pieces. Inexplicably, despite these offices being those of an upmarket financial services firm, the canvas was screwed firmly in place.

He was contemplating the low level of self-esteem an art thief would have to have in order to undertake that particular heist, when the door to the room opened and in walked a man in a smart suit. Six foot, blond, athletic build, longish hair, with eyes slightly too close together and front teeth slightly too far apart. Sturgess hadn't seen a picture of Keith Harpenden, but he didn't need to – the look of trepidation on the guy's face made it clear who he was.

Sturgess got to his feet and flipped open his ID. 'Ah, Mr Harpenden, I'm DI Tom Sturgess, Greater Manchester Police, and you're a tough man to get hold of.'

'Sorry,' said the man nervously, 'I was in a meeting.'

'Yes, so I hear. My colleague rang you yesterday, though, and I rang you very early this morning.'

'Oh, did you?' said Harpenden. 'Sorry, I've lost my phone.'

'And I'm sorry to hear that. Please, take a seat.' They both sat down. Sturgess pulled out his notepad and pen. 'Mind if I . . .'

'No, 'course not.'

'Thanks. I'll be honest, I didn't really have the time to drive all the way over here to Leeds, especially when you live in Manchester, but as my colleague and I made clear in our messages, we really need to speak to you urgently.'

'Right,' said Harpenden. 'Like I said, lost the old phone. Water?'

'No, thank you.'

Harpenden poured himself a glass of water from the jug on

the table. Sturgess noted the slight shake in the man's hands as he did so.

'So, I assume you know what this is about?'

'No.'

'Interesting. Well, I'm sorry to be the bearer of bad news but Phillip Butler is dead.'

'Really? Wow.' Harpenden was no great loss to the acting profession.

'So, did you not know?'

'I mean, yes, I . . . I heard something but, y'know, I didn't really believe it.'

'Right. Did you not think to ring your friend? See if it was true?'

Harpenden hesitated. 'Well, I . . . didn't have my phone, obviously.'

'Of course,' said Sturgess, smiling. 'That's right. You said.' He tapped at his own temple. 'My memory – not as good as it once was.'

Harpenden forced a smile in return. 'Happens to all of us.'

'That it does. That it does. So, when was the last time you saw Phillip?'

Harpenden puffed out his cheeks. 'A few weeks ago, maybe? Bumped into him in a pub. Not sure where. My memory isn't great either.'

'Sure. But you heard from him over the weekend?'

'Ehm . . .'

'No, you did. You received a text message from him.'

'Did I?'

'Yes,' said Sturgess. 'You replied to it, in fact. We've got his phone records.'

'Oh.' Harpenden shifted in his seat. 'Yes, right. I remember now.'

'What was it about?'

Harpenden pursed his lips. 'Nothing really. To be honest, didn't make a lot of sense. I think he might have sent it to me by mistake.'

'I see. Well, if nothing else, we know you had your missing phone on Sunday. That should help you narrow down the search area.'

Harpenden just nodded.

'Sorry,' said Sturgess, pulling out his own phone. 'Excuse me a moment.'

'Do you need me to . . .' Harpenden pointed at the door.

Sturgess shook his head. 'No, this won't take a second. I just . . .'

He tapped the screen on his phone. Two seconds later the inside pocket of Keith Harpenden's suit jacket began to vibrate, causing his face to flush with embarrassment.

'Would you look at that,' said Sturgess. 'I found your missing phone.'

'Yeah, no, I found it in—'

Sturgess held up a finger. 'Word to the wise, Keith. I'd stop digging. I presume a smart lad like you is aware that lying to a police officer in the course of his duties isn't the cleverest of ideas?'

Harpenden didn't say anything, just licked his lips nervously.

'I mean, I can understand it – your wariness of the boys and girls in blue. After all that unpleasantness last year.'

Keith leaned in and lowered his voice. 'There's no need to go into that, is there?'

'You being accused of spiking a young lady's drink in a nightclub? All of that, you mean?'

Harpenden sat back and his face hardened. '"Accused" being the operative word.'

'Absolutely,' said Sturgess. 'I mean, I've seen the CCTV footage. Doesn't look great, does it? Pretty damning, really.'

'All a big misunderstanding.'

'Of course,' said Sturgess. 'I spoke to a member of the team that worked the case. Seems the victim rescinded her statement, albeit after your family hired an investigator to trash her personal reputation and then, if the rumours are to be believed, slipped her ten grand to disappear. I hear she's in Australia now.'

Harpenden stood up. 'Look, I didn't . . . And I was a very different person back then. I was going through a bad time. I made some poor decisions, but I've learned from them. If you must know, I've since committed myself to therapy, I'm in a healthy relationship now, and I've found our Lord and Saviour Jesus Christ.'

'Really?' said Sturgess. 'Congrats. I'll let the missing-persons team know – they'll be thrilled. Where was he in the end?'

'If you're just here to harass me,' he turned towards the door, 'then you can contact my lawyers.'

'Sit down.'

'What?'

'You heard me. Sit.'

'Why should I?'

'No reason at all,' said Sturgess. 'That girl at reception – Yvonne, is it? She seems very friendly. Chatty. She was awful keen to know why I was here. Bet she loves a bit of a gossip.'

'This is harassment,' said Harpenden in a very quiet voice.

Sturgess leaned forward. 'And how would you describe the mother of an attempted rape victim being sent naked pictures of her daughter?'

'I didn't—'

'I. Don't. Care. You sure didn't stop it happening, did you? Were you too busy talking to Jesus to notice what was being done to clear up your little mess? And yes, I know the Harpenden name. I'm sure Daddy plays golf with the chief inspector, but believe me when I say that shit is not going to work on me. Sit down, Keith, or the next time a woman within fifty miles thinks she might have been spiked, my friends on the local force will be coming to this office and asking to speak to you.'

Harpenden plonked himself back down in the chair. His shoulders slumped in misery, all his bravado gone. 'Have you never made a mistake, Inspector?'

'Plenty,' said Sturgess. 'Not like that, though. Lucky for you, I'm not here about that. The reason I'm here is that I'm heading up a murder investigation, and because you're the last person to have communicated with Phillip Butler, I've had to waste my time driving to bloody Leeds to talk to you. So, I strongly suggest you stop messing me about and you get a whole lot more helpful fast.'

'A murder investigation? I heard it was suicide?'

Damn it, Sturgess hadn't meant to let that slip. He ignored the question. 'How did you meet Phillip Butler?'

Harpenden held his head in his hands for a few seconds before running his fingers back through his flowing locks. 'All right, fine. It was a couple of years ago. We met at a PUA course.'

'A what?'

'Pick-up artist,' explained Harpenden, looking suitably embarrassed. 'Down in London. This guy teaches you how to, y'know, chat up women.'

'Given what's happened since then, I hope you got a refund. Anyway, that was the first time you met him?'

'Yes,' said Harpenden, sitting back and folding his arms. 'We were both Manchester-based and we hit it off, so, y'know, we decided to team up. It works better with a wingman.'

'Sure. And then you hung out a lot?'

'For a while. Then, when I had my bit of trouble, we sort of drifted apart.'

'Why so?'

Harpenden's eyes narrowed. 'Would you be going out much with that hanging over you?'

'Hard for me to say, seeing as I'd never do what you did.' Sturgess was aware that he was now throwing shots at someone who was cooperating, but he didn't care. He couldn't stop himself. The man made his skin crawl. 'But you kept in touch?'

'Yeah, a bit.'

Sturgess glanced up at the bird in the tree looking at the boat. 'Did Butler ever express an interest in changing his appearance?'

'Yeah, I guess. Got his teeth whitened. Talked about getting hair plugs at one point.'

'I see. Nothing more . . . radical?'

'Radical?' Harpenden looked genuinely confused. 'Like what?'

Sturgess shrugged. 'Did he talk much about his job at Fuzzy Britches?'

'A bit. Y'know, him working for a firm who did a dating app. It naturally came up.'

'How so?'

Harpenden shrugged. 'We were on it, that's all. Same as half the city. That and a few other ones too. You know, casting the net as wide as possible.'

'Right. Did he express any interest in the occult?'

'The what?'

'The occult. You know. Magic. Vampires, stuff like that.'

Harpenden actually laughed. 'No. Why would he care about that geeky crap? Women aren't into that stuff.'

'You'd be surprised. Did Butler have any other hobbies? Interests?'

'Like what?'

'Well,' said Sturgess, sitting back, 'presumably he didn't spend all of his time trawling for vulnerable women.'

'Look,' said Harpenden, 'I don't know. I think he played a bit of five-a-side, went to the gym. That's all I can remember.'

Sturgess recalled something Siobhan had said to him that morning. 'What about his book club?'

Harpenden snorted. 'Book club? Are you taking the piss?'

'No.'

'He used to do this whole bit about how books were shit. How they'd been superseded by cinema and TV. He didn't even read the book of *The Game*, and that's, like, the PUA bible. There's no way that guy would've joined a book club.'

'You'd be surprised. I just recently met a former spiker who suddenly found God.'

Harpenden glowered at Sturgess. 'Are we finished?'

'We're finished when I say we're finished. Apart from you, did he have any other wingmen?'

'Not that I know of. He kept ringing me every couple of weeks, asking me to head out with him.'

'But you didn't?'

'No,' said Harpenden. 'Like I said, I put all that behind me. It all feels a bit ridiculous now.'

'Right. What did the text say?'

'Honestly, it made no sense. Look.' Harpenden pulled his recently found phone out of his jacket pocket and unlocked it. He went to show Sturgess a text thread. Sturgess snatched the phone out of his hand.

'Hey!'

Sturgess ignored him and read out the last text from Phillip Butler. '"What is happening to me? Is this you?"' He looked up. 'What do you think he's talking about there?'

'I've no idea. Look. That's what I texted back.'

Sturgess nodded as he read the response confirming it. Then he started to scroll up.

'You can't do that!'

It was mostly texts from Butler that Harpenden hadn't

answered. The few replies there were clearly Harpenden trying to brush him off. 'Seems like you were giving him the cold shoulder.'

'Like I told you,' said Harpenden, grabbing the phone back. 'I've left that life behind. I'm back with Jinny now. Old girlfriend of mine and we're serious. I've turned my life around.'

'Isn't that wonderful? And you didn't even have to go to Australia to do it.'

Harpenden shoved the phone back into his pocket. 'Is that all, Inspector? I've got work to do.'

Sturgess flipped over to a blank page in his notebook and handed it and his pen to Harpenden. 'I want you to write down the names of the bars you and he frequented.'

'There's a lot of them.'

'Write fast, then.'

Harpenden started writing.

'And you're sure there's nobody else he was hanging around with?'

'I've already told you,' Harpenden said, 'back in the day, we were a duo. We didn't spend our time talking to men. That wasn't the point. I don't know since.'

After a minute, Harpenden pushed back the pad with a list of ten bars written on it. Sturgess read through it. Some of Manchester's most happening hot spots, in his limited knowledge as a non-drinking social hermit.

'Are we done?'

Sturgess nodded. 'For the moment. Little tip, though – if I ring you with any follow-up questions, you'd better pick up by the second ring or I'll be ringing someone else by the third.'

'All right. I will. Just don't . . .' He glanced in the direction of the reception desk outside.

'Don't worry about it,' said Sturgess. 'Go with God.'

Harpenden got up to leave.

'Wait a sec.'

He turned around, looking as if he might cry.

'Long shot, but I don't suppose you have any idea of the code for Butler's phone?'

Harpenden leaned against the door and pinched the bridge of his nose. 'I do, actually,' he said without looking up. 'Marilyn Monroe.'

Sturgess stared at him blankly. 'What?'

Harpenden met his gaze. 'Marilyn – Butts was obsessed with her. Said she was his perfect woman. Had her singing "Happy Birthday, Mr President" as his ringtone, for Christ's sake.'

'And?' said Sturgess, still not getting it.

'He might have changed it, but try her measurements. Thirty-five, twenty-two, thirty-five.'

Sturgess all but ran out the door, back to his car. He had the phone to his ear before he reached the vehicle, leaving a voicemail for Patel from Tech.

'Manesh, it's Sturgess. Ring me back ASAP, please. I've got the code for that phone.'

One in Your Eye

A Ms Philomena Dolan has been arrested in Blackpool for scattering her father's ashes on the beach. Local police inspector Arnold Waldrom said, 'We appreciate people want to respect the last wishes of a loved one, but it is not permissible to do so on a busy Saturday in June.'

Ms Dolan responded that she was only fulfilling the express instructions laid out in her father's will. 'Throughout his life, Dad had many enthusiasms: doing loud DIY early on a Sunday morning, learning the bagpipes despite not being Scottish, and cooking fish in the office microwave even though he was a vegetarian. In short, he lived to be annoying. I think the thought of his remains ending up in the eyes, swimming trunks and ice-creams of as many people as possible really tickled him.'

CHAPTER 32

It took Stella a while to find what she was looking for, because although she'd been living in Manchester for some time, she'd spent most of that time in a stuffy old church. She wasn't used to being out in the sunshine this long. In fact, she could feel a headache coming on. Great – now she was a vampire, too.

The dot on her phone was just around the corner. She'd been listening carefully at yesterday's meeting when Hannah had explained exactly where she'd found the *Nail in the Wall*. If Vera couldn't give her answers, perhaps this Cogs guy could? Plus, there was the added bonus that, apparently, he couldn't lie to her. Everyone else had.

She walked down a cobbled side street where large bins from one of the nearby apartment buildings were waiting to be collected, reeking under the hot sun. Stella held her breath and hurried past on the far side.

She made her way through a pedestrian walkway and came out with a canal to her right. A swan sat serenely in the water, watching the world go by with regal indifference. Stella passed under an archway and there it was, the *Nail in the Wall*. She would've known it from Hannah's description – not that it mattered, for it appeared she was expected. She tutted to herself and walked up onto the pedestrian bridge that lay beside it and grabbed the rope to which a bell was attached. Not that she needed to ring it.

Banecroft stood up unsteadily on the deck and raised a glass. 'Here she is – my protégée!'

Beside him, a man who Stella assumed was Cogs, dressed as he was in a leather waistcoat, ripped jeans and a bandana, stood up to cheer her arrival. As he did so, he promptly stumbled backwards and, with much flailing of his arms and shouting 'no, no, no', fell off the boat. The accident resulted in a bulldog collapsing into hysterics, which was in itself quite the sight to see.

The fallen man's head bobbed up above the water and he spat out a mouthful of canal. 'Help me up, you sods! I can't swim!'

Banecroft didn't move. 'Shouldn't you have thought of that before you fell in?'

Cogs suddenly stopped flapping his arms. 'Oh no.'

Looking back on this moment, Stella would find what happened next hard to explain. On a still canal, the water surged abruptly and a fully grown man was tossed violently back onto the boat. It was like watching a tape of someone falling in that had been reversed, only it happened before her eyes in real time. Banecroft stepped nimbly out of the way to avoid the sodden man as he came in for a messy landing.

'Bloody hell,' said Banecroft. 'You really do have quite the way with the ladies.'

'Shush,' said Cogs as he pulled himself up on unsteady feet. He bowed theatrically to the water. 'Thank you for the kindness, m'lady.' He wheeled around at the sound of the bell being rung loudly. 'Now what?'

Stella stopped the ringing. 'I have some questions.'

'No,' interjected Banecroft, 'she does not.'

'Yes, I do.'

'She's only come here to pick me up.' Banecroft hoisted a bargepole from the deck and pushed the boat towards the shore. 'Gentlemen, it has been an absolute delight, but sadly I must be going.'

Cogs tossed himself down on some sacking beside the bulldog and looked up at Banecroft, pointing an accusing finger at him. 'How's he still able to stand up? S'not possible.'

'Gentlemen,' repeated Banecroft with a jaunty salute as the boat bumped against the bank and he stepped ashore. 'It has been emotional. Thank you for the drink.'

'Likewise, Vinny,' shouted the dog.

'Yeah,' agreed Cogs. 'Good luck with the ghost and—'

He was interrupted by the dog barking loudly.

Cogs's face dropped. 'Sorry. Bloody truth thing. Still, at least I didn't mention the—' He interrupted himself by breaking into a song which appeared to be about a maid bringing an impractical amount of stuff home from a market.

Stella stood her ground on the bridge as Banecroft walked towards her.

'C'mon, protégée, back home we go.'

'I'm not going anywhere,' she said stubbornly. 'I have questions.'

'No,' said Banecroft, 'you don't.'

He put a hand out to guide her away.

'Don't you touch me.' Stella's hands were balled into fists. She was so far beyond sick of being treated like a child. She could feel the muscles at the back of her neck tighten and, somewhere within, she felt the thing she didn't understand stir.

Banecroft looked her directly in the eyes for a few seconds before lowering his voice. 'Take a deep breath and give me sixty seconds. If you still want to talk to them after what I have to say, then fine.'

Stella clenched and unclenched her hands before drawing a deep breath and nodding.

The pair stepped down off the bridge and Banecroft directed his young apprentice into the nearby archway. She leaned against the wall with her arms folded and wrinkled her nose as the pungent waft of strong booze emanating from Banecroft's person hit her.

'Right,' said Banecroft. 'What exactly are you hoping to achieve here?'

'The truth. I'm sick of everybody lying to me.'

'And what truth are you seeking?'

'Who I am, and why someone is trying to kidnap me – again!'

Banecroft nodded. 'So you know about—'

'Yeah.' Stella cut him off. 'Little tip – next time you and your partner-in-crime fancy having a secret chat, don't do it in a cellar you've just opened up a trapdoor to. Someone standing above you will hear the lot.'

'You were eavesdropping?'

'You're in no position to have a go at me about that.'

'I wasn't. I'm the editor of a newspaper. My entire existence is based on trying to find out things people don't want you to know. Your instincts are excellent.'

Stella went to say something but stopped herself. Banecroft had thrown her by doing the most un-Banecroft thing imaginable – paying someone a compliment.

'What exactly did you hear?'

'That some psycho nutjob has gone to great lengths to kidnap me.'

'Probably kidnap you,' corrected Banecroft. 'If you're going to be a journalist, you're going to have to learn not to treat your hypotheses as fact until you've proved them, otherwise you end up in a world of hurt.'

'When did I ever say I wanted to be a journalist?'

'Never, but I've watched you in meetings. You do.'

There were many infuriating things about Banecroft, not least was his propensity for being right.

'Stop changing the subject,' snapped Stella. 'I'm sick of it.'

'Again, what exactly are you sick of?'

'On one side, I've got you, Hannah, Grace – all lying to me. On the other is everybody else who seems to want to use me for whatever this bloody thing is I have, that I don't want and that I sure as hell never asked for. I'm so tired of feeling helpless. Some people in a weird house in the middle of nowhere raised me, I've been made to feel like I was an unwanted guest my whole life. I don't know who my parents are. I don't even know who I am. I escaped because I wanted answers and I never got any. All I am is a helpless pawn in other people's stupid game. Have you any idea how utterly exhausting it is to spend your life scared of this thing inside you that you can't control? I've had enough. I want answers.' She jabbed a finger in the direction of Cogs's houseboat. 'And that idiot might just have them.'

'So you're angry?' asked Banecroft with an infuriating smile that made her want to punch his teeth out.

'Yes.'

'Excellent.'

'What?'

He leaned against a bollard and started to pat the pockets of his jacket, looking for his cigarettes. 'It's about bloody time.'

'It is?' said Stella, struggling to follow where the conversation was heading.

'Oh yes. Because if you're angry, then at least you're not scared, and I was thoroughly bored of you being that.'

'I've never punched somebody in the head before, but I'm willing to give it a go.'

'I won't lie,' said Banecroft. 'I'm a lot of people's first.' He fished a cigarette out of the pack he'd just located and lit it in a practised motion, sucking in a deep drag before letting it out. 'Would you believe Cogs doesn't allow smoking on his boat? Not even because the thing is made of wood. Apparently, it's because the dog has given up recently.'

'You're doing it again.'

'What?'

'Going off on a tangent.'

'So I am. Again – good instincts. Where was I?'

'I'm angry.'

'You are,' said Banecroft. 'And if you've noticed, your thing hasn't happened. Looks like you're learning to control it. That's good. Test passed. I can't have one of my journalists flambéing a source – it'd be bad for business.'

'How am I a journalist?'

'Because I said you are. It is my role in life to decide such things, or did you think I was referring to you as my protégée just to annoy you?'

Stella folded her arms again. 'Actually, yes, I did. Almost everything you do seems to have the exclusive objective of annoying people.'

'Yes,' said Banecroft, checking his phone. 'That way, people aren't paying attention to what you're actually doing. It's a form of camouflage.'

'Right. So your swear board was part of some bigger plan, was it?'

Banecroft shrugged. 'No, not really. Having said that, have you noticed how nobody questioned my real motive for firing the builders? See? Camouflage.'

'And what are you trying to hide now?'

'Nothing,' said Banecroft, before tossing his cigarette to the ground and stubbing it out with his shoe. 'Here is the unvarnished truth: you, my dear, have been dealt a shitty hand in life – as you ably laid out. I understand your desire for answers pertaining to who and what you are. However, you have to be careful as to how you go about it. Vera, who you saw earlier today . . .' Banecroft noted Stella's reaction. 'Yes, she texted me. I had a long chat with her just after we rescued her. To be honest, I was surprised it took you this long to seek her out. As you now know, she has no idea who you are. Similarly, from what I could determine, neither does Cogs. Not that I asked directly. The reason I'm here is to prevent you from doing so.'

'But . . .'

'Because, my young apprentice, you should never tell a secret to a man who cannot help but tell the truth. It won't be a secret any more, will it?'

'Great,' said Stella. 'So nobody can give me answers?'

'Oh no,' said Banecroft. 'That's not the case at all. There's somebody out there who can help, and they are . . .' He clicked his fingers and pointed at Stella.

'Whoever forced a builder to put a trapdoor in our bathroom.'

Banecroft gave her a round of solo applause.

'And you think they're going to just tell us?'

'Quite possibly not, but I intend to try to ask. And even if they don't, there are other ways.'

'Such as?'

Stella drew back in surprise as Banecroft threw up his hands in frustration.

'Journalism!' he roared, causing a passing cyclist to wobble violently before regaining control. 'You, under my tutelage, are going to become a not terrible journalist or die trying, and along the way, while we are learning to navigate this bizarre shitshow of a world, we will make connections, develop sources, follow leads. All that good stuff, and at the end of it, good or bad, if you do what I tell you and don't screw up too much, then you will find out what you are and what the hell is going on.'

Stella turned and walked away a few steps.

'What in the blue blazes are you doing?' asked Banecroft.

'Thinking.'

Banecroft nodded approvingly. 'Good girl. I'm going to have another cigarette.'

Stella stood there, looking down at her Doc Martens and chewing at her thumbnail. After a minute, she turned back. 'I have conditions.'

'Excuse me?'

'If I'm going to do what you say – become a trainee or whatever – I have conditions.'

'It was a take-it-or-leave-it offer.'

'Bullshit,' said Stella. 'Nothing ever is.'

Banecroft barked a laugh. 'See? This is why you're my favourite.'

'What an honour,' said Stella, rolling her eyes.

'So we're done?'

'No. Conditions.'

He winked at her. 'Just checking.'

'No more lies.'

'Excuse me?'

'No more lies,' repeated Stella. 'You lie to me again and I'm done. Gone. Out of here. I'm sick of being kept in the dark.'

Banecroft considered this and then nodded. 'OK.'

'Right,' said Stella.

'In the spirit of the new-found honesty in our relationship,' said Banecroft, 'I should tell you that if I stop leaning on whatever it is I'm leaning on, I'm pretty sure I'm going to fall over. I've been drinking with those two idiots for several hours, and

I was quite drunk when I got here. I'm really, really good at holding it together up to a certain point, and that point was five seconds ago.'

Stella detected an increasing slur in his voice and noticed that he didn't seem entirely secure sitting on his bollard.

'This is another of your little jokes, right?'

'Nope,' he said, tossing back his head and shaking it with suddenly half-mast eyes. 'It's something to do with standing up and air or something. It's basic bio . . . Biolol . . . It's body stuff.'

'Wow, you weren't kidding.'

'Hey,' he said, drunkenly waving a hand at her. 'I just outdrank a doggie. That's pretty—' He hiccupped. 'That's pretty tricky. Seeing as we are developing that dynamic duo as sources, I feel it would be bad for the paper if they were to see me collapse on my arse.'

'It might make you seem more human?'

'I rely heavily on people not thinking that. Now, it's time for you to learn the first fundidy . . . fundoodle . . . fundamental lesson in journalism.'

'Which is?'

'How to carry your pissed editor back to the office.'

CHAPTER 33

Tamsin Baladin stepped into the lift and checked her outfit in the full-length mirror on the back wall as she did so. She nodded to herself then turned back to address Robert Finch, Fuzzy Britches' head of development who remained outside in the corridor. Finch was gifted with many things, but also cursed with a flaky scalp and a chronic perspiration problem, which Tamsin assumed were responsible for his notable lack of self-confidence. The result was a terribly slouched posture and an odd twitchiness to his mannerisms, like he was carrying the weight of the world on his shoulders, as opposed to snowdrifts of dandruff.

'I told you what I wanted to have done, Robert, and I expected it to be done.'

'But your brother said—'

'I don't care what he said. I only care what I said.'

Finch pulled a particularly unattractive grimace and shifted his weight from foot to foot. It gave him the air of someone who needed the bathroom.

Catherine, Tamsin's PA, blocked the lift doors from closing and held up a clipboard with unsigned documents attached to it.

'Damn. Yes, of course.' Tamsin took the proffered pen and

278

started to sign the paper while her head of development stood there, sweating.

'Robert, who do you think runs this company – me or my brother?'

'Both of you?' he offered.

She smiled without looking up. 'My advice is – go back to your office and think about the answer to that question because believe me, once you figure it out, your life will become a good deal easier.'

Tamsin handed the forms back to Catherine, who, in turn, handed them to one of her team of assistants. That short girl with the fringe who smiled too much.

'But—'

'We're late for the thing,' said Catherine as she joined Tamsin in the lift.

'But—' persisted Finch.

Catherine hit the button for the basement and Tamsin Baladin watched the door close on her head of development, who stood there with his mouth flapping open like a particularly indecisive recently washed-up fish.

After the doors had been closed for a second, Tamsin winced. 'I thought we were getting an engineer to lower the temperature in the poor sod's office?'

'We did.'

'And he's still that sweaty?'

Catherine laughed. 'I'm afraid so.'

'God. Just looking at him makes me want a wet wipe.'

Catherine pointed at the bag she was carrying.

'Figure of speech,' said Tamsin with a grin. 'Have we heard back from that guy yet?'

'No.'

'How is that possible?'

'I don't know,' said Catherine. 'I spoke to Toby and they're sending four people up, but he emphasized that the guy was rock solid.'

'Right up until he came to Manchester to handle a pretty straightforward task and disappeared.'

Catherine nodded. 'He wanted me to give you the guy's CV – ex-Mossad and so on. He's clearly worried about losing us as a contract.'

'And rightly so,' said Tamsin. 'So . . . can I come over later?'

The other woman paused. 'Sure,' she said after a beat. 'Of course.'

The doors opened to the basement floor, where Tamsin's chauffeur, Michael, was standing to attention beside the Bentley, his six-foot-five frame always seeming even larger beneath the low ceiling.

'This thing at the town hall,' Catherine briefed him, 'and then the Lowry for that dinner.'

Michael nodded as he opened the rear door and both women climbed in.

Tamsin checked her phone. 'I don't have to if you don't want me to.'

'No,' said Catherine, 'not a problem. Don't forget to ring Nelson.'

Tamsin jutted her chin to give the slightest confirmation as the unsaid was said again.

The car began to pull away and sunlight streamed into the basement as the metal roller shutters rose in one fluid motion.

Then, abruptly, the vehicle jerked to a halt.

'What in the—' started Tamsin.

'Sorry, Ms Baladin. Some joker's blocking the ramp. Stay inside.' Michael checked his jacket pocket before exiting the car nimbly. Driving was not his only skill.

Catherine leaned forward and peered through the windscreen. 'I think it's that policeman.'

Tamsin swore under her breath and opened the car door.

Michael was standing with one hand on the detective inspector's shoulder and the other inside his jacket.

'DI Sturgess,' said Tamsin. 'Is there a problem?'

'Not at all, Ms Baladin. I was just passing and now I'm explaining to your man here that placing his hands on people in general, and on members of the Greater Manchester Police in particular, isn't the smartest of ideas.'

'Thank you, Michael. The inspector is not a threat, I'm sure.'

'Oh, you never know,' said Sturgess with a smile.

Michael stepped back and, with a nod from Tamsin, got back behind the wheel of the Bentley.

'It's worked out well that I've met you entirely by accident,' said Sturgess. 'I've been leaving you messages all afternoon to contact me urgently.'

'Really? I'm sorry. I didn't get them. There must have been some breakdown in communication.'

'Clearly. Your assistant was under the impression you'd hopped in a helicopter and were in Paris.' Sturgess bent down and peered into the car. 'Oh, there she is.' He pointed at Tamsin and raised his voice for Catherine's benefit. 'Look, I found her.'

'I have somewhere to be,' said Tamsin.

'Of course. I actually just wanted to apologize.'

'Did you?'

'Yes. I'm incredibly sorry. You see, Phillip Butler's phone – sorry, I mean the phone owned by your company – inexplicably, it disappeared from evidence some time between last night and this afternoon.'

'That is unfortunate.'

'I know.'

'Well, these things happen.'

'Oh no,' said Sturgess. 'It's very nice of you to say that, but believe me, I'm outraged by this appalling breach. Evidence in a murder investigation has gone missing.'

'Murder?'

'Yes.'

'I wasn't informed of that.'

'Well, the victim wasn't anyone you knew and we in the police aren't really supposed to tell just anyone about these things.'

'That makes sense,' said Tamsin with a smile. 'Especially as it appears your security is so lax with regards to evidence.'

'Don't worry, Ms Baladin. Whatever it takes, I'll get to the bottom of the theft of that phone. You have my word.'

'I wait with bated breath.' She turned to the car, but paused before she got back in. 'In the meantime, I'd step out of the way if I were you. With the blinding sunlight, Michael might not see you. I'd hate for there to be an accident.'

'Of course. These things happen.'

Tamsin slid into the Bentley and pulled the door shut. After a moment, the Bentley ascended the ramp, passed the waving Sturgess and eased into the evening traffic. Only then did Tamsin speak.

'Change of plans. I'm going to go and see my brother.'

CHAPTER 34

Hannah sat in the booth at the Roxy and watched the crowd at the bar. The place was doing a roaring trade, to the point that the alley outside was reasonably busy and the bar area was rammed. It was rather surreal to observe the clientele on this particular evening, though. It was 9 p.m. on a Tuesday, the Roxy's 'vampire night', and it was pretty much how Reggie had described it.

Not everyone was in fancy dress, and a lot of those who were had gone for the basic cloak and false fangs that had been Hallowe'en costume staples for generations. There was also a lot of greased-back hair and hammy fake blood in evidence. One couple had come dressed as a crucifix and a bulb of garlic, which did at least show a welcome flash of originality. Most people clearly saw the whole thing as a bit of harmless fun. Still, amongst those individuals were the people who were taking it a lot more seriously. Chief among them was the crowd in the corner, where Victor Tombs was holding court.

Hannah and Reggie had been walking in when they saw Gregory Tombs dropping off his son. Gregory had stood beside the passenger door like a chauffeur, holding up a large golf umbrella in order to shield Victor from the fading rays of the evening sun.

Victor was as pale as you'd expect someone who had consciously decided to avoid sunlight would be. His outfit consisted of leather trousers, a white ruffled shirt and the kind of leather coat that would have caused him to pass out within twenty minutes if he'd gone for a stroll in the blistering heat of the afternoon. Even in the evening, Hannah didn't fancy it as the most practical of clothing choices.

Gregory Tombs had given her a nod, no doubt aware of how open to mockery he and his son were. Not that Hannah found it funny at all. There was something desperately sad about a man who was trapped in his own guilt and left with no choice but to service his son's peculiar life choices. As she sat there, thinking about the sanguinarian lifestyle as Gregory had described it to her, it turned her stomach. So no dinner for her, and she was also staying firmly away from the booze. The day had been a long inglorious slog thanks to her self-inflicted hangover. A Diet Coke now sat in front of her, slowly going flat.

Reggie was over at the bar, mingling and interviewing people. It was all being done under the cover of a puff piece on the enduring popularity of vampires. People seemed to grow particularly excited once Reggie started taking pictures. If nothing else, they might shift a few extra copies of the next edition to people wanting to see themselves immortalized in print. One of the first things Hannah had learned since joining the paper was that the world was full of people who either really did or really didn't want their picture to appear in any form of newspaper, even *The Stranger Times*. There was a power in that.

Despite the party atmosphere, the costumes – the whole thing, really – were making Hannah's skin crawl. Her mind kept flashing back to Georgina Grant, huddled in her apartment, terrified, with the balcony door barricaded. For more than one reason she was glad she wasn't assisting Reggie with his interviews.

One of those reasons walked through the door at that minute and grimaced as he took in the throng. DI Sturgess noticed Hannah sitting in the booth and headed in her direction, forcing a smile as a man in a cloak with a collar big enough to pick up Sky Sports jokingly lunged at him, arms raised and plastic fangs protruding. The fangs fell out and Sturgess accidentally kicked them under a table, much to the now-toothless lunger's consternation.

Sturgess slid into the booth opposite her.

'Wow,' said Hannah. 'You look as exhausted as I feel.'

He leaned back and stretched. 'Yeah, it's been a long day – chatting to sexual predators, having international corporations interfering with my investigation, not to mention the senior officers trying to do the same.'

He slumped over the table and placed his head on his forearm. 'To be honest with you, I spent most of the day not actually investigating, but rather trying to figure out why everyone else is so keen to stop me from doing so.'

Hannah wasn't really listening. She couldn't help it. She was staring, transfixed, at the top of Sturgess's head. It looked entirely, unnervingly normal. The idea that an eyeball on a stalk could pop out of it was absurd. She'd be inclined to believe she had imagined the whole thing, only Banecroft kept reminding her of it on a regular basis.

Sturgess looked up. 'Are you OK?'

'Yes,' she said quickly, averting her eyes. 'Absolutely. Yes. Sorry, I'm just a bit distracted by . . .' She waved a hand in the direction of the bar area.

'Yeah. Does rather make what we're trying to investigate seem insane, doesn't it?'

'I guess.' Hannah thought back to Georgina again, huddled in her armchair, the large knife at her feet. 'So, how should this information exchange work, then?'

'Normally, I'd never consider sharing information on an ongoing investigation with a member of the hateful and untrustworthy press.'

'Thanks.'

'But, seeing as I've got the grand total of me and one overworked DS on this, I'm willing to morally compromise myself.'

'Oh, goody,' said Hannah, then instantly regretted her words as she felt her cheeks redden. It had been quite a while since she'd flirted. It was like riding a bike, in that you probably shouldn't do it in public without practising first. 'So,' she continued, looking for a segue, 'you mentioned something about sex pests?' *Oh, excellent. Well done, Hannah.*

'Yes. Turns out the last person Mr Butler texted was a gentleman by the name of Keith Harpenden. I say gentleman, but that's probably the least appropriate word for the piece of—' Sturgess stopped himself, then noticed Hannah's confused expression. 'The bloke was caught red-handed spiking a woman's drink last year.'

'Oh.'

'Yeah. And he got off.'

'How?'

Sturgess sat back and briefly ran his teeth across his upper lip. 'He comes from money and the family pulled every dirty trick in the book to make the case go away. In fact, in the end, they made the victim flee the country. Very thorough. As it is, those kind of cases are notoriously difficult to prosecute. I spoke to the lead on the investigation. She was still livid.'

'That's awful.'

'Welcome to the joys of modern policing. Anyway, this guy and Butler were mates until recently. Well, technically, Butler was his wingman. They met on a pick-up artist course.'

'I've read about them,' said Hannah. 'They're these boot-camps where guys go to learn tricks to make women sleep with them, right?'

Sturgess grunted. 'Pretty much. So, I found out Butler was a sleazy creep, but nothing about the . . .' He waved his hand in the direction of his own mouth. 'Either Keith is a brilliant actor or he had no idea what I was asking about when I mentioned cosmetic changes. The aforementioned overworked detective sergeant spent her day chasing up every cosmetic surgeon and dentist within fifty miles of Manchester, and none of them knew a Phillip Butler. So we're still clueless on that score.'

Hannah nodded at the crowd behind him. 'Speaking of the cosmetic-surgery side of things . . . Most of this lot are obviously just wearing fancy dress for a laugh, but the group in the far corner are what I guess you could call the hardcore element.'

'Couple of leather coats, long hair. Four guys, two women,' said Sturgess without looking round.

Hannah wagged a finger in his direction. 'Very impressive.'

Sturgess shrugged. 'Observation is a big part of the job. That, and mountains of paperwork.'

'Well, you've got great eyes,' said Hannah, and then wished she could take it back. 'We tracked down Victor, the group leader – that's him in the leather coat, with the long black hair. We ended up talking to his father.'

'Really?' said Sturgess. 'Let me guess, Nosferatu over there still lives at home with Mummy and Daddy?'

Hannah hesitated. 'Just Daddy, actually. Look, the guy does live a pretty weird lifestyle, no question, but his dad is a former police officer. He explained it all to us.'

'His dad is former police? I might know him.'

Hannah shook her head. 'I doubt it. He was in Glasgow. I think they moved here for a clean break. Sounds like they had a bit of trouble up there. The dad, Gregory, was very nice. Devoted to the son. He also has no idea who Phillip Butler is.'

'So he says.'

'Well, OK,' said Hannah. 'I know we can't take that at face value, but . . .' She slipped out of her bag the folder Gregory had given her and placed it on the table.

'What's this?'

'Gregory's been keeping a close eye on Victor – I mean, a really close eye. In here is a list of Victor's known associates and, more importantly, a list of some people who maybe take the thing too far, or who he just thought were a bit off.'

'Interesting,' said Sturgess.

He went to take the folder but Hannah kept her hand on top of it.

'Just . . . Look, he gave us this. He wants to help and, more importantly, he wants to protect his son from any . . .'

Sturgess nodded. 'All I'm interested in is finding out what's going on here. If it doesn't involve Victor, or his dad, I promise I'll do everything possible to leave them out of it.'

'OK,' said Hannah, removing her hand from the folder.

Sturgess picked up the file and flicked through it quickly. 'Holy crap, you weren't kidding. This is some thorough work.'

'Gregory Tombs is a security consultant these days.'

'Judging by this,' said Sturgess, scanning the last few pages, 'I bet he doesn't come cheap. So, what else?'

'Excuse me,' said Hannah, with a smile. 'I thought this was an exchange of information. The emphasis being on "exchange".'

Sturgess held up his hands. 'Sorry, I'm used to being the one asking the questions, even if I don't get answers. Let's see – Butler was a creep, still no idea where he got the dental work done, and . . . Oh.' Sturgess's face dropped. 'To put it in news-paper terms for you, I think I've rather buried the lead here.' He looked around and lowered his voice. 'We identified the source of the blood in Phillip Butler's stomach . . .'

Hannah listened in silence as Sturgess gave her the details of how the body of Andre Alashev was found. When he was done, she took a sip of her drink.

'That's . . .'

'Yes,' said Sturgess. 'It is. What's worse, I can't get anyone on the GMP side of things to take it seriously. As far as my bosses are concerned, it's a murder–suicide that needs to be signed off and consigned to history. It's got the two biggest things they don't like – the weird element and the potential to annoy powerful people.'

'Who?' asked Hannah.

'Well, I'm not sure it relates to the case at all, but Phillip Butler's employers, Fuzzy Britches, went to great lengths to get his phone back.'

'Oh?'

'Yeah. It disappeared from evidence some time between last night and about three o'clock this afternoon.'

'Isn't that—' started Hannah.

'What?' said Sturgess. 'Highly illegal? Incredibly suspicious? Hopefully, quite hard to organize? Yes – all of the above. We hadn't even managed to get into it, although we were about to. It certainly seems like they're hiding something, and I doubt it's just their latest app for sharing cat videos. Maybe it's just good old-fashioned corporate paranoia, but it's pissed me off. Something I made clear to Ms Baladin, for all the good it'll do.'

'Look at you,' said Hannah, 'making enemies amongst the rich and famous!'

Sturgess gave a little smirk. 'To be honest, it probably wasn't my smartest idea, but I hate people with money buying their own form of justice.'

Hannah felt herself smiling at him. 'You might be the only honest cop left in this cockamamie town.'

'Cockamamie? Now there's a word you don't hear much.'

'I'm bringing it back – long overdue.'

'Agreed.'

'Actually, speaking of cops in this town,' said Hannah, wiping the smile off her face. 'There was an attack last night in one of the Skyline Central buildings.'

'What?'

'Yes. A lady called Georgina Grant awoke in the middle of the night to find a guy standing over her, with the teeth and all of that. She screamed and he ran off.'

'Why didn't she call the police?'

'She did,' said Hannah. 'A couple of officers came round, reckoned it wouldn't have been possible for a man to have got in. Dismissed the whole thing as a nightmare.'

Sturgess looked up at the ceiling and spoke through gritted teeth. 'You're kidding me!'

'I'm afraid not.'

'I left specific instructions with Control to let me know if anything unusual came through. I'd better go see this woman now.'

Hannah winced. 'Sorry, I'm afraid you can't. Her sister came to pick her up and take her back home to Bristol just as we were leaving. She was pretty shaken up and, to be honest, she was angry the police didn't believe her.'

'I can imagine. This whole thing feels like it's building to something, and I have a very bad feeling about what that is.'

On cue, something smashed behind them. They looked over to see two supposedly grown men in fancy dress having a fight. Neither man gave the impression of having much experience in the field of combat, given the tell-tale awkward hugging being employed as the primary mode of attack.

The crowd parted like the Red Sea as Ronnie – all five foot five of her – barrelled through. She separated the men by grabbing them both by the hair and yanking them in opposite directions. Her actions elicited a mix of howling, swearing and finger-pointing, none of which had any effect on her. She proceeded to march the two wannabe wrestlers towards the fire exit, which she kicked open before tossing them into the night.

'And don't come back, dipshits.'

As she turned round, she was greeted with enthusiastic ap-plause. She gave an embarrassed wave.

'Sorry about that, folks.'

As Ronnie wiped her hands on her jeans, trying to remove the residue of whatever the men had used to slick down their hair, she glanced in the direction of Hannah's booth and her face fell. She pointed at Sturgess.

'Oh God, would this be that policeman friend of yours?'

Sturgess held up his phone. 'Sorry, what was that? I've been staring intently at my phone for the last sixty seconds so I didn't see or hear anything.'

Ronnie smiled. 'You two have just earned yourself a randomly assigned free bottle of wine.'

'Are you trying to bribe a police officer?' asked Sturgess.

'I'm sorry. I was talking to the couple behind you.'

'Glad to hear it. I—' Sturgess was interrupted by his phone ringing as Ronnie moved off. 'Ah crap.' He glanced at Hannah. 'It's the chief inspector. I have to . . .'

Hannah nodded. 'Of course.'

Sturgess answered the call. 'Yes, guv.' He winced. 'Well, that's not . . . I appreciate that, ma'am, but they did interfere with . . . No, no evidence of that as such, but . . .' He pulled the phone away from his ear slightly as both the volume and the pitch of the voice on the other end of the line were raised significantly.

Hannah couldn't make out any words, but the harsh tone was clear enough.

'Yes, I'll be right there.' Sturgess hung up and puffed out his cheeks.

'That seemed to go well,' said Hannah.

'On the upside,' said Sturgess, 'I wasn't very popular with her before now. I'm afraid I have to go. She wants to shout at me in person for a bit.'

'You're rather making a habit of this storming-out thing.'

'Oh God,' said Sturgess. 'I really am, aren't I?'

Hannah smiled. 'No problem.'

As Sturgess got up to leave, Ronnie passed by in the opposite direction.

'Can I ask,' he said, 'do you get many fights like that?'

'Nah,' said Ronnie. 'That was nothing. This crowd is normally good as gold. It's just this heat – turns people into animals. You've no idea.'

CHAPTER 35

Hannah pulled Banecroft's Jag into the garage and turned off the ignition.

Tired didn't cover it. She was so far beyond tired. She'd been tired a few hours ago, then she'd met DI Sturgess and subsequently joined Reggie as he interviewed-slash-chatted with the vampire crowd. She hadn't felt like it, but she wasn't the kind of person who could leave somebody else working and just go home.

In fact, she'd dropped Reggie home and then remembered, with a horrible sinking feeling, that she'd only been loaned Banecroft's beloved car on the strict understanding that she would return it that evening. It was now midnight. The idea of parking it somewhere and driving it back the following morning was briefly considered and dismissed. Banecroft was a grandmaster at noticing the exact thing you hoped he wouldn't. She'd undoubtedly receive a phone call in the middle of the night demanding its return. Or worse, the true nightmare – it would be stolen.

In that situation, resigning from her position at *The Stranger Times* wouldn't be enough. Fleeing the country wouldn't help either. Hell, even death quite probably would not prevent Banecroft from venting his rage at her. The man lived in a near-perpetual state of fury, but she'd come to realize that, despite all the evidence, there were always further levels he could reach. She imagined the car going missing would result in peak Banecroft. Nobody needed that in their life – or their afterlife. So, she'd brought the car back.

Sitting in the garage, listening to the cooling engine tick, she briefly considered falling asleep in the front seat. After all, the car was technically back where it belonged, and, despite reeking of cigarette smoke, it was certainly comfortable. Her head dipped forward and she caught herself. No, come hell or high water, she was going home. She needed a change of clothes and a shower. She climbed out of the front seat, locked and doubled-checked the car doors and closed up the garage.

The city never really gets dark. True dark. Country dark. There's always light coming from somewhere – streetlights, nearby buildings, or just bouncing off the clouds. Hannah looked up. There were no clouds. Even here, despite the light pollution, she could see a sky littered with stars. She'd always enjoyed sitting quietly and gazing up into the night. The reminder that you were on a small speck of dirt at the edge of the galaxy, where massive astral bodies were mere twinkles in the distance, certainly had the effect of putting whatever problems you had into some much-needed perspective. The sun was millions of miles away from the Earth and still it managed to warm it – too much, if anything, given that the forecast was that the heatwave would continue until the middle of next week at least. In that context, relatively speaking, the walk back to her flat wasn't that far. First things first, though – she had to drop Banecroft's keys at the office.

Hannah walked around the side of the garage and stumbled

backwards, narrowly stopping herself from letting out a shriek. She stood there feeling ridiculous. A day spent chasing monsters on nowhere near enough sleep had left her drained and jittery. That was why she'd almost screamed at the shocking appearance of a Portaloo in front of her.

It hadn't been there when she'd left earlier that morning. Grace had clearly got it in and positioned it behind the garage to prevent passers-by from seeing what the paper had been reduced to. It made sense. Grace was a woman who was very concerned with appearances. No doubt if it were up to Banecroft, there'd be just a bucket in front of the main doors.

Hannah took a deep breath, shook her head and chuckled at her own jumpiness. She needed a good night's sleep in the worst way.

'Damn it.'

In fright, she'd dropped the bloody car keys. She played the light from her phone's torch across the ground to reclaim them. Once she had them in her hand again, she straightened up, took one step forward and yelped.

The figure was standing beside the Portaloo. A man in a green anorak. 'Man' might not have been the right word. A passing car's headlights reflected off something behind her and cast enough light to pick out his distinctive teeth.

Hannah was drawing in her breath to give her shocked yelp a much-needed upgrade to a full-throated scream of terror, but she stopped as the figure collapsed onto its knees.

'Please,' said a sibilant voice. 'You have to help me. Sanctuary. Sanctuary.'

★

Hannah stood in reception and shouted, 'Banecroft!'

Stella appeared in the doorway that led up to the steeple, rubbing her eyes. 'What is it?'

'Sorry,' said Hannah. 'There's a . . .'

The door to Banecroft's office flew open and the man himself stomped into the centre of the bullpen. Hannah tried hard to focus on his eyes as he was wearing only a pair of underpants and, surprisingly, a T-shirt that read 'Frankie Say Relax'.

'What in the hell is it?' he boomed. 'It's . . .' He looked around. 'What happened to the clock we used to have on the wall?'

Stella snorted. 'You hit it with a stapler last week – when you were making a point about the Oxford comma.'

Banecroft glared at her. 'It's an important grammatical issue.'

'Yeah, but most people manage to make that kind of point in a less violent manner.'

'You remembered it, though,' he said, displaying what in some cultures might be considered a smile.

Stella shrugged. 'I remember you hitting the clock. It was our longest-serving employee.'

'Will the both of you shut up,' snapped Hannah. 'This is important.'

'It'd better be,' said Banecroft. His eyes narrowed. 'This isn't one of those booty calls, is it?'

Stella made a gagging noise. 'Sorry. I just threw up a bit in my mouth.'

Hannah pointed back at the stairs. 'There is a vampire downstairs, asking for sanctuary.'

While her words did make Hannah feel slightly ridiculous, her statement did have the rare effect of making both Banecroft and Stella shut up – for a moment, at least.

Banecroft tilted his head. 'You told me they didn't exist?'

'That's what I was told. That's what Cogs told us. That's what that awful Dr Carter woman told us. That's even what Mrs Harnforth told us.'

'And now you're saying there's one downstairs?'

'Yes.'

'Have you been drinking again?'

'No.'

'That's the second most common answer given by people with a drink problem,' said Banecroft.

'Have *you* been drinking?'

'That's none of your business.'

'And now we know what the most common answer is,' quipped Stella, earning her a caustic look from Banecroft.

'For God's sake,' said Hannah, exasperated. 'Will you stop flapping your gums and come down and meet him?'

'Hang on,' said Banecroft as he marched back into his office.

A moment later he returned with his blunderbuss. He held out the weapon. 'For our protection.'

'Could you not have found some trousers to protect us from seeing this much of you?' asked Hannah.

'Oh, don't be such a prude. The human body is a beautiful thing.'

'Yeah,' said Stella, 'but yours looks like it got pulled out of the sea at low tide.'

Banecroft stopped and studied her warily. 'Have you been watching true-crime documentaries again?'

Stella shrugged. 'I sleep in a steeple and the wifi is rubbish. All I've got is Freeview.'

'Can we—' started Hannah.

'All right,' said Banecroft. 'I'm coming.' He checked his blunderbuss. 'Stella, stay here.'

'No, thanks.'

'That's an order. There might be danger—' Banecroft felt the hairs all over his body stand on end.

Stella's right hand was glowing blue. Her eyes narrowed and, when she spoke, it was still her voice, but different. As if it were coming from several places at once. 'I am the danger.'

Banecroft and Hannah exchanged a look.

Hannah spoke in a soft voice. 'When did you learn to do that?'

The glow disappeared and Stella shrugged. 'Like I said, I sleep in a steeple and the wifi is rubbish.'

'We do need to get the wifi sorted.'

'Yes,' said Banecroft, hoisting the blunderbuss over his shoulder. 'We shall engage some local tradespeople to come in and do the work for us. When has that ever gone badly?'

Before she'd rushed into the office, Hannah had told the man in the green anorak to stay exactly where he was. As she made her way back outside with Banecroft and Stella, she wasn't sure what she was hoping she'd find – that he was still there or that he'd be gone. Part of her would be happy to find out the whole thing had been the product of her overworked and overtired imagination.

She'd grabbed the powerful torch Grace kept under her desk. There'd been three power outages since Hannah had started working there, the electrics in the Church of Old Souls functioning about as well as everything else did. You quickly learned to regularly save whatever you were working on.

She turned the corner and there he still was, the thing of which nightmares are made, looking incongruous as he stood beside the Portaloo. He had lank black hair and his skin was pale with a waxy sheen to it. His mouth hung open and he subconsciously moved his lower jaw around, as if his body were still trying to come to terms with his recently altered teeth. It also meant his sharp incisors were there for all to see. Hannah also noticed scabs on and below his lower lip, seemingly the result of him not yet being entirely acquainted with his new dental arrangement. If anything, standing there in the bright beam of the torch, he looked more nervous than they did. A state of affairs that wasn't helped by Banecroft also pointing the blunderbuss at him.

'Hands in the air, and don't move.'

'Which is it?' asked the man.

'What?' barked Banecroft.

'I have to move to put my hands in the air.'

'Obviously, put your hands in the air, and then, don't move. There was an Oxford comma between the two actions, implying a list of events happening in sequence.' He glanced across at Stella, who was standing on the other side of Hannah. 'See? I told you it was important.'

Stella muttered something under her breath. Hannah didn't

catch it all, but heard enough to know that it was a very specific opinion as to where Banecroft could stick the Oxford comma.

The man raised his hands. 'I don't want any trouble.'

'Good,' said Banecroft. 'Because if you did, I should point out that I've loaded this blunderbuss with a wooden stake made out of a church pew, and I've slathered it in garlic.'

Hannah leaned forward to take a quick look into the barrel of the blunderbuss. He wasn't kidding. 'I thought you said you didn't believe in vampires?'

'Never mind that,' interrupted Stella. 'Is that where my garlic mayo from the fridge went?'

'Condiments are the first casualty of war.'

'I don't want any trouble, I promise,' repeated the man.

'Glad to hear it,' said Banecroft, 'because rest assured, Chekhov here doesn't play games.'

'Oh my God,' said Stella. 'Seriously? He's named his gun?'

'Will you two please shut up,' snapped Hannah. 'This is serious.'

Banecroft scoffed. 'Says the only person who came here unarmed.'

'I need your help.'

'Help?' echoed Banecroft.

'Yes. My name is Leon Gibson. A few days ago, I was an ordinary guy. I don't understand what's happening to me.' There was the edge of a whine to his voice. His eyes, glinting wet in the torchlight, flicked between the three of them. 'Please.'

'How did this happen?' asked Hannah.

'I don't know. Honestly. I just woke up on Sunday morning and well, this.' He waved his hands up and down indicating himself.

Banecroft clicked off the safety on the blunderbuss. 'What did I say about moving?'

'Sorry, sorry,' said Gibson, returning his hands to where they'd been. 'Please, I mean no harm. I just need help. I can't go to the police or to the hospitals. They'll lock me up as some kind of monster. I'm not a monster. Can you help me? I'm . . . I'm a subscriber – to the paper.'

'Always nice to meet a fan,' said Banecroft, noticeably refraining from lowering the newly christened Chekhov even one inch.

'How do you know Phillip Butler?' asked Hannah.

'Who?'

'He went through the same thing as you.'

'Really? It isn't just me?' The hope in Gibson's voice was unmistakable.

'But you don't know him? Phillip Butler?'

Gibson thought for a second then shook his head. 'The name doesn't ring any bells.'

'Last night,' said Hannah. 'It was you, wasn't it? In Georgina Grant's apartment?'

He hesitated. 'Is that . . .'

'Fourteenth floor of Skyline Central.'

Gibson let out a sigh. 'Yes, I . . . It was me. But I didn't do anything. You have to understand. The hunger – God, the hunger. It's horrible. I've been trying to fight it. I . . . I caught a rat and . . .'

Hannah tried to keep the revulsion from her face.

'But I didn't. It's like – it takes over. I've been fighting it.

When I realized where I was, what it wanted me to do, I ran. I ran away. I didn't . . .' He looked at Hannah. 'Oh no, I didn't, did I?'

Either Gibson was one hell of an actor or his terror was sincere. She took pity on him.

'No, you didn't. She was scared out of her wits, but otherwise unharmed.'

Gibson's frame sagged.

'And,' said Banecroft, 'to be clear – you have not attacked anyone else?'

'No,' said Gibson. 'I swear. I've been hiding out during the day at an old abandoned warehouse, and at night, I've been walking, trying to be anywhere people aren't. Trying to fight it. Then, I thought of you. I thought if anyone might know how to stop this, it's you.'

'I'm afraid we're not in the vampire-curing business,' said Banecroft. 'You need a doctor, or a shrink, or maybe just a *Buffy* marathon.'

'Please,' said Gibson. 'If I go to a hospital, you know what'll happen. I'll disappear. They'll take me away somewhere and do experiments on me. I've seen articles about it in your newspaper. Or I'll be treated like a freak. I just want my life back. I'm getting married next year. Julia's away on holiday – she's with her mum in America. She can't know about this.'

For a moment, silence fell upon the scene. Hannah looked at Banecroft's face. She could see calculations happening behind his eyes before he spoke again.

'Two days.'

'What?' said Gibson.

'Two days,' Banecroft repeated. 'We'll give it two days to try to figure out what's happened to you, and then we'll turn you over to the police.'

Gibson dropped his hands. 'Thank you.'

'But,' said Banecroft, 'if I find out that you've lied to us – that you've attacked someone else or that you're telling porky pies about anything – then believe you me, the police will be the least of your problems.'

'OK.'

'Also, while you're here, you'll be chained up – for everyone's protection.'

'Fine.'

'Right, then,' said Banecroft. 'I suppose we'll keep you in my office. As it happens, there's an extensive collection of chains and other such paraphernalia in the cupboard in the corner.'

'There's what?' asked Stella.

Banecroft shrugged. 'It appears Barry, my predecessor, had some interesting ways of coping with the stresses of the job.'

'Ugh,' said Hannah. 'That is disturbing.'

Banecroft looked at her and then gestured towards Gibson with the blunderbuss. 'Really? *That's* disturbing.'

'Fair point,' she conceded.

'Whatever we're going to do,' said Stella, 'can we do it before somebody notices us?'

'Good idea,' said Banecroft. 'Don't want people seeing the vampire we've just adopted.'

'Yeah, I kinda meant the man in his underpants wielding a loaded firearm, but whatever.'

Banecroft ignored the jibe and took a step back. 'Now, Mr Gibson.'

'Please, call me Leon.'

'Mr Gibson,' repeated Banecroft. 'I have a strict rule of keeping things formal with anyone I may have to shoot at a moment's notice. And believe me, I will shoot you if I have to. We're all going inside, and you're going to stay in front of me – where I can see you. Any sudden movements, any funny movements – in fact, any movement at all that I deem unnecessary for the purpose of traversing from point A, being here, to point B, being my office – then you're going to be a kebab with extra mayo. Clear?'

Gibson nodded.

'And off we go.'

They walked in silence towards the main entrance to the church. A man who had seen his world fall to pieces, Gibson looked quite pathetic as he cowered before them.

Hannah and Stella fell into step behind Banecroft, who was keeping Gibson firmly in his sights. Hannah had her doubts about whether Chekhov would work in the way Banecroft had explained, but more importantly, Leon Gibson didn't seem to doubt it.

She turned to Stella. 'We'll get it fixed.'

'What?' said Stella.

'The wifi. I'll get the wifi fixed. I promise. And I promise I'll keep this promise.'

Stella laughed. 'No offence, Hannah, but you are odd.'

They'd now reached the main doors. 'OK,' said Banecroft. 'We need to negotiate the stairs. Slowly does it.'

Gibson took one step forward and a low rumbling noise immediately came from inside the church.

'What is—' started Hannah, just as the doors opposite the vestibule that led into the printing room, which also doubled as Manny's living quarters, burst open.

Manny, entirely naked and seemingly asleep, came hurtling through the air towards them. The terrible angel suspended above him was very much awake. She extended from his body in smoky tendrils, her face a mask of rage. Everyone dived out of the way as she reared up just outside the front door, right at the boundary of the area she was allowed to inhabit.

She pointed at Leon Gibson, who was now trembling on the ground just out of her reach, and screeched in a voice that sounded like a thousand tortured souls screaming from a long way away. 'Abomination! Abomination!'

Below the hissing and snarling figure, Manny slept soundly, like a baby being carried in a papoose, exhausted from his big day out. His long dreadlocks trailed behind him, floating in the air.

Hannah noticed she was hugging Stella and quickly let her go. 'You OK?'

Stella nodded.

Banecroft got to his feet slowly. 'Right,' he said. 'It looks like the landlady isn't too keen on Mr Gibson moving in.'

Gibson lay there, shaking like a leaf as he gawped in awe at the apparition. It appeared he had bitten his lower lip in fright, as fresh blood was now trickling from the scabs below his mouth. He spoke in a terrified whisper. 'What is that?'

'Best not to ask,' said Banecroft. 'She doesn't seem to be a big fan of yours.'

'What are we going to do?' asked Hannah.

Banecroft looked down at Gibson. 'We're going to have to find an incredibly understanding Airbnb host.'

'Really?' said Stella.

'What?' asked Banecroft indignantly.

'I'm going to give you a minute – see if you can get there on your own.'

'What is that supposed to—' Banecroft clicked his fingers and pointed. 'Cellar. We have a cellar.'

Stella gave a sarcastic clap.

'Nobody likes a smart-arse.'

'You're living proof of that.'

They all looked back towards the doorway at a second noise, this time from a naked Rastafarian who was yawning loudly while stretching out his arms. As he opened his eyes, confusion spread across his face.

'What g'wan? Is we sleep-walking?'

Banecroft nodded. 'In a manner of speaking.'

CHAPTER 36

Ox awoke with a start. The stifling heat in the van, coupled with the stench and the awkward position into which he had contorted himself in order to sleep in the front seat, meant that waking up in the night was both a regular and unpleasant occurrence. That and the fact Stanley Roker was such a consistent and, frankly, unsettling sleep-talker.

It wasn't that the talking was the worst part. If you were in any doubt about how badly you'd messed up your life, a noseful of the peculiarly spicy and oppressive aroma of Stanley Roker's feet would give a clearer assessment than anyone could ask for. It was Ox's second night in the van, given how he'd not yet managed to come up with any ideas on how to deal with his Fenton brothers issue.

All of the above was why Ox hadn't experienced a decent night's sleep, but still, the jarring nature of the experience was only added to by a naked Stanley kicking the back of the seat in which Ox was trying to sleep.

'Wake up, wake up, wake up,' hollered Stanley.

'All right, I'm awake!'

The clock on the dash showed 2.34 a.m.

'The thing is going off,' said Stanley. 'Quick, quick!'

Ox looked at his phone. It was sitting on the dashboard, with the app for the tracking device open. Now that his seat wasn't being booted repeatedly he could hear the beeping that indicated Williams was on the move.

'OK, relax.'

'Relax?' squeaked Stanley. 'He's getting away!'

Ox pointed at the map where a flashing blue dot was showing them the current location of Darius Williams – or, to be more technically accurate, his SUV. 'And we can see where he is, so calm down. You'll do yourself a mischief.' He shifted across to the driver's seat.

'No way. You're not driving.'

'We need to get going,' said Ox as he started the engine. 'And you, Stanley, need to put on some form of clothing.'

After ten minutes, they'd managed to track the dot and get a visual confirmation that they were indeed following Williams's SUV. Stanley relaxed a little. He really did not trust technology at all. From there, they settled back into staying mostly out of sight. The traffic was light, which made the possibility of being spotted a lot higher than in the daytime. Eventually, Williams turned right on to a road that Ox recognized.

'That's Clifton Country Park down there. I know it. Used to go out with a guy who took his dog for walks there.'

'A guy?' asked Stanley.

Ox's eyes darted to the rearview mirror. 'Problem?'

'No, I just . . .'

'What?'

'Pay attention – he's stopped.'

Ox stared at the map. 'I think he's at the car park,' he said, and pulled the van over.

The road leading down to the park wound through a normal-looking middle-class suburb, and showed few signs of life at this hour of the morning. They watched in silence as the dot remained stationary for a couple of minutes.

'Looks like he's staying put,' said Stanley. 'C'mon, we'd better go down on foot.'

The streetlights threw amber pools of light onto the pavement to guide the way down the hill. Not that they were strictly needed – a cloudless sky above gave the full moon unfettered access to the world below. A black cat froze on the path in front of them, hissed, then ran off.

'What's Williams doing down there at this time of night?' asked Ox.

'Even odds – shagging. It's almost always shagging.'

'Maybe in your world, but this guy has a smoking-hot wife at home.'

'Shows what you know.'

Ox looked across at Stanley. 'Really? You honestly think a gay fella can't judge that? I'm gay, not blind.'

'You also have no idea how marriage works.'

'And you do? Isn't your missus divorcing you for cheating on her?'

Ox was surprised by the ferocity of Stanley's movements. Before he knew what was what, Stanley had him pinned up against a large tree, his hand tight around his throat, his hot breath on his face.

'Say that again, I dare you!'

Ox pushed him away. 'Get off me.'

After a few seconds of staring eye to eye, Stanley released him. Ox bent over, spat, and heaved in a breath now that his larynx was no longer being constricted.

'That's it,' gasped Ox. 'We're done. You're mental.'

'Good. I didn't ask to have some smart-arsed degenerate gambler slowing me down.'

'And believe me, I'm sick to death of having to hang around with a fat-arsed bottom-feeding tabloid scumbag who smells like a dump on fire.'

'Keep your voice down,' snapped Stanley. 'You're causing a scene.'

'*I'm* causing a scene?'

'Shut up and come on.'

The road turned back on itself before it passed under a railway bridge. Once they reached the entrance to the tunnel, Ox and Stanley crouched down and moved slowly through the darkness, pressing themselves against the cold stone wall. When they reached the end, Stanley took a first, and then a second, longer, surreptitious glance around the corner.

To the left of the road lay a small overflow car park where Williams's SUV was parked up and empty. A much larger main car park was further down on the right, behind a closed-off barrier to prevent entry. Appearing satisfied, Stanley straightened up and walked out into the open.

'Now what?' he asked.

'Well, I don't have your finely honed journalistic instincts,' hissed Ox, 'but why don't we follow that torch?'

He pointed towards a bank of trees in which a torchlight bobbed as whoever held it walked off into the woods.

'Smart-arse.'

Ox started to walk down the road. 'You've already said that, Stanley. Don't tell me you're running out of insults?'

'I wouldn't bet on it. But then, given your gambling skills, you probably would.' Stanley sneezed.

'Shush!'

Stanley threw his hands up in the air. 'What am I supposed to do? Allergies! I'm pretty sure I've mentioned them.'

The pair fell into a frosty silence as they followed the beam of Williams's torch along the path ahead, passing in and out of patches of moonlight determined by where the trees encroached on the path. They hunched low, trying to stay close enough to keep Williams in sight, but not so close that he'd realize they were following him if he were to turn around. Ox was also aware of Stanley's constant battle to prevent himself from sneezing. They needn't have worried. Williams walked on steadily, seemingly too lost in his own thoughts to even consider anyone might be behind him.

Ox remembered there was a lake in the centre of the park. Williams was heading away from that, though, and following a trail that led to an area Ox had never visited. At least, he didn't think he had. It all seemed very different at night. There was movement in the trees surrounding them. Noises. Things scurrying about.

While he had mocked Stanley, the truth was, he too was clueless when it came to nature. At least they were in Britain, so there wasn't anything out there that could kill them. Even as the thought passed through his mind, Ox corrected himself: the man they were following had built a trap to kidnap Stella, for God knows what reason. Somebody had forced or coerced him into doing that. Odds on, there definitely *were* things in this park that could kill them.

They continued to follow the torchlight in near silence as Williams meandered through the woods. At one point, Ox had to grab Stanley, who was so focused on not sneezing that he didn't realize that the path was crossing a stream. He missed the bridge and almost fell down the bank. Ox pulled him back, but not before Stanley's arse hit the ground with a pleasingly harsh-sounding *thunk*. Ox received no thanks for dragging him up. Instead, he listened to his companion swear behind him as they continued on.

'Can you keep it down, Stanley?' he whispered. 'I'm worried that you arguing with your bruised arse might disturb the wildlife.'

'It's not my arse I'm worried about, it's my bloody camera. As a professional, I know I need to actually get some evidence. Did you bring anything?'

'I've got enough of a job carrying you, Sneezy.'

'Yeah, that's what I thought.'

The path forked to the left and rose again. Ox stood in a pile of horse shit but managed to style it out without Stanley noticing. Why did dog owners have to pick up after their mutts but the horsey set couldn't scoop up after their trusty steeds? He knew now wasn't the time, but that had always bugged him. He'd heard it explained that horse shit was a great fertilizer for plants, but this path was made of stone.

'What's that smell?' hissed Stanley.

'Classism, I reckon.'

'What?'

The path curved back to the right, still ascending, before it turned sharply left and headed downwards again. From somewhere, Stanley could hear rushing water. Williams's light turned left and disappeared, so Stanley and Ox picked up the pace, afraid of losing sight of him.

Here, the trees crowded in from all sides. Ox jumped as something moved in the undergrowth, which earned him a tut. At the bottom of the slope, they reached a gate. To their right-hand side, down a steep bank, lay a wide river. To the left, more trees. Up the path in front of them, Ox could now see two lights. One was Williams's torch as it bobbed along the ground. Another seemed to be a small ball of orange light in a clearing at the side of the path. Whomever it belonged to was obscured by the trees.

Stanley grabbed Ox's T-shirt and spoke in an urgent whisper. 'Right, look where we are. Middle of bloody nowhere. If they spot us, we're screwed. Could end up floating down that river. You stay behind me and do exactly as I say. Clear?'

Ox nodded. His extremely uneasy feeling was making him a lot less inclined to argue.

'We get a picture of whoever he's meeting and we get out. Understood?'

Ox nodded again.

Stanley hunched low and slowly opened the gate just enough to allow them to slip through. Ahead, Williams's torchlight had disappeared, leaving just the soft orb casting light. As the path curved slightly they could make out two figures in black robes standing opposite Williams in the clearing. As Ox's eyes adjusted, he was able to make out more. The figures were two men – one black and one white. At least he thought so – the white one appeared to be wearing some kind of face paint.

In front of him, Stanley stopped about sixty feet from the clearing. Ox followed suit. The soft clicking of the camera, as Stanley started snapping pictures, was barely discernible. Williams was talking now, gesticulating with his arms, trying to make a point. Ox and Stanley were close enough to hear his voice but not to make out any of the words. The other men didn't seem to be saying much.

At that moment Williams dropped to the ground and started grabbing at his clothes while the unknown duo looked down impassively. He released an animalistic yowl of pain, unlike anything Ox had ever heard before, and ripped off his T-shirt.

'Jesus!' exclaimed Ox, unable to keep silent.

He could see Williams's skin was burning. Not from the outside – Williams wasn't on fire. A couple of his tattoos had somehow come alight and were glowing red, like the filament in the cigarette lighters you used to get in cars back when that was still a thing. He clawed at his skin and Ox fancied he caught a sickening whiff of burning flesh on the breeze.

'What the . . .' started Stanley. He was seemingly unable to find any other words but kept clicking away with his camera.

'We need to get out of here,' murmured Ox. He was feeling nauseous now, and his mouth was starting to fill with the warning wash of saliva that told him he was on the verge of throwing up.

'Just a sec.'

'Please!' The agony in Williams's scream tore through the calm night. Mad with pain, he struggled to his feet and ran blindly away. He staggered into the bushes to the right of the path, stumbled and disappeared from view.

Ox didn't want to watch but found himself unable to look away. Every fibre of his being was telling him to run. All he could see now was the vegetation shaking as the still-screaming Williams thrashed about. The scream contained no words, just the desperate howls of something in a world of pain that was beyond all words.

Thanks to the summer heat, the dry bushes and whatever else Williams came into contact with started to catch alight. He was far too gone to notice. He reared up briefly but lost his footing. Ox and Stanley moved around to keep him in view.

His skin now burning an impossibly bright red, Williams tumbled down the bank before landing on the rocks below. He screamed again and, as he stood up, his arm hung by his side at a sickening angle, in a way no human arm was supposed to. He lunged forward and hurled himself into the water. As the wretched man thrashed about, steam rose around him.

'What on earth?' said Stanley.

Ox found his voice. 'We need to go.'

The two men in robes had moved from the clearing and were looking down the slope impassively. Williams would have to fend for himself – Ox was getting the hell out of here.

'Come on,' he said, pulling at Stanley.

'Just a sec,' replied Stanley as he moved forward to try to get a slightly better shot of Williams flailing about in the waters below.

At that moment Stanley crossed some invisible line. Ox felt it. A tiny shockwave passing through the air. It was as if the air itself had tightened and snapped. Half a second later, a high-pitched whine ripped through the night. Ox looked up to see the orb of light, now glowing bright red, heading straight for them.

Stanley turned and sprinted past Ox, back the way they had come. He shouted something but the deafening whine meant Ox couldn't make it out. Not that he needed to. The message was blindingly obvious.

RUN.

CHAPTER 37

Stanley ran. He wasn't running to anywhere, just away. Away from whatever the hell those two men had just done to Darius Williams, who was last seen thrashing about in the river, his skin on fire. Stanley had zero idea where he was, having quickly lost his already tenuous grip on their location in the park. He was running up a hill, his feet digging into the peaty ground as brambles and branches grabbed at his legs. He was moving as fast as he could and yet it felt horrifyingly slow. Every few steps, his feet found another root or uneven bit of ground to stumble over. When he looked back briefly he could see two angry orbs of red light bobbing through the trees behind him. In the distance he also caught a flash of flames, presumably from where the inexplicably flammable Mr Williams had rolled through the tinder-dry undergrowth. Stanley also had no idea where Ox was. As far as he was concerned, it was every man for himself.

Stanley had been here before. Not here here, but this wasn't the first time he'd encountered this eldritch woo-woo nonsense. The last time it would have killed him had it not been for the unluckiest lucky turn of events in history, when his wife had barged in, twatted the thing that was about to do God knows what to him over the head with a statue of Buddha, and then stormed out again, having wrongly accused him of having an affair. His life had been both saved and ruined in the space of a couple of minutes – hell of a night. Now all he wanted was to get his Crystal back, and to do that he had to stay alive.

He'd been running for a couple of minutes, or so he thought. His lungs were heaving and his heart was pounding in his chest at a tempo speed-metal bands might consider a bit much. He'd heard that terror was supposed to give the human body incredible abilities. Mothers lifting cars off babies and all that. Stanley's body didn't seem to be affected in that way. His chest was screaming, his legs were weak and sweat was already pouring into his eyes, further limiting his vision. He'd spent the last few weeks sitting in a dessert bar eating his pain. Now his pain was getting its own back. Blurry amoebas of light appeared before his eyes. The only thing holding Stanley up was the certainty that if he fell down, he would never get up again.

He risked a glance over his shoulder and instantly regretted it. One of the orbs was gaining on him, and someone was coming through the trees, drawing ever closer. Either his mind was playing tricks on him or he could hear jaunty whistling.

He turned back around in time to see the ground fall away in front of him as he lost his balance. With a sickening jolt, he caught a glimpse of the jagged rocks some twenty feet below. While Stanley wasn't moving as fast as he'd hoped, he still had too much momentum to stop himself from tumbling into the gaping hollow.

He braced himself. While his body wasn't good for much, it

was well used to taking a kicking. Normally, it was from the irate subject of a story. In his lifetime, he'd received proper shoeings from a footballer; a supermodel; a couple of mates of a well-known cricketer; a very large Asian woman, whose identity to that day remained a complete mystery to him; a couple of members of a choir, of all things; an irate candidate for Mayor of Liverpool; and, most recently, three hipsters, one of whom had been wearing roller-skates. It wasn't an exhaustive list, but just thinking of it certainly made Stanley feel exhausted.

Somewhere during the course of his fall, gravity left the building. While the ground was no longer throwing lefts and rights of rock, compacted soil or jagged branches into his tumbling body, the complete and sudden absence of any contact with anything was very disconcerting. Free-falling meant there was just a bigger shot coming at the end. His eyes remained tightly closed. He kept one arm wrapped around his head, primarily covering his face, while the other hand cupped his nether regions. It was reflexive. Stanley didn't know if Mother Nature's choice in targeting soft spots was the same as everybody else's, but his instincts were hard won and hardwired.

After a couple of seconds, Stanley risked opening one of his eyes and immediately wished he hadn't. He had a very good view of the hollow into which he'd been falling, and that was because he was suspended above it in mid-air. His body spun around slightly to reveal to him one of the two men he'd seen from a distance back when Darius Williams had been combusting. The orange orb hanging over his head illuminated this man in black robes. Stanley noted the clothing because he'd been trained to do so, not because it was the man's most notable feature. No, the man's face was divided into four quadrants coloured red, green, blue and yellow. Closer now, it looked less like face paint and more as if it had been inked in by tattoo or something similar, although Stanley had never seen anything like it before.

The man spoke in a calm, joyful-sounding voice, devoid of any discernible accent.

'Hello, little birdie. Didn't anybody tell you it's rude to spy on people?'

Stanley wet his lips. He was afraid to speak, in case doing so might break the spell holding him aloft. 'I wasn't. I was just going for a walk.'

'In the middle of the night, little birdie? With a camera?' As the man spoke, Stanley's camera was pulled from around his neck. He tried to grab it but his arms were no longer under his control. Instead, he watched helplessly as it floated towards the man with the quartered face.

'I do nature photography. Badgers.'

'Is that so? I'm afraid you're out of luck. There are no badgers in this park.'

'Shows what you know. Loads of the buggers. You'd want to watch yourself.'

The man smiled. The teeth revealed by his grin looked incredibly white, possibly even more so because of the oddly coloured skin around them. He looked at the camera then touched it with a fingertip, causing it to burst into flame.

'Ahhhh, that was an expensive bit of kit.'

'Look at it this way,' the man said, his smile widening, 'if our conversation goes really well, perhaps you can claim it back from your employer. Who do you work for?'

'I'm an independent nature photographer, although I've had quite a bit published in *Hedgerow Monthly*.'

The quartered man moved his hands and Stanley felt his body straighten, his arms reaching out above his head. He looked up into the perfectly clear night sky, where uncaring stars twinkled down at him.

'How do you feel about pain?'

'I'm not a big fan.'

Stanley leaned his head back to look at the quartered man, who was now beaming an upside-down smile at him. The ball of red light moved up to float above Stanley.

'Then I'm afraid you and the readers of *Hedgerow Monthly* are in for a bad night.'

The man brought his hands together in a single clap then started to draw them apart. 'I've always wanted to try this.'

Stanley felt as if something had grabbed his hands and feet. Panic started to rise in his chest. 'What are you doing?'

'You know back in olden days, when they used to have people hung, drawn and quartered?'

The tension in Stanley's limbs ramped up several notches, as if each were being pulled in a different direction.

'Well, the good news is you're not going to be hung or drawn.'

'All right,' said Stanley. 'Stop. Please. Can't we talk about this?' In desperation, he considered his options – or, rather, he tried to think of even one.

'I've already told you what I want to talk about,' said the man, moving his hands slightly further apart. 'I'm not going to repeat myself.'

'Agh. All right. All right. *The Stranger Times*. I'm doing some work for *The Stranger Times*.'

'What kind of work?'

The pain increased. Every muscle in Stanley's body was screaming in agony. 'I told you. You're supposed to stop.' Tears were now streaming down his face. 'Supposed to stop.'

'Oh, I'm not going to stop.'

'Darius Williams. Follow. Williams.'

'Is that so?'

'Please!' Stanley screamed the word, looking back at his tormentor in desperation.

That was when he saw the flicker of movement.

Something large and heavy slammed into the back of the quartered man's head. He instantly crumpled forward and tumbled into the gully, to reveal Ox standing behind him, holding what looked like half a fence post.

In a moment of blessed relief, the pressure on Stanley's limbs eased. He leaned his head forward.

'Thank G—' The red light above him flickered and disappeared. 'Oh.'

Stanley didn't scream as he fell, his body apparently of the belief that this new development was, overall, probably still an improvement on his situation. As luck would have it, he partly landed on the unconscious form of his erstwhile tormentor. However, because Stanley was never truly lucky, there was also a loud cracking noise as his right leg crashed into a rock. On this occasion, he did scream.

In the darkness some scrabbling noises grew louder, and then a pair of hands was on him.

'Come on.' Ox was towering above him but his face grew pale as he looked down at the form of the quartered man. 'Is he still alive? I haven't killed him, have I?'

Stanley couldn't believe his ears. 'You're worried about him?'

'I'd rather not kill a man.'

Stanley looked down at the man's face, whose nose was a bloodied mess from colliding with something on the way down, or possibly from Stanley landing on top of him. In spite of the man's injuries, Stanley could make out faint signs of breathing. 'He's fine.'

'Quickly, then.' Ox tried to heave Stanley upright. 'Before he wakes up.'

Stanley yelped. 'My ankle. I've broken my bloody ankle.'

Ox repositioned himself under Stanley's right arm to hold him up. 'And if your screaming attracts laughing boy's mate, odds on he'll break way more than that.'

'Wait,' said Stanley. 'Just wait a second. I just need to . . .' He leaned over to his left while Ox strained to keep him upright, then unleashed a left jab into the quartered man's testicles.

'Feel better?'

'A little.'

Getting out of the gully was hard. Because the moonlight couldn't penetrate the canopy of trees, finding their way on to a path in near-total darkness was harder. Getting all the way back to the van, moving painfully slowly while expecting something awful to find them at any moment was the hardest part of all. Stanley's body kept trying to pass out, and he couldn't blame it.

Once they reached the overflow car park, Ox propped Stanley against the barrier and headed up the road to retrieve the van. Another hill would have been too much.

Stanley noticed that Darius Williams's SUV was no longer there. He didn't have the mental capacity to figure out what that meant.

He woke up to Ox slapping him across the face.

'What?'

'You passed out.'

Stanley was sprawled on the ground. With great effort, Ox heaved him upright once more and helped him into the passenger side of the van. Stanley was dimly aware of the other door slamming shut and the engine starting.

'Hey, stay awake,' said Ox, poking him. 'Don't go passing out on me again.'

Ox threw the van into a sharp U-turn. The jolting manoeuvre sent a surge of pain up Stanley's right leg. 'Christ! Go easy!'

'Sorry.'

It was all Stanley could do to hold on and brace himself to minimize any further agony as Ox threw the van recklessly around corners to get them away from the park. Only once they'd pulled out left onto the main road did the van slow to a calmer pace.

'OK,' said Ox. 'We need to get you to a hospital.'

'Why did you do that?' barked Stanley, surprised by the anger in his own voice.

'What?' asked Ox, taken aback.

'Why did you come back for me?'

'Because . . .' Ox was unable to put the blindly obvious into words.

Stanley slammed his palm down onto the dashboard. 'I didn't ask you to do that. I'm supposed to be making my karma better, not worse.'

The van veered slightly as Ox gawped at Stanley. 'What is wrong with you? I just saved your life, you ungrateful prick.'

'I didn't ask you to.'

Ox shook his head in disbelief. 'Unreal. Just unreal.'

CHAPTER 38

He stood on the very edge of the roof and drank in the city below. This was glorious. It stretched out before him, begging for his attention. He was something different now. Andrew Campbell was, to all intents and purposes, dead; he was Mr Red now. He had shed his old skin. He was evolving. In his heart of hearts, he'd always considered himself to be a predator, but now he was more. More than he had ever imagined. He had reached the apex.

In hindsight, perhaps he should have asked the hired goon that had knocked on his door some questions before feeding on him, but he'd been hungry and excited to try out his new powers. He knew enough. Someone didn't want him to play the game and so he was going to. That was why he'd waited. It was important to select just the right target. There were bonus points to be had. A celebrity – 100 points. Video evidence – 50 points. Plus, discretionary points were awarded for degree of overall difficulty.

He looked at his phone and noticed a new dot had appeared. He clicked on it.

Oh my. How delicious.

CHAPTER 39

The human mind, thought Hannah, was, in many ways, a wonderful and wondrous thing. Its basic functionality: reasoning, memory, the capacity to make cookie-dough ice-cream, the self-control to resist the temptation to consume cookie-dough ice-cream for every meal. All of that was very impressive, and that was before you took into consideration the great achievements accomplished by people using their minds, not to mention the weird stuff like how the mind can get damaged and somehow the person wakes up new and improved – speaking a language they didn't know or possessed of the sudden ability to play the piano or to read the entire terms and conditions that come with every Apple product without their head exploding.

So yes, in general, the human mind was awesome in the true meaning of the word. It was just that Hannah's was, at that particular moment, being a massive pain in the arse. She had been beyond exhausted two hours ago, before the admittedly massive dose of adrenalin that comes from a vampire, an actual teeth-and-all vampire, rocking up to your place of work and pleading for sanctuary.

Except for getting Leon Gibson's name, basic info and the

assurance that despite his physical appearance and the cravings he was experiencing he really didn't want to bite anyone, they hadn't managed to extract much in-depth information from him. Once Banecroft had decided that they weren't going to report Gibson to the police or try to drive a garlic-sauce-covered stake through his heart, the priority had become to secure him – for his own and everyone else's safety.

This endeavour had been complicated by the, well, whatever you could call the spirit that cohabited Manny's body, making it very clear that Gibson was definitely not welcome in the Church of Old Souls. They'd got around this by installing Gibson in the building's cellar, which recent evidence had proved the spirit could not enter. He'd been restrained using items from the box of bondage gear supposedly left in Banecroft's office by his predecessor. Hannah had been way too tired and freaked out to ask any questions, although she had fetched a pair of Marigolds from the office kitchen before touching any of it.

She'd felt awful watching as the whimpering Gibson, monitored by Banecroft and his blunderbuss, secured himself to a ten-foot-long chain attached to the cellar wall. She knew on some level he was a terrifying monstrosity, presumably capable of the same kind of atrocities as the late Phillip Butler – namely ripping out another man's throat. Still, in that moment, he was a pathetic, frightened man, bewildered by what his world had become and lacking any explanation for why it had happened to him.

So, after all that, Hannah had eventually treated herself to a taxi home. She'd staggered into her flat and barely managed to undress before she collapsed onto her bed some time after 1 a.m.

It was at that point that her mind, in direct contravention of every request from the rest of her body, had gone to work. What did all of this mean? Everyone – the Founders in the guise of Dr Carter, the Folk in the guise of the man to whom Banecroft had spoken, and Cogs, who was, well, Cogs, a man who could apparently speak only the truth – had assured them that vampires didn't exist. They were an allegory. Now two of them had turned up. Who was behind this and why? Should she tell DI Sturgess about this latest development? They'd promised Gibson not to go to the authorities yet, but . . . but what?

As if all of this wasn't enough, there was the stuff with the trapdoor and somebody trying to kidnap Stella. Could it be related? Hannah hadn't the foggiest. When she'd tried to bring it up with Banecroft earlier, he'd dismissed her concerns by saying that he and the 'special operations' team were handling it. She didn't know who that was supposed to involve, although Ox hadn't been seen for the last couple of days.

All of this was running around in her head. Perhaps she should have just come home earlier, without taking Banecroft's car back, and . . .

'Ah, damn it!' Hannah shouted up at her own ceiling. She'd dropped off the car but the bloody keys were still in her bag.

'Well, I'm not taking them in now. He can wait,' she muttered to the ceiling.

It said nothing back.

'He doesn't need his car now. It's, like, two in the morning. Even Banecroft must sleep some time.'

The ceiling continued to say nothing.

'I'm going to sleep.'

The ceiling's silence was starting to feel very judgemental.

'Oh, shut up,' said Hannah, clambering out of bed.

Then, because the human mind can be downright perverse – not in a Barry-the-former-editor way, although yes, also in that way – Hannah got dressed in her running gear. She'd run into the office, drop off the keys, and then run back home again. Both her body and mind would be rendered into a state of such total exhaustion that they would agree to enjoy the four or so hours' sleep that would be allowed to them.

It was only once she'd left her flat in the middle of the night, dressed for a jog, and passed a drunk bloke who'd blacked out with a traffic cone on his head, and a couple who appeared to be working hard on making themselves into a trio, that Hannah realized a lack of sleep meant that maybe she wasn't thinking clearly. Who the hell went for a jog in the middle of the night? Apparently, she did.

She made it to the office in just over twenty minutes, a personal best made possible by the fact that every time she tried to stop and walk for a bit, a drunk person appeared out of nowhere and wanted to chat. People really were friendlier up North, whether you wanted them to be or not. She let herself into the Church of Old Souls, glancing over at the cellar door before she did so. Everything seemed to be in order.

As she climbed the stairs, Hannah was surprised to hear voices. She reached the first floor, careful to avoid the fourth step from the top that still needed fixing, and realized the voices were coming from the bullpen, the door to which was slightly ajar. A shaft of light spilled out across the floor of the reception area and Hannah walked quietly towards the gap. She didn't know why she was sneaking – after all, she worked here, she was the assistant editor, in fact, and her desk was in there. Still, she tiptoed across the floor.

Placing her eye to the crack in the door, she saw Banecroft leaning against a desk on the far side of the room. Hannah carefully nudged the door open a tiny bit further. At first, she didn't understand what she was looking at. Then, as her exhausted mind caught up, she slapped her hand over her mouth to stop herself from yelping audibly.

She had only met him twice, and briefly at that, but she was certain of what she was looking at. Sitting at the spare desk near the window was Simon Brush, wannabe reporter for *The Stranger Times*, who never got to be one, given he was murdered a few months ago, during Hannah's first week on the job. She was looking at a dead man. Then she realized that technically, seeing as she could see the wall behind him, she was looking *through* a dead man. Also known as a ghost. Hannah rubbed her eyes.

Banecroft, who had been uncharacteristically if not unprecedentedly quiet, spoke again. 'As you can see, Stella put together a collection of all the stories we've done about vampires in the last ten years.'

'Yes,' replied Simon. 'She is very thorough.'

'Indeed. None of which explains the gentleman currently sitting in our cellar.'

Simon said nothing in response to this.

Banecroft shifted around slightly. 'So, I was wondering if we could talk some more about the other thing?'

Simon said nothing and Banecroft sat there, looking afraid to speak. Something about him looked so utterly different to the man she knew. Eventually, it dawned on her what it was. Doubt. Banecroft was many things but included in that multitude was a cast-iron certainty that he was right about essentially everything. The man she was looking at now didn't have that. He looked anxious – desperate, even. Somehow, it made him look so much smaller.

Luckily, Hannah still had her hand over her mouth, which was why she managed not to scream when somebody tapped her on the shoulder. She spun around to see Stella stepping back and holding her hands in the air.

Hannah slowly let out the breath she'd been holding and waited for her heart to locate itself in her chest once more. 'Bloody hell, Stella,' she whispered. 'You nearly scared the life out of me.'

'Sorry, but . . .'

Hannah felt suddenly awkward, realizing that she'd been caught eavesdropping. 'I was just . . .'

'Is he talking to Simon again?'

'Again?'

Stella dipped her head in the direction of her bedroom, indicating that they continue their conversation there. Hannah followed, being careful to walk quietly and say nothing until they were both inside, with the makeshift door pulled across. She looked around for seating options and decided on the crate in the corner – the only available seat that wasn't also a bed. They both spoke in a whisper.

'Is there a . . .'

'Ghost?' prompted Stella.

'Right. One of them, currently sitting in the office, talking to our boss?'

'Yes.'

Hannah shook her head. 'That's . . .'

'I mean, in case you haven't noticed, we sort of got attacked by a werewolf a while ago, not to mention a crazy wizard-type dude. I'm – well, who knows what I am, and, oh yeah, there's, like, a vampire in the cellar right now!'

'Well, when you put it like that . . .' Hannah shook her head again. 'How long has this been going on for, then?'

'I dunno. Weeks.'

'Why didn't you say something?'

'About our boss having late-night chats with a ghost?'

'Yes. That.'

Stella leaned back against the door. 'Because he didn't say anything.'

'But . . .'

'Do you know what he does? Simon sits there, reading whatever's on the desk, and Banecroft makes some painful small talk, then builds up to asking him about his dead wife.'

'Oh.'

'I don't . . .' began Stella. 'Look, I don't understand. She's dead, right?'

'That's what I've been told.'

'Banecroft keeps asking about her. Like, he thinks she isn't really gone. He said at one point that he knew she wasn't dead, despite what everyone told him. He gets himself worked up and then Simon disappears.'

'Oh,' said Hannah. 'That sounds . . .'

'Awful,' concluded Stella. 'I've stopped watching because it felt so intrusive.'

'What does Simon say?'

'Not much. Thing is,' said Stella, 'I know this is gonna sound stupid but, it's like Simon is one of those bots you get for customer support. He can only answer certain questions and say certain things, but Banecroft keeps trying to ask him something outside the programming.'

Hannah put her elbows on her knees and cupped her hands under her chin. 'Wow. That is bleak.'

'Yeah, I know. I mean, I know he's big bad Banecroft most of the time,' Stella cocked a thumb back in the direction of the office, 'but that version of Banecroft . . . Man, it's tragic.'

'And it's every night?'

'I don't know. Don't think so, but it's hard to say. Like I said, I listened a few times but after a while, it just felt like I was in someone's most private space, uninvited.'

Hannah nodded. 'I'll talk to him about it. Once we've . . . y'know . . .'

'Dealt with the vampire in the cellar and the nutters who tried to turn our shower into a kidnap trap?'

Hannah could feel herself redden. 'Oh, you know about that?'

'Yes,' said Stella, 'I do. You're not the only person who can investigate round here.' She waved away Hannah's apology before she could even start it. 'Forget it. I'm just saying, given all of the above, exactly how shocked can you be to find out ghosts exist?'

Hannah sighed. 'It has been a very long day.'

'Speaking of which . . .' Stella looked Hannah up and down. 'Did you just jog into work in the middle of the night?'

'Yes.'

Stella shook her head. 'Hard as this is to believe, I think you might still be the biggest weirdo in this building, and that really is saying something.'

Hannah smiled. 'Thanks.'

Bad Doggie

It has long been noted that most of the dead bodies found in the UK are located by dog walkers. However, researchers at Salford University looking into this phenomenon for the first time have unearthed some shocking results. According to chief counter-upper Rachel Reeker, 'We were shocked to discover that canines are responsible for 90 per cent of body finds. We were particularly alarmed to realize that one particular dog – a Labrador called Bobo – has apparently been behind eighteen finds in the last four years alone. Now, maybe he's just a dog with a very good sense of smell, or maybe he has a terrible secret. Either way, we'd just like to talk to him to find out.'

Bobo's location is currently unknown. His last owner mysteriously died when the brakes on his car failed while taking his cat to the vet.

CHAPTER 40

Natasha Ellis slammed shut the door of her hotel room. Immediately, she pulled off her high heels with one hand, and held her phone to her ear with the other.

'Come on, come on, come on, come on! Pick up!'

After the sixth ring, it answered. Jared sounded as if he'd just woken up. 'Natasha, babes, is everything all right?'

'All right?' sniped Natasha. 'All right? No, everything is not all right. That event was a total disaster!'

Jared sighed. 'OK, sorry to hear that. Can we talk about this in the morning?'

Natasha heard a female voice in the background, no doubt Jared's bitch of a wife. Always acted so damn snooty towards her.

'No, we cannot. When you became my manager, you said it would be a twenty-four-seven full-service gig. It sure don't feel like that.'

Somewhere else in the background, a baby started crying. 'I will do everything I can for you, Natasha. You know that. There's just nothing I can do at . . .'

The wife snapped something and a door slammed.

'. . . what I'm reliably informed is three in the morning.'

'Are you laughing at me, Jared? Am I a joke to you?'

'No, Natasha, no. I just . . . OK, what was the problem?'

'What was the problem? The same as last time, Jared – you had me booked for an event with a bunch of Z-list nobodies! How do you think that makes me look? I have a brand to maintain here.'

'Wait, hang on – what's-his-name was there, wasn't he?'

'No, he wasn't. How the hell does somebody open a nightclub in Manchester and not get a Premiership footballer? Half the population of this town must be footballers – it's all they've bloody got to do up here.'

'Ah, Natasha – tell me you didn't say that. We can't afford another Newcastle.'

'No, I didn't say anything, and even if I did, there was nobody there to hear it. I didn't see any press. Just as well, too – they had me judging a best pecs competition. And then I had this sleazy DJ creep trying to get me to make out with the winner. I mean, Jesus.'

'Right,' said Jared. 'That should not have happened. I will get on to the promoter first thing and rip him a new one.'

'Promoter? That guy? Coked out of his mind. Three times he introduced me to some Trisha woman who does the weather. The weather! Talk about a ridiculous job.'

'Trisha Banks – I think she's a trained meteorologist.'

'So? What do I care?' Natasha was shouting again. 'I came third on *Love Mountain*! Do you know how hard that is? There's, like, eighty million people in this country, and only one came third. That's literally impossible.'

'I mean . . . three people have managed it since, but—'

'So you *are* taking the piss out of me.'

'No, Natasha, but it's three in the morning. Can we discuss this tomorrow? By which I mean later today.'

'I want a car. In the morning, I want a car to pick me up.'

Jared exhaled loudly. 'We discussed this – you have a train ticket. You're, like, five minutes' walk from the train station – just get on the train. It's even an open ticket. Get on any train you like.'

'The train is for losers. I have four million Instagram followers. I can't be seen with losers.'

'It's first class, sweetheart. It's a much higher class of loser. You might meet an MP.'

Natasha threw herself on the bed. 'Do you know how many other managers I could've had before I gave you a chance?'

'Two.'

'What?'

'Sorry, that's how many you did have before me.'

'Screw you, Jared. That's it – you're fired.'

'OK.'

'You're not taking me seriously, are you?'

'No, Natasha, I am. Just like I took you seriously when you fired me twice last week.'

'Do you know what you'd be without me, Jared?'

'Asleep.'

'Nothing! You'd be nothing! I am a beloved national fucking treasure.'

'Oh for . . .' Jared's voice changed suddenly. 'No, you aren't. That's it. I can't handle this any more. You take up half my time and you make me bugger all money. I manage people who are only

famous for being famous, and even amidst that group of delu-
sional half-wits you are absolutely the worst. You made my PA
cry last week – a job that, incidentally, if you hadn't managed to
hook up with two other fame-hungry fucknuggets in the same
night on national TV, you wouldn't be qualified for. We're done.
I don't give a shit any more. You and your horrible attitude can
go make somebody else miserable.'

'What?' Natasha sat up. 'Jared, we're just talking here. Two
mates, messing around.'

'No, Natasha. We're done. People don't ring up their mates
and give them dog's abuse at three in the morning. You chase me
constantly, begging me to get you work – like it's my fault you've
crippled yourself by buying a house you can't afford. Then I get
you whatever I can find, and all you do is bitch and moan about
it. You're a reality star that people vaguely remember, not Princess Diana. Wind your neck in.'

'I'm . . . I'm . . .'

'Now, until your next manager gets you the L'Oréal ads or the
gig presenting the MTV Awards or, I dunno, the job reading the
Six O'Clock News that you so clearly reckon you deserve, you've
got that Insta promo to do before you go to bed or that'll be no
money either. Get the script right, do not improvise, just get it
done. I'm hanging up now.'

'Jared?'

The line went dead.

'Jared? Jared?'

Natasha hurled the phone across the room, where it thumped
into the wall.

A voice from the room next door shouted back angrily, 'Keep it down! Some of us are trying to get to sleep!'

'SCREW YOU!'

Natasha ran her hands through her hair. 'This is bullshit. I don't need that loser.'

Ten minutes later, she dragged herself up off the bed. She tried to ring Jared again but it went straight to voicemail. He'd call back and apologize in the morning – 'course he would. He had to. They needed each other. Maybe she shouldn't have rung him at 3 a.m., though? No. Screw it. She had to work at this time. Anyway, Beyoncé's manager picked up the phone whenever she rang. In fact, he probably stood outside her door at all times, just in case something came up. Tomorrow Natasha would check who it was, see if they wanted to have a meeting. Discuss her options.

She went and turned down the air-con as low as it would go, for all the good it did. That was the thing with bloody England – it didn't get enough hot weather to have any idea what to do with it. When she'd spent that week in LA, everything had been cool. They'd had air-con outside. Britain could learn a lot.

She looked at her phone. Christ – she still had that damn promo to do. She sat down at the desk and started fixing her make-up. Two years ago, there'd been someone to do that for her too. There was no question – Natasha Ellis needed a reboot. There was no point getting back together with Marcus or Kai – she'd tried both of those avenues and the media interest had been weak at best. They'd then pitched that reality show where all three of them ran a hotel in Blackpool, but Channel 5 had passed.

She needed something radical. She could go lesbian, maybe? Had anyone done that? That could work. Everybody loves a lesbian. She might get some work on the Pride circuit again too. It'd been long enough that they must have forgotten that joke by now. Bloody gays – so sensitive! The annoying thing was she didn't even understand what was homophobic about it. In all honesty, she'd just been repeating what she'd heard from that Sammy guy, but she couldn't say that. 'Please don't blame me, I was only repeating something I heard from my dealer.'

Right. She would do this one drop, get to bed and figure out her next move over breakfast. Jared would be sorry. She was going to get back on top. Natasha Ellis was a fighter, an entertainer and, possibly, a lesbian, once she'd checked a few things.

She looked herself up and down in the mirror and nodded. *Looking good, girl.* She fished the script out of her suitcase and started to read through it. Whoever wrote this stuff at the agency always made her sound like a total airhead. She reached for her phone to ring Jared to complain about it, and then thought better of it. Just get it done. She reread it. Screw it – as long as she said, 'These Renaldy eyelashes are amazing – they stay on as long as you do,' then that's all they'll care about.

She pulled out her kit – telescopic phone stand, halo light, additional highlighter. This gear was the best money she'd ever spent. One of the lighting crew on *Love Mountain* had shown her how to make even live videos pop – invaluable when you're somewhere like a hotel room. And the telescopic stand made it look as if someone else were holding the phone, so you didn't look like you were alone.

She took the empty champagne bottle and ice bucket she always brought with her out of her suitcase and set it up in the background. Then she took the bottle and filled it most of the way up with water from the bathroom tap. It needed to look open but full – party girl, not alcoholic.

She jumped as the curtain twitched.

'Holy shit!' She moved across the room and looked behind the fabric. The door to the balcony was slightly ajar. Down below, the city was still looking pretty lively. She stepped outside and peered over the railing. 'What a shit hole! SHIT HOLE!'

She felt better after that, and stepped back inside and closed the door behind her.

'Shut up!' the voice from the next room was yelling. 'I've got work in the morning!'

'Right,' she said out loud, oblivious to the complaint. 'Got to make sure the voice is in working order. Red lorry. Yellow lorry. Red lorry. Yellow lorry. Red lorry. Yellow lorry.' She didn't really know what that did but some actor had said it when they'd both appeared on that panel show.

She went back to the desk and sat down. All things considered, the image on the phone was pretty good. The wallpaper was hideous but there was nothing she could do about that.

Something moved behind her.

Her eyes darted to the mirror, but there was nothing there.

'Jeez, I am jumpy tonight. Must be that fake-assed champers they were feeding us. Bunch of cheap losers.'

She gave the phone one last check. Big smile – teeth were good. Make-up good. OK.

She hit the button and the countdown to the live stream appeared on the screen.

Three . . . two . . . one . . . live!

'Hey, party people, your girl Natasha here, coming to you from Manchester! OMG, I've just been out' – she caught herself – 'at an incredible club opening.' She wasn't giving those a-holes a free promo. 'And wow, what a night. They really know how to have a good time up here. So many hot guys' – wait a sec – 'and girls. Some real foxes . . .' Never too early to lay some breadcrumbs for the reboot. 'Those Manchester ladies have it going on.' Time for the money shot. 'And I'll tell you what, girls . . .' Lean in, show those eyes really popping. 'These Renaldy eyelashes are amazing—'

On the phone display, a figure in a red hoodie appeared and disappeared in an instant, sweeping Natasha out of shot and leaving the viewers looking at some not terribly nice wallpaper and a champagne bottle full of water sitting in a bucket.

Off camera there came a blood-curdling scream.

'Right, that's it,' the voice from the next room hollered. 'I'm calling the front desk. You're in trouble now!'

CHAPTER 41

DI Sturgess stood out on the balcony and took a few calming breaths. In the hotel room behind him, the body of Natasha Ellis was a bloody mess on the floor. One of the forensics had commented in hushed tones that he'd never seen anything like it. Sturgess had looked at the man's colleague and not said a word. He knew for a fact she had – he recognized her as having worked the scene at the body of Andre Alashev, the night watchman whose corpse they'd discovered two days ago. This whole thing was a nightmare.

It could be an actual nightmare. Certainly, it had started in the middle of the night. Sturgess took a second to enjoy the thought that perhaps this wasn't really happening and it was all just playing out in his mind. Maybe he'd eaten too much cheese? Maybe he hadn't been woken by a panicked call from Control informing him that a woman had been attacked by a 'thing', live on social media? He felt his phone buzz in his pocket again but ignored it. It confirmed this was real. Even in his nightmares, his phone didn't go off this much.

The hotel – in fact, every hotel in Manchester – had started receiving panicked calls asking whether Natasha Ellis was staying there. A poor night porter had gone to check her room, having also received a noise complaint, and found the body. He was downstairs right now, being assessed by a paramedic to ascertain whether he needed hospitalizing for shock or just a really stiff drink. Sturgess didn't blame him for being freaked out. As a copper, he'd seen a lot in the line of duty, but this was stomach-turning. It looked more like an animal attack than something one human being could have done to another.

As far as Sturgess understood – as he maintained a wilful ignorance of these things – Natasha Ellis had been live-streaming across several social media platforms when she'd been attacked. He'd mistakenly thought that the timing meant that it wouldn't get too much attention, which showed exactly how little he knew. It might have been 3.30 a.m. in Manchester but it was 7.30 p.m. in LA. The clip had gone viral and been splashed all over some entertainment websites straight away, the kind unconcerned with confirming sources. India, meanwhile, had woken up to it. The protocols in place to remove sensitive material from social media and so on had kicked in but, as the liaison with whom he'd spoken had informed him, unofficially, the horse had already bolted.

The initial response was many people believing that the whole thing was a hoax, a big publicity stunt designed to rejuvenate a flagging career. As soon as Sturgess had seen the footage, he'd known it had been otherwise. As well as the live recording, some stills from the stream had gone everywhere. You couldn't clearly make out the attacker's face under the red hood, but the teeth – or, to be more exact, the fangs – had been remarkably visible. Within thirty-five minutes of receiving the call, Sturgess had been standing over the body of Natasha Ellis, who looked set to achieve a much higher level of fame in death than she'd ever managed in life.

He had two detectives going through the hotel's CCTV footage, but the night porter swore that the last guest to come in had been Natasha Ellis and she'd been alone. Since then, the doors had been locked – the hotel was particularly hot on security after a spate of recent rather embarrassing break-ins to guests' rooms. New cameras had been installed on every door and in every corridor. Nobody was seen going into Natasha Ellis's room after she'd entered. That meant they'd either somehow got in there hours before and waited for her, or they'd got in from the balcony. From his current position, Sturgess looked up, down and across. They were nine storeys up and none of the neighbouring balconies were particularly close.

He'd just got off the phone with the chief inspector, who was demanding to know how the hell this could have happened. Several hours ago Sturgess had received an in-person bollocking from her about the importance of not pissing off prominent members of the business community, and his failure to recognize that his investigation was not the most important thing on the planet. Now, all of seven hours later, he was hanging up the phone having being bollocked by the same woman for not making the same investigation a high enough priority. The one he was being expected to conduct with just himself and one overworked detective sergeant. Of course, the murder of Natasha Ellis wasn't his case at all, technically, but even the CI lacked the will to pretend that perhaps this was a coincidence.

The bodies weren't identical in their injuries. Alashev's had been considerably less messed up than poor Natasha Ellis's. Her attack looked like it had involved much more of a frenzy. While they were referring to it as a body, in truth it was no such thing. What they had were remains. The poor girl had been ripped limb from limb. Blood spatter was on every surface of the room, including the ceiling.

Given what had followed on from the Alashev attack, it was pretty clear that Phillip Butler had been horrified by what he'd done and had chosen to take his own life. Ellis's attacker, on the other hand, looked alarmingly like someone who enjoyed their work. Greater Manchester Police had already put the call out for a man in a red hooded top, but Sturgess didn't hold out much hope on that front. Then there was the element that nobody had dared to speak aloud: no ordinary human had the strength to do this.

Sturgess was roused from his thoughts by the sound of a throat being cleared behind him. He turned around to see DS Wilkerson looking about as cheerful as he felt.

'One second.' Sturgess fished a walkie-talkie out of his pocket. 'Sturgess for Steen.'

'Yes, guv?' came the answer.

'Danny, I can see press milling about down there. Can you tell the uniforms to only let in people if they can show a keycard and verify they're on the register? And nobody, and I mean nobody, leaves until we clear them.'

'Understood.'

Sturgess shoved the walkie-talkie back into his pocket. 'So?'

'We've completed the check on all the rooms, guv. All guests present and accounted for.'

'Anything suspicious?'

'Well,' said Wilkerson, 'there was one unusual one.'

'Unusual how?'

'We knocked on a door on the third floor. Noise inside, no answer. Had to get the manager to open it. Bloke inside wearing a rubber suit – tied to the bed and covered in custard.'

'You're kidding?'

Wilkerson shook her head. 'Guy explained. He has a "friend" . . .'

'Hooker?'

'Hooker,' confirmed Wilkerson, 'who ties him up, leaves him there all night and then comes back and lets him out in the morning.'

'Right.'

'Look on the bright side. That's one guy we can take off the suspect list.'

Sturgess nodded. 'That's something, I guess.'

'So what's our next move, guv?'

'DI Clarke will be here within the hour to relieve me. You'll report to him. I've been taken off the case.'

Sturgess was slightly heartened to see Wilkerson's look of genuine outrage. 'That's bullshit. How are they justifying that?'

He shrugged. 'The usual. Listen, there was a report filed night before last by a woman staying at Skyline Central. Says she woke up to find a man with those "teeth" in her room. I only found out about it last night.'

'What? How did we not know this before now?'

'A couple of uniforms responded and told her she must have been dreaming.'

Wilkerson threw up her hands. 'Unbelievable!'

'I know, but now you're going to need to chase her up. I believe she's gone home – to Bristol, I think it was. I asked for you to be sent the details.'

'How did you hear about it?'

'My friends in the press.'

'Do you mean the—'

'I do. Best not to mention the source to Clarke, though.'

' 'Course not.'

'I'll brief him, but you know what he's like.'

'A pig-headed, cloth-eared, close-minded, tit-ogling, stink-breathing, stat-chasing disgrace to the force.'

Sturgess smiled. 'That is way too specific for you to have come up with just now.'

'Unofficially, myself and a couple of the other female detectives might've had a little competition. Mandy won as she set hers to the tune of one of the songs from *Hamilton*.'

'The woman has skills.'

'Yeah.' Wilkerson paused for a second. 'Seriously, though, guv – we need you on this. Whatever it is, it sure as hell isn't anything we've seen before. Isn't there anyone you could talk to?'

The phone in Sturgess's pocket buzzed again. His mysterious benefactor, Concerned Citizen, was losing their mind. If anything, they were even more pissed than the chief had been.

Sturgess decided to ignore the message. He wasn't beholden to them, whatever they thought.

'Nope,' said Sturgess. 'Look, Clarke might be a windbag, but he'll follow procedure with all this heat on it, and they'll be throwing resources at it. Just keep your head down and do the job.'

Wilkerson glanced over her shoulder at where the forensics team were still hard at work. 'I wish I shared your confidence. I don't think procedures were designed with this in mind. I mean . . .' She lowered her voice. 'The state of the body. I know we're supposed to be all rational about this, guv, but honestly, maybe it's time to consider that this is what it actually looks like? Maybe we should start saying the V-word? I mean, I don't know – perhaps all these stories come from somewhere.' She shuffled her feet. 'Sorry. Ignore me. I've not had much sleep.'

Sturgess tried to stretch out his back. 'Between you and me, I rang Dr Mason. Got him out of bed and asked him to go and confirm that Butler's body is still in the morgue.'

Wilkerson raised her eyebrows.

'It is, but I swear to God, part of me wanted to ask if two armed officers could accompany him when he checked. I know that sounds crazy but, well . . .' He nodded towards the room.

'How the hell is this going to end?'

Sturgess turned back around and looked down at the crowd that was already gathering outside the hotel's front entrance. 'Badly.'

CHAPTER 42

Ox finished speaking and, for a moment, the entire room fell silent. Then Hannah yawned.

'Really?' said Ox. 'I explain how the man we were following unspontaneously combusted and then two wizard monks, or whatever they were, chased us through the woods at night, almost killing him' – he jabbed a finger towards Stanley Roker, who was currently sitting on two chairs, one of which was supporting his right foot clad in a surgical boot – 'and you yawn? Which bit did you get bored at?'

'Sorry, sorry, sorry,' said Hannah. 'I've had about zero sleep.'

'She's hungover,' said Banecroft.

'I am not.'

'You were hungover yesterday.'

'That was an entirely different day.'

'Ah, but you said you've not been to sleep, which means it's still technically the same day.'

'For the love of all that is holy, will the both of you shut up,' said Grace. 'I have a question.'

'Is it . . .' began Stella, with a pointed nod in Stanley's direction, 'how come the new guy has ice-cream and nobody else does?'

Stanley had limped in on crutches, with Ox trailing behind him, carrying a tray loaded with six tubs of ice-cream. Stanley had proceeded to sit through the update on the vampire story, including the revelation that there was now one chained up in the basement, as well as Stella's update regarding the earlier reports of the attack on Natasha Ellis, which had prompted the emergency meeting, and then Ox's recap of his traumatic night, while steadily making his way through tub after tub of ice-cream. He'd barely even looked up as Banecroft had explained to him that if he felt tempted to run to any newspapers with the vampire story, he would break Stanley's other ankle. Hannah didn't have a lot of experience of office environments, but she was fairly sure that most of them weren't quite so blasé about senior management issuing threats of physical violence.

'It's nine in the morning, child,' said Grace, giving Stella a stern look. 'You don't have ice-cream for breakfast.'

'Ah, but according to him,' said Stella, pointing at Banecroft, 'it's actually still yesterday, so this would qualify as an evening snack.'

'I didn't say it was still yesterday for you,' said Banecroft.

'Even if it was,' interjected Grace, 'you shouldn't be eating ice-cream late at night either.' She turned her disapproving gaze – the one where she threw in that lemon-sucking face that Hannah dreaded seeing – upon Stanley.

Hannah reckoned Grace had been holding back, as Stanley was a visitor, but now her patience had run out. Aside from anything else, Hannah knew that Grace also had quite the sweet tooth.

To his credit, the target of her gaze seemed utterly unfazed by it.

'I broke my ankle for you lot,' said Stanley, without looking up from running his plastic spoon round the bottom of tub number four. 'I'll eat ice-cream wherever I like.'

'We need to get this meeting back on track,' said Reggie. 'Although I have to say that going forward, the rule should really be: if you're bringing ice-cream, you should bring enough for everybody.'

'He did,' said Stella.

'If,' bellowed Banecroft, 'you're all quite finished. I don't know if anyone has noticed we have rather a big issue?'

'The thing in the cellar,' said Hannah.

'These nutter monks,' said Ox.

'I'm out of action for six weeks,' said Stanley. 'Who is compensating me for that?'

'Impending type two diabetes for some of us,' said Stella.

'No,' said Banecroft. 'None of the above. What does the sign outside say?'

Reggie sighed. 'This is no longer a church. Please go bother God somewhere else.'

'Not that bit,' said Banecroft. 'The bit above that bit.'

The room remained silent.

'I'm not going to continue until somebody says it. I went out and changed it weeks ago expressly for this purpose.'

Grace sighed. 'The Stranger Times Newspaper.'

'Bingo!' exclaimed Banecroft. 'Give the lady her prize. Newspaper. We have an edition coming out on Friday and, seeing as you've all been having a whale of a time gallivanting about, we're tragically short on articles.'

'That's your top priority?' asked Reggie, which earned him a withering look.

'No,' said Banecroft, 'that is my *only* priority. Luckily, seeing as the existing investigative journalism team has dropped the ball quite so spectacularly . . .'

'That is unbelievably harsh,' said Ox.

'I mean, really,' agreed Reggie.

'. . . I have added an additional journalist to the team.'

All eyes turned to Stanley, who was digging into tub number five with no noticeable fall-off in enthusiasm. 'I've not said I'm joining.'

'Not you,' said Banecroft. 'Stella.'

Stella looked taken aback as everyone turned in her direction. 'Hello.'

Grace stood up.

'There's no need to . . .'

Whatever else Stella had planned for the rest of her sentence was lost as Grace swept her into a bear hug and muffled her words with her bosom.

'I'm so proud of you!'

Everyone else echoed the sentiment, although not as emphatically.

'We don't have time for workplace bonding,' said Banecroft.

'Shut up, you silly man,' said Grace.

'Seriously, Grace,' said Hannah, 'I think Stella might be running out of oxygen.'

'Oh right,' said Grace, releasing her.

Stella made a show of gasping for air theatrically. 'So . . . much . . . bosom!'

'Oh hush, you!'

Once Grace had sat down again, still beaming, Ox stood up, snatched the remaining tub of ice-cream from Stanley's grip and handed it to Stella.

'Here, I got you this.'

'What the hell?' asked Stanley, not a hint of levity in his voice.

'Oh, be quiet. I saved your ungrateful life last night.'

'And when we stopped off at the shop, I told you that you could get a tub for yourself if you wanted one.'

'After spending the last two days in your company, I doubt I'll ever eat ice-cream again.'

Banecroft kicked over a wastepaper basket. 'With Grace's big friend in the sky as my witness, if you don't all quit with the sickening bonhomie, I'm going to become testy. Stella – double page spread on vampires, the history of false claims, scares, yada, yada, yada. On my desk by four p.m.'

'Yes, boss,' said Stella, failing to suppress a smile.

'Stanley . . .'

'I'm not writing anything until—'

'One-page anonymous description of your, let's call it "experience" with the, whatever the hell it was that your wife caught you diablo in flagrante with. If that thing is out there, maybe one of the loons will be able to identify it.'

Stanley nodded reluctantly. 'I can do that.'

'I have no doubt,' said Banecroft. 'Now, these homicidal monks and combustible tattoos that Sundance over there described – I assume you got pictures of them?'

'I did, but then the monk torched my camera.' Stanley held up his hand to stall Banecroft's response. 'However, I do have pictures of Williams's tattoos that I took a couple of days ago – when he was working on one of the sites.' He looked at Ox pointedly as he said it. 'They're up in the cloud.'

'Fine,' said Banecroft begrudgingly. 'Hopefully that'll be enough. How many quarter-faced men can there be, after all?'

'There are plenty of two-faced ones,' muttered Hannah.

'Oh God, the jilted housewife is about to kick off.' Banecroft rolled his eyes, then nodded at Stanley and Ox. 'You two are coming with me, see if we can't get some answers about what happened last night.' He nodded in turn at Reggie and Hannah. 'You two, get down to that hotel and pump your police sources for information. Do whatever it takes.'

'What it takes,' said Hannah, 'is asking politely.'

'Is that what they're calling it now? OK,' said Banecroft, clapping his hands together. 'It's going to be a busy day. Try to screw up as little as possible.'

'Inspiring as always,' said Reggie.

Grace's hand shot up. 'Excuse me?'

'Why are you raising your hand?' asked Ox.

'Shut up,' said Banecroft. 'I like it. New rule – everyone has to raise their hand from now on. Yes, Grace?'

'As I said about ten minutes ago, I have a question: what about the man downstairs?'

'I thought you were much more into the man upstairs?'

'As always, your hilarity is matched only by your personal hygiene.'

'There's no need to be personal,' said Banecroft, kicking off a Mexican wave of eyebrow-raises around the room.

'The man downstairs – in the cellar,' repeated Grace.

'What about him?'

'Does he have food? Water?' She wrinkled her nose. 'A bucket?'

Banecroft arched his eyebrows, inadvertently completing the wave. 'Interesting. Yesterday we didn't know vampires existed, now we're wondering how they take a—'

'My point is,' interrupted Grace, 'we can't just leave him tied up down there. We have a duty of care. Otherwise it is not Christian.'

'Well,' said Banecroft, 'unless there's some mention of vampires in the Bible that I missed, neither is he.'

'But—'

'All right, all right. Fine. Take some money from petty cash, go down to the butcher's, get some very bloody steak and, I don't know, figure it out. I assume we have a bucket somewhere?'

'Manny will have one,' said Ox.

'Best not to bother him,' said Hannah.

There had been an uncharacteristic amount of loud stomping and banging from Manny's room downstairs. Nobody had gone to check, but Hannah had a strong feeling that his other half remained extremely unhappy about their guest in the basement. The sounds were those of a man having an argument with himself.

'Fine. Go buy a bucket too. Let's just hope he doesn't need it until you get back.'

'They normally sleep in coffins,' said Ox, 'which aren't typically en suite.'

'Never seen one take a dump in a movie,' mused Stanley.

'Well, no,' said Reggie, 'but you don't see that happening in many movies, vampire or otherwise, do you? Dame Judi Dench has established the most magnificently diverse oeuvre of work in her illustrious career, and at no point in it has there even been the implication of a visit to the water closet.'

'Funny you should say that,' said Stanley. 'Got a bit of hot goss on that very subject.'

'Which you will not be sharing,' said Banecroft, clapping his hands. 'C'mon, everybody – move, move, move! I've had more than enough of this paranormal crap.'

As they stood, the sound of a throat being pointedly cleared drew everyone's attention to the doorway, where Dr Carter was standing, looking less than happy.

'Buggeration,' said Banecroft. 'Apparently not.'

CHAPTER 43

Hannah showed Dr Carter into Banecroft's office then went and stood in her by now established spot beside the window. She had now met the woman a sum total of four times, so it wasn't like she knew her well, but still, it didn't take much to see that she was flustered. The normally immaculate Dr Carter was sporting a coffee stain on the skirt of her business suit and was wearing only one earring.

A small part of Hannah felt very unkind for enjoying the sight ever so slightly. Another part reminded the first part that the woman in question represented a group of individuals that were as close to evil as you were likely to find. *Yes*, said the first bit, *but we've all spilled a bit of coffee. There's no call to be mean.*

Dr Carter took a seat and looked Hannah up and down. 'Is that appalling smell coming from you?'

I take it back, said the admonishing part of Hannah's brain. *Nail the cow.*

'No, it isn't, but you have—' started Hannah, before being tragically interrupted by Banecroft slamming the door on his way through it. He wasn't particularly angry, it was just his chosen way to close any door.

'I do wish you'd ring before turning up,' he barked. 'That way I could make sure not to be here.'

'At least if you were out, I'd think you might actually be doing something.'

Banecroft slumped into his chair.

'What the hell is going on?' snapped Dr Carter.

Banecroft scratched his head with one hand while he rummaged round the desk with the other, trying to find his cigarettes. 'Lots of things are going on – could you narrow down your area of interest a little?'

'You know what I mean. I get woken up in the middle of the night to find out some "thing" has attacked and killed a woman in central Manchester and the entire planet is somehow interested in it. I told you to keep a lid on this story.'

Banecroft's head snapped up and he spat out the cigarette he'd just placed in his mouth. 'Excuse me? That is not what we agreed. I'm not here to "keep a lid" on anything. I said we would look into the matter of Phillip Butler's death, and that is precisely what we have been doing.'

'And have you made much progress in that area?'

'Enquiries are proceeding.'

Hannah tried to focus on one of the many stains on the carpet – the large alarmingly red one. She did not have the world's greatest poker face and she guessed Banecroft was about to be rather economical with the truth.

'Proceeding?' scoffed Dr Carter. 'How comforting.' She leaned forward. 'The people I represent are very upset.'

'The people you represent are very upsetting.'

Carter sneered. 'Glib, as always. Have you forgotten the rest of our arrangement? Because I haven't. You screw me on this and believe me, we will be taking an interest in your little friend.'

'Don't you dare come into my office and threaten me.'

'I'd do it elsewhere but you never seem to leave, and seriously, what on earth is that smell?'

Hannah nodded at the blunderbuss propped up in the corner. 'Garlic sauce left out in a hot room.'

Carter glanced at the weapon and then back at Banecroft. She dipped her head in Hannah's direction. 'Your cleaner isn't doing a very good job.'

Right, thought Hannah. *That is it. Any minute now . . .*

'Well,' said Banecroft, 'when your upset and upsetting bosses fire you, let me know if you want the gig.'

Dr Carter got to her feet abruptly. 'Trust me, sweetie, you would not like me when I'm angry.'

'I don't like you now.'

She lowered her voice. 'Is there anything you would like to tell me before I leave?'

'Yes,' said Banecroft. 'You're missing an earring and there's a coffee stain on your skirt.'

Damn it, thought Hannah.

Carter snatched her handbag up off the floor. 'You have until the end of the day.'

'Or what?'

For a moment Carter looked as if she were about to say something, but then she headed for the door.

'The end of the day,' she repeated. 'And get an air freshener!'

The long-suffering door slammed again.

Banecroft retrieved his cigarette and lit it. 'Is it me, or did she seem a little tense?'

'Do you think she's serious?' asked Hannah.

Banecroft blew a smoke ring towards the ceiling. 'Pah. If you're not being threatened, you're not doing the job properly.'

'In which case, we seem to be nailing it.'

Banecroft scratched at something enthusiastically. Thankfully, Hannah's view of it was obscured by the table.

'On the upside,' he said, 'we've got something she hasn't.'

'The stench of rancid garlic mayonnaise that we will never get rid of?'

'I meant the other thing.'

Banecroft tossed the last of his cigarette into a mug where it sizzled and died. 'Come on, it's time we interviewed our vampire.'

He grabbed the blunderbuss from its spot in the corner.

'Can't forget Mr Chekhov,' said Hannah. 'I was worried my nausea might clear.'

'That's probably the result of your drinking problem.'

'Oh, do shut up.'

CHAPTER 44

As the cellar doors opened, a whimper issued from inside.

'Close it, please. Please!'

The voice was a croaky, lisping thing. Banecroft turned on the light and closed the door behind them.

Hannah paused for a moment to give her eyes time to adjust to the dank room after the glorious sunshine outside. The pathetic creature that was now Leon Gibson gradually came into focus, cowering in the corner. Either he'd deteriorated considerably overnight or the light of a new day just made him appear all the more dreadful. His head poked out from the anorak pulled tightly around him. His skin was pallid and glistened with sweat. His eyes were wide, bloodshot discs, and his bottom lip had scabbed over again from where the new and unwelcome overdeveloped incisors had bitten through. Hannah was not a fan of vampire movies but even she knew that these creatures of the night were supposed to be rather suave and dangerously sexy individuals. Gibson was none of that. He looked more like a victim than any great alpha predator.

Beside her, Banecroft pointed the blunderbuss in Gibson's direction.

'Is that really necessary?' asked Hannah.

'I'm hoping we don't have to find out.'

She raised her voice. 'Leon, are you OK?'

'Cold. Hungry.'

'Right,' said Hannah. 'Well, we're trying to sort you out something to eat, and I think I saw a couple of blankets over here.' She crossed the room to where a couple of dust sheets were covering something. She pulled them off. 'Oh, for God's sake.'

'What?' asked Banecroft.

'Nothing, just . . .' Hannah surveyed the towers of tins stacked before her. 'Yet more inexplicable Spam.'

She edged towards Gibson to give him the sheets.

'Don't get too close,' warned Banecroft, which earned him a scowl from Hannah.

Still, she did find herself stopping about seven feet short and tossing the sheets in Gibson's direction. He snatched at them and pulled them around himself.

'Is that any better?'

'I . . .' Gibson licked his lips. 'Thank you for helping me.'

'That's OK,' said Hannah.

He looked from her to Banecroft and back again. 'Why is this happening to me?'

'We were rather hoping you could help us with that,' said Banecroft.

'How would I know?'

'Well, did you notice anything unusual before it happened?'

Gibson shook his head.

'Had you met anyone unusual? Eaten or drunk anything unusual?'

Gibson shook his head again. 'Nothing. I started feeling weird on Friday night, I think, and . . . I woke up like this on Sunday morning and – what day is it now?'

'Wednesday,' said Hannah.

'Really?'

'And you didn't meet any of the others like you?'

'No. I didn't know there were others until you said. Are you sure there are?'

'I'm afraid so.' She winced, realizing from Gibson's pensive look that she'd inadvertently revealed more than she'd intended.

He pointed a long-nailed finger at her. 'Oh no. What . . . what did they do?'

'It doesn't—'

'Tell me. Please?'

'There was an attack last night. A woman was killed.'

'Oh God,' said Gibson. 'It wasn't me. I swear.'

'We know,' said Banecroft. 'You were here already when it happened. Otherwise, rest assured, you wouldn't be here now.'

Gibson recoiled under his blankets and whimpered.

Hannah put her hand out and tried to sound comforting. 'Don't worry. You're going to be OK. We'll figure this out.'

Banecroft made a scoffing noise.

Hannah spoke to him out of the side of her mouth. 'Your bedside manner is awful.'

'We don't have time for niceties,' said Banecroft. 'Mr Gibson, you are neck-deep in doo-doo. Your only chance is to help us in any way you can.'

'I will.'

'Good. Then take me through everything that's happened in the last week and don't leave anything out.'

Gibson did so, but there was a notable absence of a timeline in his account. As he kept saying when pressed, all of his focus was on the hunger and trying to fight it.

'Tell me more about the hunger?' said Banecroft.

Gibson stared at the floor for such a long time that Hannah wondered if he was ever going to speak.

'It wants you to hunt. It . . . It's exactly like you see in the films. The stupid bloody films. Oh God, I'm a monster.' He looked up at Banecroft and his blunderbuss. 'Maybe I should let you use that. End me before something terrible happens.'

'No,' said Hannah quickly. 'Don't think like that, Leon. We'll figure this out. You have my word.'

'We're not making any promises,' said Banecroft pointedly.

Gibson met his eye. 'If it needs to be done, then . . .'

'Don't worry.' Banecroft patted Chekhov. 'It will be.'

Before Hannah could find the transition the conversation desperately needed, the cellar doors were thrown open and the room was flooded with sunlight. Gibson howled. Even Hannah and Banecroft threw up their hands to protect their eyes.

Grace strode down the steps, holding a plate in one hand and a large glass in the other. Stella followed in her wake, looking embarrassed to be carrying a bucket.

'Please close the door,' urged Hannah.

Stella obliged as Grace gave the room a disapproving look before clearing her throat.

'Hello, everybody.' Her tone was forced. 'I have brought some much-needed nourishment and . . . some other things for the patient.'

'Patient?' echoed Banecroft.

'Yes. The poor man is sick. Now, where is he?'

Grace's eyes followed the direction in which the blunderbuss was pointed. The moment when her vision adjusted enough to be able to make out Leon Gibson clearly was obvious to everyone.

'Oh my.' She took a step back and her cast-iron façade faltered for a moment.

Hannah was impressed by how quickly her colleague recovered.

'Hello, Mr, ehm . . .'

'Gibson,' offered Hannah.

'Gibson,' repeated Grace. 'Sorry you are unwell.' She held up the plate. 'I wasn't sure what you might need so I have brought you a steak.' Her face dropped. 'As in the meat and not . . .' She looked at the glass in her other hand. 'Also, some lemonade. Everyone likes lemonade.'

'I don't,' said Banecroft.

'You are not included in everyone and you never have been.'

'I always suspected.'

Grace moved forward.

Hannah pointed at the floor. 'Maybe just leave them there, Grace.'

Grace nodded. 'Oh right, yes. That would be best.' She set them down on the cool flagstones. 'There you go, Mr Gibson.' She turned and took the bucket from Stella. 'And there is a bucket if . . . you need a bucket.'

'Thank you very much, Grace,' said Gibson weakly.

'You are most welcome.' She pulled a pamphlet out of her pocket. 'Also, here is a pamphlet with some thoughts and prayers in it, if you would be interested in letting the light of our Lord Jesus into your life.'

'That's very kind,' said Gibson.

Grace placed the leaflet beside the glass of lemonade and nodded, pleased.

'Poor sod,' said Banecroft. 'Not only has he got the whole fang-fest to deal with, but he's also being Jehovah-Witnessed while he's chained to a wall and can't get away.'

Grace's head snapped round. 'Do you think it speaks badly of you, Vincent, that you have worse manners than the monster?' Her face fell again. 'Oh, I'm very sorry, Mr Gibson. I didn't mean to call you a . . .'

'And yet,' said Banecroft, 'I'm the one people accuse of having a poor bedside manner.'

Hannah raised her voice. 'We'll leave you alone to eat and, y'know. And don't worry, Leon, we'll sort this out.'

Banecroft swung the blunderbuss over his shoulder as he turned to leave, and gave it a pat. 'One way or the other.'

The Play Is the Thing

By Reginald Fairfax the Third

The Chorley Amateur Dramatic Society's production of *Hamlet* was plunged into confusion this week after it became apparent that it was being haunted by a better version of the play.

The production, which many local theatre-lovers have criticized for being woefully inept, has been beset by paranormal intrusions. The company's artistic director and abysmal Prince of Denmark, Roger Robinson, who critics have branded shouty yet largely incoherent, explained, 'It's been a nightmare. Every night while we are clearing the set away for the Zumba classes in the morning, we are inundated with the ghosts of dead actors giving their interpretations of the piece. It's hard not to take it as a criticism, and it's been terrible for company morale.'

Robinson's wife, Amanda – herself terribly miscast to cover the roles of both Hamlet's mother and Ophelia, his love interest, which gives the piece sexual tension in all the wrong places – added, 'It's bad enough getting poor reviews from the living, but now we're getting them from the dead as well. I said we should stick to doing musicals. Audiences loved our version of *Cats*.'

It gives this publication no pleasure at all to offer the correction that the company's version of *Cats* was, in fact, also dreadful. However, it was, at least, difficult to hear the anguished screams of both the living and the dead over the wailing that the Chorley Players believe approximates singing. Despite objections from multiple planes of existence, their desecration of *Hamlet* runs until the fifteenth of this month, and is to be avoided like prawns that have been left out in the sun for a week.

CHAPTER 45

'Excuse me. Sorry. Sorry. Excuse me.'

Hannah was barging through the crowd at the back of the large conference room in the Hilton Deansgate as politely as she could. It was rammed with press. While she felt bad for pushing, everyone else was too, and as far as she could tell, she was the only one who felt compelled to offer any apologies. She'd already been walloped twice in the shins by flight cases containing some kind of broadcast or camera equipment.

She'd never been to a news conference before that morning, and she was now about to attend her second. The first had been the one given by the Greater Manchester Police where a Detective Inspector Clarke gave a statement during which he looked quite smug, said nothing and asked everyone to remain calm. He then nodded, glass-eyed, and looked a lot less smug as dozens of journalists, who were anything but calm, shouted questions at him that he did not answer.

In contrast, this press conference seemed to be a complete free-for-all. The number of journalists seemed to have doubled in the last hour, and a lot of them looked as if they might have travelled in from overseas. Natasha Ellis really was big news now.

As soon as Hannah had left the cellar after interviewing Leon Gibson with Banecroft, she'd headed straight down to the Ridgemount Hotel where the body had been found. On the way, she'd attempted to ring DI Tom Sturgess but he hadn't picked up. She told herself that odds on, he was having a particularly busy morning. Still, she did feel a little put out about it.

When she reached the hotel, it was entirely cordoned off by the police. They were aggressively turning everyone away, press or otherwise, and guarding all possible entrances. Following DI Clarke's disastrous presser, Hannah had stood about and been patronized by 'proper' journalists for an hour. She had smiled, nodded and not risen to the bait. They could scoff all they like – they were all in *The Stranger Times*' area of expertise now.

As she ploughed her way through the crowd towards her intended target, another little thrill ran through her. All of these hacks could scrabble about, desperate for any kind of angle, but she had the mother of all exclusives sitting in the cellar. No, they weren't going to use it but still, for one of the few times in her life, Hannah Willis felt like she knew something that nobody else did, and there was a little cheeky buzz in that.

She nimbly stepped over what appeared to be two esteemed members of the press having a heated argument about a plug socket, and slipped into the space that the gentleman in shades and a baseball cap had opened up for her.

She stared fixedly at the stage at the front of the room, making every effort to look casual as she spoke. 'Hello, Tom.'

'Ms Willis,' said DI Sturgess. 'You have an excellent eye.'

'Two of them, in fact.'

374

'Indeed. There are local journalists in here who didn't see through this stunning disguise. Well done you.'

'Well, you probably haven't been dodging their calls all morning.'

'Oh no,' said Sturgess, 'I most definitely have. If it's any consolation, of all the calls I didn't pick up this morning, yours was the only one I felt bad about.'

Hannah caught herself smiling and turned away to prevent him from seeing. 'Shouldn't you be busy being elsewhere?'

Sturgess lowered his voice further and leaned in slightly. 'DI Clarke is in charge of this investigation now. I briefed him and I've been told to toddle off home.'

'That's not fair!' said Hannah, slightly louder than she intended, which caused a couple of heads in front of them to turn in their direction.

Sturgess took a sip from the can of Diet Coke he had in his hand and waited for the heads to lose interest. 'Thanks, but I knew it was coming. Given what this week has been like so far, Clarke is welcome to it. Besides, just because I've been told to go home doesn't mean I am.'

'I'd expect nothing less. So what are you doing here?'

'Morbid curiosity.'

'Really?'

'I don't know what this is, but I've got a really bad feeling about it. This city is a lot of things, not least is a pile of kindling always in danger of finding a match. I did mention that to DI Clarke but, well, he might've been too busy shouting at people to pay any attention.'

Hannah gave him a sideways look. 'I take it you two aren't the best of friends, then?'

'Did I not hide that well? He's a monumental—'

Whatever Sturgess was about to say was lost as the room exploded into a cacophony of camera clicks and shouted questions. A quartet of people emerged from a door at the front of the room. Hannah hadn't been an avid fan of *Love Mountain*, but she vaguely recognized Marcus Mangan and Kai Peters as having been contestants on the show with Natasha Ellis. A nervous-looking blonde woman with a clipboard directed the two younger men to take the seats on the stage at either side of the podium. The other man – an older guy in his forties, in a black suit with a dark red shirt and tie – stood at the podium and waited a few moments for the din to die down.

'Thank you all for coming. My name is Jared Holland and I am . . .' His voice faltered. 'Sorry – was Natasha Ellis's manager. I know you all have a lot of questions and we'll answer for you what we can, but before that, please can we all remember that beyond the story here lies a real person. Natasha was a beautiful soul. So full of life and concern for those around her. I actually spoke to her last night, as I often did, after she'd finished her appearance here in Manchester, and she was charming, funny, gracious – an absolute delight to work with. To me, she wasn't a client, she was family.' He stopped to wipe a tear from his eye. 'And this is a very real tragedy. She may have come from humble beginnings, but Natasha Ellis had a warmth and a popularity with everyday people that few entertainers could match.'

A journalist at the front scoffed loudly, which earned him a look from Holland.

After a second Holland continued. 'I'll always treasure her last words to me. We'd been discussing how best to handle her many charity commitments and she said to me, "Jared, I just want to thank the people for all they have given me." He looked down, as if to gather himself, before raising his head again, all professionalism. 'And now, ladies and gentlemen, I know you'll want to hear from two people so dear to our Natasha – Marcus Mangan and Kai Peters.'

On cue, both men stood up simultaneously and made for the mic. Jared had a quick word with them both – whatever he said, at least one of them ignored. Following a bit of undignified shoving, Kai Peters, thanks to his stockier build and lower centre of gravity, got most of the podium.

'Tasha was a wonderful woman and a right good laugh. She meant the world to me.'

Marcus Mangan, he with the flowing blond locks that had sold quite a bit of anti-dandruff shampoo before he got caught calling it 'smelly crap' on an open mic, raised his voice. 'She was the love of my life.'

'Yeah, well,' said Kai, 'mine too. In fact, I'd asked her to marry me.'

'We were having a baby together!'

Jared stepped forward and, as subtly as possible, tried to remove the pair from close proximity to the mic. 'OK, well, as you can see, emotions are running high.'

Kai pushed Jared's hand away and shouted, 'I will not stop until I've found the bastard what done this!'

'I'm offering a ten-grand reward for information that helps the police make an arrest,' added Marcus.

'I'm offering twenty grand for two minutes in a room with the bastard first!'

At that point, Marcus pulled a wooden stake out of his back pocket. 'I'm going to stake the fucker!'

The mic cut out and Marcus and Kai could no longer be heard over the clamour of questions. The two men, however, seemed primarily concerned with pushing each other, like boxers at a weigh-in that was getting out of control.

What happened next was unclear from Hannah's position all the way in the back, but it looked like the stage collapsed.

The room was in uproar, with journalists trying to climb over each other to reach the front. Hannah could see that in addition to the fight at the front of the room, two other skirmishes had broken out.

She turned to Sturgess, who mimed a match being lit, followed by an explosion.

CHAPTER 46

Banecroft stepped inside the door and allowed his eyes to adjust to the light. The Kanky's Rest looked more or less as he had left it. To be fair, people who had last been there during the seventies would probably say the same thing. The pub appeared to be untouched by time and, possibly, disinfectant. Ox trooped in behind him and held open the door for Stanley as he hopped in on his crutches.

'Right,' said Banecroft. 'I'll do the talking.'

'OK,' said Ox. 'I'll handle any singing.'

Stanley looked down at his surgical boot. 'If we're relying on me for dancing, this plan is a non-starter.'

Banecroft rolled his eyes. 'Oh good, you two are a little double act now. How delightful.'

As he walked towards the bar, Banecroft realized that the place didn't look *much* the same, it looked *exactly* the same. Margo, the seemingly unmoving woman in black with the long dark hair, was seated in the same spot, with the man in the thick overcoat beside her, talking to himself. The red-headed woman was still throwing darts – scoring nothing but bullseyes despite ignoring the board to inspect the newcomers, an expression of utter boredom on her face. And then there was . . .

'Here,' said Stanley with a whisper, 'there's two women knitting something in the corner – and it looks like it's got eight legs.'

John Mór stood watching the trio from behind the bar, his long arms stretched out wide on the counter. 'Gentlemen.'

Banecroft nodded. 'Mr Mór.'

Inside Banecroft's pocket, his phone started to ring. He fished it out and quickly rejected the call.

'Bad business last night,' offered John Mór.

'Which bit exactly?'

'That poor girl at the hotel.'

'Ah yes.'

'If you've come here looking for information, then I'm afraid I've nothing new to tell you. My people are as confused as anyone.'

'Que sera.'

Banecroft winced as his phone rang again. 'Excuse me.' He rejected the call again and set the device to silent.

'So, what can I get you gents?'

'I'll have my usual,' said Banecroft.

'A Coke, please,' said Ox.

'I don't suppose you do a chocolate fudge sundae?' asked Stanley.

'He'll have a Coke,' said Banecroft. 'A Diet Coke.' He looked at Stanley. 'Even I am beginning to think you have a problem.'

'Go on over to the snug,' said John Mór, 'and I'll bring your drinks over. Let the fella take the weight off his leg.'

'Thank you,' said Stanley huffily. 'At least some people have a bit of consideration.'

★

After a couple of minutes, mainly taken up with Stanley trying and failing to get his foot into a comfortable position, John Mór arrived with their drinks on a tray. He doled them out, then set down a pint of stout for himself and sat down behind it.

'So, if this isn't about that thing, then what is it about?'

Stanley and Ox looked at Banecroft.

'We had reason to hire a builder to do some work at our offices. We became suspicious when he and his lads went above and beyond. Turns out they were there to assist somebody in kidnapping a member of my staff.'

'Bloody hell,' exclaimed John Mór.

'Yes,' agreed Banecroft, 'I wasn't particularly pleased either. We wanted to find out who was behind it, so I set my two bloodhounds here on the trail. They followed this builder to a meeting at – where was it?'

'Clifton Country Park,' supplied Ox.

'Clifton Country Park,' repeated Banecroft, 'where he met two gentlemen. How would you describe them?'

'They were wearing robes,' said Ox. 'One black fella, one . . . sorta white fella. He had his face painted in, like, quarters.'

'What colours?' asked John Mór.

'Red, green, blue and yellow,' said Stanley.

'Are you sure?'

'The bloke tried to rip me in four – you could say he made quite the impression. I imagine I'll be waking up screaming at the thought of his face for quite some time.'

John Mór pursed his lips and nodded. 'I can see that. How come he didn't?'

'Excuse me?'

'He tried to rip you in four. How'd you get out of it?'

Stanley nodded begrudgingly in Ox's direction. 'He stopped him.'

John Mór turned to Ox. 'You a practitioner?'

'A what?' asked Ox.

'I'll take that as a no. How'd you take down this brother, then?'

Ox shrugged. 'There isn't a man alive that doesn't need to pause for thought after taking a fence post to the back of the head.'

John Mór nodded appreciatively and tilted his head towards Stanley. 'You're lucky to have such a good friend.'

Stanley looked extremely uncomfortable at the notion.

'So, you know who it was?' asked Banecroft.

'No, but I know what he was. At least, what he considers himself to be. The quarters mean he's a novice in the Ceathramh.'

'The what?'

'Ceathramh,' repeated John Mór. 'Meaning "quarter" in old Gaelic. Symbolic of the four elements. They're part cult, part militia. Only they don't exist any more. Haven't for a long time.'

'Since when?'

John Mór turned his pint around slowly. 'Since the Accord was signed.'

'Am I correct in assuming they might not have been wild about that?'

John Mór jutted his chin. 'At the end of any war, there are those who want to keep fighting. Nature of the beast.'

'Well, it appears someone is getting the band back together.'

'That is . . . not good news.'

'You're telling me,' said Stanley.

'If you don't mind me asking, how'd you break your foot?'

'I was floating in the air when my colleague walloped your mate in the back of the head.'

'Whoever this lad is, he's no friend of mine. I assure you of that.'

'Do you know where we could find him?' asked Banecroft, which earned him a look of surprise from John Mór.

'Seeing as I didn't know they existed until a minute ago, how would I? And more importantly, what would you do if you did find them? I'm not sure the fence-post trick would work a second time. My advice would be to stay out of their way.'

'I'd love to, but unfortunately, they put themselves in my way. They came looking for us.'

'They came looking for the girl, you mean?'

Stanley looked round the table, aware of how things had suddenly become very tense. There was a long pause.

'What girl?' asked Banecroft.

'Like I told you before,' said John Mór, 'people notice things. All I know is there's a girl working for you and she's unusual.'

'And what exactly have you heard she is?'

John Mór took another drink. 'Take it easy. I don't know and I don't want to know. I'm just saying what I heard.' He turned his attention back to Ox and Stanley. 'Did you hear any names? Anything like that?'

The pair shook their heads.

'All we saw,' said Ox, 'is Darius Williams – that's the builder's name – going to meet these two guys, then . . . Well, his skin . . .'

'What about it?'

'The tattoos on it – they started burning. I mean, like, from the inside. The guy rolled down a hill into the river and was still going. He set a load of the park alight. I could still see some of it burning when we left. It would've made the news only, well . . .'

'Right. The hotel thing,' said John Mór. 'What did these tattoos look like? Can you describe them?'

'I can do you one better than that,' said Stanley, pulling his phone from his pocket. He tapped it a few times then handed it to John Mór. 'I took some pictures earlier in the week when we were following him. I sent them to my tattoos guy and asked if they were gang insignias or something. He said he'd never seen them before.'

John Mór studied the images and nodded as he scrolled back and forth through them. 'He wouldn't have done. I, on the other hand, do recognize them. These are not ordinary tattoos.'

Banecroft leaned in. 'How so?'

'You've heard the phrase "the pen is mightier than the sword"?' The table nodded. 'Well, in your world, that is figurative, but not in ours. These marks mean that you're indebted to someone. An unbreakable form of collateral because, well, you've seen why.'

'How does that help us?' asked Ox.

'Because each mark shows to whom you owe the debt originally. Only the original inker has power over you, unless they pass it on.'

'Or sell it on?' said Banecroft.

'Exactly.'

'The dangers of getting into debt over your head,' mused Stanley, which earned him a sour look from Ox.

'I'll go talk to the man whose design that is and let you know.'

'No, you won't,' said Banecroft. 'We're going with you.'

'He won't like that.'

'Do you think he'll like it more or less than I like someone attacking my staff?'

'He don't like new people.'

'I don't like any people. Sounds like we'll get on famously.'

'I'm going now.'

'No time like the present.'

Banecroft pulled his phone out of his pocket and read a message on the screen. 'Ah, having said that, it appears something has come up requiring my immediate attention. Can we do this tomorrow?'

'No,' said John Mór. 'As I said, I'll report back.'

'Not even close to good enough.' Banecroft nodded at Stanley and Ox. 'You will take my associates with you.'

'This isn't a school trip.'

Banecroft held up his phone. 'Or, I could blow this off and come with you. That whole nasty business with the guys with the fangs? I take it you and your people are fine with that not getting resolved, then?'

John Mór leaned back on his stool. 'Fine,' he said with a sigh, before looking at Ox and Stanley. 'Do me a favour, though – keep your mouths shut and, for the love of all things, don't ask the man for ice-cream.'

CHAPTER 47

Reggie was standing across the road from the house of Gregory and Victor Tombs, nervously drumming his fingers on his chin. There was a crowd forming, or, as Reggie was trying not to think of it, a mob. It was hard to say at what point a group of people stopped being the former and started being the latter, but Reggie could feel that time approaching.

When he'd arrived, there'd been a few people milling about. He'd elected not to ring the doorbell, on the grounds that doing so would attract a lot of attention from the dozen or so individuals who were dotted around. Instead, he'd tried to ring the phone number Gregory Tombs had given them, but that had gone to voicemail with the standard network message. He'd also tried ringing and texting Hannah, who'd only belatedly responded to let him know she was on her way. He had no idea what she would do when she got here or what difference it would make, but he still hoped she'd show up soon. The crowd was growing by the minute.

Twenty minutes ago an older lady from across the street had come out and asked some of the people sitting on her wall what the hell they were up to.

'We're making sure that freak don't leave,' said one of the more confident youths in a baseball hat.

'What are you on about?' barked the old lady before she looked in the direction of the Tombs' house and the realization dawned on her. 'You leave 'em alone. That Mr Tombs is a nice man. Always helping out. He filled in the hole in my wall last winter.'

The youth sniggered. 'Oh yeah, filling in your hole, is he?'

The old lady moved forward. Reggie shifted towards them too. He didn't want to intervene, but he would if he had to.

Instead, the old lady bent down and peered under the peak of the young man's cap. 'Seymour Reed, is that you?'

The smile fell from the youth's face.

'Yo, Funk – is that your real name?'

'Shut up, bellend.'

'It is, isn't it?' said the old lady, wagging a finger. 'That's you, Seymour. Taller, and a lot more spots than the last time I saw you, but I never forget a face.' Her words were greeted with more guffaws as the kid turned bright red. 'I know your nana – she'll be hearing about this. You mark my words. Used to be a nice boy and now look at you. Behaving like a hoodlum, trying to intimidate little old ladies.'

'I wasn't. I . . .'

'Making lewd remarks.'

'I didn't.'

'Oh, do me a favour, ya little shit. I'm old, not daft. Filling in my hole? You act like sex was invented five years ago. How do you think you got here? I was young in the sixties. I could tell you tales that'd make your spots fall off.' She dropped into a remarkable impression of his voice. '"Filling in your hole, is he?" Look at the state of you – no self-respecting girl would let you within a mile of her hole. And as for the rest of you . . .'

At that point, a neighbour stepped out and wisely guided the woman back inside. She looked over her shoulder as she was escorted away. 'If my Jonny was still alive, he'd have gone through the lot of you like shit through a donkey. Get off my wall!'

It said something for the presence of the woman and her dearly departed Jonny that the kids did move. The majority hung about while Seymour went home, possibly to talk to his nana.

Some members of the growing crowd seemed to be waiting with purpose, but others were just there to see what happened. Reggie was more than a little relieved when Hannah came running around the corner.

'Where have you been?'

'I was up at the press conference,' said Hannah, looking about. 'There's a lot of people here.'

'I know.'

'Do you reckon Gregory knows?'

'I've no idea,' said Reggie. 'He's not answering his phone.'

'Did you try knocking on the door?'

Reggie nodded towards the crowd. 'Just walking up and ringing the doorbell is going to attract a lot of attention. Either the Tombs are in, in which case you'll be told to bugger off or end up trapped in the house with them. Or they're out, in which case people will have nothing but you to focus on.'

'I've seen you defend yourself,' said Hannah.

'That's as may be. But odds are odds, my dear.'

'What about the police?'

'I called them. Long story short – if an actual riot kicks off, I should call back.'

'Oh, for—'

Whatever Hannah was about to say next was lost in the hub-bub as a couple of SUVs pulled up at the end of the road. Several men got out and amongst them was Marcus Mangan, he of the ten-grand bounty on Natasha Ellis's killer.

'Oh crap,' said Hannah.

'I'm not an avid fan of such downmarket television,' said Reggie, 'but is that not the chap from that awful reality show?'

'I'm afraid so.'

They watched as the men stopped and talked to a few people then marched purposefully down the road towards the Tombs residence. *There*, thought Reggie sourly. *That was the point.*

People fell in behind the group of men, the crowd swelled and then disappeared as it became a mob. From somewhere a 'freaks out' chant popped up and was taken up by those intoxicated by the thrill of being in a group large enough to circumvent the social norms.

Marcus Mangan stood at the front, his muscles flexing, his eyes bulging. A film crew had appeared from somewhere, and the cameraman was running backwards in front of Mangan. The appearance of the camera made some people rush to the head of the mob in order to be seen, and prompted others to cover their faces for exactly the opposite reason.

'I'm ringing the police again,' said Reggie, then realized he was talking to nobody. He looked around and, in a moment of pure horror, saw that Hannah – all five foot six of her – was now standing at the bottom of the path leading to the Tombs' front door, her hands out, facing the mob and preparing to make a reasoned argument.

Reggie guessed this was her first riot, and possibly her last.

Hannah tried to sound a lot calmer than she felt.

'Please, listen to me. These people had nothing to do with this.'

'Who are you?' barked Mangan.

'I'm a journalist and I've been following this story. These people had nothing to do with it.'

'Bullshit!' came a shout from the crowd.

'Fake news!'

'I just want to talk to 'em,' said Mangan.

'OK, but . . .'

The crowd surged, pushing Hannah back as it made its way towards the front door. 'No, just hang on.'

Then, Reggie was beside her.

'Wait!' hollered Hannah as one of the men beside Mangan grabbed her and tried to drag her away.

'Unhand her,' demanded Reggie.

'Make me.'

The man collapsed to the ground. Hannah didn't see what happened but suddenly Reggie was in front of her.

'Stay back,' he ordered.

A couple of fists flew. One of which Reggie blocked, the other he didn't.

'Stop!' screamed Hannah.

Another surge came out of nowhere and Reggie found himself under a mass of bodies that fell onto the ground.

'Get off him!'

At that point the air was rent asunder by the loudest sound Hannah had ever heard – a screaming siren of such intensity that people scattered, tumbling to the floor. She clamped her hands over her ears and curled up next to the front door.

The door opened unexpectedly and Hannah saw a pair of legs rush past her while hands simultaneously grabbed her and dragged her inside. She looked up to see Victor Tombs wearing ear protectors. He looked a lot more frightened than frightening. A couple of seconds later, Gregory stumbled back through the door, dragging Reggie behind him. He quickly slammed it shut then jammed a series of metal bolts into place. He hit a button on the wall and the deafening sound stopped.

Gregory pulled off his ear protectors. 'Ten out of ten for bravery, Ms Willis, but minus a million for common sense.'

'How did you . . .'

'Security consultant, remember?' he said with a grim smile. 'Heaven help the burglar that tries to get in here. I'm afraid your friend is a little worse for wear.'

'I'm fine,' said Reggie, trying to staunch the flow of blood from his nose. He looked down. 'Although I fear this waistcoat is a write-off.'

'Oh God,' said Hannah. 'Reggie, I'm so sorry.'

'You can make your apologies later,' said Gregory. 'We need to move.'

Where they needed to move to was a basement beneath the house, accessed via a set of stairs from the hallway. They made their way through a room that contained a drum kit, some amps and a couple of guitars on stands, and entered a smaller room. This one had a bank of four flatscreen monitors on the wall, a mic and a laptop sitting on a table in front of it.

'Wow,' said Hannah.

'It pays to be prepared,' said Gregory.

They looked on as people picked themselves up outside the front door. Gregory snatched up the mic. 'This is the police. Back away from the door. You are on private property.'

Many of the members of the crowd did move back, but most of them stayed put outside the front gate. The video feeds didn't have audio but even without it, the demonstrative gestures made it clear a disagreement was taking place.

'Do you think that'll hold 'em off, Dad?' asked Victor in a surprisingly soft voice.

'Not for long, but fingers crossed the police actually show up, even if it's just to arrest me for impersonating an officer.'

The mob was re-forming before their eyes as the shock wore off and was replaced by anger.

Gregory picked up the mic again and flipped a switch. 'To the three lads climbing over the back wall, I really hope ye like dogs.'

He clicked off the mic and saw Hannah looking at him.

'I don't have a dog.'

'Jesus, Dad,' said Victor. 'It'll be burning torches in a minute.'

As if on cue, Hannah noticed the crowd on the left-hand side shift to make room and a flicker of flame became visible.

It wasn't a torch, though. Hannah realized this as the Molotov cocktail flew through the air and crashed against the front door.

'Oh my God,' she said, 'they're going to burn the house down.'

'Just as well we've got good insurance,' said Gregory. 'Time for plan B.'

He reached across and placed his hand on two points on the wall. A section of it that had previously looked very normal slid away. Gregory flicked a switch to turn on the lights that revealed a tunnel.

'You're kidding,' said Hannah.

'Always be prepared,' said Gregory. 'That's what the Boy Scouts taught me.' He grabbed two torches from a mount on the wall, turning one on and handing the other to Victor. 'It runs for fifteen feet then it meets a sewer, I'm afraid.' He looked at Reggie, whose nose was still bleeding. 'You OK to walk?'

'Absolutely.'

'Good man. Victor, take the rear.' Gregory ducked slightly and headed into the tunnel. 'I hope none of youse have a sentimental attachment to your shoes – it's about to get a wee bit Shawshank.'

CHAPTER 48

Ox held open the door and he and John Mór tried to help Stanley out of the taxi, but he brushed them off with poor grace. Stanley had been a miserable sod before the events of last night, but now he seemed to be in a slightly different kind of foul mood. Ox had driven him to the hospital and stayed with him all night. He had no idea what the angry outburst at the park had been about, given that he'd saved Stanley from being ripped apart by some quarter-faced nutjob and then carried him back to the van. Shock, possibly? Certainly, while Ox's experience of saving people from a horrible death was limited, Stanley nevertheless seemed ungrateful, verging on downright belligerent, about it.

The taxi had dropped them off on a side street in the Northern Quarter. Ox was pretty sure there used to be a sex shop down here. He'd been once, as a kid – on a dare. His mate Dazza had reckoned that because Ox was Chinese, they wouldn't be able to tell what age he was. In hindsight, the fact he was under five foot and clearly scared shitless might have been a clue. He'd walked in, made eye contact with the girl behind the counter, who was, as it happened, also of Chinese extraction, and had turned to get out of there so fast that he'd crashed into a display while trying

394

to get around another shopper. Looking back, Ox wondered if getting caught in that downpouring of dildos had been a formative experience.

The sex shop was gone, replaced by an estate agent's. Ox couldn't help but think that, if anything, this development had lowered the tone of the area.

He turned to John Mór. 'Where to from here?'

The big man pointed to the sign above his head. Ox looked up. 'You're kidding me?'

'No, I'm not. It's this man's base of operations.'

'A karaoke bar?'

John Mór shrugged. 'We've all got to be somewhere. Do I need to go back over the need for the two of you to be quiet?'

Stanley snorted. 'I've dealt with more dodgy sods than you've had hot dinners.'

'Not like this guy, you haven't. Did you enjoy last night's experience?'

'No.'

'Then don't be fooled. The people you dealt with there had to come cap in hand to this man.' He pointed at the doorway. 'Be respectful and, more importantly, understand this isn't your turf. Let me handle it or you might not be walking out of here. Got it?'

Stanley nodded.

John Mór looked at Ox.

'Mate,' Ox said, 'I don't even want to go in here except I've been told I have to. I'm not saying a word.'

'Good. The man we're meeting is called Ferry. Come on.'

★

395

Given that it was now mid-afternoon during a heatwave, the basement karaoke bar was surprisingly busy. A couple of groups sat chatting amongst themselves around tables in the darker corners. Up on the stage, a member of the city's Chinese student community was knocking out a passable rendition of 'Wind Beneath My Wings'. Karaoke might have been a Japanese invention but Ox's family gatherings testified that the Chinese had taken to it. The Bette Midler wannabe was being cheered on by a table of half a dozen friends while being ignored by the rest of the bar.

The hostess, an attractive woman with dark red hair, wide eyes and a knowing grin, all wrapped up in a silk dress that shimmied as she walked, came over to greet and seat them.

'John Mór,' she purred. 'This is an unexpected surprise.'

'How've you been, Nancy?'

'Oh, y'know. Chained to this place. Rumour has it the sun's come out and people are losing their minds.'

'More than you know.'

She leaned in slightly. 'Delighted as I am to see you, I take it this isn't a social call?'

'You are correct.'

'Take a seat and I'll let him know you're waiting.' As she turned away, Nancy waved to the barman and pointed at the trio. 'On the house for our good friends.'

The barman waited as Stanley manoeuvred himself into position on a stool and then the others sat down either side of him. 'What can I get you gents?'

'I'll have—' started Stanley, but he was interrupted by John Mór.

'Three bottles of beer, please.' He pointed down at the fridge behind the bar. 'The front three there look good.'

The barman nodded.

'Why can't I—'

'Because,' said John Mór, leaving it at that. 'Remember what I said.'

'Fine,' said Stanley. He nudged Ox. 'When we're done here, will you go around to the Spoonful of Sugar for me? I'll treat you to whatever you want.'

Ox gave Stanley a long look. 'Really?'

'C'mon.'

'Fine. But only if you're good.'

Stanley's only response was to stick out his tongue.

The barman delivered their beers and the three of them watched the stage in silence as the Chinese girl failed miserably to cope with the octave change.

'It's a tough song,' said Ox.

'Difficult choice,' agreed John Mór.

'Can I ask a question?'

John Mór nodded.

'That woman, the hostess . . .'

'Nancy. Believe me, she is not your type.'

'Yeah,' Ox agreed. 'You've no idea how right you are. Thing is, though – her eyes. There was something . . .' He lowered his voice. 'She isn't what you'd call your ordinary girl, is she?'

John Mór gave a slight nod. 'You could say that.' He gave Ox a sideways look and raised an eyebrow. 'That was a very good spot. Most people would have no idea.'

'Most people haven't seen what I've seen.'

'Fair point.'

The song changed and a couple of giggling girls stood up on the stage, accompanied by the first bars of 'Footloose'.

'How come,' started Stanley, 'everybody wants to be a singer these days? You don't even need to be able to sing any more. I got given the original tapes of a certain artist's album a few years ago, before they'd "sweetened" it. Jesus H, I tell you. Awful.'

The other two men nodded.

'Do you want to know who?'

John Mór shook his head. 'No, thanks.'

'I stopped looking for new music in nineteen ninety-nine,' said Ox.

Stanley tutted. 'The two of you are just as bad as the papers. I paid five grand for them tapes – nobody was interested then either.'

A man in his twenties emerged from behind a curtained-off area at the back of the room, rubbing his shoulder.

'Can I ask another question?' said Ox.

John Mór gave a sideways glance. 'You can ask.'

'How does this thing work – with the tattoos, I mean?'

John Mór looked around to make sure they weren't being observed. 'All right, I'll explain it – if only to stop you from getting the urge to ask awkward questions in there. You know that scene in *The Godfather*, when everyone comes to him asking for favours?'

Ox nodded.

'Well, it's like that, only in return, you get a mark on your skin. An obligation, we call it. The size, all that, depends on what you ask for, how big a thing it is. The person who holds the rights to it can then call on you and demand repayment.'

'Like a loan?' asked Stanley.

'Sort of. It can be financial but more often it's something else.'

Ox couldn't resist looking at the proliferation of tattoos along John Mór's arms.

The big man gave a half-smile. 'Some tattoos are just tattoos.'

Stanley leaned in. 'And they can sell your obligation on?'

John Mór scanned the bar again. 'They're not supposed to, but yes, people do. Mostly, it's a way of having a guaranteed fair deal between parties. Although some individuals made it into more of an enterprise than was intended.'

'This is all basically loan-sharking?' asked Ox.

'Definitely do not use that word,' warned John Mór as he noticed Nancy emerge from behind the curtain and wave them over. 'In fact, best not to use any words – to be on the safe side. Remember our agreement.'

Ox wasn't sure what he was expecting to see behind the curtain, but the reality was surprisingly ordinary. Two men were seated there on a sofa, half-drunk pints of beer on a table in front of them.

The man in the flat cap and neatly pressed Burberry shirt spoke first. His facial hair was white and carefully sculpted, giving him a look best described as steampunk musketeer. His accent was pure Manc. 'Big John, to what do we owe this undoubted pleasure?'

John Mór took the extended hand. 'Mr Ferry.' He nodded at the man's companion, a gentleman with long black hair and a decidedly shaggier beard. 'Riley.'

'John,' replied Riley. 'How's Margo?'

'Same old same old.'

'Do pass on my regards.'

'Sit, sit,' invited Ferry, and John Mór, Stanley and Ox took the three stools on the opposite side of the table. 'Everyone all right for drinks?'

When they all confirmed they were, Ferry nodded at Nancy, who silently withdrew.

'And who are your friends, John?'

'This is Ox and Stanley – they work for *The Stranger Times*.'

Ferry had been reaching for his drink, but stopped and fixed John with a look. 'You bringing the press to see me, John?'

'It's not like that. You have my word.'

Ferry relaxed a little and proceeded to pick up his pint. 'All right. So what is it like, then?'

'Last night, they were attacked by two men who, it appears, are at least calling themselves members of the Ceathramh.'

Ferry looked briefly at Riley. 'There's no such thing any more.'

'That's what I said, but one of them had the quarters.'

'That doesn't prove anything,' said Riley.

John Mór nodded. 'You might well be right. Here's the thing, though. They had the obligation on a man who was bearing your mark.'

Riley leaned forward. 'John, it feels like this little friendly chat might be about to get unfriendly?'

'Doesn't have to. I didn't come here looking for trouble. I came looking for answers.'

There was a pause in the conversation, prompted by an unduly warm reception for the kicking 'Footloose' had just taken.

'What business is it of yours?' asked Ferry.

'The man in question, his name was . . .' John Mór looked at Ox pointedly.

'Darius Williams.'

'Got himself hired to carry out some work at *The Stranger Times*. Only it was a front for an attack.'

'What kind of attack?' asked Riley.

'Doesn't matter. You know the rules. They're supposed to be left alone.'

Ferry laughed. 'Would you listen to that, Riley? Man comes into my place of business and accuses me of breaking the Accord. Isn't that a hell of a thing?'

Ox could feel the tension rising. The idea of running flashed into his mind but was dismissed. The door suddenly felt like it was a long way away.

'I'm not accusing you of anything, Mr Ferry. I'm not saying you knew why the man wanted Williams's debt. I'm just saying he had it, and I'm politely asking if you could see your way clear to giving me a steer in the man's direction.'

It was Riley's turn to laugh. 'You expect Ferry to turn

snitch? Do you not reckon that might be bad for business if it got out?'

'I'm assuming this man didn't tell you what he'd be using your obligation for when he acquired it.'

'Of course not,' snarled Ferry, the conviviality dropping away.

'And I know you'd not have given it to him if he had. The way I see it,' John Mór continued, 'you'd just be allowing me to sort out the mess that this man dragged your good name into.'

Ferry opened his mouth to speak, then it dropped open wide, aghast. In the background, the opening riff of 'Wonderwall' could be heard. The bar fell abruptly silent except for the music. Riley was halfway off the sofa, just as the intro was finishing, when the music cut out.

A couple of seconds later a flustered-looking Nancy stuck her head around the curtain. 'Apologies, boss. It's the new guy running the decks. I told him, but he must have forgot.'

Ferry fixed her with a hard look. 'Remind him in a way he won't forget.'

Riley picked up his pint and noticed Ox's confused expression. 'That's the boss's song. Everybody knows that.'

Ferry waved it away and the uncomfortable atmosphere eased slightly as the seemingly uncontroversial choice of 'Angels' by Robbie Williams kicked in. He sat back on the sofa and took his time rearranging himself. When he'd finished, he looked at John Mór again.

'This is a liberty, John.'

'I'm just trying to keep the peace, Mr Ferry. You know I wouldn't ask if I didn't have to.'

'I'm surprised you need me. The man in question is an old friend of yours.'

Ox felt the big man tense beside him and straighten up on his stool.

John Mór and Ferry locked eyes. 'That's not possible.'

'You calling me a liar, John?'

'He's . . . he's dead.'

Ferry smiled. 'That's what I thought too, until he walked in and sat down right where you are now.'

'And you didn't think to tell me?'

'What did you just—' started Riley, but broke off as Ferry placed a hand on his arm.

'All right, calm down. For old time's sake, I'm going to put what John here just said down to shock, as we know that normally he isn't that suicidally stupid.' Ferry drained his pint and belched loudly. 'Now, unless there's anything else . . .'

'I need a location.'

'You're pushing it now. How am I supposed to know that?'

John Mór didn't reply, just sat there impassively.

'Fine,' said Ferry with a sigh. 'Nancy will give it to you on the way out, but you didn't get it from me.'

'Understood.'

Ferry waved his hand and John Mór got to his feet. 'Thank you for your time.'

'Yeah,' said Ferry, sounding none too pleased about it.

The trio turned to go.

'And, John.'

John Mór turned back.

'Just so we're absolutely clear, you ever turn up here again with the bloody press in tow, and you and I will have some serious words.'

John Mór nodded.

On their way out the door they picked up a piece of paper from Nancy. Only when they got outside did Ox feel like he could breathe normally again.

CHAPTER 49

Cogs lay on the sun lounger on the deck of his boat with his eyes closed, enjoying the peace and quiet. The reason it was so peaceful was that he'd put up the 'closed' sign and slipped on a pair of noise-cancelling headphones. They were the best investment he'd ever made. Not that he'd actually bought them – he'd got them off a builder who'd wanted to know if Cogs thought that wearing glasses made him look more intelligent.

He didn't open his eyes as the wet nose of a bulldog nudged against his leg. 'I don't care what it is, Zeke – closed is closed. It's been a stressful week – I need a little quality me time.'

Zeke nudged his leg again.

'Look, just go in the plant pot. It's fine. That thing probably needs the water anyhow.'

Zeke nudged much more persistently at Cogs's leg, forcing his non-owner to open one eye and lift the sunglasses he was wearing.

'What is your problem?'

Zeke nodded towards the bridge.

'No,' said Cogs, waving his hand in that direction without looking. He raised his voice. 'Whatever it is, come back tomorrow. Even truth needs a day off.'

He was about to close his eyes again when his own bell came crashing down onto the deck beside him. He leaped to his feet and snatched off the headphones. 'What the . . .' He looked across at the bridge. It was that posh bird from *The Stranger Times*. 'What in the hell are you doing? You nearly got me with that.'

'I need to talk to you.'

'No, no, no, no, no! This is not how we do that, sweetheart. Read the sign.' He tried to point to it. 'It's . . . Where's the sign gone?'

'I knocked it over,' said Zeke.

'Why'd you do that?'

'Because I'm a dog. Your day off is a week off in dog years and the record player is broken.'

'What?'

'I need to talk to you,' repeated Hannah loudly.

'And I said we're closed. You can't keep coming here and breaking the rules not to mention the bloody bells. Those things ain't cheap, you know? You're already on a warning, and for the love of all gods, don't you dare start singing!'

'It's important.'

'Just once,' began Cogs. 'Just once, I'd like somebody to come here and say that it isn't important. The answer is a firm no.'

He nearly lost his footing as the boat, seemingly of its own accord, moved towards the bank.

'What in the hell?'

Zeke chuckled. 'Looks like the boss is overruling you.'

Cogs looked down at his companion. 'You can forget that steak from the freezer.'

'That's a dangerous thing to say to a creature with big teeth who knows you sleep in the nude.'

The houseboat thunked against the grey stone bank just as Hannah reached it from the bridge.

'Whoa, whoa,' said Cogs. 'Easy does it, sweetheart. We've got a system. Tribute.'

'I'm not here to ask you something, I'm here to make a complaint. You lied to me!'

Cogs looked down at the dog and up again. 'I wish I could, darling, but I can literally only tell the truth.'

'He's right,' said Zeke. 'He can't do it.'

'Well, then,' said Hannah, 'can you explain to me' – Cogs and Zeke exchanged a look as Hannah looked around her twice and then leaned in to speak in an urgent whisper – 'how a vampire killed a woman last night?'

'Couldn't have done. Vampires—'

'Don't exist,' finished Hannah. 'So you keep saying. Then how come I've got another one sitting in the cellar beneath our offices right now?'

'That's not possible.'

'Really? Are you suggesting I'm lying? You need to turn on the news. The city is in uproar.'

'Ahhhh,' said Zeke. 'That might explain the three lads I saw earlier, running about with baseball bats. I did notice they didn't have any baseballs with 'em.'

Cogs shook his head. 'Read my lips, love – vampires do not exist. If I'm lying, I'm dying.'

'So how do you explain the attack? And the visitor in my cellar?'

'Ehm . . .' said Cogs, scratching his armpit. 'This visitor of yours, how long has he been a . . . y'know?'

'About four or five days.'

'Right. Did he get bitten by another one?'

'No,' admitted Hannah. 'He just woke up and sort of was one.'

'Did he, I dunno, drink a potion, read something off a scroll, get jiggy with a mysterious individual, chop down a particularly nice tree?'

'No, he swears he did nothing.'

'OK, let me put it this way. You ever opened the oven and found a lovely cake sitting in there, all baked and covered in icing, despite the fact that you never put one in?'

'Ohhhh, I love cake,' observed Zeke.

'No,' said Hannah.

' 'Xactly,' said Cogs. 'The world might be a lot more inexplicable and mysterious than you imagined, but the law of cause and effect still applies. Mostly. Now, what do you think is more likely – a man suddenly becomes a vampire for no reason or he's lying to you?'

Hannah stopped to consider this. 'Oh.'

'Yeah,' said Cogs. 'I'd have a chat with your boy again, if I was you.'

'Right.'

'Because – and I'll say it again and let this boat sink beneath the waves if I'm lying – vampires do not exist. Or at least they didn't until your mate turned up. So something, somewhere is taking the Michael.'

Hannah nodded. 'OK, then.' She turned to go.

'Whoa there, love. Hang on.'

She turned back and looked at him.

'Not for nothing, but something that can turn a man into something that don't even exist, well, you're dealing with something dangerously powerful. You watch yourself.'

Cogs and Zeke watched as Hannah ran back over the bridge.

'I like her,' said Zeke.

'Me too.'

The boat rocked.

'Not like that,' added Cogs quickly.

The boat softly glided back to its position in the middle of the canal.

'That's proper wrecked my mellow buzz, that has.' He looked down at Zeke. 'What do you fancy for lunch?'

'Steak and ice-cream.'

Cogs sighed. 'Screw it. World's going to hell, might as well go down swinging. Let's open that sambuca too.'

Alien Husbandry

Mrs Darlene Debray claims that the universe has a vendetta against her, after losing a third husband in ten years to alien abduction.

Mrs Debray, an alligator farmer from Coopersville, Florida, says that her husband, Billy Bob, was taken last week. 'There was one of 'em big old lights in the sky, and I told him to stay inside, but he insisted on going out and taking some potshots at it with his AR-15 that we have for home protection. Next thing I know, Billy Bob's fat ass is being tractor-beamed up into the sky and I'm single and ready to mingle.' She added that she likes long walks, piña coladas, men who know how to treat a lady, and greyscale in an alligator.

The Coopersville Sheriff's Department has been quoted as finding Mrs Debray's explanation for the repeated disappearances of her husbands hard to swallow, and has applied for a search warrant to examine the stomach contents of her farm's 400-pound alligator that goes by the name Prenup.

CHAPTER 50

What everyone else does.

That's what Chief Inspector Clayborne, in her infinite wisdom, had told Sturgess to do. She'd said it right after she'd ordered him to go home. He'd asked her what he was supposed to do there, and that had been her answer – do what everyone else does. Sunbathe in the garden, read a book, get drunk. Those had been her specific suggestions, before she'd immediately reiterated that what he was definitely *not* to do was find himself within a mile of the Natasha Ellis murder investigation. On that point, she had been rather emphatic. She'd even said that she didn't care what anyone else thought about that – a clear reference to his mysterious benefactor, Concerned Citizen.

Not that Sturgess reckoned that person would be on his side for much longer. He'd ignored CC's texts demanding an update, then had received a final one stating that he was utterly useless and their relationship was over. Sturgess's relationship experience was limited, but at least he now knew what it felt like to be dumped by text. That would give him something relatable to use next time he was having an awkward chat with Dr Charlie Mason. 'Yeah, he/she said it was me and not them.' Thing is, they were right. He'd been working on this case for three days now, and it felt like he was getting nowhere. Each new fact seemed to lead to more confusion rather than less.

The Natasha Ellis murder was the Greater Manchester Police's worst nightmare. Never mind the internet, the mainstream media was filled with wild speculation about what the live-stream footage showed. They were trying to investigate it while, at the same time, working to dismiss the most outlandish theories being pushed to explain it.

The unspoken agreement had been that Sturgess would be permitted to investigate this kind of nonsense on the very strict understanding that it and he stayed out of the public eye. Now that he had failed so emphatically in sticking to that brief, the chief inspector's main objective was to get him as far away as possible from the investigation, and from anyone with a microphone. Her tone of voice had implied that if she had access to a massive catapult, Sturgess would, at that moment in time, be hurtling towards the sun.

So he'd decided to embrace his new normal and do what everyone else does. He wasn't getting drunk but he was damn well doing the other stuff.

The grass in the back garden was under a foot tall, which Sturgess judged to be pretty good going. He opened the shed, ignored the rustling noise that meant that something had taken up residence inside, and grabbed the sun lounger the previous owners had left behind. He opened it and watched it fall apart before his eyes. OK, he would just lie on the cushioned bit, then – that was fine. The sun was in outer space, so what difference would an extra couple of feet make? He made himself the closest he could to being comfortable, opened the can of Diet Coke he'd brought outside with him, and ignored how half of it fizzed over the only pair of shorts he owned. He then opened the 832-page biography of Alexander Hamilton that his sister had bought him a couple of Christmases ago. Right, where had he got to? Ah – page four, OK. Normality, here he came.

He read almost two sentences then slammed the book shut. He was missing something, and not just sunblock – although, also sunblock. He started to scroll through the notes on his phone that constituted his only record of the case.

Phillip Butler lived alone. The report from the officers down in Berkshire who had dropped over to give his mother the news stated her belief that he hadn't been in a relationship and that he didn't have any serious hobbies, except the gym and the odd bit of five-a-side football. Despite Wilkerson's extremely thorough efforts, no doctors or dentists had been traced that knew anything about the dramatic changes in his appearance. He worked at Fuzzy Britches and they mourned his loss while going to extraordinary lengths to get his phone back. The last person Butler had texted was Keith Harpenden, a grade-A sleazy bastard with whom he'd apparently gone cruising for women – so there was at least one hobby his mother hadn't known about. Could picking up women be classed as a hobby? Sturgess was literally the worst person to ask. The closest thing he had to a hobby was the almost two sentences of the book he'd just . . .

He scrolled up to double-check his memory wasn't failing him, then quickly searched through his contacts.

She picked up on the third ring. The sounds of people, music and laughter filtered through from the background. She was probably out somewhere in a beer garden with friends.

'Hello?'

'Hi, Siobhan – it's Tom Sturgess here.'

'I'm sorry, who?'

'Detective Inspector Tom Sturgess.'

'Oh, right.'

'Is that the new boyfriend?' shouted a rather drunken female voice.

'Shut up, April.' The sound was muffled for a few seconds. He guessed Siobhan Regan was moving away from her friends for a little privacy. 'Sorry about that.'

'Not at all. I am really sorry to bother you again—'

'Yeah, it's not a great time, to be honest.'

'Sure. Just quickly – you mentioned Phillip Butler was in a book group?'

'Yeah,' said Siobhan, sounding confused at the question.

'Do you know who else was in it?'

'I don't. Look, we really didn't hang out much outside of work.'

'Right. Did he mention anything else about it?'

'No. I think he was a bit embarrassed. Didn't fit with his image, I guess. I only knew because I met him while he was heading into it.'

'I see,' said Sturgess, trying to sound casual, 'and where was that exactly?'

CHAPTER 51

Driving instructors will often emphasize the importance of keeping both hands on the wheel at all times when the vehicle is in motion. It should therefore go without saying that trying to execute a sharp turn through a set of gates while both of your hands are endeavouring to light a cigarette is really something to be avoided. That incredibly specific detail doesn't come up much in driving lessons. It has, in fact, only ever been pointed out twice – on both occasions, the person driving the vehicle at the time was Vincent Banecroft.

On the day Banecroft went on to pass his driving test first time, Patrick, the instructor who'd had to endure the stresses of teaching him, resigned in protest at a system that was broken beyond belief. He retrained in a less stressful profession and ended up being awarded a medal for his work as a bomb-disposal technician.

In Banecroft's defence, the person he'd just hit with his Jag was his employee, and he'd only hit them a little.

'Jesus!' shouted Hannah, the employee in question.

'What?' hollered Banecroft, winding down the window.

'You ran into me!'

'Oh please, it was just a nudge. And what on earth are you doing standing in the middle of the gates?'

Hannah held out her arms in indignation. 'I work here!'

Seeing as the gates in question were the ones that led to the Church of Old Souls, she was dead right on that point.

'Yes,' said Banecroft, 'but we've given you a desk. I mean, I've told several members of staff to go and play in the traffic in the past, but I'd all but given up hope of someone taking me up on it. And you're standing with the evening sun behind you. Frankly, it's testament to my catlike reflexes that you're still alive.'

'My hero.'

'You're welcome.' Amongst Banecroft's many annoying habits was his infuriating ability to ignore sarcasm when it suited him. 'So, was this an attempt to end it all?'

'No. I just got here. Actually, I was trying to ring you, but you weren't picking up.'

'Of course I wasn't. I was driving, and some of us take road safety seriously.'

Hannah resisted the urge to hurl her phone at Banecroft's head. She'd invariably miss. As she watched him park, Hannah decided that while she was definitely not going to forget this incident she would file it away to bring up at a more appropriate time. There were more pressing matters at hand.

'What are you doing back here?' asked Banecroft, getting out of the car. 'Did Stella ring you?'

'No,' said Hannah. 'Why? Has something happened?'

'Not exactly,' said Banecroft. 'Off her own bat, my protégée did some digging regarding our guest.'

'You mean . . .' said Hannah, pointing towards the doors to the cellar.

'Yes, poor ickle Leon Gibson, the world's saddest vampire. Stella did a social media search on him. She dug up a very long rant posted ten months ago by a woman of his acquaintance. Apparently, he is quite the sleazoid with the ladies.'

'Just like Butler and his mate.'

'Exactly,' said Banecroft. 'Peculiar though it may be, it is a link.'

Hannah nodded. 'Funnily enough, I went to see Cogs – to inform him that, despite his assurances to the contrary, random people were becoming vampires. He made the point that whatever's been happening, it definitely won't have been random, and that something powerful must be behind it.'

Banecroft nodded. 'I think it's time we had another chat with Mr Gibson.'

'I agree.'

'But first,' said Banecroft, 'why are your shoes covered in excrement?'

'Long story.'

'Give me the highlights.'

'Reggie and I went round to the house of Victor and Gregory Tombs.'

'The wannabe vampire and his daddy?'

'Yep. We got there just ahead of an actual mob, led by some acquaintances of the late Natasha Ellis. Things are getting completely out of hand.'

'And the footwear?'

'The mob was setting their house on fire so we had to escape through a sewer. Oh, and Reggie's in hospital.' She felt instantly guilty for not leading with that. 'His nose got broken in the fight.'

'With the Tombs family?'

'No,' said Hannah, 'the mob. The Tombs family dropped him off at A and E – on their way to an undisclosed location.'

'Which is?'

'What bit of "undisclosed location" are you struggling with? Victor Tombs might be a bit odd, but unless I'm way off, he isn't the villain here.'

Banecroft nodded. 'OK.' He turned towards the cellar doors. 'I think it's about time we found out who is.'

CHAPTER 52

Banecroft threw open the doors and the evening light spilled into the cellar. Hannah entered first and heard a whimper from the corner of the room. There was no denying that Gibson cut a pathetic figure, huddled there under his anorak and a couple of dust sheets. She noted the pieces of raw steak that Grace had brought him were now lying, sucked dry, on the plate. The glass of lemonade sat beside it, flat and untouched. She refrained from checking the bucket.

'Please, shut the door.'

'No,' said Banecroft, striding in, Chekhov over his shoulder. 'This time I don't think I will.'

Gibson's bloodshot eyes fixed them like those of a trapped animal. 'What's . . . What's wrong?'

'I was rather hoping you would tell us, Mr Gibson. All of this always smelled a bit off, but I'm afraid your assertion that you've no idea what is happening to you has now taken on the distinctively pungent aroma of total bullshit.'

'I don't know what's happening,' snapped Gibson. 'I've no idea what this is.'

'Maybe not, but I bet there's still something eating away at your conscience, isn't there? Something you've done that pissed off somebody. In this life, if we do something that really, really winds other people up, nine times out of ten we know it. Take it from an expert in the field. And I think you've got more of an idea than you're letting on. We need to know what it is right now, because there's something out there like you only worse. It's already killed, and I'm guessing it isn't done.'

'I already told you, I've got no idea.' As Gibson poked his head out, Hannah noticed that he had begun to foam at the mouth slightly. 'You're supposed to be helping me. All you've done is chain me up, and now you're accusing me of something, and I don't even know what.'

'Did you know Phillip Butler?'

'I already told you – no. I don't know anybody by that name.'

'Because here's the thing,' said Banecroft. 'Everything you've told us, and everything we know about him – there's nothing that links either of you to the occult.'

'I told you that.'

'Yes, but the thing you do both have in common is a rather chequered dating history.'

'What?'

Hannah took out her phone. The signal down there was poor. 'Excuse me a sec,' she mumbled.

Banecroft shot her a look but she ignored him entirely. There was something in the way Gibson had phrased it: 'I don't know anybody by that name.' She left Banecroft to continue his interrogation and moved towards the open door, typing in a Google search as she went. In the background she could hear Banecroft reading Gibson the text of the social media post in which a woman laid out his crimes.

After a minute Hannah returned. 'Right, Leon. Let's try this another way. I want you to be honest with me. Can you do that?'

'Yes. Of course.'

She took a step forward, which prompted Banecroft to hiss, 'Careful!'

Hannah looked back at him and then at Gibson. 'It's all right. If Leon wanted to hurt me, he could've done so last night. He understands we're the best chance to stop whatever's happening to him – don't you, Leon?'

He nodded.

It didn't take much to be good cop to Banecroft's bad. Just being the person who wasn't pointing a blunderbuss loaded with horrendously off garlic mayonnaise was enough.

Hannah took another step forward and showed Gibson her phone. 'You don't know the name, but do you recognize this man?'

There was a moment, before Gibson could throw up any defence, when his eyes told the story. 'I – I don't know him.'

'No,' said Hannah, pointing at the picture of Phillip Butler, 'but you've met him, haven't you?'

He paused for a moment then nodded.

Hannah lowered her phone and took a step back. 'You need to tell us now, Leon. Everything.'

'It'll sound worse than it is.'

'Try us,' said Banecroft.

Hannah put her hand on the muzzle of the blunderbuss and gently directed it away from Gibson.

'Talk.'

'It was a couple of months ago. I got approached by this guy in a bar, asking if I wanted to take part in a product trial. I thought it was a wind-up initially, but they said I'd be paid for it and everything. It was to test a new dating app. Real cutting-edge stuff. He talked me into it.' Leon shifted and averted his eyes as he spoke. 'They brought you in to take these personality tests.'

'Where?' asked Banecroft.

'Rented offices on this industrial estate. Sat there, answering questions, and then we had to sign all these non-disclosure things. After all of that, they showed me the app. It was this new thing – they referred to it as XR29 because they said it wasn't even named yet – all very hush-hush.'

'Aren't there lots of dating apps already?' asked Hannah.

'Not like this. This – this one told you where the women were. Like, their exact locations, and info about them.'

'How did it do that?'

'I don't know.'

Hannah and Banecroft looked at each other. This explained why Fuzzy Britches were so incredibly keen to get their employee's phone back.

'I thought maybe the women had signed up for it – maybe. At first. They just wanted us to test it out. We were all guys out looking for women anyway. It just, y'know, it showed you where all the hot single women were, and told you a bit about them.' He ran a hand across his sweaty brow. 'Worked great. Cut out loads of the guesswork. And we got paid. All we had to do was attend a meeting once a week and tell the guy about the experience.'

'What guy?'

'I don't know. Some guy. There were six of us, including him. None of us used our real names or could hang around or talk about it outside of the group. We all had codenames.' Gibson shrugged. 'I was Mr Green.'

'So,' said Hannah, 'this app just told you where the single women were and their names?'

Leon briefly met her gaze then looked away again. 'At first. They were constantly adding features.'

'Like what?'

Despite often hearing the phrase, Hannah had never seen somebody squirm before. Gibson's shoulders hunched forward and his hands played nervously with the zip of the anorak draped on top of him, as if he were expecting heavy rain to fall.

'The thing was . . . Look, I'm not an idiot. It must've been reading emails and I dunno what else. It knew all this personal stuff about the women. Insecurities. Medical stuff. Bad experiences. Fears. Soon, it was just feeding you targets with locations and lines of attack.' He pulled the anorak around him tighter. 'Their language. Not mine.'

Hannah thought she might be sick. 'So, all of these women – this app was telling you their most intimate secrets so that you could use them to get them to sleep with you?'

'Look, I know it sounds bad. I was in a very bad space mentally.'

'Shut up,' said Hannah, real venom in her voice now. 'Please, stop making yourself out to be the victim here.'

'I'm . . .' Leon Gibson went to say something then stopped and lowered his head in shame.

Hannah turned away and went to leave, but Banecroft laid his hand on her arm to stop her.

'Tell us the rest.'

'What rest?'

There was a real snarl in Banecroft's voice. 'You think you're the first sleazy arsehole I've met in my life? I used to edit a tabloid newspaper. Tell us the rest.'

'I didn't want to—'

'Tell us!'

'All right, fine,' said Gibson, holding back his head, suddenly defiant. 'The guy said to make it fun, and to make sure we were testing it to the max, they gamified it. You got points – for a phone number, how many women you slept with, if they were famous, that sort of thing.'

'And?'

'I didn't, all right, I didn't! But some of the other guys, they started using the function where you got bonus points for sharing pictures and videos. OK. I get it. All right? It was a terrible thing to do. I deeply regret it.'

'Sure,' said Banecroft. 'You're a new man. But only because somebody or something made you into one.'

Hannah pulled her arm away from Banecroft and headed for the door. She didn't want to look at Leon Gibson ever again.

'I've got a sneaking suspicion,' Banecroft continued, 'but just for fun, how about you tell me where this collection of classy gentlemen met every week?'

CHAPTER 53

Sturgess banged his fist on the door with the 'closed for private function' sign on it. He peered through the window, cupping his hands around his eyes to block out the dazzling light of the setting sun behind him. The Roxy looked deserted. He banged loudly for a second time. All he needed was some information. Butler's book group that was clearly not a book group had met here once a week. There might be CCTV footage. Failing that, somebody would have taken the booking for the meeting room they used. There would be something.

He took a step back as the door he'd been hammering swung open. That was odd. He'd tried it when he'd first arrived and it had been locked, he was sure of it.

He walked in slowly past the unoccupied ticket booth. 'Hello? Hello?'

There was no response. He'd been in the bar-cum-restaurant area twice before, but such places always looked smaller and shabbier when unoccupied. Sturgess started to wonder if maybe there was another door outside that led directly to administrative offices upstairs when suddenly organ music started to play. He walked through the empty bar towards the double doors at the end.

The main auditorium was large and impressive. Restored to its original pre-war look, the seats were upholstered in red velvet and, in the corner, stood a concession stand that sold popcorn and candyfloss. The three aisles sloped down towards the stage, with its massive screen, upon which was playing out an old silent movie: a bald-headed vampire with hideous teeth and impossibly thick eyebrows was menacing a young woman dressed in white, who was screaming her lungs out for all she was worth. All of this was set to the swelling music that seemed to fill the empty venue more than should be possible.

The auditorium contained one other person. At the organ beneath the stage sat a young woman. Her flowing blonde hair had an eerie, translucent quality to it as it swished back and forth while she played.

The music wasn't just loud. It seemed to fill the space physically as well as aurally, the melody ominously dramatic. The hairs on the back of Sturgess's neck stood to attention as the air crackled with an unseen energy.

He shouted hello again, but received no response. A part of him felt the urge to turn and flee, but it was shouted down by his curiosity. He started to walk down the centre aisle. On the screen, a card flicked up: *Come, my dear. I have something to show you.*

The actress screamed again. It appeared to be her main role in proceedings.

'Excuse me?' said Sturgess as he reached the organ. 'Hi, I was wondering if . . .'

Up close, the woman's long blonde hair wasn't just shiny, it was glowing. His sense of foreboding grew stronger. Step back.

Move away. Run. Do something. Instead, he found his feet rooted to the spot. Like a deer in headlights.

The woman both turned around and didn't. One version of her remained playing the organ while another stood in front of him and smiled.

'Ronnie?'

It was the Roxy's manager – only not.

The woman's mouth moved and a voice came out, although something was off – as if the audio hadn't been dubbed correctly.

'Hello, Inspector. So glad you could make it.'

The golden hair surged forward and wrapped itself around Sturgess, enveloping his entire body. It coiled tightly around him, binding him, and raised him off the floor. The urge to scream overwhelmed him but no sound would come.

He hung there, suspended in mid-air, while below him the woman clapped her hands excitedly.

'Oh, this is excellent. You are just what we need.'

Then the voice changed, as if several people were saying the same line in near but not exact unison.

'Come, my dear. I have something to show you.'

CHAPTER 54

Mr Red danced a few giddy steps before he leaped to the next rooftop. Having been trapped inside all day, watching the world tremble before him, it was joyous to be out in the sweet night air once again. There was a glorious scent of panic all around – he could taste it. The footage of his latest prize had exceeded anything he could have hoped for, travelling around the world as it had done. The bonus points would be enormous. The fact that the girl had been live-streaming at the time had been a happy coincidence. It was so much better that way.

Now, of course, the world was looking for him, but then, he had skills the world wasn't ready for. He jumped to another rooftop and looked at the phone in his hand. The problem with announcing his arrival in quite such an emphatic fashion was that he had set the bar so high. He'd been thinking about it all day. After such a strong beginning, how could he bring the Manchester part of his adventure to a fitting close?

The only solution was to go for multiple targets. Really rack up the points. Then, at the end of the night, he could steal a car or force someone to drive him. Take the show on the road. West

428

to Liverpool, east to Leeds, or Sheffield, maybe? There were so many choices. The world truly was his feast.

Then, he stopped.

The night was suddenly filled with music.

Such music. Swooping and soaring under the perfect moonlit sky. It rose up to engulf him in a sweet embrace and wrap itself around him. Calling him home.

He stretched his arms out wide and roared with unrestrained delight.

He was in need of a finale, and here it presented itself. Where better than the place it all began?

CHAPTER 55

Grace looked out of the window at the crimson sunset hanging low over the city. She did enjoy a good sunset. If you were in the office at just the right time, the light through the old church's stained-glass window could be spectacular, casting shimmering sheets of bright colour that made the shabby and tired place look magical, if only for a little while.

Down below, she caught sight of Banecroft's Jag, with Hannah in the passenger seat, as it pulled out of the gates and drove away at high speed.

'Wait! They're back . . . Where are they going? But . . .'

Grace threw up her arms in consternation. This week had been difficult for many reasons. There was the bathroom situation. She wanted to sort out somebody to come in to fix and finish the job, but she couldn't do that until Banecroft gave her the go-ahead. She'd also been watching the news as the city went into meltdown after the attack on that young lady from that awful TV show. While Grace didn't approve of such programming, she could only feel sorry for the poor girl, having met such a horrible end, and for her family too.

More than anything, Grace was annoyed because, despite

trying to ring several of the members of staff of the newspaper, nobody had got back to her with an update. She wanted to know what was going on. As it was, she'd spent most of the week stuck in the office, alone more often than not, except for Stella, who had a tendency to stick to her room. Part of the fun of working at *The Stranger Times* was feeling involved with things. If she was going to feel like a secretary, she could do that somewhere else, and it would definitely pay better.

She sighed. Still, she understood everyone was busy, and she supposed they were all doing what they could, given the heavy fall of crazy that had been dumped on them within the space of a week. It would just be nice to know what was going on. To feel useful.

Grace went to get her bag.

She heard the sobbing before she'd even opened the doors to the cellar. She'd decided to bring the poor man Gibson some more raw meat and another drink, and, Grace shuddered, to offer to empty the bucket. As she switched on the light, the pitiful creature cowered in the corner.

'Mr Gibson, are you OK?'

His voice came out hoarse between ragged sobs. 'It burns. Oh, sweet Jesus, help me – it burns.'

'What does?'

He held his hands up limply. 'The shackles. I don't know what happened. I . . . I was reading the pamphlets you gave me, and I decided to accept the light of our Lord Jesus into my life, then the metal shackles started to burn.'

'Oh dear.' Grace looked around. 'Let me try and ring Mr

Banecroft again.' She put the plate of meat and the drink down on the steps.

Gibson doubled over in pain. 'Oh God, please help me. Please!' He tried to stand but collapsed to the ground.

'Oh no.' Grace clasped her hands to her chest. 'Mr Gibson? Are you OK? Mr Gibson?'

She pulled out her phone. Damn it. No signal.

'Mr— Oh no!'

Gibson had started to convulse. Grace turned around, grabbed the keys to the shackles that were hanging on the nail by the light switch and ran across the room.

'You will be OK, Mr Gibson. Hang in there. I will help you.'

After some fumbling, Grace managed to get the shackles off his ankles. Then she moved on to his wrists. As she did so, she started to sing 'Bringing In The Sheaves' – to calm herself as much as anything. Once she'd released the last manacle, she stood up and quickly moved back.

'Mr Gibson, are you OK? I got the shackles off you.'

Gibson rolled over and lay there breathing heavily for a moment, almost hyperventilating. Then, gradually, he seemed to calm.

'Are you feeling OK now?'

He looked up. 'Yes, thank you.'

'OK,' said Grace. 'Now, if you just stay there, I'll try and . . .'

Grace looked behind her at the food and then gasped as she turned back. Gibson was right in front of her.

She took a couple of steps back.

'Mr Gibson, Leon – you should stay over there for a minute and . . .'

As she looked into his eyes it felt as if the bottom fell out of her stomach. There was something in his gaze. It spoke to a deeper thing than the mind. It was the innocuous log drifting down the river, the rustle in the bushes, the movement you see out of the corner of your eye.

Grace kept edging backwards towards the steps.

'You need to control yourself . . .'

He smiled at her, stretching the skin on his face and causing a couple of the scabs on his lips to reopen. Grace's heart thumped faster and faster in her chest. He moved so quickly, putting himself between her and the door. She feinted to the left but he was in front of her before she could move any further. There was no escape. She kept inching backwards, the only choice open to her.

'The Lord is my shepherd I shall not want. The Lord is my shepherd I shall not want.'

Grace felt the cold stone of the wall press against her back. Her bracelets jingled as she held up her index fingers in the shape of a cross.

Gibson laughed, his face a hideous mask of ravenous madness.

'Please,' begged Grace softly, her body shaking as the monster stood before her. She clamped her eyelids shut, not wanting to bear witness to the final moment.

There was a change in the air. Like the seconds before a torrential downpour. Grace risked opening one eye.

Gibson had turned his back on her. A warm blue light was radiating from something behind him, growing to fill the room.

Grace angled her head to look around him.

Stella was standing there, her entire being surrounded by the light.

Gibson threw a hand out in front of his face. 'This is a . . . misunderstanding.'

'No,' said Stella. 'I understand what you are perfectly.'

Her voice sounded different – as if there were an oscillation to it, as if powerful waves were rising and falling within it. Grace realized that the light didn't just surround Stella, it was coming from her. Emanating from every fibre of the girl's being.

'I'm . . . I need help,' pleaded Gibson. 'I have a problem.'

'You were going to hurt her.'

'No, I wasn't.'

'Don't lie to me!' snapped Stella, and the colour around her intensified.

Gibson crumpled to the floor, as if the light itself was pinning him down.

'Stella, dear . . .' started Grace.

'Are you OK?'

'Yes, thank you. Everything is fine. Don't do anything you might regret.'

'Listen to your friend,' said Gibson. 'You don't want to hurt anyone.'

'Why not? Lots of people seem intent on hurting me.' Stella looked at Grace. 'You should get out of here.'

'No, Stella,' said Grace, trying to sound a lot calmer than she felt. 'This isn't you.'

Stella bunched her fists and her eyes widened. 'I'm beginning to think it is.'

Gibson struggled to crawl a few inches to his left. It seemed like the weight of the world was pinning him down. 'You don't mean . . .' He trailed off and gazed into the distance, mesmerized.

After a couple of seconds Stella looked over at Grace, suddenly unsure.

'What are you doing?' Stella asked Gibson.

Gibson didn't move his head. 'Can't you hear it? The music. The wonderful music. Calling me home.'

Stella turned and tilted her head to one side, as if also listening to something. Grace couldn't hear anything.

In a flash, Gibson shot past Stella and was out the open door behind her. She watched him disappear into the night. Grace moved towards her, trying not to show her fear.

'Stella? Are you OK?'

The blue light faded so quickly it was as if it had never been there, save for the waning memory of it imprinted on Grace's vision. As Stella turned back to face Grace, she became that same teenaged girl again, smiling sheepishly.

'I'm fine. You were the one that was being attacked.'

'But you're OK?'

'Yes.'

'Good. In that case, I'm going to faint now.'

The last thing Grace recalled was Stella's arms around her, catching her before she hit the floor.

CHAPTER 56

Dr Carter tried to force a smile. No, not a smile. Given the circumstances, that might seem too flippant. She needed to look composed, though – in control, that was the most important thing. She turned back to her desk. Perhaps she should be sitting down? Did that look in control or more nonchalant?

Before she could decide, a pinging noise came from the monitor and the large screen changed from black to red. It took a certain kind of mind to demand a video call and then disable their own feed. She assumed it wasn't because he didn't know how the technology worked, although he was several centuries old. Her guess was that the old bastard enjoyed watching people squirm.

In the absence of any other options, Carter stood to attention.

'What the hell is going on, Carter?'

'There have been some unforeseen issues, sire,' she said, trying to sound calm.

'Issues? This is a total disaster. It's all over the world media.'

Dr Carter nodded. 'It is, my lord. As I pointed out last year, with the changing media landscape—'

'Don't even think about it, Carter. You were in charge of this debacle. Don't you dare turn around and use it to try to score points.'

'That was not my intention, my lord.'

'Your value to this organization is based on the fact that, until now, you have shown an aptitude for dealing with tricky situations. If that has run out, then so has your usefulness.'

Dr Carter gave a tight smile. Now was not the time to rise to that kind of bait. 'Whatever this is, it has nothing to do with us and, from what I can gather, the Folk are as mystified as we are.'

'Mystified?'

Damn it, that was not a good choice of words. She tried not to wince. 'I meant only that this is something new, or, quite possibly, something very old. Perhaps some of the old powers—'

'The old powers did not make silly monsters to frighten children.'

'No, my lord, but something involved here is very powerful. Perhaps an old power has attached itself to—'

'Speculation,' boomed the voice. 'Your house is on fire and you're still throwing out wild theories about what might have caused it. I thought you had those newspaper people looking into this?'

'I have, my lord, but as far as I can tell, they haven't found anything concrete yet either.'

'As far as you can tell?'

'I did warn you, sire. Vincent Banecroft is not a man who can easily be controlled.'

'Yes, well, we'll see about that. And your pet policeman?'

'DI Sturgess has been removed from the case.'

'Has he? Perhaps his superiors have the right idea. Maybe I will send in—'

'Respectfully, my lord, there is no need for that. While the situation has escalated, I am confident I can regain control of it and turn this to our advantage.'

'How do you intend to do that?'

Dr Carter ran a hand through her hair. 'In the same way I have always done in the past, my lord. Humbly, I ask for your patience to let me work.'

'Hmmmm. Very well, but be aware, Doctor – you are in a precarious position. What is supposed to be given to you can be given to others instead.'

'Thank you, my lord. If the purpose of this call is to deliver that threat, rest assured I have well and truly received it.'

'Doctor, do not take our previously warm relationship as a licence to take liberties. You are on very thin ice given what a royal screw-up this has been.'

Out of the corner of her eye, Dr Carter noticed the figure of her assistant hovering. 'I apologize, my lord. If you'll excuse me for a second.' She quickly muted the call. 'Not now, Jeremy. I said I was not to be disturbed.'

'I'm sorry, but . . .'

She turned to look Jeremy full in the face. 'What?'

'It's DI Sturgess. Something's happened.'

CHAPTER 57

Hannah looked out of the window as the world whizzed by in the darkness.

'You seem distracted,' said Banecroft from the driver's seat.

'To be honest, this is the first time I've been in a car driven by you. I was busy watching my life flash before my eyes.'

Banecroft huffed. 'There is nothing wrong with my driving.'

On cue, a car in the oncoming lane honked loudly.

'What the hell was his problem? He was on the other side of the road.'

'I think the problem was that so were you.'

'Pffft. People.'

Hannah decided to study the back of her hands, in the hope that trying to stay calm would mean her body would be limp during the crash that was inevitably going to happen. She had a vague idea that if you're physically relaxed you have a better chance of avoiding serious injury. A few weeks ago they'd run a story about a drunk man falling off the top of a football stadium and essentially bouncing before, incredibly, walking away unscathed. There'd been some references to science. At the very least, she certainly felt like she could use a drink.

The car lurched to the left, which resulted in somebody some-where screaming.

'So,' said Banecroft, 'exactly what do we think is going on? I mean, *I* know, but I wanted to check that you've been paying attention.'

Hannah took a deep breath. 'OK, as far as I can see – Leon Gibson, Phillip Butler and the four other members of this sleazy little cabal were having their weekly meetings in the back room at the Roxy, and something or someone took notice.'

'All right, but why turn them into vampires?'

Hannah closed her eyes and patted her hands on her knees. She needed to think. 'Be quiet for a second.'

'What?'

'Just shut up a minute . . .'

The car screeched to a halt and there was a lot of honking. Hannah tried to block it out. Someone behind them blasted their horn particularly aggressively, prompting Banecroft to wind down his window.

'Why don't you take your horn and shove it up your—'

'Vincent!' cried Hannah, not opening her eyes.

'He started it. Ha – the idiot's getting out now. He's . . .' Banecroft's tone changed. 'He's actually quite big. These lights must be due to change . . . Let's assume they have.'

The Jag accelerated hard, forcing Hannah back in her seat. There was an awful lot of horns blaring for the next few seconds, and then the noise stopped.

'Christ,' said Banecroft, 'even I thought that was dangerous.'

Hannah opened her eyes and slapped the dashboard. 'The films!'

'What?'

'Think about it. Something – or someone, or whatever – is seeing this six-pack of sleaze meet there every week. Sees them taking advantage of vulnerable women. It comes to see them as . . .'

'Monsters,' finished Banecroft.

'Exactly. Like it sees in the films the Roxy shows. Whatever this thing is, assuming it's based there, it's experiencing the world through the lens of cinema, and so it's turned these men into something it understands.'

'Makes sense,' says Banecroft. 'Although, let's be honest, call this thing "it" all you like, but I'm going to assume it is a woman.' He took his hands off the wheel to gesticulate wildly, which did nothing to improve his driving. 'The Roxy's ghost! Of course. The weeping girl!'

'What?' said Hannah.

'It was in the file Stella prepared for me. The weeping girl with golden hair, jilted at the altar and left a broken woman. When the place was an old music hall she used to play the organ before she killed herself.'

Hannah slapped the dashboard again. 'Oh, for God's sake. Ronnie – the manager. She told me they were getting sued because male members of staff were getting hassled.'

'Angry ghost?' asked Banecroft.

'Maybe,' said Hannah. 'Although there's a big difference between whispering things or messing with a knife to transforming presumably six men into monsters. Cogs said that it'd take something incredibly powerful to do that and . . . Wait a sec!' Hannah bounced up and down excitedly in her seat.

'What?' said Banecroft, turning to look at her.

Hannah grabbed the wheel and turned it towards her, so that only the wing mirror was clipped by the large delivery truck they had been careering towards. 'Holy crap! Watch the road, you insane Irish reprobate.'

'All right, all right,' said Banecroft, facing front again. 'But what are you jumping up and down about?'

'Cogs. When I first met him he said something about the old ancient whatever were rising. Old magic. Looking for somewhere to go.'

'And you reckon it attached itself to this ghost?'

'I dunno,' said Hannah. 'Maybe. Best explanation we've got. Suddenly, instead of crying her eyes out, the organ player has a whole lot more power.'

'And she's using it to take her revenge on men. As a wronged woman yourself, whose side are you on here?'

'Give it a rest,' said Hannah. 'Just because my soon-to-be-ex turned out to be an arse, doesn't mean all men are. A lot of people have happy marriages. I mean . . .'

Hannah glanced at Banecroft. Improbably, he was using his time in control of a speeding vehicle to simultaneously light another cigarette. Ghosts, marriages – in one way this felt like a good moment to bring up the Simon thing, but still, it felt horribly intrusive.

'What?' asked Banecroft through a cloud of smoke.

'Open a window,' replied Hannah.

'If you need to pass wind, do it on your own time.'

The car screeched to a seatbelt-testing halt.

'We're here.'

CHAPTER 58

Once Hannah was out of the car, she felt considerably better. Living through a near-death experience can often lead to feelings of euphoria. She was sure she'd read that somewhere.

In contrast to her two previous visits to the Roxy, the venue was very quiet. Music and laughter could be heard spilling out of various nearby apartment buildings as people enjoyed the warm night air. The Roxy, in contrast, stood funeral still. Only low-level lighting was on inside, although the neon sign still flickered above the main entrance. It and the two streetlights gave the alleyway the look of one where toughs would hang out in a James Dean movie. A woman Hannah vaguely recognized was standing outside the door. As Hannah got closer, she realized it was the waitress who'd served her the first time she'd been there.

'Hi – is it closed?'

'It's not supposed to be,' said the woman. 'I've no idea what's going on. We're meant to be screening *Ferris Bueller's Day Off* tonight. We've had people turning up and leaving angry. I've been here for nearly an hour.'

'Is Ronnie about?'

'No, and she isn't answering her pigging phone either.'

'Have you tried hammering on the door?' asked Banecroft, earning him the kind of withering look you can only get from someone who has worked in the service industry for far too long.

'No. Over a hundred people have tried to get in here, and would you believe that blindingly obvious idea has not occurred to *any* of them?'

Hannah gave an embarrassed smile while Banecroft ignored the comment entirely.

The woman turned to Hannah and pointed at the blunderbuss Banecroft was holding. 'Why's he got a weapon?'

'Mainly to stop people attacking him when the smell hits them.'

'What sm—' The waitress blanched as the stench finally reached her. She turned away, her hand cupped over her mouth. 'That is rank!'

Banecroft walked up to the door and thumped on it loudly. He somehow managed to look surprised when his efforts elicited no response.

Hannah stood beside him. 'What are we going to do?'

'As soon as she leaves,' said Banecroft, 'I'll keep watch and you kick it in.'

'You are quite the gentleman—'

Hannah broke off as the door suddenly opened.

'That's . . .' started Banecroft. 'That was locked a second ago.'

And then the world was turned on its side. At least, that's what it felt like. Hannah found herself falling through the door as if gravity had been flipped sideways and she had no choice in the matter. Banecroft grabbed her with his free hand but he couldn't pull her back. Instead, he too was dragged inside. The door slammed behind them and then, as if the switch had been flipped back, the world returned to near normal.

'What the hell just happened?' said Hannah, looking around.

'I don't know,' said Banecroft, 'but being in here doesn't feel as desirable as it did thirty seconds ago.'

They watched as the waitress tried the door but it was locked again. She glared at them through the glass.

Hannah moved forward apologetically and tried her luck with the door, keener to get herself out than to get the waitress in. She examined the locks, which didn't seem to be engaged, and then strained at the handle. 'It won't open.'

Banecroft stood behind her. 'Really? I'm quite new to dealing with this woo-woo nonsense, but were you expecting the suddenly magical door through which you were dragged to let you leave again? You seem to have very little appreciation of narrative integrity.'

'Wait a sec,' said Hannah, slapping the pockets of her jeans then pulling out the old brass key for the front door of the Church of Old Souls. 'I've got the key. I thought magic isn't supposed to work on you if you have one of these in your possession.'

'Hmmmm,' mused Banecroft. 'Maybe this woo-woo is a different type of woo-woo.'

'Or a more powerful one.'

The waitress was waving her arms and shouting something at them, but Hannah couldn't hear anything. All she could do was shrug and smile apologetically.

'I'm just . . .'

Hannah stopped mid-sentence. The waitress slapped her hand to her neck as if she'd been bitten. She looked briefly confused before she collapsed to the ground.

'What in the . . .'

Men – or, at least, figures – in all-black body armour, complete with balaclavas, ran down the alley.

'Oh Christ,' said Banecroft. 'Not this lot again.'

It said something about how freaked out Hannah was by whatever had dragged them into the cinema, that the arrival of a mini army of storm troopers didn't bother her much. It was as if she were capable of only so much shock, and she'd already reached her limit. Besides, as Banecroft pointed out, this wasn't the first time they'd encountered the troops.

At some point later, Hannah might sit around and marvel at how insane her life had become that these events didn't feel that unusual, but right now she pointed at the unconscious waitress and shouted after the men, 'Oh, c'mon! At least pick her up.'

The troopers fanned out in a semi-circle around the door. Banecroft and Hannah watched as one of them attempted first to open the door and then to kick it in, all to no effect.

One of them drew something out of a backpack.

'I think we should stand back,' said Banecroft.

They did so and watched as the storm troopers attempted to blow the door off. All their efforts generated was a lot of smoke and some quite confused body language.

At that point Dr Carter came striding down the alley, staring through the glass at Hannah and Banecroft as she did so.

Banecroft waved cheerfully. 'Look who it is.'

Carter stood in front of the door and, as the storm troopers encircled her, threw out her hands, closed her eyes and mouthed something. For a few seconds her body shook visibly from the strain, then she stopped, defeated.

Banecroft approached the door and knocked on the glass. When Carter looked at him, he pointed at her and shouted, 'DID YOU' – he jabbed a finger at the ground – 'WANT TO COME IN HERE?'

She gave a tight smile and nodded.

He scratched his head theatrically before wagging his finger in the air as if he'd just had a brainwave, then he pointed at Carter again. 'You' – he indicated her skirt – 'still have a coffee stain! On your skirt. COFFEE!'

This elicited some sign language from the doctor that required no formal training to decipher.

'While I'm sure you're enjoying yourself,' said Hannah to Banecroft, 'have you failed to realize that whatever dragged us in here is, apparently, strong enough to keep her and her mini army out?'

'Oh no,' said Banecroft, 'I definitely have not. I appear to be a man trapped in a building inhabited by a powerful man-hating entity. That has not escaped my attention.'

'Good.' Hannah looked around them nervously. 'In light of that, are you sure that using it as an opportunity to taunt the woman outside the door is the wisest of moves?'

He puffed out his cheeks. 'Well, if you're going to take all the fun out of it.'

Just then, the sound of organ music seemed to fill the entire room. Hannah looked down at her feet, aghast as they started to walk of their own accord towards the auditorium.

'What the hell?'

It took every inch of her self-restraint not to scream. She could feel her legs. She could feel her feet as they rose and fell. She just had no control over what they were doing.

'Where are you going?' asked Banecroft.

'I have no clue.'

Banecroft hefted the blunderbuss onto his shoulder and waved through the window to Dr Carter and her men.

'Bye, kids. I think the show's about to start!'

CHAPTER 59

Hannah's feet walking entirely independently of her was the most horrible feeling. She was no longer in control of her own body. Like a marionette with someone else pulling the strings.

'Where exactly are you going?' asked Banecroft for the second time.

'I don't know, do I? I'd have thought that was obvious.'

'Right. Hang on.'

He hurried a few steps ahead, placed Chekhov on the floor and stood in front of Hannah, his arms outstretched. He raised his voice. 'I command you to stop walking!'

Hannah had to admit that, despite her horror at being a puppet under someone else's control, and the dread in the pit of her stomach as to where all this was heading, a part of her was still thrilled to experience the sensation of firmly kicking a man in the testicles.

Banecroft crumpled to the ground.

'That wasn't me!'

His response was lost in a fit of coughing and groaning. Hannah's body, which she was starting to think of as something

449

separate to her, stepped nimbly around him and continued on its merry way.

'Banecroft, help me! I don't like this. I don't like this at all!'

Her hands flew out in front of her and pushed through the swing doors that led to the main auditorium. The music swelled dramatically as she entered. The space was bathed in the flickering monochromatic light from the massive screen that dominated the stage. It showed a caption card that read *THE HERO ARRIVES*. Beneath it, on the stage itself, was Sturgess, tied to a chair.

Hannah looked around. It appeared to be her, Sturgess and one other person in the auditorium – to the front left of the stage a figure with eerily translucent blonde hair was playing the organ. Hannah hadn't seen the instrument before, but she guessed it didn't normally look like this. It was changing colour from green to red to blue, pulsing along with the music.

The card on the screen changed. *Help!*

'Hannah!' hollered Sturgess. 'Is that you?'

She shouted to be heard over the music. 'Sort of.'

'Can you come down and untie me?'

Hannah tried to shrug but her shoulders appeared to have joined the rebellion. All she seemed to have left was the ability to turn her head and speak. 'I'd like to. I'm not in control of myself at the moment.'

'What?'

The card on the screen changed. *I'll save you, my darling.*

'Hang on, I think . . .' Hannah's legs started to move much more quickly now. 'Yep, here I come.'

She smelled Banecroft – or, rather, Chekhov – before she heard him.

He was behind her, panting to catch up. 'Where are you going now?'

'Really? You think that's a sensible question?'

'Don't get narky with me. I'm the one who has recently sustained a testicular assault.'

Hannah continued her walk down the central aisle. The light from the screen grew brighter still as she stepped out of the shadow of the balcony that ran across the back half of the auditorium.

Banecroft managed to pull up alongside her, his gait noticeably altered. He looked across at the blonde woman enthusiastically playing the organ. 'I'm guessing that would be our host?'

'Looks like it.'

Hannah reached the end of the aisle and stopped. The woman's face was now clear to her.

'Ronnie?'

'You know her?' asked Banecroft.

'It's Ronnie, the manager – only it isn't. She doesn't have long blonde hair and she doesn't play the organ.'

The music fell away slightly as the woman's head turned towards them. Hannah felt a sensation like her ears popping, which was quickly followed by a strange shimmy in the air. Suddenly, where there had been one face, there were now three, as if superimposed on top of each other: Ronnie screaming, a blonde woman smiling, and a golden light that was featureless and only vaguely human in shape.

With difficulty, Hannah focused on the face in there that she recognized – Ronnie's – whose mouth was opened impossibly wide, caught in an awful, never-ending screech of anguish.

'Ronnie! Hang on, we'll—'

The air vibrated once more and there was a single face again, nominally Ronnie's, but with long flowing blonde hair, and the unnatural golden light in her eyes.

'Oh God, I think she's been possessed,' said Hannah.

'Well,' said Banecroft, 'takes one to know one.'

The card up on the screen changed again. *Please, help me! I'm so weak and feeble!*

'I get it,' said Banecroft. 'It looks like you're acting out your very own movie.'

'Super.'

'A badly written one.'

Hannah spoke through gritted teeth. 'While it is a very you thing to do, are you sure slagging off the all-powerful entity is the best of ideas?'

'Well, if she can't take a bit of constructive feedback . . . This is how we ended up with awful *Dr Dolittle* reboots.'

'Will you focus!' snapped Hannah, as the music started to rise in intensity again.

'All right. No need to be snippy. You're obviously here to save Sturgess.'

'How's that supposed to—' Hannah's train of thought was derailed as her body turned abruptly to the right, in the direction of the stairs leading to the stage. 'Fantastic. We're off again.'

'Not much of a rescue, is it?'

'Will you shut up with the criticism!'

'What's going on?' shouted Sturgess.

'Hang on,' replied Hannah. 'I think we're coming.'

Sure enough, she started to walk up the stairs. It was all rather awkward. Whatever had control of her didn't seem to be moving her ankles, so every step was all knee and hip. As she reached the stage, Hannah could see that Sturgess's chair was, in fact, some kind of prop throne.

'Quick, untie me,' he said.

'I can't,' said Hannah. 'Banecroft?'

She managed to turn her head to see Banecroft standing at the top of the stairs, his back to her. He was staring up at the large balcony.

'I've just figured it out,' he said.

'What?'

'The film. You're saving PC Plod all right, but not from her . . .'

As Hannah's eyes adjusted, she was able to just make out the indistinct outlines of four individuals standing up in the darkness. 'Oh no.'

As they watched, a figure dropped down from the balcony and landed in the central aisle – Leon Gibson, unmistakable in his green anorak.

'Leon?' said Hannah. 'How did you get out?'

'I . . . I don't know what's happening,' shouted Leon, sounding as terrified as Hannah was feeling.

'OK,' yelled Sturgess, 'whatever's going on, somebody really needs to untie me right now.'

Another figure dropped into the left-hand aisle and started walking down the auditorium towards them.

'From a narrative perspective, this all makes sense,' said Banecroft. 'The baddies needed to be established, which is why this lot have been running around for the last couple of days. Now they've done bad shit, you, the hero, are justified in—'

Hannah screamed as she noticed something hurtling towards her from the side of the stage. She clenched her eyes shut, so only felt her hand, independent of her, shoot up and snatch the thing out of the air. She opened her eyes to discover she was holding a large metal spike. 'Oh God.'

A third figure dropped down into the right-hand aisle.

'Yep,' said Banecroft, sounding smug. 'That's what I thought.'

The card on the screen above them changed once more. *Don't worry, I shall protect you, my sweet virgin betrothed.*

Banecroft pointed at the card. 'Wait, what? Hang on a second.' He raised his eyebrows quizzically at Sturgess. 'Are you?'

Sturgess's face turned red with fury and embarrassment. 'Untie. Me. NOW!'

'All right,' said Banecroft. 'Keep your knickers on. Apparently, you're good at that.'

Hannah sensed Banecroft moving across the stage but her eyes remained fixed on the aisles. Behind Leon Gibson, a fourth figure descended. This one was wearing a red hooded top. It wasn't just that which differentiated him, though. Unlike the others, who looked utterly terrified, this guy was wearing a broad smile.

Banecroft's voice came from behind her. 'I don't want to worry anyone unduly, but I'd bet the farm that Red there is the gent who recently became an internet sensation.'

'The ropes!' shouted Sturgess. 'Untie the ropes!'

'I can't untie them because they're not tied. There aren't any knots. It's just . . .'

'Figure it out,' snapped Sturgess.

'Someone's a little tense. Wonder why?'

Hannah ignored the bickering. All of her attention was on the four figures moving towards the stage.

'Oh God.' She looked with dread at the metal spike in her hand. 'Somebody do something.'

Hannah turned to read the latest card on the screen. *You shall not lay a finger on this sweet virgin, you ungodly monsters.*

'Wow,' said Banecroft. 'There's definitely a theme developing here, Detective. Are you, like, religious or something? Or is it a medical thing? Nothing to be ashamed of. Happens to the best of us.'

'Shut up.'

'All right, hang on.' Banecroft pulled his lighter from his pocket. 'I'm going to burn 'em off.'

As soon as he flicked the lighter into life, Banecroft experienced a sensation he'd not known since he was a toddler – that of being picked up and raised in the air. 'What the . . .' Nothing was holding him. He was just floating upside down, ten feet off the ground, Chekhov still waving in his right hand, a useless lighter in his left. 'Oh no. I do not like this.'

Hannah glanced behind her. 'What are you doing?'

'Does it look like this is my idea? Do you think I've known how to fly for ages and just decided not to mention it?'

Down in the central aisle, Hannah noticed the man in red had moved past Leon Gibson. In fact, Gibson and the other two figures appeared to be moving against their will, much like her, but not Red. He stalked forward with great purpose, his eyes alight with a terrible enthusiasm.

She knew with great certainty where this was heading, and tried to strain with all her might to pull herself away, but nothing below her neck was under her control. 'I need help here.' She could hear the panic in her voice.

Banecroft waved Chekhov about as he rotated slowly like a kebab rotisserie. 'Could all four of you gentlemen please stand in a line? I've only got the one shot, so I'm afraid you're going to have to share.'

'I'm not killing anybody!' Hannah screamed down at the figure playing the organ.

'Yes, you bloody well are,' roared Banecroft. 'Stop being selfish. We have an edition due out on Friday and you're my assistant editor. This is kill or be killed.'

'Talk to her,' yelled Sturgess.

'What?'

'The . . . whatever. Talk to her.'

'Woman to woman,' added Banecroft.

If Hannah had control of anything other than her head, she would have leaped back in shock – 'Ronnie' was standing beside her. The music played on, even though the seat at the organ was now empty.

The four, for want of a better word, men had now reached the stage. Red surged towards Hannah but was pulled back, as if being restrained by invisible arms. He snarled like a caged animal.

Hannah turned to Ronnie and friends. In the golden eyes before her, she could see the lights flickering, as if being projected from within, and which reflected back at her the image of her own terrified face. 'Please, I know what you want, but I won't kill these men.'

Out of the corner of her eye Hannah noticed a new card. *They are monsters.*

'OK,' she said. 'Yes, they are awful people, but I'm not. I don't want to take a life.'

The card changed again. *You will be a hero.*

'No,' said Hannah, 'I'm just me. And this? This isn't heroic.'

She tried not to focus on the fact that the anorak-clad figure of Leon Gibson was coming closer and closer.

'Please? I get it, I do. You're angry. The man who left you at the altar was horrible. So are these men. Hell, so was my ex-husband, but that's just them.'

The card changed. *Kill the monster.*

'No,' said Hannah, but even as the words left her mouth, her hand rose and held out the spike. She wasn't going to have a choice.

'What about the good guys? There are good guys.' With an effort, she nodded in Sturgess's direction. 'That guy.'

The card flipped again. *He is the virgin sacrifice.*

'He's just not met the right girl yet,' said Banecroft, which everyone ignored.

'Ehm, right,' said Hannah, clueless as to what to do with that. 'He's still a good guy, though.'

Leon Gibson took another step forward. He was right in front of Hannah now. So close that she could see the terror in his eyes. The certainty that he was going to die. She tried to concentrate on her hand, to will it back under her control.

'Don't. Make. Me. Do. This.'

One more step and Leon Gibson's life would be over.

A desperate thought flitted through Hannah's mind and she leaped on it. 'Banecroft!' she shouted.

'What now?'

'Shut up,' she said and turned to look into the eyes of the one who had control of her. 'That man. That shattered mess of a man up there. Him. Look at him.'

Ronnie's head turned slowly and Hannah saw the image reflected in them change to Banecroft's upside-down face.

'If you can see what these men are, then you can see him too. He was a king of the world. Then his wife died, and now look at him. Drinking to numb the pain, riddled with guilt and sorrow. A twisted mess of a man who spends his nights pleading with a ghost for any word of the woman he loved. That's love. Real, brutal, awful love. Look at that.'

The music held a single note, unwavering.

In front of Hannah, the point of the spike was now prodding Leon Gibson's chest. His face was a mask of wordless dread.

Above her, Banecroft started to slowly descend until he was floating upside down in front of Ronnie. She reached out and placed a hand gently on his cheek. Images flashed across the golden eyes in rapid succession, too quickly for Hannah to see.

The figure of Ronnie tilted her head towards the stage floor and her mouth curved down at the edges, from a smile to a frown.

The world held its breath.

After what felt like minutes but must have been only seconds, Ronnie lifted her head and looked Banecroft directly in the eyes. Her hand softly stroked his cheek. A voice unlike anything Hannah had ever heard spoke. It sounded like a chorus singing softly. 'Such pain. Such love.'

Banecroft's mouth opened but no words came out. His eyes filled with tears.

The voice spoke again. 'Enough.'

The force slammed into them like an unexpected wave in an otherwise peaceful ocean. Everyone standing on the stage was scattered to the floor. Banecroft hit the ground with a graceless thump and an expulsion of expletive-filled air. For a moment, the only thing still upright was a featureless golden figure standing over the crumpled form of Ronnie. Then, with a *pop*, it was gone.

As Hannah shook her head to clear her mind, she realized that her body was once again under her control. She sat there and enjoyed the sensation of wiggling her fingers and toes.

A figure loomed over her. DI Sturgess. 'Are you OK?'

'I guess so. You?'

She took his proffered hand and allowed him to pull her up. 'I've had better days, I guess. Certainly less weird ones . . .'

Hannah caught the movement out of the corner of her eye at the same time Sturgess did. Three of the four men were sitting on the stage looking shell-shocked, running their hands over their now no longer unduly fanged faces. Their nightmare over.

But Red . . .

Inexplicably, Red was still the nightmare he had embraced.

With a snarl, he hurtled towards them at an inhuman speed. Sturgess barely had time to reach a hand across Hannah before . . .

There was a bang, a flash of motion and Red disintegrated in a shower of dust.

Hannah turned to where Banecroft was sitting with a stunned expression on his face, clearly as shocked as anyone that Chekhov had worked. He placed the still-smoking blunderbuss carefully down on the stage next to him.

'You know how you meet someone and instantly think, me and him aren't going to get on?'

They all looked back at where Red had been moments before. All that remained was a red hoodie and a wickedly sharp stake fashioned from old church pew and covered in rancid garlic mayo.

Banecroft laughed.

'What's so funny?' asked Hannah.

'Oh,' said Banecroft, 'I was just imagining DI Snow White here trying to explain all of this in a police report.'

CHAPTER 60

Hannah was lost for words. Now the adrenalin had worn off, every inch of her ached. She was sitting in one of the booths at the end of the Roxy's bar, nursing a glass of wine and considering never moving again for the rest of her life. Ronnie appeared before her, bottle in hand, a grin on her face.

'Top-up?'

Hannah laughed and shook her head. 'I'm fine, thank you. How are you so chipper?'

'Right, well, not going to lie,' said Ronnie. 'I came to, sitting on our stage, not a scoobies how I got there, and then I saw a gee-zer disintegrate into dust. Never been so freaked out in my life. If that wasn't mental enough, some tooled-up army types came crashing through every door and window imaginable, and, not for nothing, in a listed building them doors and windows cost a fortune to replace. I mean, that and, obviously, spectacular breach of civil liberties and all that . . .'

'Sure,' said Hannah.

'But then,' continued Ronnie, 'see that short blonde over there with the politician's wife hairdo?'

Hannah sniggered. That really was the perfect description of Dr Carter's look.

'Well, she gave me her card and said if I forget everything that happened, we'll be receiving a contribution that'll cover the bloody organ restoration, a full refurb of the whole place – windows and all – and she'll represent us in the court thing for free.'

'That's an excellent deal,' said Hannah, raising her glass in a toast.

'I know. Especially as I'm being paid to forget a whole lot of stuff I don't remember anyway. I'll leave you the bottle.'

Before Hannah could protest, Ronnie did just that and walked away whistling a cheerful tune.

At least someone was happy. Hannah's brief chat with DI Sturgess had been, well, a mix of a lot of things. Confusion mainly, as on this occasion he'd seen the storm troopers that accompanied Dr Carter to such events. He and the good doctor had had a rather terse conversation, now that he knew her responsibilities extended far beyond practising the law.

'Turns out,' Sturgess had said, 'that Dr Carter is the invisible hand that has been controlling my bosses and, lately, me, for quite some time.'

Hannah nodded. 'You're taking it rather well.'

He shrugged. 'It's not like I didn't know something rotten was going on, but now I know. If that makes sense?'

'You know everything?'

'What do you mean?' He'd given her a suspicious look. 'What else is there?'

Hannah had stood there with a grin plastered across her face as she couldn't come up with anything to say. What she'd wanted to say was, 'She's put some freaky one-eyed parasite in your head that allows her to see everything you see,' but from all Hannah had been told, there was a very good chance Sturgess would be dead before the end of the sentence. So instead, she'd just kept smiling back at him.

'About the other thing,' he said, looking awkward.

'What other thing?'

Sturgess, a full-grown man, had reddened like a schoolboy.

'Oh, forget that,' Hannah said with a wave.

'No, I want to . . . I just . . . I'm really dedicated to the job and I haven't – hadn't – met the right girl . . .'

'Sure.'

'And I . . .'

'Yes.'

'But I . . .'

'Right.'

'Still I . . .'

She'd ended up kissing him to shut him up. That, and the fact she'd wanted to. As soon as she'd done it, though, her bastard of a mind gave her the image of that horrible eyeball in his head, wriggling around, and she'd pulled away.

'OK, then,' she said, covering.

'Right,' said Sturgess with a smile. 'That was . . . good. Nice. Good.'

There was something ever so slightly adorable about a grown man blushing.

'I should probably get a move on,' he continued. 'I have to go and conspire with the woman in charge of the highly illegal private army about how we're going to explain what happened here to my bosses at the Greater Manchester Police and, y'know, the general public.'

'That does sound like it'll be tricky,' said Hannah, smiling back. 'You OK with that?'

'Oh no. I'm beyond freaked out by pretty much everything that I've seen today, and I'm going to need a whole lot of questions answered, but at the same time, I'm quite keen to see the city not descend into total chaos.'

'That does make sense.'

'And besides,' added Sturgess, 'engaging in cover-ups and conspiring with powerful people is really what I got into policing for.'

Hannah nodded. 'Word of advice – if you want a new truncheon or something, now would be an excellent time to ask for one.'

He laughed. 'That's how they get you.'

Sturgess had then gone into a huddle with Dr Carter, which Banecroft had also invited himself along to. Hannah, meanwhile, had experienced a brief moment of panic before she rang and confirmed with Grace that while Gibson had escaped, everyone at the office was fine.

That out of the way, Hannah picked up her glass of wine. Banecroft plonked himself down opposite her and snatched up the bottle.

'Not my usual but needs must.' He drained an improbable

amount before setting the bottle down, belching loudly and wiping his mouth.

'So,' said Hannah. 'Everything sorted?'

'I assume so. Satan and the Virgin Mary over there are cooking up a cover story.'

'Will people buy it?'

Banecroft read the label on the bottle. 'What you have to realize is that there will be nothing else on the shelf. Obviously, the video of that poor girl's death is a problem, but luckily, we live in the times we do. With technology, it's possible to make it look like anyone did anything, so explaining away the truth just became a lot easier.'

'Right,' said Hannah. 'Well, that's . . . good?'

'Nope. Awful, but the horse has long fled the barn.'

'OK.'

They sat there in silence for a few seconds.

'I'm sorry,' said Hannah eventually.

'For what exactly?'

'I . . . I used you and your situation at the end there.'

Banecroft turned his head and looked out of the Roxy's large windows and into the night. 'It's fine. You improvised well in the circumstances.' He shifted in his seat. 'How do you know about Simon?'

'I saw.'

'I see.'

'How long has—'

'A couple of months.' Banecroft hunched forward and looked Hannah directly in the eye with such intensity that she had to stop herself from pulling back. 'Look, I know how it might seem, but I've always known that there was something very wrong about Charlotte's death. All right, maybe that's just the desperation of a grieving man, maybe I'm insane, but after all we've seen in the last couple of months, anything is possible.'

Hannah nodded. 'True. If you want help, or if you just want to talk about it . . .'

'Good God, no. Can't think of anything worse.' He tipped the remains of the bottle into his glass and downed it in one. Once done, he fished a packet of cigarettes out of his coat pocket.

'You can't smoke in here,' said Hannah. 'Or, indeed, in pretty much any building.'

Banecroft pointed over his shoulder. 'About an hour ago I smoked a murderous vampire that was about to go on a rampage in there. I think I'm entitled to one cigarette.'

'Oh,' said Hannah, 'thank you, by the way.'

'For what?'

'Saving me from that thing.'

'Pah,' snorted Banecroft. 'You're assuming you were the tastiest thing there. How sexist. Could have been after me, or the Virgin Mary.'

'Please stop calling him that.'

'Yes,' said Banecroft, cupping his hand around his lighter and the cigarette, 'that is a thing that will definitely be happening.'

He blew a plume of smoke towards the ceiling. 'So, has it occurred to you yet?'

'What?' asked Hannah.

Banecroft tutted. 'Disappointing.'

'I will smash that bottle over your head.'

'Four,' said Banecroft.

'What?'

'Have a think.'

Hannah sighed and rested her forehead on the table. She could sleep for days.

She sprang back up again. 'There were four vampires.'

'Correct.'

'And the late Phillip Butler makes five.'

'He does.'

'Leon said there were six of them. He said it a couple of times. Where the hell is the sixth one?'

'Where indeed,' said Banecroft, whose smug smile lasted a further three full seconds before the smoke from his cigarette set off the sprinkler system.

CHAPTER 61

At around the time Banecroft's cigarette was setting off the Roxy's smoke alarm, Ox found himself huddled by a ditch in the middle of nowhere. He wasn't a big fan of the countryside in the daylight and it turned out he hated it a lot more in the dark. The last time he'd been in the great outdoors at this time of night, he'd ended up carrying a hobbling, broken-down tabloid hack back to the van after mistakenly stopping someone from killing the ungrateful sod. He was really starting to miss his desk. All of this fresh air was going to be the end of him.

After they'd left the karaoke bar, John Mór had walked back to the Kanky's Rest in near-total silence. Stanley's crutches rendered him entirely incapable of keeping up with the big man's angry strides – Ox had been forced to virtually run to do so – so he'd flagged a taxi and met them there. It was noticeable that as John Mór marched down the pavement, he didn't need to dodge anyone. There was something about a six-foot-eight man striding purposefully towards people that made them clear his trajectory.

As soon as they'd got back to the pub, John and a few of the regulars had gone into the back room for a conference, one to which Stanley and Ox had not been invited. Afterwards, John Mór had come out and sat down with them.

'Right, then. I'll be going to see the man who's behind your little problem this evening – to warn him off. Your boss wanted to be kept in the loop and, given that it was you who were infringed upon, I reckon you've got that right. So, if you want, you can come as observers, providing you shut up and do as I say when I say it. You've already seen what these people can do, so I reckon you don't need warning again.'

'Definitely not,' Ox had said.

'Especially not me,' Stanley added. 'In fact, I'm off this particular ride.'

'Fair enough,' said John Mór. Then he'd turned to Ox. 'You?'

Ox had instantly regretted his words, but he'd nodded and said, 'I'll go.'

Stanley stood up awkwardly. 'I got something I need to handle.'

'OK,' said Ox. 'Take care of yourself.'

Stanley had given Ox a funny look and, without saying anything else, had left. He was an odd bloke. Mind you, as Ox had spent the next couple of hours sitting in the Kanky's Rest, his definition of 'odd' had already expanded considerably. A lot of unusual characters had come in and out and, from what Ox could judge, most of them hadn't been there for a pint.

Eventually, John Mór had led Ox out the back and into a battered old Range Rover. The woman with the long black hair from the pub had been sitting in the back seat. In near silence they'd driven out to somewhere in the country and Ox had watched the road zip by through a hole in the vehicle's floor.

Eventually, they'd pulled into a lay-by. John Mór had killed the engine and turned to Ox.

'You remember what we discussed?'

'I'm going to do what you say when you say it.'

John Mór nodded. 'Let's go.'

Ox had opened the passenger door to follow John Mór. 'Isn't she . . .' He checked the back seat. The woman with the black hair was no longer there.

'Stay close to me.'

The two men had then walked across several fields in the dark – the kind of dark you don't get in the city. The only light was coming from the moon and stars. Ox had mentioned his phone had a torch but he'd received not much more than a growl in response.

Eventually, after they'd jumped over a few gates and Ox had stood in enough cow shit that his trainers were undoubtedly a write-off, a light had appeared in the distance. It turned out to be a thatched cottage, with a large Audi parked outside it.

John Mór had pointed to a gap in the hedgerow and spoke in a whisper. 'You stay there. Anything happens to me, run.'

'Where to?'

'Away.' John Mór gave him a smile, which didn't reassure Ox in the least.

Ox then watched the big man walk along the hedgerow a little before hopping nimbly across a ditch and through a larger gap. As John Mór approached the front door of the cottage, a light came on, illuminating the whole house. After a moment, Ox realized what was particularly odd about the light was that it didn't have a source. It was as if the ground itself had just lit up.

Thirty feet from the door John Mór stopped and raised his voice. 'Jacob.'

After a minute or so it opened, and a short-haired, dark-skinned man in black robes emerged, his hands crossed inside the sleeves, keeping them hidden from view. It was one of the men from the country park – the one Ox hadn't walloped with a fence post.

The man gave a broad smile. 'Hello, John. Nice to see you.'

'Can't say the same.'

'How long has it been?'

'You know well. Let's not pretend this is a social call.'

The other man shook his head. 'And we used to be so close.'

'Things change.'

'That they do.'

'Like, for example,' John Mór continued, 'you used to be dead.'

Jacob laughed. 'Not quite, but let's just say it suited me for that to be the widely held belief.'

'I believe you're in the plumbing game these days?'

'It's good to diversify,' said Jacob with the kind of shit-eating grin you'd get from someone selling you a car you already owned.

As he listened, Ox noticed the outline of another figure in black robes moving silently across the ground ahead of him, working his way behind John Mór. Ox couldn't see the guy's face, but his best guess was that it was the quarter-faced fella to whom he'd introduced the business end of a fence post to the night before.

John Mór carried on talking, oblivious to the danger. 'I noticed your robes. You're in the Ceathramh now?'

'I have seen the true light.'

'Sure you have. Or at least you've found something that suits your longing for chaos.'

'So cynical, John. Once we fought side by side, like brothers.'

'And then we made a peace.'

'You did,' said Jacob. 'I didn't.'

Ox's eyes remained fixed on the other figure. It was now standing fifteen feet behind John Mór. There was the faintest of flashes as something metallic in the man's hands caught the light. Ox started to creep forward. Despite John's instructions, he was going to have to charge at the sneaky bugger currently standing in the big man's blindspot and hope for the best. He got down on his knees and began to crawl through the gap in the hedge in front of him.

John Mór cleared his throat. 'Men like you, you never find peace. You love the war too much.'

Jacob gave a mock frown. 'You wound me, John. Once we wanted the same thing.'

'Not any more. I'm here to warn you off.'

'Is that right? Hell of a way to treat a former comrade-in-arms.'

As Ox pushed through the hedgerow, he could do nothing to stop the incredibly loud rustling.

'If it's any consolation, our history is the only reason you're not dead already.'

'Threats, John?' Jacob shook his head. 'It has come to this?'

John Mór nodded. 'It has, and if you wanted to take the moral high ground, maybe don't try and ambush me.'

Ox had just got to his feet on the other side of the hedge when a ball of light appeared above the head of the robed figure crouching in John Mór's blindspot. The woman with the long black hair hadn't been there a second ago, but now she was. The long nails of her right hand dug into the throat of the younger man with the quartered face. With some satisfaction, Ox noticed that the psycho's nose was still a mess from their meeting the night before.

Jacob laughed. 'Just checking you'd not entirely lost your edge, serving booze to the Folk even as you lead them to oblivion.' He raised his voice. 'Hello, Margo. Nice to see you again.'

The woman didn't move.

Jacob lowered his voice. 'She never liked me.'

'She has always been an excellent judge of character.'

'Do you think she would stand aside, let the two of us go at it, once and for all?'

'I'm not here to fight you, Jacob.'

'No? Isn't there a part of you missing it, though? The thrill of it?'

'Some of us don't find death so intoxicating.'

Jacob shook his head. 'You really shouldn't admit weakness like that. It's two on two, and while Margo has the jump on my apprentice, I'm betting you're not the man you once were.'

'I might not be,' said John Mór, 'but you're not going to find out.'

To Ox, it looked as if the big man just flicked his beard with his hand, but all around the cottage, balls of light appeared in the surrounding fields. Ox could vaguely make out figures standing beneath them.

'Like I said,' continued John Mór, 'one and only warning. You and the boy come within one hundred miles of the city again and you're done.'

Jacob looked around slowly, counting the lights. Then, he parted his arms deliberately and raised his hands, still smiling. He raised his voice to address the crowd. 'Some of you know me, I bet. Some more might know the legends. John Mór and I, we were something in our day. Whether he likes it or not, a war is coming. For too long the Founders have taken from us. Drunk our life's blood. Drained us dry. A day of reckoning is upon us.'

John Mór tilted his head. 'Are you done?'

For the first time, Jacob's face showed irritation. 'Do you have any idea what the girl is, John?'

'I don't know and I don't care.'

'One day you will, believe me.'

John Mór pointed at the Audi. 'Both of you, get in and drive. Don't stop for at least two hours.' He pointed at the sky. 'You will be watched.'

Jacob pointed in the direction of the cottage. 'Can I—'

'No.'

'I need the keys.'

'If you've forgotten how to hotwire a car, then you're walking.'

Ox watched as Margo, in the blink of an eye, went from standing behind the quarter-faced man to beside John Mór. Jacob gestured to the other man that he should head for the car and slowly, as if being careful to make no sudden movements, they got in. After a few seconds, the car kicked into life and they drove down the long driveway and into the darkness. Above his head, Ox fancied he heard wings flapping, but it could have been his mind playing tricks on him.

John Mór watched the car disappear from sight then nodded again. All the lights went out.

The big man turned back to walk towards Ox. As he did so, the cottage behind him burst into flames.

CHAPTER 62

Ferry looked up from his pie and mash as Stanley Roker limped into the room. In the background, someone was doing a karaoke version of the D:Ream classic 'Things Can Only Get Better', which was inadvertently true. Certainly, they couldn't get any worse.

'Back so soon?' asked Ferry. 'This is an unexpected treat.'

Stanley took the seat opposite and set his crutches down by his side.

'So,' continued Ferry, looking up at Riley, who was standing behind Stanley, 'my associate tells me you'd like to make me an offer.'

'That's right,' said Stanley, nodding nervously.

'Your friend owes the Fenton brothers . . .'

'Twenty thousand pounds,' supplied Riley.

'Twenty thousand pounds,' repeated Ferry. 'And you'd like to assume his debt?'

'That's right.'

Ferry smiled. 'What a lucky boy he is to have a friend like you.' He gave Stanley a long, hard, assessing look. 'What's he got over you?'

'Does it matter?'

'Not as such, but I like to know what I'm buying. It's a lot of money.'

'All you need to know,' said Stanley, 'is that you'll get it back with the agreed interest in three months.'

Ferry's lip rose a little into a warning sneer. 'I'll be the judge of what I do and don't need to know.'

'Sorry,' said Stanley, with a nervous gulp. 'I meant no disrespect.'

'I'm glad to hear it. So I ask again – you don't grab me as the self-sacrificing type, so what has he got on you?'

Stanley paused for a moment then spoke in a soft voice. 'Karma.'

'Excuse me?'

'He saved my life.'

Ferry rubbed his chin and nodded slowly. 'Life debt, eh? Interesting.'

'Just . . .' started Stanley, raising a finger. 'Can I clarify . . .'

'Of course.'

'After this, the Fentons will leave him alone?'

'Yes.'

'Are you sure?'

Ferry squinted. 'Do you think I am who I am if people don't do what I say?'

'OK, sorry. I— Sorry.'

'You need to watch your mouth,' growled Riley.

'Apologies,' said Stanley quickly. 'I'm new to this.'

'Are you sure you want to do it?'

Stanley thought for a second and nodded. 'Yeah. Yeah, I do.'

'If you're sure,' said Ferry. The big man slowly rolled his head around his neck then nodded at Riley.

'Lift up your right sleeve.'

With a shaking hand, Stanley did as he was told. 'Is this going to hurt?'

Ferry gave him a wide smile. 'More than you can possibly imagine.'

EPILOGUE 1

Tamsin Baladin was having a very hard time resisting the urge to punch the wall. She knew it wouldn't do any good, of course, but then nothing else they had attempted in the last few days had done much good either.

She raised her hand to cut off Dr Fuentes, for fear he would drone on for another fifteen minutes, mixing medical terminology with excuses and prevarications. Everything she'd heard had told her that the man was the best, and she'd paid a great deal of money to have him transported to this undisclosed location buried deep in the Cheshire countryside that didn't appear on any maps. However, so far, for all the good it had done, she might as well have asked the local GP to pop round.

'You told me, Doctor, that you could fix this.'

'Respectfully, Ms Baladin, that is not what I said. You have to appreciate that what we are dealing with here is outside of the boundaries of ordinary medicine.'

'Really?' said Tamsin, making no attempt to keep the sarcasm out of her voice. 'Did you think I was unaware of that?'

'As I said, if I could do some tests on the others who have made a recovery—'

'We've been through this. We are working on it. In the meantime . . .'

'I will continue doing what I can.'

'Thank you.'

Tamsin turned and left the laboratory, letting the door slam shut behind her.

As she entered the main room, she looked across at the large two-way mirror that made up most of the far wall. It was turned off, so all she could see was the reflection of the room she was in, rather than the horror show that lay on the other side. Stupid Alan. As a child, her brother had been an impetuous, petulant idiot and, as far as she was concerned, all that had changed since was that he had grown taller.

In a way, she blamed herself. The signs had been there. Ever since that incident at university his warped sensibilities in certain areas had been apparent. The psychiatrist had called it 'an unhealthy attitude towards women'. At least he had, right before Alan had refused to keep going. And still, she had ignored the warning signs and protected him.

While she'd like to think she'd done that purely out of frater-nal love for her twin, her brother's genius had made her massively rich. Sure, he wouldn't have got there without her – that was one thing the official, sanitized version of their history got right – but still, they needed each other. Collectively, they were responsible for the monumental success of Fuzzy Britches, but Alan's 'issues' always lurked in the background.

In the early days, she'd kept a close eye on him and guided the development to prevent him from leading it in directions it should not have gone. They'd agreed that Alan should leave all of the public-facing stuff to her. As the company had rapidly expanded, she'd gone to great lengths to ensure that those around her brother would inform her if he strayed from the agreed path. She'd tactfully made sure that his 'needs as a man', as her mother would so diplomatically put it, had been accommodated – in such a way that the women in question were paid a great deal of money to forget his name.

For all she had done for him – hell, *because* of all she had done for him – there had been bitter, acrimonious arguments, and she'd been aware of Alan's growing resentment towards what he saw as her interference in his life. That was why, while she'd been vaguely aware that he had a couple of little side projects going on, she hadn't investigated their exact nature. How she regretted that now. She couldn't have expected this, of course – whatever the hell this was – but even a devout atheist such as herself had to recognize that there was an element of divine retribution to it. If her brother had been anyone else, she would have delighted in firing him. Instead, she had ignored, placated and essentially indulged his toxic tendencies, and this is where they had ended up.

Within hours of Phillip Butler's death, they'd known what he'd been involved in. Butler had been part of a group that her brother had been using to test the new app he'd been developing in secret, running off the back end of Fuzzy Britches. Good God, if the regulators found out – or the media – they would be ruined.

She'd got hold of Alan's records immediately and gone looking for the other 'testers', as they'd been euphemistically branded. Initially, Tamsin had been focused only on wiping all trace of the application off the face of the earth – she'd not expected there to be any link to the bizarre death of Phillip Butler. Then, one of the security team had died while attempting to contact Andrew Campbell. They'd been lucky in that they'd managed to recover the body before the authorities did. By this point Alan's behaviour had . . . Well, the true nature of the problem had begun to make itself known.

Tamsin looked at the two-way mirror again. This whole thing had become a nightmare. Like some Faustian pact, or perhaps a biblical one. 'I am not my brother's keeper.'

She'd been so wrapped up in her thoughts that she hadn't noticed the stranger's reflection staring back at her until the woman waved.

Tamsin screamed. The woman who was sitting at the desk in the middle of the room seemed entirely unperturbed by Tamsin's reaction. She simply smiled at the CEO and raised a cup of cappuccino that she had seemingly helped herself to from the machine in the corner.

'Ms Baladin, so lovely to meet you at last.'

The woman was blonde, middle-aged and very definitely not meant to be there.

'How did you get in here?'

'Well, not to blow my own horn, sweetie, but, as the kids would say, "I got mad skills."' At which point she unleashed a giggle that could grate cheese.

'Security! Security!' hollered Tamsin.

'Oh, please – do calm down, dear. Frankly, I'm a little disappointed. I was expecting more grace under pressure than this.'

Tamsin threw open the door. 'Secu—'

The word died in her throat as she saw the two figures slumped on the floor in the hallway outside. She briefly considered running, but instead, she closed the door and turned back to the woman sitting behind her desk, drinking her coffee.

'OK, then. Who exactly are you?'

The woman put down the cup. 'There we go. I knew you'd rally. You may call me Dr Carter. Charmed to meet you. Big fan!'

'And I'll ask you again – how did you get in here?'

Dr Carter sighed. 'Word to the wise, poppet – from one who has perhaps a couple of years on you. You need to live more in the moment. What matters is that I am here, and what you need to know is why.'

Tamsin folded her arms. 'Well?'

'I'm here to help.'

'We don't need any assistance, thank you.'

'Really?' asked Dr Carter with a broad grin. 'Well, that's tickety-boo. I'll go back to the people I represent and tell them that the mighty Baladin twins have the situation under control.' She pushed herself away from the desk, ready to leave.

Tamsin noticed Dr Carter's eyes flick meaningfully towards the two-way mirror. It was only when the doctor got to her feet that Tamsin realized that the woman was tiny – even in six-inch heels she barely touched five foot.

'One thing before I go, though,' said Carter. 'When did you find out?'

'About what?' Tamsin said after a brief pause.

'Your brother's little side project?'

'I don't know what you're talking about.'

In response, Dr Carter unleashed one of those giggles that Tamsin had already decided ranked amongst her least favourite noises.

'Oh, come now, Tamsin. No need to keep secrets between us gals. Your brother was developing a – I mean, could you call it a "dating app"? Does seem rather too sweet a description, doesn't it? I'd personally go with "predator assistance technology" but you run that by the marketing folks and let me know. That bit you are all too aware of, of course, but I'm guessing you don't understand what happened next, do you?'

Tamsin kept her expression deliberately blank, keen to give nothing away.

'That's what I thought.' Dr Carter sat back down. 'Well, long story short, a powerful entity with a penchant for old movies happened to take notice of your brother's little group. I mean, in all honesty that was sheer dumb bad luck for all concerned. Of all the bars in all the world, they had to walk into hers. And she decided the best way to deal with this beastly behaviour was to turn them into something actually beastly.'

'A powerful entity?' repeated Tamsin with a sly smile. 'What exactly is that supposed to mean?'

'Still trying to hang on to that rationality, sweetie? How's that working out for you?'

Tamsin ignored the question. 'And where do you come into all of this?'

Dr Carter waggled her eyebrows. 'Let's just say I'm a concerned citizen. Particularly when naughty boys with pointy teeth are running about the city, frightening the cattle. Not your brother, interestingly. We know he was one of the six, in those little meetings. Fun as his prosthetics-and-wig thing was, we confirmed that. I'm guessing you realized he was, ahem, not well, before he could get out and about.'

'You'll have to forgive me, Doctor whatever you call yourself, but I'm really not in the mood for fairy tales. My brother is unwell, but I'm sure he will recover. Good luck getting anyone to believe this hokum.'

Dr Carter spun around in the swivel chair. 'Hokum?' She laughed again. 'Oh, I knew I was going to like you. Even now, so logical, so in control.'

She leaned forward to the Newton's cradle that had been a gift from Tamsin's parents, which Tamsin kept on her desk despite never using it. Carter lifted one of the ball bearings and allowed it to fall – an action that normally would have caused the ball on the far end of the six to swing up and back, and so on and so forth. On this occasion, once they collided, all six ball bearings simply glided off their moorings and headed slowly through the air towards Tamsin.

'I'm afraid, Dorothy, you're not in Kansas any more.'

Tamsin felt her breath catch in her throat, before she softly croaked, 'How are you doing that?' She watched as the six balls started to slowly circle her head.

'Occam's Razor, dear: magic.'

Tamsin gawped at the balls until Dr Carter clicked her fingers and they stopped moving.

'Focus,' instructed Dr Carter. 'That's it. Now, you currently have that security consultancy you pay a lot of money out looking for the surviving trio from your brother's little focus group. You won't find them. Know why?'

Tamsin stayed silent.

'That's right – we have them. Not as prisoners.' Dr Carter smirked. 'We're not monsters, after all. Let's just say they were all keen for a fresh start in life, and we provided that, while, of course, having access to them and their phones, should we need any evidence.'

'So this is blackmail?'

'Oh Tammy, Tammy, Tammy, I don't like that word.'

'I don't care what you like, you odious witch.'

Dr Carter clutched her chest. 'Oh dear. Word of advice, sweetie – might be best not to insult someone who, with a literal flick of her finger, can send a steel ball bearing ripping through that big brain of yours.'

Tamsin licked her lips but held her tongue.

'Apology accepted. Now, as it happens, you have impressed my employers. They realize that as an organization, perhaps we have fallen behind the times, and we need someone like you, who is possessed of skills and sensibilities we do not have. I'm here to recruit you.'

'And what do I get?'

'Good question. With our assistance, this little affair goes away. You don't need to worry how it will affect your future share price, because we will make you a very generous offer to come aboard as your silent partners. We can also divert a certain detective inspector of your acquaintance from looking into things as, believe me, he does not stop when he is on the scent, unless someone stops him.'

'I can handle one policeman.'

Dr Carter stuck out her chin. 'Normally, you probably could. Him, though – if we let him off the leash . . .' She sucked air through her teeth theatrically. 'Personally, I've long said the man needs to get laid – although until recently, I'd no idea how much. I digress. We will also do what we can to fix your brother's little problem.'

'What problem?'

'I'm only guessing, dear, but seeing as you're keeping him locked away underground in this rather delightful undisclosed location, I'm guessing he's more than a little under the weather.'

Tamsin locked eyes with Dr Carter. The other woman didn't blink. Eventually, Tamsin nodded and turned her attention to the six ball bearings still floating around her head.

'And this?' she asked.

'What?'

Tamsin smiled. 'You have me at a disadvantage, I concede that. On the other hand, you wouldn't be here if your organization didn't need me. So, if I'm to assist you, I want this.' She pointed at the ball bearings. 'Power. Real power.'

Dr Carter smiled. 'You started poorly but you're finishing strong. I knew we were going to get along. We'll talk. First, though . . .' Dr Carter indicated a folder on the desk. 'We need to cover up this mess, for all of our sakes. Andrew Campbell – the gentleman in the red hoodie who made himself and poor little Natasha Ellis so famous. We have here freshly minted, authentic-looking evidence of how he was obsessed with the V-word.'

'Vampires?' asked Tamsin.

Dr Carter winced momentarily, as if a bad smell had wafted by her. 'Yes. That. And how he faked everything to make basic murder look like something other than what it was. He then burned himself alive, blah blah blah . . . We'll spread those crumbs in the traditional media but what we really need is for you to give it some social media juice. We want it trending like a new iPhone.'

'Not a problem.'

'Excellent.'

Dr Carter stood up. 'That's what I like to hear. So, just how bad is your brother?'

Without saying a word, Tamsin moved across to the two-way mirror and flipped the switch to turn it on. Part of her was pleased to see the look of revulsion ripple across Dr Carter's face as she saw what Alan had now become.

'Oh my,' said Dr Carter. 'That is . . .'

'Yes,' said Tamsin. 'It is.'

Alan stared out at them from behind the glass. He smiled as if he could see them. Maybe he could.

Behind him, written on the wall in blood, were the words 'I am Mr White'.

EPILOGUE 2

Banecroft slapped the alarm into silence in one fluid motion. He hadn't managed to sleep. His head was full of too many questions.

He listened for a moment. Then, outside in the bullpen, he thought he heard the noise he'd been waiting for. The soft sound of a page turning.

He moved quietly across the office. As he opened the door, relief washed over him. Simon was seated at his usual desk. Part of Banecroft had wondered, now that others knew that Simon was coming here, whether Simon might stop. The thought had previously occurred to him that Simon's visitations might have all been in his head. Perhaps his own guilt and regret about Charlotte's death had mingled with his regret about Simon's and come up with this unhealthy cocktail with which to torture himself. At least now he knew that wasn't the case. Simon was as real as anything in the peculiar ensemble Banecroft's world had become.

The young man sat there, reading through a copy of that week's edition of *The Stranger Times*. They had chosen to report Manchester's great vampire scare in diplomatic language. They had offered up the official story but done so in such a way that those in the know would pick up on some subtle references. Banecroft was increasingly aware that his life was becoming just that – a series of compromises for the greater good. Still, he'd found a way to protect Stella – at least for the moment – and tomorrow's problem could be tomorrow's problem.

'Hello, Simon.'

Simon didn't look up from what he was reading. 'Hello, Mr Banecroft. Exciting edition this week.'

'Yes. It's rare we get a big story like that happening on our own doorstep.'

'That's true,' agreed Simon.

'Would you like to hear what really happened?'

Simon looked up. 'Oh – yes, please.'

Banecroft experienced that disconcerting feeling of watching the boy's eyes widen with excitement while, at the same time, being able to see through to the chair on which he was sitting.

'Righto,' said Banecroft, wincing slightly.

When had he ever said 'righto' before in his life? He coughed to clear his throat.

'But first, do you remember that question I asked you? About my wife, Charlotte.'

Simon nodded. 'Are you sure you really want to know?'

Banecroft clutched at the desk he was leaning back against. Simon rarely engaged with the question. With an effort, he kept his voice calm. 'Yes, please, Simon. I have to know.'

'There's a full moon tonight,' observed Simon.

Banecroft nodded. He couldn't push too hard or . . .

Simon's head twitched suddenly. 'Ouch.'

'Are you OK, Simon?'

He twitched again and grimaced in pain. 'Agh. Agh!'

Banecroft took a step forward. 'Are you all right? Can I help you?'

Simon started to thrash about. Unsure what to do, Banecroft moved closer. As he tried to touch Simon's form, his hands passed through it, becoming terribly cold and causing Simon to scream. He withdrew them.

'I'm sorry. I'm sorry, Simon.'

Above his head, two light bulbs shattered simultaneously. Banecroft staggered back, broken glass crunching beneath his slippered feet. 'Please. I didn't mean to . . .'

'Lumpy?'

Banecroft froze. It couldn't be. Something in him wouldn't allow him to believe.

'Lumpy, is that you?'

The voice was unmistakable. It was coming from Simon, but it was not his.

Banecroft's voice came out in a hoarse whisper. 'Charlotte?'

'Lumpy, thank God. You have to help me. I'm in so much trouble.'

'Of course, what do you—'

'Please, help me. I'm in so much trouble.'

Banecroft stepped towards Simon again. 'Just tell me what to do. Charlotte? Charlotte?'

And then the figure of Simon began to fade away.

'No, Simon. Don't go. Simon? Charlotte? Come back! Please. Charlotte?'

FREE STUFF!

Hello, C. K. (or Caimh) here. Thanks very much for reading *This Charming Man* – I hope you enjoyed it. If you did, then your *Stranger Times* journey doesn't have to end here. If you hot-foot it over to thestrangertimes.co.uk you can sign up for my newsletter and get a collection of *Stranger Times* short stories, including one that spills the beans on what happened to Stanley Roker on that fateful night that wrecked his marriage. You can also hear that tale and lots more on *The Stranger Times* podcast, which features loads of short stories written by me and read by some of the finest comedians available in my price range.

The next book in the series, *Love Will Tear Us Apart*, will be out on February 9th 2023, assuming we all live that long.

Before that, though, up next are the acknowledgements for this book, written by *The Stranger Times*'s resident conspiracy-corner columnist, Dex Hex.

Cheers muchly,
Caimh (C. K.) McDonnell

ACKNOWLEDGEMENTS

C. K. McDonnell, if that really is his name, would like to thank
the following people, for both the vital part they have played
in bringing this book to life and their role in assisting
the global elite to pull the wool over the eyes of you, the
sheeple.

Simon Taylor, editor, who lovingly guided this book through the
editorial process when not engaged in his main job of hiding the
fact that The Beatles were replaced with androids in 1969.

Judith Welsh, managing editor, who ruled over the process with a
loving iron fist despite having the Roswell alien trapped in her
basement. She was ably assisted by Josh Benn, who feeds it when
she goes away on birdwatching weekends.

Rebecca Wright, whose rigorous attention to detail greatly
improved this book, while her unwavering support for the satanical
cult running the British rail system makes the lives of everyday
people so much worse.

Marianne Issa El-Khoury, who designs a lovely cover but should be roundly condemned for helping to cover up the fact that Switzerland has never existed and was invented only as a way for cuckoo-clock companies to avoid paying tax.

Phil Evans, who made sure this book actually got produced. A challenging task given that he is also part of the team of people responsible for the world paper shortage, which was caused by them replacing the moon with a papier-mâché replica.

Marketing supremos Sophie Bruce and Ruth Richardson, who do an excellent job convincing people to buy this book while also organizing the black market in second-hand human organs stolen from people who fall asleep on late-night buses.

PR guru Tom Hill, who gets the word out better than anyone while simultaneously making sure that no members of the lame-stream media slip up and admit that the world is not only flat, but also exists entirely in the imagination of a bloke called Brian from Dudley.

He would also like to thank the UK and International sales teams, who do an excellent job while sacrificing a frankly appalling number of goats.

Uber agent Ed Wilson, who does a reasonable job of agenting considering so much of his time is taking up maintaining the ludicrous cover story that cricket is a sport and not the ongoing experiment in weather control that it so clearly is.

And finally, to Mammy and Daddy McDonnell, Wonderwife, Diller and Jackson, who have successfully hidden the fact that the author of this book is, in fact, three chipmunks high on caffeine.

ABOUT THE AUTHOR

Born in Limerick and raised in Dublin, C. K. (Caimh) McDonnell is a former stand-up comedian and TV writer. He performed all around the world, had several well-received Edinburgh shows and supported acts such as Sarah Millican on tour before hanging up his clowning shoes to concentrate on writing. He has also written for numerous TV shows and been nominated for a Kid's TV BAFTA.

His debut novel, *A Man With One of Those Faces* – a comic crime novel – was published in 2016 and spawned The Dublin Trilogy books and the spin-off McGarry Stateside series. They have been Amazon bestsellers on both sides of the Atlantic.

This Charming Man is the second book in his Stranger Times series, the first being *The Stranger Times*.

C. K. McDonnell lives in Manchester. To find out more, visit whitehairedirishman.com

Read on for an exclusive look at the
first pages of the third book in
The Stranger Times series . . .

LOVE WILL TEAR US APART

CHAPTER 1

Tristram Bleeker's mind went blank. Staring down the wrong end of a gun will have that effect on a man. His mouth was dry. His palms were sweaty. He found himself utterly incapable of summoning a single coherent thought.

Not that he had much experience of these things, but it was not a normal gun. Instead of the typical straight barrel, the muzzle of this one flared out like the bell of a trombone. He kept his eyes fixed down the centre line of it, as if he might discern the spark in the darkness that would herald the eventful end to his previously uneventful life. It was like looking into the nostril of an irritable dragon. One that could barbecue you with a single breath.

'Do I need to repeat the question?' asked the voice at the other end of the weapon. It sounded oddly weary, as if Tristram were the tenth or so person it had held at gunpoint that day and the process was becoming entirely tedious.

Tristram's lips moved but no words emerged.

The voice tutted. 'This is not going well.'

It wasn't. In these circumstances, the cliché was that your life should flash before your eyes, but that wasn't happening for Tristram. Instead, the first ten minutes of his interview kept replaying in his head, over and over, as if his mind were trying to process how things had reached this alarming state of affairs. He must've done something very wrong at some point. Tristram was good in interviews – everybody said so. He was personable, articulate and a master of brevity. He'd been warned to expect the unexpected today and, to that point, he thought he'd dealt well with the curveballs thrown his way. Then he'd found himself staring down the barrel of this weird gun.

'The question,' said the voice, sounding increasingly irritated, 'was . . . how well do you handle pressure?'

'I . . . I . . .' stuttered Tristram.

'Never mind. I think we have our answer.'

Tristram was dimly aware of the sound of one of the doors being opened behind him. A female gasp followed. 'Vincent!'

'I'm in the middle of something, Grace.'

'I can see that. Put that horrible gun away this instant.'

After what felt like a very long time, the dragon's head turned away and was replaced by the face of a man who looked in need of a shower, a shave, a decent meal and about a month's worth of sleep. It belonged to the individual who had been holding Tristram at gunpoint: Vincent Banecroft, editor of *The Stranger Times* and former Fleet Street legend.

The view of Banecroft's face was only a minor improvement on that of the gun. His eyes were sunken and dark. For a moment, his eyelids closed and Tristram wondered if perhaps Banecroft were about to fall asleep, but then they shot open again abruptly. A master of multitasking, Banecroft placed the gun down beside him, sneered across the table and lit a cigarette.

Grace, the friendly matronly black woman from behind the reception desk, appeared at Banecroft's shoulder, bearing a tray loaded with two mugs and a plate of biscuits.

'Sorry about that, Tristram. Mr Banecroft can be a little . . .'

'Insightful,' finished Banecroft.

Grace's brow furrowed. 'I am pretty sure that is not the word I was looking for.'

'It should have been.' Banecroft held aloft two sheets of paper, which Tristram recognized as his CV. 'Mr Bleeker here, who is applying for the role of assistant editor at this publication, has a first-class degree in journalism from the University of Leeds, followed by seven years' experience working for a mixed bag of publications, ranging from national newspapers to more special-ist magazines, and it is his dream to work here because of his lifelong interest in the paranormal. His portfolio is frankly out-standing and his references so glowing that the reader is required to wear protective eyewear or risk permanent damage to their retinas while perusing them.'

'I know,' said Grace, before adding pointedly through gritted teeth, 'he is perfect for the job.'

'Exactly,' said Banecroft, as he dropped Tristram's CV into the wastepaper basket at the side of his desk then casually flicked cigarette ash after it. 'My point being – if it looks like a duck, walks like a duck and quacks like a duck, I find myself highly suspicious as to why it is applying for the role of the bread-loving aquatic bird we are so ducking desperate to fill.'

Grace's face scrunched up for a second before she shook her head. 'No. You have lost me.'

Tristram coughed and was surprised to realize he had recovered the power of speech. 'I think what Mr Banecroft is trying to say is that I am overqualified for the role.'

'No. I am not trying to say anything. What I am saying is that you are perfectly qualified for the role. Too perfect. Now, run along before I lose my temper, and do let your handlers know that if they try this kind of thing again, next time I will not take it in such good spirits. Speaking of which . . .'

Banecroft picked up the bottle of Irish whiskey that sat on his desk and poured himself a healthy measure, then kept pouring past the point of unhealthy all the way to death wish.

'There's clearly been a misunderstanding here,' said Tristram, trying to sound jovial. 'Nobody has sent me.'

'Right.' Banecroft patted the gun. 'Well, you've got until the count of ten before I shoot you. Then, if nobody claims the body after a week, I shall offer your corpse a full and grovelling apology.'

'Vincent!' exclaimed Grace. 'You're being unreasonable. Even for you – and that really is saying something.'

'Four,' announced Banecroft.

'OK,' said Tristram. 'I get it. You're testing me.'

'Nope. Five.'

Tristram failed to keep the edge of panic from his voice. 'What happened to one through to three?'

'I said what I was counting to, never said where I was counting from. Six.'

Tristram looked up at Grace. 'He's kidding, right?'

The woman gave an expansive shrug, which resulted in a

splash of tea spilling over the lip of one of the mugs. 'With the good Lord as my witness, I cannot promise that.'

'Seven.'

Tristram got to his feet. 'You people are crazy!'

Banecroft picked up the gun. 'Sticks and stones may break my bones, but Chekhov here will make you holier than Grace. Eight.'

'I will be reporting you to the police.'

Banecroft raised the gun while looking up at Grace. 'Holier? Do you get it? I thought it was quite good.'

'It was not,' said Grace.

'You've no appreciation of wordplay. That's your problem. Nine.'

Tristram turned and ran for the nearest exit. En route, he tripped over one of the many piles of books on the floor and crashed headfirst through the door. In his hurry, he'd left through a different door from the one he'd come in, and this was how he came to find himself sprawled on the threadbare carpet of an open-plan office area.

Three people were seated behind desks and drinking mugs of tea: a portly white man in a three-piece tartan suit, an East Asian man tossing a yo-yo up and down, and a black teenaged girl with purple hair, who didn't look up from her phone.

Tristram pointed behind him in the direction of Banecroft's office. 'That man is a monster.'

His words were met with a round of nonchalant nods. Then, the portly gent in the three-piece suit turned to his colleagues. 'I have to say, these new biscuits are a bit dry.'

CHAPTER 2

Grace opened her notepad to a fresh page as Banecroft slumped into the chair he traditionally occupied for these meetings. It occurred to her that if they lost any more staff, he would soon be able to stay in his office and they could go to him, rather than him having to stomp ill-temperedly out to the bullpen.

'Right,' Banecroft began. 'Let's get this parade of ineptitude kicked off, shall we? Grace – please do the honours.'

She spoke as she wrote. 'Weekly editorial meeting. Present – the staff of *The Stranger Times*.'

'Remaining staff,' muttered Ox under his breath, still fiddling with his yo-yo.

'What was that?' snapped Banecroft.

'I was just pointing out that we are the remaining staff. Since we lost Hannah.'

'Lost? We haven't lost her,' said Banecroft. 'She isn't stuck down the back of the sofa. She walked out on us and went scurrying back to the philandering phallus she was supposed to be divorcing.'

'Why, though?' asked Reggie, readjusting his waistcoat.

Banecroft threw up his hands in exasperation. 'We have gone

over this several times in the last three weeks. She just informed me she was leaving and then she left. All of you seem to be having difficulty grasping these two salient pieces of information.'

'But what did you say to her?' asked Stella.

'How is that relevant?'

She pushed her purple hair out of her eyes. 'Because, boss, you have a tendency to say truly awful things in the way other people have a tendency to breathe.'

Banecroft shot a look at the young girl. 'And yet, I am somehow seen as the kind of easy-going cuddly boss who can be slagged off in a meeting by an apprentice reporter and that reporter can inexplicably still expect to have her job at the end of it.'

'You can't fire me. You ain't got enough staff as it is. I'm currently second in line for the job of assistant editor.'

'Hang on,' said Ox. He pointed at himself and then at Reggie. 'Which of us do you think is below you on that list?'

'Both of you,' interrupted Banecroft with a shrug. 'Grace is clearly number one.'

The idea made Grace feel queasy. 'Don't you dare,' she warned. 'Perhaps you should just ring Hannah and apologize?'

'For what?'

'Everything,' said Stella.

'Anything,' offered Ox.

'Being you,' concluded Reggie.

'All right,' said Banecroft, leaning forward. 'First things first – you are all skirting dangerously close to mutiny. Second – as it happens, I have attempted to ring Hannah. Not, I hasten to add, to apologize, but rather to see if the woman has come to her senses. Her phone keeps going to voicemail.' His eyes scanned the group. 'Has anyone else had any luck getting hold of her?'

The paper's remaining staff avoided meeting his gaze. Grace had been trying Hannah's phone several times a day but had received no response beyond the single word – 'sorry' – that her former colleague had texted on the first morning of her absence. Grace knew for a fact that none of the others had had any more success.

Banecroft folded his arms as he sat back in his chair. 'That's what I thought. You can all keep pretending this is somehow my fault, but the reality is she walked out on all of us.'

Nobody had anything to say to this.

Since Hannah's shocking departure, morale in the office had taken a nosedive. She had worked there only a few months, yet had somehow become the glue that held them together. In the weeks that followed, the cloud of depression that hung over the place had manifested itself in the form of petty squabbles and hurtful remarks among the group. Reggie had even got into a disagreement with Manny, the perpetually relaxed Rastafarian who ran the printing press on the ground floor. Having an argument with Manny was like trying to punch a cloud.

Everyone felt as if they'd lost a friend. Worse than that was the unspoken realization that the person they thought was a good friend apparently wasn't. True friends don't just up and disappear out of your life.

'Now,' said Banecroft, 'if we're all done having our little tantrums, we have a newspaper to publish.'

'To do that,' replied Grace, 'we really do need an assistant editor.'

'We can muddle through for another week until an appropriate candidate comes along.'

'Really? Last week's edition had two page sevens.'

'And,' added Reggie, 'a crossword that had the clues from three weeks ago reprinted alongside the wrong puzzle.'

'Yes,' agreed Grace, who had been fielding irate phone calls about the error ever since. She'd had no idea that people took crosswords so seriously. There had technically been a death threat. 'Technically' because, as Ox had put it, the intersection in the Venn diagram of individuals who complete crosswords and those who firebomb buildings was either empty or humanity was already doomed. 'Not to mention the story about Mr Adam Wallace's ghost frequenting that lap-dancing club in Chinatown and inappropriately touching the ladies.'

'Ah,' said Ox. 'That makes sense. That geezer outside this morning . . .'

'Was the very much alive Mr Wallace,' confirmed Stella. 'Accompanied by his missus, who was proper vexed.'

'I admit,' said Reggie, 'that I received some very bad information regarding that story. However, while the reports of his death have been greatly exaggerated, I believe the ones about his behaviour are accurate.'

'Still, though – not exactly paranormal, is it?'

Reggie looked affronted. 'You can talk. At least I can spell. You submitted a half-page article about an unidentified frying object over Bolton.'

'That's nowhere near as bad as—' Ox stopped. He looked across the room at Banecroft, whose chin had dipped on to his chest and eyes had closed.

Of the many things worrying Grace, this was the thing that concerned her most of all. Vincent Banecroft had never been what you would call healthy, but in the last few weeks he had really gone downhill. Falling asleep mid-conversation had become a new and alarming trend. His distracted, listless air also alarmed her, and while describing Vincent Banecroft as being more irritable than usual was akin to accusing the sea of being more wet, he was. He really was. His fury, while often unjustifiable, had always felt as if it had some sense of purpose behind it. Now, however, it seemed entirely scattershot.

All that aside, the effects of whatever was going on were being felt on the paper itself. What she had begun to think of as the 'old' Vincent Banecroft never would have allowed all the recent screw-ups to get past him. It was as if he were only half here. Going through the motions.

Grace looked round and saw the faces of her other colleagues mirroring her own concern. Then Banecroft broke the tension by passing wind loudly. It appeared to wake him up, and his eyes flashed suddenly.

'Now,' he said, without missing a beat, 'if you've all finished, I would like to remind you that it is not your job to point out other people's screw-ups. As editor, that is both my job and my privilege.'

Stella folded her arms huffily. 'It's the job of the assistant editor to make sure the screw-ups don't happen in the first place. That's why we need one.'

'And we will get one, eventually.'

'I thought it was gonna be that woman who wore all the scarfs and smelled of patchouli oil?'

'We had a fundamental disagreement.'

'What a shock,' said Reggie, which earned him a particularly dirty look from Banecroft.

'The woman didn't believe in double letters.'

'I'm sorry?'

'Case in point – she didn't believe the word "sorry" should have two Rs in it. Said it was wasteful. Bad for the environment.'

This last statement was met with confused expressions all round.

'I don't—' started Stella.

'Not just that,' continued Banecroft as he placed his slippered feet upon the desk and tipped his chair backwards to balance on its rear legs. 'She also believed that capital letters were elitist and punctuation was divisive.'

A long moment of quiet followed as everyone in the room tried to figure out exactly how such rules would work. Eventually, it was Ox who broke the silence. 'Even for this place, that is odd.'

Stella raised her hand. 'What about that nice old dude who was in reception last week? Big white beard. Looked like Santa.'

Banecroft turned to Grace and raised an eyebrow. 'Would you like to field this one?'

Grace blessed herself. 'He said he could not work on full moons as he needed to make a' – her face twisted into a sour expression – 'blood sacrifice.' She blessed herself again.

'That's right,' said Banecroft. 'Looked like Santa but loved him some Satan.'

'But . . .' Stella faltered, 'he had leather patches on his elbows. Leather patches,' she repeated forlornly.

'And the bloke from this morning?' asked Ox.

Banecroft gave him a blank look.

'Really?' Ox continued in disbelief. 'Came flying out of your office, like, twenty minutes ago, claiming you'd threatened to shoot him?'

'Oh, that one. Yes, he was too good to be true.'

Ox looked at the others with wide eyes before turning back to Banecroft. 'What does that even mean?'

'Clearly a Trojan horse sent by our enemies in a transparent attempt to destroy us.'

'More fool them,' shot Ox. 'We don't need any help doing that.'

Reggie shifted in his seat and straightened his waistcoat. 'Do you not think that is, perhaps, a touch paranoid?'

Banecroft yawned before responding. 'Have you been here for the past few months? You can't be paranoid if you have documented proof that people are literally out to get you. There's still a dent in the wall from the werewolf and I can't be the only one who, every time I take a dump, remembers the hidden camera installed in the new bathroom by the loony cult?'

'Maybe,' conceded Grace. 'Or maybe you're finding fault with all the candidates because none of them are Hannah?'

'Yes, that's it. You've found me out. I'm in love with that woman I was constantly at loggerheads with.'

'Judging by the sarcastic tone you employed while making that statement,' she responded, 'I am going to assume you have never, ever seen a romantic comedy film.'

'Have you lot been eating brownies with the Rastafarian or something? Look, if it will stop you all clucking like tedious hens, as it happens, I have the assistant editor situation in hand.'

Grace's eyebrows shot up her forehead. 'You do?'

'Yes. I'm going to ask Stanley Roker to come in for a chat.'

'Stanley?' echoed Stella. 'The fella you called the worst kind of tabloid-scribbling parasite? That guy?'

'Yes.'

'Stanley's all right,' said Ox softly.

'I'm not saying he isn't,' she replied. 'But he' – she bobbed her head in Banecroft's direction – 'said he wouldn't trust the guy as far as he could throw this building.'

'We don't need to like or trust him,' said Banecroft. 'You all liked and trusted the previous assistant editor and look where that got us. Stanley Roker is many things, and while several of those things are reprehensible, one of them is that he is an individual with extensive experience in the newspaper business. He may have written some fetid tripe over the years, but it has always been correctly spelled and fact-checked fetid tripe. Now, we need to move on.'

'Quite right.'

The staff turned as one towards the corner of the room from where the new voice had come, Banecroft doing so vigorously enough to send himself toppling back in his chair and on to the floor. One of his slippers liberated itself from his foot and hit him on the head.

He got to his feet and joined his colleagues in gawping at the woman who was sitting behind a desk on the far side of the room, peeling a satsuma. She was rotund, about sixty, and was wearing a wax jacket and deerstalker hat. Her face was heart-shaped with ruddy cheeks, and she looked as if she would be more at home tramping around her country estate with a couple of collies than sitting in a newspaper office in Manchester. By way of greeting she gave them a cheerful grin.

'Who the hell are you?' asked Banecroft.

'Elizabeth Cavendish the Third, but please call me Betty.'

To Grace's ears, she sounded similar to one of those useful posh people who appeared on TV occasionally. The type that owned a lot of land but were still happy to shove a hand up a cow's rear end if the situation required it.

'How long have you been sitting there?'

'Long enough.'

'And, more importantly, how on earth did you get in here without any of us seeing you?'

She shrugged, popped a segment of satsuma into her mouth and chewed briefly before answering. 'I'm a woman of a certain age. The world has got very good at ignoring us – Hollywood in particular. Unless you're Meryl Streep or Helen Mirren, you just have to hang around and hope someone needs a grandma at some point. And don't get me started on the gender disparity among newsreaders.'

'What?' said Banecroft.

'Should I pick any free desk?' asked Betty, waving a hand about. 'Or is there a system?'

'What?' repeated Banecroft, with the air of a man about to lose it. As soon as he got a grip on exactly what 'it' was.

'Sorry,' said Betty. 'I've got ahead of myself again, haven't I? I do have a tendency to ramble. I must apologize. Chitty-chatty Betty. That's what the girls called me at school. Children can be so cruel, can't they? One girl – Dorothy Wilkins – once stuck chewing gum to my seat. Horrible little thing. Wonder where she is now. Probably married to a government minister. All the worst ones are. Anyway, yes – with apologies to the frankly awful-sounding tabloid chappie you mentioned, I am the new assistant editor.'

'Over my dead body,' snorted Banecroft.

Betty wrinkled her nose. 'Well, that would certainly explain the smell.'

'Let me get this straight – you thought the best way to apply for the job was to sneak into the building, join a meeting to which you weren't invited, and then insult me?'

Betty looked genuinely perplexed. 'Have I insulted you? I mean, I'm fairly sure you've insulted most of the people in this room during the course of this meeting, but I don't recall me or anyone else insulting you.' She popped another slice of satsuma into her mouth and chewed contemplatively. 'What surprisingly thin skin you have.'

'Let me save you some time. You've definitely, one hundred per cent failed the interview. Now, will you be leaving of your own volition, or shall I get Chekhov to show you out? That is the name of my—'

'Blunderbuss,' Betty finished. 'Yes, I know. Very clever. That will not be necessary. I will be going nowhere, though, as I'm afraid you have crucially misunderstood something. I am not applying for the role of assistant editor; I have already been given it.' She pulled a letter from one of her jacket pockets and held it up. 'I have here a missive from this newspaper's proprietor, Mrs Harnforth, explaining as much. A copy of it has just been emailed to' – Betty pointed – 'Grace, is it not?'

Grace nodded.

'Hello. Lovely to meet you. I've heard only good things.'

'Impossible,' said Banecroft.

'Excuse me?' said Grace, affronted.

'Not you.' Banecroft gave a dismissive wave and focused his attention on Betty. 'You cannot be the assistant editor as I and I alone have the ability to hire and fire.'

Betty popped in another piece of satsuma. 'Entirely incorrect.'

'It is in my contract.'

'You do not have a contract.'

'I have a verbal contract.'

Betty raised an eyebrow and looked round the room. 'Oh dear. Do you have any witnesses to this contract, as Mrs Harnforth clearly doesn't remember it?'

'It was an implied contract.'

This earned Banecroft the double-eyebrow raise. 'Let's just let that phrase percolate for a minute, shall we?'

Banecroft stamped his foot. 'Fine. I resign.'

Betty nodded. 'While obviously we are very sad to see you go, the newspaper thanks you for your service. On the upside, you have to admire how dynamic and fast-moving an organization we are. I mean, I've only been here five minutes and I've already been promoted. Not a hint of a glass ceiling. How refreshing. The *Six O'Clock News* could learn a lot from us.' She tossed two final satsuma segments into her mouth, chewed expansively and gulped them down, before favouring the room with a benign smile.

Grace looked at her colleagues and then back to Banecroft. The vein in his forehead was throbbing. She had a sudden urge to flee the area and take every piece of breakable furniture with her.

Betty swallowed. 'I see you're still here. Shall we assume that resignation was merely a joke that didn't hit the mark?'

Banecroft spoke through gritted teeth. 'I wish to speak to Mrs Harnforth immediately.'

Betty got to her feet. 'I'm afraid that is impossible, but as I am here as her representative, I will be delighted to discuss your concerns.' She waved a hand in the direction of the door to Banecroft's office.

The two of them locked eyes for an uncomfortable amount of time. Any passing polar ice caps would have gone up in a puff of steam had they been unlucky enough to get caught between the pair. Betty held her smile throughout. Eventually, Banecroft took a step towards the office.

'Lovely,' said Betty, sounding cheerful. 'And look on the bright side – I am a massive fan of punctuation.'

LOVE WILL TEAR US APART
C. K. McDonnell

Love can be a truly terrible thing.

Marriages are tricky at the best of times,
especially when one of you is dead.

Vincent Banecroft, the irascible editor of
The Stranger Times, has never believed his wife died despite
emphatic evidence to the contrary. Now, against all odds, it
seems he may actually be proved right; but what lengths
will he go to in an attempt to rescue her?

With Banecroft distracted, the shock resignation of assistant
editor, Hannah Willis, couldn't have come at a worse time.
It speaks volumes that her decision to reconcile with her
philandering ex-husband is only marginally less surprising than
Banecroft and his wife getting back together. In this time of
crisis, is her decision to swan off to a fancy new-age retreat
run by a celebrity cult really the best thing for anyone?

As if that wasn't enough, one of the paper's ex-columnists
has disappeared, a particularly impressive trick seeing
as he never existed in the first place.

Floating statues, hijacked ghosts, homicidal cherubs, irate
starlings, Reliant Robins and quite possibly several deeply
sinister conspiracies; all-in-all, a typical week
for the staff of *The Stranger Times*.

Love Will Tear Us Apart is the third outrageously funny
novel in C. K. McDonnell's *The Stranger Times* series.